IN THE GREEK MIDWINTER

MANDY BAGGOT

Boldwood

First published in Great Britain in 2023 by Boldwood Books Ltd.

Copyright © Mandy Baggot, 2023

Cover Design by Leah Jacobs-Gordon

Cover Illustration: Shutterstock

A CIP catalogue record for this book is available from the British Library.

Paperback ISBN 978-1-80549-370-9

Large Print ISBN 978-1-80549-371-6

Hardback ISBN 978-1-80549-369-3

Ebook ISBN 978-1-80549-372-3

Kindle ISBN 978-1-80549-373-0

Audio CD ISBN 978-1-80549-364-8

MP3 CD ISBN 978-1-80549-365-5

Digital audio download ISBN 978-1-80549-366-2

Boldwood Books Ltd
23 Bowerdean Street
London SW6 3TN
www.boldwoodbooks.com

For Springsteen, the best cat in the whole world. 23 April 2003-30 June 2023. Sleep tight.

1

ST AGNES CHURCH, LITTLE PICKERING, WILTSHIRE, UK

'Stick him with the sword! Right in the guts! Now... thrust and slice! Nathanial, remember what we talked about. I want to see the menace begin in your soul, translate to the eyes, and come to absolute fruition in your sword! This is Herod you're fighting! The tyrant who ordered a massacre of innocents!'

Geoffrey himself gave a roar from his position in the pews, the noise echoing all around the holy pillars and back again, startling Bonnie so much that she dropped half a mince pie right into Jen's lap.

'Bonnie!' Jen exclaimed, brushing crumbs into her hand, and then wondering what she should do with them.

'Sorry,' her best friend replied. 'But I wasn't quite ready for him to shout like he was introducing wrestling.'

Jen focused back on the dramatisation on the red carpet at the front of the church before a candlelit altar. While one of her hands held the pastry crumbs, the other was using a pen to make notes. And, right now, none of them were particularly positive. Had she given Geoffrey too much of a free rein on this project?

Next, in a crescendo of cymbals, cellos and clarinets, many

heads of plastic baby dolls rolled across the performance area like footballs and then there was an explosion! What looked like blood burst from cylinders at either side of the 'stage', coating everything and everyone in range with bright red liquid. Bonnie screamed, the rest of her mince pie dropping to the floor, while Jen got to her feet, notebook and crumbs flying, shifting out of the pew.

'Geoffrey, there's blood all over the church!' she shouted. 'And the vicar has evensong in twenty minutes!'

Geoffrey looked as if he needed some of the red liquid injected into him to replace what had drained from his face. 'Those weren't... meant to go off... until the actual performance.'

Jen surveyed the damage. Pools of red on the ancient flagstones. All Geoffrey's actors' faces covered and dripping like they had roles in *Evil Dead*. The beautiful grey stone pillars decorated with holly and ivy now resembling a crime scene. And the performance had been way too dark even for the historical society's Christmas party. It was going to have to be back to the drawing board for that and somehow getting St Agnes cleaned before the village congregation arrived.

'This is a sign,' Bonnie whispered, arriving at Jen's shoulder, 'that Paris is calling and you must go.'

Jen sighed. 'It seems I can't even go back to the office and brainstorm this dramatic piece until after I get elbow deep in Cillit Bang.'

'Think of Paris,' Bonnie said, making her voice dreamlike as if she were in a cutesy, fuzzy festive TV commercial. 'The romantic mist over the Seine. The creamy, sugar-sweet *chocolat chaud*. The Eiffel Tower and David down on one knee with the kind of solitaire that every Disney princess dreams of.'

Currently Jen's view was not the golden lights of France's most famous landmark, nor a ring to rival Aurora's. With this crimson concoction of Geoffrey's dripping off things she hoped didn't predate Dame Judi Dench, it was hard to remember that in a few days she wasn't going to be here in Little Pickering.

'I can see it now,' Bonnie carried on as centurions, or whatever it was Geoffrey's actors were supposed to be, palmed their faces, shaking blood-tinged fingers in the air. 'Chocolate-filled croissants for breakfast, chocolate-coloured poodles trotting around the boulevards, a cream and chocolate Chanel bag for your best friend's Christmas gift...'

The minutes were ticking by, and the vicar was nothing if not punctual. Geoffrey seemed to be stuck like one of the statues of Jesus carved into the marble, mouth agape at the chaos he himself had created. There was only one thing for it: to lead by example. It was time for the CEO of Christmas Every Day to be the competent, capable and professional manager and business owner that she was.

Jen shrugged off her bright red coat and pushed up the sleeves of her spruce-green jumper.

'Right now,' Jen said to Bonnie, striding towards the door to the vestry, 'the only gift I'm looking for is the bucket-shaped kind.'

2

CHRISTMAS EVERY DAY, LITTLE PICKERING, WILTSHIRE, UK

'Are you sure you don't want some?'

Bonnie had morsels of a Greg's triple chocolate muffin underneath her fingernails as she devoured the treat in Jen's car. Greg's was like Greggs, except it wasn't a national company, it was run singlehandedly by Greg and the business premises also combined the Little Pickering post office and an Amazon hub locker.

Jen looked at her own hands. In comparison to Bonnie's, she had red staining under her fingernails that made her look like she had either had a fight with a bingo dabber or had murdered someone. She wasn't quite sure how she was going to get rid of it yet and she had one last meeting before she could sign off for the evening. Not that she ever really signed off from work. Business owners didn't often get the luxury of clocking off or 'leaving things until the morning'. Particularly small businesses who relied on repeat business, reputation and recommendation. Jen had managed to assure the vicar that if the staining on his altar cloths didn't come out in the wash, or if they returned like some sort of ode to the Turin Shroud, she would hire a team of professional cleaners but she wasn't certain he was going to let her use the church for rehearsal space again.

'You should just get Geoffrey to do the nativity,' Bonnie said between bites.

'I've been organising the dramatic piece for this group for four years now and we did a spin on the nativity in year one and year three. Year one was *The Three Wise Hens* and year three was *What if Jesus Had a Twin.*'

'Christ!' Bonnie exclaimed. 'I mean, not Christ.'

'Actually, that *was* what we called the twin,' Jen answered.

'How did I miss that one?' Bonnie asked, licking her chocolatey fingers.

'Well, I think you were going through your salted caramel phase,' Jen said. 'A bit like you're going through this chocolate phase now.'

Bonnie stopped chewing. 'Are you food shaming me?'

'No,' Jen said. 'But back at the church you said the word "chocolate" about a million times and when you get that kind of obsessed about something it usually means there's something on your mind, so why don't you tell me now before we get to the point where you're locking yourself in one of my Christmas rooms with the Ferrero Rocher and pledging yourself to the ambassador.'

'I did that *once!*' Bonnie exclaimed, scrunching up her Greg's bag and dropping it onto Jen's rubber car mat.

Jen waited, knowing her friend was about to open up. Bonnie had been opening up to her since they'd first met at the retirement home five years ago. Sitting on reception, Bonnie had lifted her head from the magazine tucked under her computer keyboard and asked Jen if she thought her face was square or oval and, if it *was* square, did she know any contour tricks. Over a weak nursing home tea, their friendship had begun. Bonnie was one of only three people Jen trusted. Actually, she supposed it was four now with David.

Bonnie sighed and hugged her bag to her body. 'OK... there is something.' She sighed again. 'My sister. She's moved back home.'

'Oh no,' Jen said immediately.

As much as Jen knew Bonnie loved her sister, she also knew that Bonnie thought her parents favoured high-profile lawyer Andrea. Andrea lived in London. Andrea once went to a party attended by Anton Du Beke. Andrea had never eaten a whole packet of Oreos for breakfast.

'I swear she's only done it because Mum's literally just finished redoing the spare room and Andrea loves a bit of ochre.'

'That can't be the only reason,' Jen said, turning a little in her seat.

'Well, she mentioned something about splitting up with "Jules" and then she burst into tears. But she's always been so dramatic. Her crying about something is more on demand than BBC iPlayer.'

Jen had only met Andrea once. It had been at a Boxing Day meal – a pretentious spatchcock turkey gifted to Andrea by a client – and whether Bonnie's sister knew it or not she had spent the whole meal telling everyone around the table how much better London was compared to Little Pickering.

'I don't even know if Jules is a real person. She's never talked about a Jules before and suddenly she's crying like she's watching the ending of *It's a Wonderful Life*.' Bonnie shivered. 'But what I *do* know is the thought of her being at home all the time, with no end date, is filling me with dread. And apparently making me talk about chocolate all the time.'

Then Bonnie gasped.

'Can I move in with you? Why didn't I think about it before?

Your flat is even nearer to the vets! I'll be able to get at least ten minutes more shut eye before I start work.'

Bonnie had swapped the nursing home reception for the vets a year ago now. According to Bonnie it was more euthanasia but less all-round excrement.

Jen felt panic starting to build and she squeezed in her core, using that inbuilt emotion-controlling tactic she'd perfected over the years in every foster placement she'd lived in. *Don't show anything. People will use it.* She might trust Bonnie, but that didn't mean it always came naturally.

'You don't want to live with me,' she said as calmly as she could.

'I don't want to live with my sister,' Bonnie said, her breath beginning to steam up the car windows so much that the shining outline of the converted barn that housed Christmas Every Day began to disappear in the blur of condensation. 'And you're going to France in a couple of days, so if I move in then, you won't have to set your lights to come on on a timer or get Natalia to water the plants.'

Think, Jen, think.

And then it came to her. Natalia – her assistant. Another person she trusted.

'Actually, Natalia's moving in,' Jen said fast. 'Tomorrow.'

Bonnie went to say something else and Jen knew she had to make it clearer.

'With her brothers.'

Bonnie screwed up her face in confusion. Was it any wonder? Because it did make zero sense. But she kept talking anyway.

'I needed as many elves on board for the flash mobs. Natalia's brothers are between jobs and Natalia's house... has rats.'

'Rats?'

'In the loft,' Jen said. 'Horrible. A whole family of them eating away at the... beams.'

Bonnie sat stock still and Jen knew she'd gone too far. She stopped talking and waited for Bonnie to call her out.

'Jen,' she began. 'I'm not stupid. You know that, right?'

She did know that. Bonnie was as switched on as the Little Pickering Christmas lights right now. But Jen couldn't show weakness. She dug deep, knowing she could claw her way out of any situation. Like that family of fictional rats in the loft of a three-bedroom terrace...

'What's going on?' Bonnie asked. 'It sounds very much like you don't want me moving in with you.'

Jen couldn't bring herself to say anything else. She pulled at the door handle and stepped out of the car into the icy evening chill. She breathed deep, taking comfort in the bright strings of lights around the eaves of the barn, the thick spruces that marked the entrance lit up in gold, silver and green, the reindeer and sleigh made from recyclable materials...

'Jen,' Bonnie said, out of the car too and following her as she walked towards the barn. 'You're worrying me now.'

'Don't worry,' Jen said, pulling her keys from her bag and slipping a brass one into the lock on the thick wooden door. 'I'll put the kettle on.'

* * *

'How long?' Bonnie asked, her hands wrapped around a hot chocolate, sitting on the bright red sofa in Jen's open-plan office.

'Not long.'

'Days? Weeks?'

Jen shook her head.

'Please tell me that means it's only been hours!'

'It's been... since September,' Jen said, sipping at her hazelnut coffee. Internally, she cringed. Bonnie would be hurt that she hadn't told her, but when you had spent a lifetime keeping things to yourself it was hard to change the default.

'Let me get this straight,' Bonnie began, taking a baby marshmallow out of the top of her mug and squeezing it between her thumb and forefinger. 'You moved out of your flat and you've been living here at the office since September, and you never told me.'

Jen took another sip of her drink. 'I didn't tell anyone.'

Did that make it better?

'Jen!'

Apparently, it did not make it better. Jen didn't say anything else.

'Does David know?'

Jen shook her head. 'I said I haven't told anyone.' And she hadn't been planning to tell Bonnie either. 'Because, you know, after Christmas, things will hopefully be better.'

Hope.

You always had to have hope or what else was there? Things weren't so bad. Yes, she might have had to cut costs and move out of her flat, but she had the business, and the business had four display rooms with plentiful cupboards for her clothes and one now housed a sofa bed she could squirrel away behind garlands of tinsel and a framework of candy canes. Milo, who owned the gym below had also asked no questions when Jen said her shower at home was broken and was it possible to use his facilities. With light, heat, her favourite pillow, her teddy bear, Bravely, the fancy coffee/hot chocolate machine and running water shared with martial arts enthusiasts, she had everything she needed. Things could be a whole lot worse.

'Is the business really in trouble?' Bonnie asked, her brown eyes studying her intently.

Jen shook her head. 'It's a lean spell, that's all. You know how it is, summer is always more difficult when your speciality is Christmas.'

She had known that from the outset when she created the company. But Jen knew a business had to be driven by passion and her heart was always powered by December. Yes, she could diversify, might be forced to if momentum didn't pick up, but she truly believed this situation simply required her to work harder, make people see their lives would be incomplete without an event provided by Christmas Every Day. Except in a few days, she was leaving the business and all the events in Natalia's capable hands while her boyfriend, David, took her to France.

'You should have told me, Jen,' Bonnie continued. 'You should have said *something* before you started sleeping in a Santa cupboard.'

'It's not a cupboard,' she protested.

'You could have moved in with me.'

'And Andrea.'

'She's not there yet. In fact, if you needed somewhere to stay, then Andrea wouldn't be able to come!'

Jen shook her head. 'I'm going to Paris, remember?'

'And you really don't sound as excited as I thought you'd be about that.'

'Well, I've obviously got a lot on, and this is the business's busiest month so it's not the ideal time to go away.'

And she had told David that, suggested they revisit the idea in the new year, but according to him, never having had a break for Christmas was as bad as never having watched *Elf*.

'But it's Paris,' Bonnie reminded her. 'The pavement cafés. The Arc de Triomphe. The chocolate... sorry.'

'I know,' Jen said, suddenly hit with the fact that there were many people who would give all their festive roast potatoes for this kind of opportunity.

'And it's *David*. Handsome, intelligent, funny David. The only person I've ever seen you get mushy over.'

Mushy. Jen wasn't sure she would recognise mushy if it pied her in the face.

'Jen, he's going to propose in Paris, you know that, right?' She put her hot chocolate down on a side table decorated with silver fir cones.

'What?' Jen's heart jolted more uncomfortably than it had when Geoffrey's blood cannons had coated the knave.

'You've been dating for over six months. It's Christmas. It's Paris. I'm telling you, he's going to ask you to marry him.'

Now Jen felt sick. The coffee began to push its way back up her throat. She swallowed, tried to maintain equilibrium.

'It hasn't been that long.'

Was that all she had? Questioning the timeline of her relationship with David and asking Bonnie for the answers?

'It was June. The weekend of my mum's birthday.'

Jen frowned. *Had* it been that long? All she remembered about June was the Christmas in Summer stall she'd had at the Little Pickering fête to drum up business and then that phone call from the nursing home saying Kathleen had had a fall...

Kathleen – another trusted friend.

'Jen, trust me, you're going to come back from Paris with a rock the size of Dwayne Johnson on your finger.'

Jen had no idea what to say. She managed some kind of half-nod. Someone asking her to marry them. *David* asking her to marry him. Being together forever. A family...

'Jen,' Bonnie said, looking at her with wide eyes now. 'If David asks, you *are* going to say yes, right?'

'Well, I mean, we haven't ever talked about anything like that.'

'You don't talk about things like that *before* the proposal. Otherwise, it wouldn't be very romantic, would it?'

But if marriage was on the cards, perhaps you might have told the man you'd been dating for apparently over six months that you had moved into Christmas Every Day's Lapland room and were sharing showering facilities with would-be power lifters...

It was then that Jen's mobile phone erupted on the coffee table between them. A rising crescendo of 'Santa Baby' filled the space and a name flashed up on the screen. *David.*

'Ooh!' Bonnie exclaimed. 'Here we go! He'll have arranged a Parisian winter picnic before you jet off.'

Jen picked up.

A roaring sound – wind or perhaps rushing traffic – met her ears.

'Jen... can you hear me?' It was David but his voice sounded muffled and so far away.

Jen stood up and stepped towards one of the windows. 'Just about, but it's really noisy.'

'Jen, I don't know how to say this but... we're not going to be able to go to Paris on Friday. There's a work emergency and I'm the only one qualified to sort it out. Believe me, I've really tried to get someone from HQ to step up but it's a non-starter.'

'Oh,' Jen replied, disappointment arriving. 'Well, can we move our flights? Go away after you've sorted out the problem?'

Or perhaps in January...

Bonnie was mouthing a shocked 'what' and her expression of bitter disappointment was perhaps one Jen should have been echoing.

'The problem isn't here,' David said. 'I'm at Bristol airport now. I've got to fly to Greece.'

'Greece,' Jen said.

Bonnie was now making shapes with her arms which Jen had no idea how to decipher.

'Yeah, I know,' David continued. 'Athens. Not exactly Paris, is it?'

Jen had no idea what Athens was like in comparison to Paris because travelling wasn't exactly the preferred pastime for someone who had always just craved stability in her locality, a home to fit into. She went to say something, but David carried on.

'The size of this issue – I think I'm going to be there for the whole of the holidays. It's shit, I know. I'm really sorry, Jen. If there was anything I could do then...'

Bonnie was shaking her head and looking somewhere between furious and frustrated. Jen didn't know how to react or what was appropriate to say to someone who allegedly had been going to propose but was now not going to see her over Christmas at all. She was seconds away from feeling relief that she could focus on the business but there was a part of her that had been looking forward to seeing somewhere different, being treated, not working...

'Listen, I've got to go now,' David said. 'The gate's going to be displayed at quarter to. I'll text you, OK?'

'David, wait, I mean, give me a second to—'

'Speak later, OK? Bye.'

The dial tone sounded loud and clear.

3

LITTLE PICKERING CARE HOME, LITTLE PICKERING, WILTSHIRE, UK

'This smells like arse!'

'Kathleen, you know you're not supposed to swear like that.'

'I said it smells like arse! That's not swearing, that's stating facts!'

Jen couldn't help but smile as she stood at the door of the day room where Kathleen Ockenden was vigorously shaking a forkful of food at one of the care workers. The climate inside the nursing home was in sharp contrast to the chilly weather outside, the radiators pumping the air up to Caribbean levels that had Jen unbuttoning her red coat. She stepped into the room then, passing the artificial Christmas tree decked in gold, red and a rather unfortunate yellow, and made her way over to the woman who had been more of a mother to her than any other.

'You have a visitor, Kathleen,' the care worker said. 'Perhaps Jen can get you eating the turkey casserole.'

'Pigs might fly! In fact, give that muck to the pigs and see what they make of it.'

Jen smiled at the assistant and then sank down into the seat that had just been vacated. She picked up the plate and gave it a sniff.

'Smells like arse, doesn't it?' Kathleen said, taking a tissue from the sleeve of her red and white spotted cardigan and wiping her nose with it.

'It smells like some part of a turkey,' Jen said, putting the plate back down.

'Turkey arse,' Kathleen countered and then she laughed, light flooding her bright blue eyes.

'Causing trouble as usual, I see,' Jen said, raising an eyebrow. And then her demeanour cracked. 'Well done.'

Kathleen shook her head, white curls bouncing. 'Got to keep people on their toes, Jen, never forget that.'

Jen nodded. Keeping people on their toes was just one of the mantras that Kathleen and her late husband, Gerald, had passed on to her over the years since they'd first met in nearby Salisbury. Kathleen and Gerald had run a party shop on the high street and from the moment a thirteen-year-old Jen had seen the Christmas window display – sparkling reindeer; an old-fashioned Santa Claus in a silver-edged suit, sitting in a rocking chair; real iced gingerbread men on platters – a piece of her had come alive. She'd gone inside and breathed in the scent of pine and fir trees, peppermint and caramel, her fingers tracing over the spirals of ice lights and packs of winter fancy dress – angel wings and halos, The Grinch, Santa's little helpers. Jen had wanted to soak it all up, shower in it, stay there amongst the brightness and the sequinned gloriousness as it presented her with so much unequivocal joy. Instead, Gerald had chased her out with a broom, worried she was one of the 'delinquents' who had stolen three wise men and a baby the day before. But the spikes of Gerald's broom on the backs of her leggings-clad calves hadn't deterred her. Salisbury might have a cathedral and fantastic coffee shops, but it was this party store that was the real attraction for her. It offered a bright, hopeful haven amid a life that had been anything but. She'd gone back, day after day, any small chance she got, until her visits got more regular – the same time of day, for longer and longer – and Kathleen started offering her something to eat and drink. *Just what we're having for our dinner.* And Jen began to pitch in. *Jen, could you pass the rainbow streamers down, I've got a display to do for the Guildhall.*

When Gerald died, some five years ago now, Kathleen had withered too. Within six months of his passing, everyday things she had usually done with vigour became difficult, until the stairs to the apartment above Fancy Occasions were too much and social services were tipped off, much to Kathleen's fury. Jen had offered to help, move in, keep the shop going, but Kathleen was furious at that idea too. The only thing Kathleen *hadn't* been furious about was Jen pilfering as much of the stock as she wanted before the owners of the chain took everything back. It was a sad day when Fancy Occasions closed, had its bright window displays removed, the glass covered over with black blinds until it became a waffle café, but it had also been the start of Jen's Christmas Every Day venture and she was determined to make that a success as much for her as for Kathleen. She felt that Kathleen seeing a little part of something like Fancy Occasions was what kept her going.

'Have you come to remind me you're going to Paris?' Kathleen asked, poking a gnarled finger at her water glass as if she wanted to transform it into a glass of sherry.

'No,' Jen said. 'I've just come because I always come to see you.' She sighed. 'And Paris… it's off.'

'Off,' Kathleen said, as if she were talking about a rancid cheese.

Jen nodded. 'David has to work.'

'But *he* booked this trip! What happened? Did he forget to ask for the time away?'

Jen filled Kathleen in about the work emergency and David's trip to Greece.

'Sounds like poppycock to me,' Kathleen said bluntly, folding her arms across her chest. 'Sounds as if he's leading you down the garden path.'

That had always been one of Kathleen's favourite phrases, along with something about not casting a clout until May was out. Jen still didn't know what that meant. Should she tell Kathleen that Bonnie thought the garden path might be leading to a proposal? She went to say something, still a little unsure exactly what, when Kathleen carried on.

'Only one way to find out really.'

'Ask him if he's serving poppycock?' Jen suggested with a half-smile.

'Tell him you'll go with him,' Kathleen said. Then she pointed a finger. 'Or better still, surprise him! Turn up in Greece without saying anything!'

Jen was already shaking her head. She hated surprises. Yes, her business quite often carried the element of surprise – festive birthdays, anniversaries, and no shortage of proposals – but that was fine because those were surprises for other people. When it came to the unexpected, Jen's life had never been blessed with the happier end of the surprise spectrum. Surprise – you're moving foster placements again. Surprise – no one remembered your birthday. Surprise – not knowing Bible quotes could mean you miss out on dinner...

'I wouldn't ever do that,' Jen replied. 'Besides, David's got to solve this work issue, it's not going to be the same as being in Paris when he doesn't have computer... or technical things... to fix.'

'What is it then?' Kathleen asked, an eyebrow raised and

slanting with suspicion. 'What exactly has happened that only King David can fix?'

Jen's mind went back to that telephone conversation. What had David actually told her was wrong?

'Well, he didn't elaborate because I don't know much about what he does,' Jen said.

'And what *does* he do exactly?'

'Important things with computer servers.'

'Ah,' Kathleen said, picking up the fork bearing turkey bits. 'Computers. The things meant to show us the world so we don't have to visit places in person. And he's had to go to Greece.' Her laugh tinkled.

Now Jen felt that Kathleen thought she was stupid. That wool was being pulled over her eyes somehow – another Kathleen saying. Was it? Why hadn't David given her a better explanation? He hadn't even given her a second to ask him anything and there had been no text from him yet. But she also knew Kathleen had never liked David. He had been the only boyfriend she'd introduced to her and afterwards, all Kathleen had said was 'very charming, very *very* charming'. Three verys meant the exact opposite of the statement.

'Tell you what,' Kathleen said, twiddling the fork a little. 'I'll eat some of this arse, if you promise to get to the bottom of David's issues.' She paused. 'The computer ones, at least.'

Jen was about to shake her head but then she reconsidered. She knew Kathleen would be snacking on Tuc crackers later but she'd really rather have her eating something else. That was more important than a broken server, or whatever it was.

'Keep people on their toes, Jen,' Kathleen reminded her. 'Like I said.'

'Eat your turkey,' Jen encouraged. 'I'll call David, find out what's going on.'

'Good,' Kathleen said, putting the fork in her mouth and immediately pulling a face as if it was the most awful substance known to man.

'Now, let me tell you about what happened at the church today.'

'Did Edna Warren get struck down by a godly lightning bolt while she was singing "In the Bleak Midwinter"?'

'Believe it or not, it was far more dramatic than that.'

4

GREG'S, LITTLE PICKERING, WILTSHIRE, UK

'Elf Number Three was the best,' Bonnie said, sinking her teeth into a chocolate-loaded bun that was drizzling maple syrup.

It was the next morning and Jen, Natalia and Bonnie had been conducting interviews for more seasonal elves. Jen had a good team of all-year-round elves, reindeer and Santas, plus Geoffrey's group of actors and, for anything specialised, she brought in outside help on an ad-hoc basis. However, come December, there weren't just more events but *bigger* events and that meant a larger number of employees, hence temporary staff.

'Elf Number Three look like Vladimir Putin. No one want to look at Vladimir Putin over brandy pudding,' Natalia answered, not even looking up from her iPad, which was balanced on her lap.

Bonnie gasped as if she'd just been witness to a discovery that was going to change the planet forever. 'Oh my God, Natalia! You're right. I *knew* he reminded me of someone!'

'Only villain role for this man. Herod. Grinch. Scrooges.'

Jen sipped her drink. A caramel latte without the caramel or the latte... a black coffee she was imagining tasted better because skipping a couple of these luxuries was keeping money in her company's bank account. The only reason they were having these meetings here and not at the office was because she hadn't had time to deconstruct the sofa bed and because she liked to challenge her potential staff to perform a little in public. If they couldn't pretend to be an elf in front of her, Natalia and today, Bonnie, plus Greg and members of the Little Pickering Knitting Circle, then they weren't ready to take the performance to her clients.

'I agree with Natalia about Elf Number Three,' Jen said.

'Head of baby. Eyes of devil,' Natalia concluded.

Between the not-caramel-not-latte and a plate containing a chocolate and coconut flapjack Bonnie had also bought, Jen's phone vibrated and a text message appeared on screen.

'It's David,' Bonnie said, leaning forward before Jen could.

'Thanks, Bonnie,' Jen said, swiping the phone up.

'He has fixed thing that is broken?' Natalia asked. 'He fly from Greece to Paris and meet there?'

Both her best friend and her very capable assistant seemed incredibly invested in the contents of this text message. Jen held her phone but did nothing further. She had tried to call David last night after she had moved nutcrackers and silver swans in order to set up her bed, but there had been no answer. After five other tries and still no response, she had left him a voicemail. This text was going to be in reply to that.

'Why you not open message?' Natalia asked.

'I am,' Jen said. 'I will.'

'Now? Or in new year?' Natalia asked.

'Ooh, there's another one,' Bonnie said.

Her friend had goo from the bun all over her chin and could apparently still see the screen of Jen's phone, despite the fact Jen was half-shielding it. Why was she half-shielding it?

'It's a photo! Of Greece!' Bonnie declared very loudly, so much so some of the knitters in their midst almost lost stitches.

'Is not picture of inside of computer mainframe? Because he is working?' Natalia added.

No, it wasn't wires and motherboards, it was ruins, the famous ones with a name that wasn't coming to Jen straight away. Columns of ancient stone against a ludicrously blue sky. She went on to read the message that accompanied it.

Stepped out to get lunch and this is the view. Not the same without you.

As Jen let David's words settle on her she realised that Bonnie had got up and was standing behind her.

'Stepped out to get lunch and this is the view. Not the same without you,' Bonnie read aloud.

There was a collective 'aww' from the knitting ladies and Greg, who was now leaning his elbows on the counter as if he hadn't been making more muffins but had been paying attention to this instead.

'I told you!' Bonnie exclaimed. 'He misses you! He was going to propose on this trip!'

'He was going to give you ring?' Natalia asked, stopping the iPad slipping from her lap.

Jen shook her head. 'No. I mean... that's just Bonnie's theory.'

'You should go to Greece!' Bonnie said, still at full volume. 'It might not be Paris but if David's got time to take photos of scenery like that he's going to have time to take you up to a rooftop restaurant and get on one knee. And Paris, I mean, everyone does it there. Not everyone does it in Athens!'

'I do it outside British Embassy,' Natalia informed them.

Jen couldn't think, couldn't feel anything, except the scrutiny from everyone around her. Kathleen had said 'keep people on their toes' and 'go to Greece' but equally Jen knew her old friend didn't trust David for some reason. Should she be taking action? Leaving the UK for somewhere as planned? Or would she be wiser to stay here at the helm of her business?

'I take it back!' Bonnie carried on. '*You* shouldn't go to Greece. *We* should go to Greece! It makes perfect sense! You can go off and do romantic stuff with David when he has a break from the heroic CPR of laptops or whatever it is he's doing, and then, when he has to work, we can tour Athens and see how they celebrate Christmas! Meaning I don't have to spend a second with Andrea!'

'Greece have good food,' Natalia said. 'Better than snails of French.'

'I had a Greek boyfriend once,' one of the knitting ladies commented. 'He was very inventive.'

Suddenly Greg's felt as hot as a building whose foundations were on the Equator. Jen made for the door and a bit of Little Pickering drizzle. Once outside, she leaned her head against the glass of the Christmas window display she always helped Greg change up each year. Angels were holding miniature cakes and sausage rolls on shiny silver platters sitting on a small version of the food truck Greg brought out when he went mobile for events.

She closed her eyes and took a deep breath. Natalia was a fantastic assistant and everything had been arranged around this trip to Paris.

It might not be Paris. David might have to work most of the time. But as today's photo proved, they could have moments together. Moments together in Greece. Maybe spontaneity *was* what was needed. Maybe taking a chance would get rid of any doubts she had about the relationship...

Jen lifted her head off the glass and eyeballed a festive mouse in a ballet tutu.

'Don't be afraid to fail. Because failure or success means the same thing. You were brave enough to try.' That quote had been on a picture in her first social worker's office. She had stared at it for hours one day when they were trying to find somewhere else for her to go. She didn't always feel brave, but she definitely always tried. She wiped a finger over the window. She'd made her decision.

5

ATHENS INTERNATIONAL AIRPORT, ELEFTHERIOS
VENIZELOS, ATHENS, GREECE

'Look at the decorations! Jen, look, you could basically hold a
Christmas event in this airport. It's so much better than that lame
stack of presents and a few fairy lights at Luton.' Bonnie heaved in
a breath, still pointing at the ceiling. 'There are stars and sparkles
and gold moons...'

As Bonnie continued to list off the airport's festive attributes,
Jen zoned her friend's voice out and tried to ground her thoughts.
She was in Greece. Athens. She had let Bonnie book – and pay for
– a flight here plus a room at a hotel called Plaka. Apart from
creating a Christmas company from the ground up, it was, without
doubt, the craziest thing Jen had ever done. The day before
yesterday she was interviewing for elf positions and now she was
in another country clutching her new acquired-for-the-Paris-trip
blue British passport. She took a deep breath and looked to the
sliding glass doors ahead of her, opening and closing as people
arrived or departed. The centre of Athens and their hotel was a
metro or taxi ride away. Presumably this was where David was
based as he had taken a photo of the ruins Jen now knew was the
Parthenon on top of the Acropolis. She had replied to his text and

the photo, under Bonnie and Natalia's scrutiny and with their input:

Wish I was there!

Why four words needed so much thinking about, Jen hadn't been sure, but in the end she had sent it while Natalia and Bonnie were still arguing back and forth about what emojis should be added.

Three hours later and Jen had a reply.

Me too x

For Bonnie, that had been the game-changer that powered her into woman-on-a-mission mode. Wizz Air flights had been booked, the hotel had been found and somehow, using the kind of persuasive skills only Bonnie seemed to possess, she had talked retiree, Susan, who Bonnie had replaced at the vets, into coming back for a couple of weeks. Meanwhile, at Christmas Every Day, Natalia was already ready to take the reindeer by the antlers and steer the business through December. Jen knew she had been desperate to 'decapitate' the festive Russian dolls on Jen's desk ever since one of their happy clients had sent them.

Suddenly Bonnie was clamping her arm. 'You OK? Not having second thoughts, are you?'

Jen wasn't sure she had really had first thoughts. And now, as she fished her phone out of the pocket of her trolley case, the only thing she was thinking about was why her phone still hadn't connected to any network.

'Because I am loving the Greek festive vibe!' Bonnie continued. 'There's the music! And the decorated trees! And we aren't even out of the airport yet. I have a feeling that Athens is going to give London a run for its money!'

Bonnie was excited. Bonnie was the kind of excited Jen should be. This wasn't what she did – jetting off on a whim – jetting off at all. She was content wrapping herself up in the Christmassy glow she'd created in Little Pickering, where she felt safe. Being here was a step into the unknown.

'Taxi or metro?' Bonnie asked. A taxi sounded more expensive and Jen had to be frugal. Although at the end of yesterday's visit, Kathleen had dipped into her handbag and produced a wad of cash she'd pressed into Jen's hand before she left and that Jen had changed into euros at Greg's. But it was her definite intention to pay it back.

'Right, I'll decide,' Bonnie said, pulling Jen towards the glass doors. 'I say taxi. I'll pay.'

'Bonnie, you can't pay for everything. You paid for the flights. I know you paid Greg to take us to the airport and—'

'And you have no idea how grateful I am for an escape from living with my sister for a week.' She gave Jen's arm a squeeze. 'No idea, OK? So, roll with it. Besides, as soon as we catch up with David, I'm sure his credit card might be able to swing a Greek dinner.'

Jen didn't have a chance to say anything else before a gust of actually quite warm air whirled around them and they were outside the airport underneath a crazily blue winter sky.

6

BAR PÁME, PLAKA, ATHENS, GREECE

'One special meze and extra *dolmades*, a gift from us.'

Astro Salvas gave a smile to the three customers, then laid the two huge platters of food on the table. As expected, a gasp of appreciation met the air, directed towards the mix of meatballs, sausages, chicken and pork *souvlaki*, crispy feta parcels sprinkled with sesame seeds, pitta breads and homemade chips. As soon as he had turned from the table and was heading back towards the bar, his smile dropped. His uncle, Philippos, the bar's owner, was on a stepladder, twisting tinsel around the iconic stone surround in front of the beer taps. With the bar more cave than café with its stone walls and bottles resting on holes carved out of the rock, it was both traditional and cosy as much as it was contemporary and funky. And garish Christmas decorations had no place here.

'What are you doing?' Astro snapped.

'Before you say anything,' Philippos began. 'I—'

'I have already said something,' Astro interrupted. 'I asked what you are doing.'

'Astro, have you seen the other bars and restaurants? They have had decorations everywhere since the middle of November.'

Philippos was still standing on the ladder – two of the steps warped close to breaking – half the tinsel in his hand, half trailing across the stones like an ugly glittery worm.

'I try not to look,' Astro answered. 'Why do you think I wear my hood up from the middle of November until we are in the new year?'

Philippos dropped his hold on the worm garland and it drooped. 'Astro, it has been seventeen years.' He sighed. 'But I know that the passing of time does not change anything. And, I also know this season may not be as lucrative as the summertime, but Greece wants to be an all-year destination. They advertise a Greek winter, more people they come.' He paused, wet his lips. 'I just think that Eleni... your mother, she would want us not to miss out on these opportunities. In the time she had with us she would seize everything coming her way, no?'

Astro had frozen to the spot the second Philippos had said 'seventeen years'. One hundred years could have passed, it made no difference. His mother had died on Christmas Day when he had been just seven years old. On that Christmas Eve, she had read him a story about Saint Vasilis, kissed him goodnight, tucking the bed covers around him and tickling his neck the way she always had, and left him with the babysitter while she went to work. He had never seen her alive again. An aneurysm they'd said, something growing inside her she had never known about. He hadn't understood what that was at seven, but he had looked into it later.

Often Astro wondered if she *had* known about the weak spot or at least sensed that something was wrong but had put off going to see the doctor, or, more likely, was unable to get an appointment around her waitressing job. The memories he had of his mother always involved her trying to juggle a multitude of things – her work, taking him to school, fun low-cost trips with him at the weekends, more work. That Christmas Day morning, when

Philippos had arrived at their apartment, red-eyed, his then short, dark beard speckled with the light snow that was falling, Astro had known that his life was going to change. It was like suddenly realising that everything that had gone before was only a too-short preparation for what was to come...

'No.'

Astro said the one word a little too loudly and it was tinged with anger and despair. But he held his ground, his green eyes fixed on his uncle, wanting to make his point totally clear, needing to see that golden trail of disgustingness fall back into whatever box it had come from.

'Astro—'

He changed tack, trying to nullify the feelings that were crawling up over him like a clutter of spiders. 'Bar Páme is not like anywhere else the rest of the year. Why does it have to be like everywhere else now?' He forced a smile. 'What happened to individuality? Our bar being unique.'

By the expression on Philippos's face, Astro had a feeling that this approach wasn't working either. He found he had nothing else to say.

The radio began to play something with jingling bells and it set his teeth on edge.

'*My* bar,' Philippos began, one foot hitting the rung below on the ladder. 'Needs every cent it can get... or I might have to let Marjorie go before the new year.'

'What?'

'That is business, Astro. And, I am afraid, if I do not make this place into a grotto that Saint Vasilis would be proud of, then tourists looking for the festive spirit are going to find it somewhere with decorations I do not have.'

When Philippos stepped on the next rung of the ladder, it gave way, sending him sprawling to the floor. At the same time, the golden sliver of tinsel unstuck itself and landed on Philippos's beard.

'Are you OK?' Astro asked, offering out a hand.

Philippos gave a grunt, heaving himself up from the floor and brushing the garland away from his mouth.

'The decorations are going up, Astro. Be it today or tomorrow. And, by the end of this week, the Christmas music will be loud, there will be serviettes with holly berries on them and *melo-makarona* will be going on the menu.'

Astro bit the inside of his lip. That Greek treat was as festive as it got. They were cookies with honey, cinnamon, cloves and nutmeg. He had made a cupcake variation with his mother the year she died and he had got so much syrup in his hair she had to cut pieces out of his fringe. Now he was going to have to serve it to their customers. The thought made him want to vomit. He stamped his foot down on the tinsel snake. Fuck this time of year!

7

HOTEL PLAKA, PLAKA, ATHENS, GREECE

It had taken around forty-five minutes to get from the airport to the hotel, through quite substantial traffic, but Jen had felt her shoulders relax a little as they passed the sparkling Christmas decorations en route. Despite the warmth compared to England, this city was geared up for the winter season, from the tall, decorated spruces on the corner of dramatic marble squares, to large twinkling almost stage-sets of stars hanging above the carriageways below those ruins David had sent a photo of. The Parthenon. There it was now in late evening, lit up and glowing against the clear darkening sky.

From where they sat on the hotel roof terrace, a carafe of red wine on the table, it was like somehow being part of classical civilisation. And tonight Jen would be sleeping in a king-sized bed next to Bonnie and Bonnie's multitude of chocolate snacks she had tipped out of her cabin bag.

Or was she going to be at a different hotel, in a different bed, with David? Jen's eyes went to her phone that was next to the rather delicious oaky red wine.

'Still nothing?' Bonnie asked.

'No,' Jen said, wrapping her hands around the wineglass. She sighed, feeling a tension invade her neck muscles. And then she said what was actually on her mind. 'It's a bit weird, isn't it?'

'Well, he did say he was working all the time.'

'I know. But people have to go to the toilet, don't they? And have you ever peed and not checked your phone afterwards, in that minute or so after washing your hands and getting back to work?'

'To be honest,' Bonnie said, fingers walking their way towards the Bombay mix they'd been given with their drinks. 'I'm usually checking my phone even when I'm meant to be looking at the weekly diabetes readings for Mrs Curtis's Jack Russell.'

'So why hasn't David answered my calls and messages?' Jen was asking the universe as much as Bonnie or the Greek gods who all seemed within touching distance here.

'Remember that David doesn't know you're here yet,' Bonnie said, then took a sip of her drink, looking like she hung out on Greek roof terraces on a regular basis. 'He thinks you're coordinating the latest Christmas proposal or a cranberry product launch. Back in the UK.'

Was her sense of urgency because she was here and not there? Because she had acted on a whim and didn't yet know how David was going to react? Or was it a generalised feeling that his delays in responding were something much more than his work issues? There had been times when he had gone radio silent for whole weekends but he had always eventually replied with a valid excuse. But, for some reason, this felt different...

'Well, how long do I give it? I mean, what if he doesn't respond at all tonight? Or in the morning? Because I don't know the name of his hotel or where the company's based here or—'

Bonnie lifted her phone from her jumper-clad midriff where it was residing attached to a lanyard around her neck. 'But you know the name of the company he works for, right? So, we can just search it up and get an address.'

Jen shook her head. 'God, it sounds stalkerish now.'

'Give me the name of the company. We don't have to call them or hunt them down or do anything tonight. But, on the very slim, off-chance that David doesn't answer until the morning we'll have somewhere we can head to tomorrow.'

This was Bonnie being super sensible. It didn't always happen naturally. Jen took a glug of the wine and sat back in her seat, enjoying the sensation of warmth and not having to wear her fit-for-minus-thirty-degrees coat over her long-sleeved top.

'It's Tex Spex.'

'You're going to have to spell that for me,' Bonnie replied.

A few moments later and Bonnie still seemed to be looking. Such an uneasy feeling had taken hold of Jen.

She put her wine on the table and sat forward in her seat. 'Can't you find it? Did you spell it right?'

'Yes, I did. It's probably Safari playing up. It's all ads and suggestions you don't need these days, isn't it?'

Jen could sense the panic in her voice and her fingers sought, not the nibbles, but her own phone, the display still as black as the night.

'OK, let's think logically,' Bonnie said.

'What? You never think logically. You're the girl who still thinks there's a chance that Cillian Murphy's going to walk into Greg's one day and order a toastie.'

'It *could* happen!'

And whilst Jen had distracted Bonnie with that thought, she was going to search for Tex Spex herself. There it was. Muted greys and red, a bit like if the Terminator had designed a tech company website.

Our offices. Jen began to look down the list alphabetised by country. *Belgium. France. Germany. Spain. United Kingdom.* Where was Greece?

 She might have dipped in and out of many schools along her educational path but she knew that Greece should be right after Germany. And even if whoever made the website was alphabetically challenged, it should be there somewhere. It wasn't. There was nothing. Jen shivered as the temperate weather clashed with the ice-cold concern chilling her insides.

'You didn't find an office in Athens,' Jen stated. Her voice was like something from a sat-nav, stating facts and directions, emotionless.

'No,' Bonnie said. 'But, you know, websites can be out of date, or it could be a new office. Like, maybe they took over another company called something else previously and that's why they're having this big problem with whatever David's been called in to fix and...'

Jen wondered how long Bonnie could keep talking. She got to her feet and walked to the edge of the roof terrace.

Leaning on the surround, she looked out over the city as her brain tried to fill in the blanks. Greenery almost entirely covered the wall opposite, and iron bistro tables and chairs were set out on the tiles of a neighbouring terrace.

There being no office for Tex Spex in Athens was one thing. Yet the idea that David wasn't *working* here but doing something else entirely was another thing altogether? Or was he even here at all... Had she travelled four hours to get somewhere to see someone who was somewhere else? Now her mind was whirring and Bonnie was still talking as if she was in charge of relationship algorithms.

'He's lied to me,' Jen interrupted.

'We don't know that yet.'

'Come on, Bonnie,' she said, walking back towards the table, where she picked up her glass of wine and slugged back the contents. 'We've flown all this way and he's not answering my phone calls or my messages. And what might have started out sounding like a cool surprise is now feeling like a huge mistake.'

She slumped down into her chair. Now there was emotion. Now she felt completely stupid, in the middle of unfamiliar circumstances she had no control over. She hated feeling like that, it took her right back to all those many authority figures making decisions about her welfare...

'It's not a mistake,' Bonnie said quickly, getting up and dragging her chair around the table until it was alongside Jen's. 'This is... an unexpected glitch in the programme, that's all.'

'Computer maintenance talk, Bonnie? Not OK.'

'Sorry, I just meant that there has to be more to it and we are literally jumping to conclusions just because Tex Spex doesn't have an office here.'

Bonnie had made the last sentence sound like she was saying 'just because Tesco doesn't stock that particular brand of cereal'. Jen appreciated her efforts – kind of – but she was far more cynical than that and expected the worst from every life scenario.

'At best, he's working for someone else or he's here for another reason he didn't feel he could tell me about,' Jen said. She sighed. 'Worst case, he's not here at all and he's lied to me. About this trip. About Paris. About possibly everything.'

Everyone lied to her. Always. Why should it ever be any different?

'It can't be that,' Bonnie said, a flat hand moving to her chest. 'Because David's nice. The nicest guy yet.'

Nice. Jen had always had an issue with the word 'nice'. It didn't really mean anything at all. It perhaps got across that something wasn't deeply offensive but simply there, minding its own business, being OK. It wasn't keeping anyone on their toes...

'He hasn't responded to my last text message or any of my calls,' Jen reminded her. 'That isn't nice.'

She got to her feet again. When had she started to let the actions of someone else dictate what came next? She was a boss bitch – literally.

'No,' Bonnie agreed. 'But—'

'Right, well, you paid for us to be here and... we're here. And it's somewhere neither of us have been and I need a distraction... from David and... from worrying that while my back is turned Natalia is going to make every Christmas event we have lined up Ukrainian-themed.' She sighed. 'And, as lovely as this roof terrace is, there's a whole city down there we should explore.'

Don't show weakness. Take ownership. Keep going. There was nothing to be done tonight. It was almost eight o'clock. Close to six in the UK. Offices would be shut. Answers would have to wait.

'I am starting to get hungry,' Bonnie admitted, standing up.

'Then let's go and find somewhere authentic and most importantly, cheap,' Jen said, picking up her phone.

8

BAR PÁME, PLAKA

'Astro! Your pigeon is on table four outside!'

Marjorie was shouting across the bar to him, something Philippos was always telling her not to do. Yes, the music might be a little louder in the evenings but none of their customers needed to know about their problems, even pigeon-sized ones. As Marjorie bustled back through the swinging doors that led to the kitchen, Astro followed her, almost tripping over two pencils and a hair grip as they fell out of the pocket of her jeans.

'Marjorie,' he said, bending to pick up the items and almost colliding with one of their casuals carrying two bowls of *gigantes plaki* – a traditional dish with butter beans. 'You dropped these.'

She ignored the items Astro was offering and instead picked up the next dishes for service. 'I do not have time for this. I also do not have time for your pigeon eating customers' food and scaring people away.'

Astro deposited the pencils and the hair grip on the worktop. 'How do you know it is *my* pigeon? The city is full of pigeons.'

'Astro, it still has the red polish you painted on its claws.'

Marjorie said no more, and shifted past him and back out into the bar with her next meals.

'Astro,' the chef called, the burners on the hob roaring. 'If that pigeon does anything to ruin my reputation I will—'

Astro didn't hang around to hear the threat he knew was coming. He pushed his way out of the kitchen and back into the bar, making sure his uncle was busy serving drinks and not about to comment on the bird too.

Stepping outside, he took a deep breath and looked out over the tables and chairs that were dotted up and down between the stone steps that led to and from the Acropolis rising above this area of Athens. It was alive tonight, nearly all the seats taken, even the cushions on the steps. Any that weren't occupied by people served as a rest stop for the local cats, which were curled up in balls. He had always liked how the golden lights swirled around the branches of the trees, but now everything seemed to be on course for an opening night in Las Vegas. Doors were wrapped with shiny red and gold ribbons like they were gifts waiting to be opened, a white-bearded man in a red cloak was everywhere, like a spectre, and if there was a spare window ledge or square inch of wall, it held snowmen or reindeer or flashing icicles. Plaka's vibe the rest of the year was cosy yet classy, vibrant yet relaxed. Now all it seemed to be missing was the Coca-Cola truck...

Ignoring the décor, Astro scanned the tables looking for Peri, his pigeon. Calling Peri *his* pigeon sounded crazy, but it had been that way for the past year. One morning the mottled bird – in shades of grey, white and brown – had tapped at the window of his loft apartment above the bar as if he was knocking at a door. And the tapping hadn't stopped until he had paid the bird attention and offered up a crust of bread. It hadn't been a one-time thing. Peri had come back, day after day until Astro was buying seed and

Peri was strutting into the space to eat at the table. But no one liked pigeons picking at their restaurant meal...

Except he couldn't see the bird anywhere. Until...

'Peri!' he exclaimed as the bird landed on his shoulder. He quickly picked him up, letting him settle on his hand. 'You need to sit outside our apartment. Or find somewhere else for scraps.'

Peri responded by cooing affectionately and bumping his head against Astro's apron. Astro ran a finger over the little thing's head and then tickled under his throat, across his bib the way the bird seemed to like it.

'What is that you say? You hate all the pictures of the chubby man in red, a saint that Greeks do not even believe in? I agree.'

He kissed the top of the bird's head, who then walked up his arm and nestled in at his elbow.

'Listen,' Astro whispered. 'You stay away from the bar and tonight I will bring you Christmas biscuits so they cannot go on the menu tomorrow. OK?'

What was he doing? Talking to a bird... The patrons at table six were staring at him, probably thinking he was mad. Well, if there was one thing guaranteed to make him mad, it was this season!

'Astro! Philippos said he needs a little help in here!'

He jumped at the sound of Marjorie's voice as she moved past him and on to serve another table. Peri jumped too, taking flight, and fluttering in front of Astro's face.

'*Ela!* Go!' he ordered the bird.

KLEPSIDRA CAFÉ, PLAKA

'I have no real idea what's in this, but I am in love!' Bonnie announced, wiping her mouth with a serviette.

The menu had said the meal was called *gyros*, but their waiter had pronounced it very differently. It comprised of a large plate full of slivers of meat, lush fleshy tomatoes, bright red onion, golden fries, a large dollop of tzatziki and pitta bread cut into triangles. When the first plate had come out, Jen had expected that it was theirs to share, but very quickly there were two! And it was really delicious. She hadn't realised how hungry she was until the scent of grilled meat, spices and garlic had wafted up her nose and drawn them both into this eatery. The taverna was like something you'd see in a guidebook encouraging travellers to enjoy tradition and history – a picture-perfect representation of Greece, its culture, and its architecture.

They were sat outside, the locals recognisable by being bundled up in jumpers and coats, despite it currently being the temperature of the UK in May. Metal tables had pots of basil at their centre, a sprinkling of tinsel to set the festive vibe, and multi-coloured striped cushions adorned wooden chairs. There were doors with peeling paint beneath ancient archways sitting alongside modern street art and less appealing straight-up graffiti but, somehow, it worked. And soaring above them was the Parthenon that seemed visible from a different angle wherever you were in the city.

'If you'd told me when we were interviewing elves that I'd be in Greece a couple of days later I'd never have believed it,' Bonnie continued.

Jen took a sip of her second glass of red wine before answering.

'Can we pretend, just for tonight, that jumping on the plane here had nothing to do with David?' Something was awry, she knew it. But if she let it fester, this delicious food and beautiful setting was not going to get the attention it truly deserved. 'Maybe we could – I don't know – pretend it's research?' Jen offered. 'I mean, how can I be a Christmas expert if I haven't experienced the Christmas build up in other countries?'

'Right,' Bonnie said, pointing a finger that was slick with the dip from her plate. 'Exactly. We can see how the Greeks do it and then you can offer Greek Christmas-themed events next year. Starting with food options that include whatever the waiter said this feast was called.'

Jen smiled, putting an oregano-sprinkled fry into her mouth, and savouring the subtle flavours. This was momentarily better. This was like her sticking her head inside one of the decoration-filled trunks in her office until she almost believed the latest overdue invoice had disappeared, or squeezing Bravely Bear until the scent of peppermint in his tummy shrouded every bad feeling...

'It feels a bit magical here, doesn't it?' Bonnie whispered, as the sound of a light guitar suddenly drifted through the air. 'The whole we're-not-really-supposed-to-be-here-but-here-we-are kind of thing plus the fact the little bars and restaurants we passed are all oozing their own buzz.'

Bonnie was right. Perhaps it was simply landing somewhere previously unthought about until now and it being theirs to explore. Each narrow street and paved or cobbled walkway provided something that was worthy of a photo. Near to their hotel, restaurant tables spilled onto pavements, yellow street food trucks served hot doughnuts and kiosks were situated every few metres selling everything from magazines, beer and wine to hardback copies of *Anna Karenina*.

Jen felt her phone buzz in her bag. The temptation to look and see if it was David was strong but now she was 'researching' she really didn't want anything to intrude. Not even a message she'd been waiting the whole day for.

'Are you going to check it?' Bonnie whispered.

Jen sighed. 'You heard it vibrate from over there?'

'Sorry. It's up to you. Pretend I didn't say anything.'

Except she *had* said something. Jen put down her knife and fork and took her phone from her bag. Her reaction was for some reason one of relief instead of disappointment.

'It's Kathleen,' she said, clicking on the message. She smiled as she read it. 'She says Natalia brought her *borscht*.' There was a photo too. Natalia and Kathleen in festive paper hats over the delicious-looking soup. Kathleen was sticking out her tongue. 'She also asks if you've fallen in love with a Greek yet.'

Bonnie laughed, mouth full of *gyros*. 'Yes! A Greek dish! This one! Tell her that.' She held a chip aloft.

Jen texted a quick reply and snapped a photo of her glass of red wine before putting her phone away again.

'How's Kathleen doing?' Bonnie asked.

'She's grumpy,' Jen answered. 'That's how I know she's OK. The second I go and visit and she's smiling or doesn't have anything to complain about, I'll know to call the doctor.'

'Have you... told her about not having your flat any more?'

'No!' Jen exclaimed. 'Of course I haven't. She would... try to give me money, much more than the money she insisted I have towards this trip. She barely has enough to pay for her care. And she would worry. And I don't want her to worry about anything other than being bitchy to her carers.'

It wasn't just that Kathleen would worry about Jen's living arrangements either. Jen knew that she would be concerned about Christmas Every Day and Jen was damned if she was going to let what happened to Fancy Occasions repeat itself. The business was more important than her current living arrangements. If it turned out she couldn't keep these particular premises, she'd downsize. Over the years, she'd pretty much learned to sleep in whatever space was available.

It was then that Jen realised what she'd said had come out harsher than she had intended . Bonnie was the very last person she should be being harsh to. 'Sorry.'

'Don't be sorry,' Bonnie said. 'I'm your friend. I *want* you to share how you feel with me. That's what friends are for.'

Jen nodded. 'Yes. I know the concept.'

'Jen, I mean it,' Bonnie said. 'I know you're crazy independent. I get that it's always been that way and why it's been that way but... if someone offers help, it's not against the world rules to take it.'

She nodded again. Bonnie was being kind – that was who she was. But Bonnie didn't know how accepting help for her had usually always come with a consequence. A return favour to be called upon. An alibi. Worse.

'God! Let's not get too deep,' Bonnie said, changing her tone. 'Let's have a look at the map and see where we're going to go next.'

'OK,' Jen agreed.

But her concern was that she would have no idea what came next if tomorrow threw up more curveballs.

10

BAR PÁME, PLAKA

Astro gritted his teeth. He had almost perfected the mouth shape so it looked like his grimace was a smile for the customers. Somehow mistletoe had appeared over the door. A large bunch of green leaves and plump white berries were fixed to the frame. It was hanging from a hook that had been set in the middle of the smoky mark of a cross Philippos had made with a candle at Easter. On both sides of the frame were trails of icicle bunting. Astro had spent his evening, in between service, surreptitiously removing everything else Marjorie had tried to put up inside the bar every time she had turned her back. Astro knew he couldn't fight this forever – not if his uncle's mind was made up – but, for tonight, it was important to him that he made his stance clear. Christmas was not being comfortably welcomed in his life. If Philippos really wanted this situation, then he was going to have to accept it wouldn't come easy.

Astro sat down on a vacant step, resting his back against the trunk of a tree growing up through the slabs and took out the tiniest sketch pad from the pocket of his jeans. With the stub of the pencil he untucked from the wire rings of the notebook, he began to draw the things around him quickly. The face of a dog, dark fur scruffy around its mouth. A woman having a loud telephone conversation using her hands to gesticulate. Two guys at a nearby table laughing, bottles of Mamos in their hands. Two women walking up the steps towards him, dragging an inflatable candy cane...

What?

He stopped drawing then and watched the scene before him. Others were looking too. The Christmas decoration monstrosity was bouncing into this cool vibe and invading like a loud clown arriving at a business meeting. And it was getting ever closer to Bar Páme's tables, threatening to knock over the candleholders and plants...

Astro got to his feet. '*Na stamatiesi!* Stop!'

He now couldn't even see the women behind the giant red and white cane and he didn't know what to do. His first thought was to burst the inflatable before it broke something or caught fire on a patio heater.

He picked a fork up from the table and prepared to do just that.

'What are you doing?' One of the women appeared. She had blonde wavy hair that just touched her shoulders and earrings that looked like golden angels. Her coat was Santa Claus red but the expression on her face was not the happy kind children expected to come from that man.

'What are *you* doing?' Astro snapped back. 'Because another step and your... *thing* will collide with my tables.'

'Sorry!' The other woman came into sight, dark brown curls almost down to her waist. She was a little out of breath. 'That was my fault.'

The woman in red took a step towards him, her eyes meeting his. Hers were brown. The colour of almonds. And at the moment they were radiating annoyed energy and it was all directed at him.

'So, if you don't like something you attack it with cutlery?'

Cutlery? It was not an English word Astro was familiar with. But then her gaze went from him and landed slap bang on the *piroúni* – fork – in his hand.

Before he could come up with a response, the candy cane started to take flight on a sudden breeze, rising up and disturbing the branches of a tree, before heading towards a pushchair holding a small child...

'I let it go! Oh, God!'

The cry had come from the woman with brown hair and Astro was already jumping into action as the candy cane went rogue. He pulled the pushchair out of the way and simultaneously, as if he were an expert in shepherding out-of-control festive pieces, guided the inflatable back down to the ground. As he took a breath – disaster averted – a few patrons broke into applause. It was then he realised he was still holding the fork.

Next there was a loud miaow, followed by a yowl, then a loud pop and then a hissing sound met the air as a black and white cat disappeared off up the steps and down a path. Astro suddenly realised what had happened and he really couldn't have been happier.

'Did you fork the candy cane?' the blonde-haired woman accused him.

'It was not me,' Astro answered, the candy cane already beginning to wilt, somehow still under his control. 'It was the cat.'

'Because cats often use forks,' she said, shaking her head and looking even more annoyed.

She had misunderstood, so he clarified. 'He has made this happen with his claws. Not a fork.'

It was the brown-haired woman who answered him now. 'Oh

no! And we didn't take any photos to send to Natalia or for Instagram!'

Astro did not know why anyone would want a picture of a monstrosity like this now squealing, depleting effigy of a mint sweet. And just how long was he going to have to stand here holding on to it so it didn't suffocate any of Bar Páme's customers?

'Did you bring this to Greece?' he asked.

The brown-haired woman started to laugh. 'Do you have anything to declare, madam? Yes, I have an inflatable candy cane in my backpack and I'm not afraid to use it.'

'It was a gift,' the blonde-haired woman said. 'From a nice man selling bracelets on the street.'

Astro shook his head. 'I am afraid you were marked. Check your bags and your pockets. See if you still have everything you came with.'

Then he made a grab for the top of the candy cane, dragged it downwards, squeezing, then plunged in the fork. He tore a hole in the thin plastic. The action set off a whoosh of air as finally the thing began to deflate a whole lot faster.

'Marked?' the blonde-haired woman asked.

'Oh my God!' the other woman said, beginning to pat herself down and then unfasten her bag. 'Like for pickpockets!'

'As she said,' Astro said, manhandling the cane until he was able to start folding it into a manageable lump. Finally, it was almost air-free. He was going to dump it in the nearest bin. 'Most times they give you a bracelet or a badge. It is so another member of their group can pick you out as easy to steal from.' He dropped the scrunched-up inflatable to the ground and kicked it out of the way until such time as he could bin it. 'I am guessing anyone who happily takes something so large and obvious would be the simplest prey of all.'

'Phew! Everything is still here!' the brown-haired woman said.

Astro noticed that the other woman hadn't even checked her bag and was narrowing her eyes at him. As if *he* had done something wrong.

'What if the guy who gave us the candy cane was just being nice?' she suggested. 'It's rather negative to assume that someone who gave us a Christmas decoration was using it to steal.'

Astro shrugged. 'It is the way of the world.'

'Not at Christmas,' the woman answered with absolute conviction and a steely gaze.

'O-K,' the brown-haired woman said, taking her companion by the arm. 'Now you've poked the Christmas obsessive with a Scrooge stick, we're just going to go into this bar and order some drinks.'

'This bar?' Astro clarified. 'Bar Páme?'

'Is that OK? Or is someone going to give us a certain type of drink that says we're ripe for being taken advantage of?' the blonde-haired woman asked with more than a fair degree of annoyance.

'No,' he answered. 'Because this is my uncle's bar.'

Why had he said that in an unwelcoming way? Philippos needed customers. Things were so desperate, he was even determined to turn the bar into a grotto.

Before the women could make a different decision, he put that smile/grimace in place and gestured with his arm. 'Please, *páme*, let me show you the best table.'

11

They opted to sit outside again. It was a real novelty to be able to have a drink alfresco in the winter and here, in the middle of this pathway of steps with golden lights in the trees, tables and chairs squeezed into any space, it was the perfect people-watching spot.

'Sorry about the candy cane,' Bonnie said, winding the strap of her bag around the leg of her chair as if someone might whip it away from her at any moment.

'It wasn't your fault,' Jen answered. She poured herself some water they'd been given into a tumbler. 'The man who gave it to us was quite insistent.'

'In a kindly way?' Bonnie asked. 'Or in a "my associates are going to rob you blind" type of way?'

'I think in a kindly way. I don't have anything missing either,' Jen said, pouring Bonnie a glass of water too. 'And you don't need to keep touching your bag with your foot. I don't think it's going anywhere.'

'Sorry,' Bonnie apologised again. 'I just feel that... it's because of me we're even here and... I wish David would just call you and make everything all right.'

'Everything *is* all right,' Jen said in a tone that was slightly calmer than she was really feeling. 'We agreed that tonight was about experiencing Athens and that's what we're going to do. Even if some of it involves a puncture wound and a grumpy waiter.'

'Grumpy but really hot,' Bonnie said, sitting forward a little.

Jen's gaze went across the path to the tables just outside the door of the beautiful stone building and the man who had burst the candy cane. He was whisking away plates and expertly skipping around a group of cats all looking for the slightest sliver of a falling scrap. He had a presence about him somehow, a confidence, a filling of the space he was in. And with his short dark hair and green eyes, she could see why Bonnie had labelled him 'hot'.

He'd said his name was Astro, before suggesting they both order cocktails containing brandy and Cointreau. Already a little buzzed from the wine she'd had with their *gyros* meal, a cocktail sounded perfect – despite not knowing how much they were going to cost – and Bonnie had rapidly said yes for the both of them.

'Is that your phone?' Bonnie said suddenly, leaning against the table, her eyes on Jen's bag.

'What?'

'It's vibrating. I can hear it.'

Jen had put her bag on the spare chair next to her and unless Bonnie had developed the kind of hearing some superheroes would kill for, there was no way she would be able to hear it, right?

'I switched it to silent for a reason,' Jen reminded her.

'It's not stopping... Oh, it's stopped.'

'See, no drama.'

Despite the sounds outside on the city street, loud conversations and Greek music, the phone rumbling somehow again drew their attention.

'It's David,' Bonnie gasped. 'I can sense it.'

Jen's stomach started to churn and she knew it wasn't from

their delicious meal. This was nerves or maybe even terror. Why did it feel like terror?

'Answer it!' Bonnie ordered. 'Before he gives up!'

Jen was torn between doing as Bonnie had suggested or analysing the 'before he gives up' element. But she made a move for the bag, unzipped it and took out her phone.

David.

'It's him, isn't it?' Bonnie said, eyes wide. 'Answer it!'

Jen stood up and answered the call. She took a few paces away from the table, went down several steps and stopped in a nook a few bars down.

'Jen! Is everything OK? You took a long time to answer. I was worried.'

She didn't immediately know how to respond to that. *He* was worried?

'Jen?' David said again when she made no reply. 'Where are you?'

The time had come. She steeled herself. 'I'm in Athens. The Plaka District. Whereabouts are you?'

She was met with a silence that elongated rapidly until: 'Wow, Jen, for a second there I thought you were serious. Way to give a guy a heart attack.'

Why would she be giving him a heart attack if she was in the same city as him? She sucked in her core and gave him her answer. 'I *am* being serious.'

'What?'

'You sent that photo and said you wished I was there, so Bonnie organised the rest,' she explained. 'So, tell me where you are and we can find each other. Or you could come here, it's a place called Bar Páme, and we've just ordered cocktails so—'

'I think *you* said you wished you were there. Athens, that is, not... I mean, I said "me too" because...'

David stopped talking but Jen had already caught the vibe. Coupled with her already pulsing insecurities about this situation, she pressed the FaceTime button and waited. Why wasn't he accepting her FaceTime?

'David, accept my FaceTime or I'm ending this call!'

'Give me a second... no... wait—'

Whether it was inadvertently or not, the video call connected and Jen's jaw dropped the second she saw the background behind David.

She couldn't believe it.

'You're in Paris!'

'Jen, don't do this now.'

'"Jen, don't do this now?!" What the hell does that mean?'

She watched him on screen. The lights of Paris were right there and he seemed to be moving location and then... was that... the actual Eiffel Tower?

'You need to calm down,' David told her, presumably in a less public location that looked very much like a rooftop restaurant.

Calming down was the very opposite of what Jen was intending to do.

'Don't tell me what to do, David. Why are you in Paris? And why does Tex Spex not even have a branch in Greece?' She had no idea why she had bothered to ask that last question because it was now quite apparent that David was nowhere near Greece, nor had he ever intended to be.

'I was going to talk to you about this when I got back but...'

'But what? I'm waiting. You know, in actual Athens, not the iStock version you obviously sent me!'

'So, the thing is... I really like you, Jen, but...'

Wasn't there always a 'but' when it came to relationships? All it really signified, in most situations, was the beginning of the end. Jen went down a step from her position, nestling herself between the edge of an unoccupied table and a roaring patio heater.

'But there's something you should know,' David continued.

'Something other than the fact that we were supposed to go to Paris *together*? That I've taken time off work at a critical period for my business to go to Paris with you and now I'm in Athens and you're—'

'Married.'

Jen gave an involuntary shudder and she lost composure – and her balance, her elbow knocking two menus off the table next to her. Had he said *married*? She blinked in disbelief at his image on her phone screen. All of a sudden it was like looking at David for the first time again and making lots of reassessments. He *did* look older than his profile photo on the dating website. There *was* an air of superiority about him like Kathleen had once said. He was only good-looking when he was smiling, and he wasn't smiling now. His expression was kind of blank, like there was nothing going on behind his eyes. Why hadn't she picked up on these things before?

'But, you know, it only changes things if you let it,' David said sheepishly.

Jen didn't know what to say. She was in emotional freefall yet what David was following up with was something that seemed to suggest this was a mere blip in their relationship journey. She couldn't believe what she was hearing!

But, what she felt stronger than anything else, was stupid. She had let her guard down because Bonnie and Natalia had said she should. She had let these dates with David develop into weekends away and a shared purchase of a yucca plant that really wasn't thriving. She had got close to thinking that perhaps she should share her no-flat issue with him and her concerns about the business. He had almost been someone she trusted. Almost. And now she was finding out he hadn't even been truthful about his single status. She wasn't his girlfriend, she was his *mistress*.

'Say something, Jen.' He smiled then, but whether he had tried to get across 'sincere' or not, Jen wasn't buying it.

'Is your wife in Paris with you?' she asked, turning around and walking back up the steps, oblivious to the people she was passing by, knocking into, eyes focused on her phone screen.

David sighed, his eyes roving over to his left. 'That's not really relevant. If you...'

He was still talking, but Jen wasn't listening. What was there to hear? He had lied to her about everything for almost six months. And now she had travelled to Greece for him. She wanted to throw up.

'Jen, it's really not that big a deal. Think of it like this—'

'I'll tell you exactly how I will think of it,' Jen said, powering up the steps, still seemingly against the flow of absolutely everyone else. 'I will think of it as one of the biggest mistakes of my life. I will forever regret listening to Bonnie and Natalia, who told me I should do online dating, and I will be writing a very detailed letter to that website suggesting they carry out a thorough audit of all their members to ensure married people cannot pass themselves off as single quite so easily!'

'Jen—'

'Fuck off, David. We're done.'

With tears of humiliation stinging her eyes and the bustle of the night-time crowd around her, Jen didn't see the top of the last step before Bar Páme. It was only the ground that caught her.

12

'Drink,' Astro said.

Jen cradled the bulbous brandy glass in her hands, still stunned from her fall and the fallout after her FaceTime with David. Her chin was throbbing with pain and she couldn't quite remember what had happened after her face had met the stone step. And now she was sitting at a table inside some kind of cave bar with the waiter, Astro, standing opposite her, observing her as if she might hit the ground for a second time.

'This isn't the cocktail I ordered,' she said, sniffing at the brown liquid inside the glass. The alcohol smelled so strong her head recoiled a little. Was this even a legal drink?

'No,' Astro said. 'It is only the combination of spirits. For your shock.'

Her shock. Yes, and that wasn't only the coming together with the ground. David was *married.* She took a slug of the drink and it ripped its way down her throat.

'*Ochi.* No. Not so fast.'

Now Astro was looking at her like it wasn't only her chin she had thumped. Almost as though she was a curiosity. Perhaps that was what she had been to David. Well, screw David and screw other people's opinions. She was and always would be the conductor in the orchestra of her life. She threw back the drink. All of it.

'What are you doing? Are you crazy?' Astro erupted, dropping the holder of serviettes he had been arranging.

Wow. The drink *was* strong. It was taking every bit of restraint she had not to cough as her chest expanded in reaction.

'Where's... Bonnie?' Her voice rasped.

'Your friend?' he asked. 'She is with Marjorie. After she bend over you on the ground, she rip her trousers.'

Now Jen started coughing. It felt as if she had demons to expel from inside her and they were not taking no for an answer.

'You drink too fast. As I said.'

'I'm just... loving Greece so far. People... marking me out for a bag snatch and... attacking Christmas decorations with a fork and... giving me lethal substances to drink!'

'If only you were here in the summer. Then the sun would also be roasting you like lamb on a spit.'

He took a bottle down from a shelf and passed it to her. She unscrewed the cap and glugged it back, momentarily wondering if it *was* the water she presumed it was and not *ouzo,* which the Greeks seemed to drink just as readily here. Finally, she could catch her breath.

'What are you doing?' she asked him.

'What?'

'You have something scrunched up in your hand.'

'No, there is nothing.'

It wasn't nothing. She could see something glittering red, tiny pieces of it peeking out from between his fingers.

'I can see it,' Jen continued. 'It's tinsel.'

'This?' Astro said, unfurling his hand. 'In Greece this is called *poúlies*. And it is going in the trash.'

Jen took in the cave bar anew. It was the very best example of rustic yet on-trend, with its rough stone and warm uplighters in arched nooks, strings of golden fairy lights, earthenware pots and iron tools that looked like they might have been found in an archaeological dig. But, unlike the streets outside and the taverna they had eaten dinner in, there were barely any festive adornments in here. Marrying that with the fact that Astro had seemed horrified by the inflatable candy cane, Jen could jump to only one conclusion.

'You're a Christmas hater,' she stated. 'Aren't you?'

'Do I get a badge to wear on my chest?'

'You really *do* hate Christmas. Oh my God.'

'I think it is more strange that people are so obsessed with it.' He scrunched the tinsel in his hand again. 'It is not natural to bring real trees inside your house unless you are using them for firewood.'

Jen gasped. 'There is something wrong with you.'

'Because I do not want my uncle's bar to contain bells and angels?'

'Well... yes.'

Astro laughed then and its sound took Jen by surprise. It was soft and light – in complete contrast to his views about her very favourite thing.

He pulled up a chair, twisting it the wrong way and sitting astride it. 'OK, why not tell me something there is to like about Christmas.'

Jen smiled and twisted the cap back on the water bottle. 'This won't work.'

'Exactly,' Astro said. 'Because there is nothing to like about it unless you fall for the hype and the shiny things they put in the stores.'

'No, it won't work because your mind is set,' Jen continued. 'No matter what I say, you are not going to give Christmas a chance.'

He laughed again. 'Give Christmas a chance? You speak of it like it is an abandoned puppy that only needs love.'

He stood up and moved across the room. At that same moment Jen saw Bonnie rushing down the bar, side-stepping customers to reach her.

'Are you OK? Ooo, your chin looks a bit red. Sorry I left you but honestly, I bent down and *riiiip*! I just knew my booty was being exposed to every Athenian in the vicinity so once Astro had picked you up, Marjorie, that's the waitress, she shielded me with some menu boards until she got me somewhere she could stick the Greek equivalent of Wonder Web on my trousers.'

Finally, Bonnie inhaled and then she took Jen's bottle of water.

Astro had picked her up? Oh God, now she was starting to remember. It had all hit her at once, including the pavement, and it was as if she didn't know what to do. Jen watched Astro now. His fingers were peeling off some tape that was holding a white rattan star in place on the wall.

'Anyway, never mind my wardrobe malfunction,' Bonnie said. 'What did David say that made you swan dive to the ground?'

Perhaps it was because she wanted to avoid this conversation, but Jen was distracted by Astro taking down the star. She watched him slide it behind a coffee machine on the edge of the bar so it was out of sight.

'Jen?'

'Yes,' she said, finally meeting her friend's eyes.

'What did David say?'

Jen swallowed, her throat dry, as the FaceTime came flooding back. 'David... is in Paris.'

'What?!'

'Yeah.' Jen nodded. 'And he's there... with his wife.'

This time the drink Bonnie reached for was the brandy glass. She tipped it back, drinking the tiniest of dregs that remained, and then held the glass aloft.

'Astro, can we have two more of these?'

13

What was wrong with him? The bar was busy now, he had tables to keep served with drinks and food, yet Astro found his interest returning to the two women in the corner of the bar. Well, one woman in particular, the one Marjorie had now told him was called Jen. The one who had defended Christmas as if the season was her very best friend. The one with soft waves of blonde hair and eyes the colour of ripe acorns.

'Astro, what are you doing?'

It was Marjorie, sneaking up behind him. He wasn't certain how long he had been standing there with the tray containing three bottles of Alfa beer and a coffee.

'Taking these outside to table two.' He made to move off.

'I was not talking about the drinks, I was talking about the festive decorations I have been putting up, which you have been taking down.'

'No,' Astro answered, shaking his head. 'Some have fallen and I have put them somewhere safe. Others, they were knocked over by...' He paused and then he indicated Jen and Bonnie. 'These women.' He swallowed. 'They seem to want to, I don't know, throw their arms around and, you saw, they fall into the street.'

Marjorie gave him one of her special looks. One she could hold for a very long time. One that he always had to look away from. The second he blinked he knew he had lost this contest.

'Just for tonight, Marjorie,' he pleaded. 'You know—'

'Yes, Astro, I do know.' She planted a firm hand on his shoulder. Her next words were spoken softly. 'But I also know that your uncle has bills he has not paid. And I know that I am not family and I cannot cook like Chef so I will be the first person who has to leave and—'

'Marjorie—'

'No, Astro, this is the best place I have worked. Philippos is the kindest boss and I do not have to wear clothes that show my ass to get tips.'

Now he felt like a child. His uncle had bills he hadn't paid. Marjorie loved this job. He thought about his mother then. How hard she had always worked to keep paying for essentials, holding back a little so he could have small treats like all the other kids. It was only one month, and after that, all the garish madness would be consigned to cellars and attics again and the city could return to normal.

'OK,' he told her. He pulled a string of tinsel out of the front fold of his apron and then a string of silver bells from the pocket of his jeans, and gave them to her. 'And the star, it is behind the coffee machine.'

Marjorie shook her head. 'Perhaps if you think a little less about the decorations, you will have more time to stare at the girl you carried into the bar like a Herculean.'

Straight away, before he realised it, Astro's eyes were back on Jen. What was it about her that was drawing his attention? It wasn't as if he was immune to attractive women, but no one had made him look more than once for a very long time.

'Bonnie is very talkative,' Marjorie continued. 'They arrive only today. They do not yet know how long they will stay.'

He swallowed, watching Jen sip the final drops from the second round of strong drinks he had brought them some thirty minutes ago now.

'I am saying, if you like her, you will need to act fast,' Marjorie said.

She pocketed the decorations Astro had given her and then took his tray from him.

What was the point? If he wanted female company, there were plenty of places to go in the city where likeminded singles too busy for a relationship could get to know one another. Philippos had warned him that starting anything with a tourist was only asking for trouble.

He took the tray back from Marjorie. 'Table two are waiting for their drinks.'

* * *

'These drinks are numbing things a bit, right? I mean, they're numbing the news a little for me, but are they in any way lessening the impact of David being married for you?' Bonnie asked.

The truth was, Jen didn't know how she felt apart from duped. She felt like someone who had been scammed out of their life savings by an online lothario. If she actually had any life savings. Or savings of any kind. For some reason she nodded.

'Jen, please, you've barely said anything, and I read online that internalising your feelings and not sharing can cause a 35 per cent higher risk of having a stroke.'

Jen sighed. 'It's probably higher than that if you internalise your feelings whilst drinking these Greek spirits.' She ran her index finger around the rim of the glass.

'You should be getting angry,' Bonnie said. '*I'm* angry! I'm *so* angry! Because I trusted him! And I encouraged *you* to trust him!'

'You did,' Jen answered.

'Oh God!' Bonnie shrieked. 'You blame me, don't you? Because you didn't want to sign up for that dating app and I said it would be OK because my auntie met Kevan on it and everyone loves Kevan and—'

'I don't blame you,' Jen said. 'It was my decision to sign up. I wanted to see if meeting guys that way would be better than waiting for Cillian Murphy to walk into Greg's.'

She managed a small smile.

'I know but I've been going on and on about you going to Paris with David and saying I thought he was going to propose and—'

'Bonnie, it's fine,' Jen said. 'Honestly, if it's anyone's fault it's mine. I should have trusted my gut that people will take advantage any chance they get and the more you give, the more there is for them to take.'

Now Jen was feeling something. Darkness. Disappointment. It was similar to how she had felt when she was a teenager and the next foster home turned out to be even worse than the one before. Back then she would have slipped Bravely Bear up her jumper so no one could see her hugging him, put her headphones in her ears and played a medley of Christmas hits until she was so warmed by the lyrics, the melody and Bravely's soft fur next to her skin, that a fuzzy festive coat of armour protected her from any other emotion.

'I don't want you to feel like that,' Bonnie said, reaching for her hand. 'Because there are good people in the world. Like Kathleen. And Natalia. And me... when I'm not shooting my mouth off about engagements at the Eiffel Tower.'

'I know,' Jen said, giving Bonnie's hand a squeeze. 'But that's only three people in a very big world.'

She shrugged, resigned, hatches battened down.

'Well, I'm not letting what David's done make you feel that way about the universe!' Bonnie announced.

'It's OK.' Jen was suddenly feeling so very tired. 'Can we just go now? Sorry, I think it's the early flight and—'

'And that wanker pulling a stunt like that.' Bonnie got to her feet. 'Yes, we'll go to bed, sleep on it and in the morning we can work out our whole Athens festive tour!'

Jen swallowed. She shouldn't be here. That was the bottom line. Flying here was a mistake. She needed to get back to England, throw herself into the business, forget David and this impromptu Greek break and find her equilibrium again.

'Bonnie, we can't stay,' she said. 'Longer than tonight, I mean.'

'What?'

'We came here because David said he was here, but he isn't here. And I have a business that needs me as much as I need it right now and to be really honest with you, the thought of losing that hurts me so much more than losing a man I found out I never really had in the first place.'

'Jen, let's think about this,' Bonnie said as Jen got to her feet and began pulling on her coat.

'There's nothing to think about. I'll find a way to pay you back for the flights and tonight at the hotel and then we'll forget we ever did something so spontaneously stupid over a creep who wasn't worth it.'

With her coat now buttoned up and her resolve back in place, Jen headed for the exit.

14

ASTRO'S APARTMENT, BAR PÁME, PLAKA

A sharp pinprick of pain woke Astro. Another hit came quickly, then a third. He snapped open his eyes and there was Peri, head bobbing up and down and side to side, not cooing softly but aggressively and now the pigeon's feet were moving like he was performing a traditional *kalamatianos* dance on Astro's chest.

'*Kalimera*, Peri,' he said, offering a finger to the bird who hopped on board.

The room felt cold and from his now sat-up position he could see condensation on the glass of the small windows that looked out over the rooftops and roof terraces. Peri fluttered over to the stool Astro used as a nightstand and settled on top of a book about sculpture which Astro was currently struggling to get time to read.

There was a knock on the door. Astro grabbed for his T-shirt.

'Astro, are you awake?' the voice called.

His uncle. Astro checked his watch in case he was late for work. Seven a.m.

'I am here,' Astro called. 'Come in.'

The T-shirt over his head, he dragged up his jeans and ran his hands through his hair.

The door opened and Philippos entered. Straight away, Astro was struck by how exhausted his uncle looked. There were dark rings under his eyes and his skin seemed drawn, cheekbones more pronounced than usual and highlighting the grey flecks in his beard.

As if Philippos could read his thoughts, he put his hand to his jaw.

'I need to trim my beard, right? Before it is me that looks like Saint Vasilis.'

'Is everything OK?' Astro asked. 'Because if you are still thinking about the decorations for the bar, I said to Marjorie last night that—'

'I need to be somewhere else this morning. Can you set everything up? Be ready to open at nine?'

'Nine?'

'There are many tourists, Astro. If we are not open early, we will miss out and we cannot afford to miss out.'

Perhaps this was his opportunity to ask about those bills Marjorie had mentioned…

'I will be back for the lunchtime rush and Manos said you can call him if you need an extra hand before then.'

Before Astro could say anything else, Peri rose into the air, crapping on the wooden boards as he flew across the room to the small kitchen area in the far corner.

'Astro! That bird is a hygiene risk!' Philippos exclaimed. 'How long has it been coming inside?'

'I had no idea he was here until this very second,' Astro lied, padding barefoot towards Peri who was now sitting on the arc of the mono tap over the sink. Moving with a deft sleight of hand, Astro threw a tea towel over the packet of bird seed on the counter. He picked up the pigeon and headed over to the window. Peri was just going to have to wait for his breakfast until his uncle was gone to wherever he was going.

On that topic...

'So, where are you going so early? Have you started going to church more than on Sundays?' he asked, opening the window, putting the reluctant pigeon on the sill, and quickly shutting the glass again.

'Church,' Philippos said, shaking his head. 'I start to wonder if faith has any place in this life any more.'

Now Astro knew something was wrong. Even when Philippos had been distraught at Eleni's death, he had gone to church. A young Astro had sat next to him on the uncomfortable wooden chairs, listening to his uncle whisper for forgiveness as if her death was the result of something he himself had done.

'I... could come with you on Sunday if you like?'

Philippos's face broke into a smile as he laughed. 'Are you kidding? You hate going to church. Last time you wore head-phones and we had black looks from the congregation because they could hear Shawn Mendes louder than the litany.'

Astro did hate going to church. He hated it almost as much as he hated Christmas, but that wasn't the point. If Philippos needed him then he was there, like his uncle had been for him his whole life.

'I won't wear my headphones,' he offered.

Philippos placed a hand on his shoulder and patted it. 'Astro, you do not have to do that. The only things I ask of you are to open up early this morning and to tolerate the festive decorations. Everything else... will be OK.'

Everything else sounded monumental. But as Astro went to reply Philippos spoke first.

'Oh, before I forget,' he said, slipping his hand into the pocket of his jeans before drawing it out again. 'Marjorie found this when she was clearing up last night. She told me to give it to you and said something like you would know what to do with it.'

Philippos unfurled his fingers and in his palm was an earring shaped like a golden angel. Astro knew exactly who that belonged to – Jen. But what was he supposed to do about it? However, apparently that question didn't stop him from reaching out to take the small gold object.

'*Ta léme*,' Philippos said, heading back out.

As his uncle closed the door, Astro was left wondering how he was going to find the woman who had burst into his winter in a city this big.

15

SYNTAGMA SQUARE

'What time is this meant to happen again?' Jen asked.

'Every hour, presumably on the hour, but I'm not 100 per cent,' Bonnie answered, her head in a pamphlet the receptionist had given them. 'I'm not sure we're in exactly the right place.'

They were here to see the changing of the guard and the place was a beautiful, tiled square, a bubbling fountain at its centre, people passing back and forth towards a wide flight of steps at one end. All the trees were decked with golden lights and the Christmas centrepiece was a large spruce at least twenty metres tall, a shining star at its peak. Strings of lights, wrapped gifts and icicles decorated the branches. The streets they'd walked down to get here were bordered by high-rises, towering up at the edge of very busy roads – cars, buses and motorbikes all speeding as if the tarmac might at any second burst into flames.

Jen breathed in the air, a lot cooler than it had been when they'd arrived yesterday and enough of a temperature drop to warrant her coat done up. It was beautiful here, but her head was still scrambled from the events of yesterday evening. Between telling Bonnie they needed to go back to the UK last night and now, there had been plenty of discussion over Bonnie's chocolate snacks after midnight and the delicious breakfast this morning. But what had really settled it was that there were no Wizz Air flights back to London today. And seeing as Bonnie had already shelled out for their tickets and Jen's finances were drier than over-air-fried kale, booking entirely new flights with another airline wasn't really an option.

With her mouth around perfect scrambled eggs, baby sausages, a Greek pastry featuring spinach and a mound of feta cheese, Jen had agreed to see how today went and to check in with Natalia and Kathleen later. A decision about anything else could come after that. As for David, he had phoned twice and left her two texts saying how sorry he was and asking to talk. Except Jen got the feeling that the only thing David was really sorry about was having been found out. As far as Jen was concerned, there was nothing else to talk about.

'Ah! Here we are!' Bonnie exclaimed, lifting her head from the guidebook, finger on a rather small map inside. 'We need to climb those steps and the parliament building should be on the other side. What time is it?'

'About three minutes to nine,' Jen answered.

'Ooo, we'll have to run! Quick!' Bonnie started to pick up the pace.

'But, if it's every hour then—'

'Come on!' Bonnie called from ahead, hair flying in the breeze.

* * *

'Are they even real, do you think?' Bonnie asked. 'They're standing so still.'

Having crossed a road that felt like the equivalent of Brands Hatch just as the starter dropped the flag, they were now standing outside the parliament building, in front of which was the Tomb of the Unknown Soldier and two sentries in traditional dress: hats with tassels, navy smocks with pleats, white stockings and heavy shoes with pom-poms on top. The whole ensemble was majestic in all the right ways.

'They're real,' Jen whispered, the way she used to the moment she got captivated by one of Kathleen and Gerald's new window displays.

And then movement began, slow and steady, replacement sentries arriving from the left with a khaki-clad escort.

'Wow,' Bonnie said in as quiet a voice as Bonnie could ever manage. 'It's so...'

'Like a dance,' Jen said.

She reached into her bag for her phone to take a photo and then she had second thoughts. This was a moment to savour, to enjoy exactly as it happened and commit to memory rather than camera roll. As the sentries leaving their duties swapped with their comrades – long steps, shoes slapped to the ground – Jen's fingers went to graze her earring... It wasn't there.

'Amazing,' Bonnie said as the new guards took their post and the others left, presumably for a sit down somewhere.

'Bonnie, I've lost my earring,' Jen said, having already confirmed the left one was still in place.

'Here?' Bonnie asked, gaze dropping to the ground and scanning the near vicinity.

'I don't know. I mean, I think it was there when I went to bed last night.' The truth was she couldn't remember and that meant it could literally be anywhere. And how could she possibly find a small earring? The hope would have to be that it was in the bed at the hotel. But one shake of the sheet from the maid and, if it was between the covers, then it was going to be whisked off to be wrapped up and sent whizzing around in a wet drum with every other cotton item in the hotel.

'Not the angel ones!' Bonnie exclaimed, now looking at Jen's ear that still had an earring in it. 'The ones Kathleen and Gerald bought you.'

Yes – that was why she was on the verge of panic. Apart from Bravely Bear, they were the only items that meant anything to her. They had been a Christmas present. She should have taken far more care of them.

You shouldn't even be here.

'Yes.' The word caught in Jen's throat.

'Well,' Bonnie said, eyes back on the ground now. 'We will just have to retrace our steps and—'

Jen shook her head. This wasn't the loft office where there was a vague chance of discovery if she looked closely enough. This was a Greek city with hundreds of people treading the same pavements with drains and cracks and a myriad of places a small piece of jewellery could disappear into.

'We're not going to find it.'

'No,' Bonnie said. 'I'm not having that kind of pessimism this early on a bright, if slightly chilly, Athens morning. There is *every* possibility we can find it.'

She linked arms with Jen and pulled her close.

'Just like there is every possibility we're going to get mown down by a yellow taxi if we stop to look on the pedestrian crossing.'

'Well, let's hope it's not there then. I mean, chances are it could actually be stuck in your knickers or something. One time I lost a ring for three days like that.'

'I have no idea how to respond to that.'

'Eyes down,' Bonnie ordered, still squeezing her arm. 'We are going to find it, OK? Because if anyone deserves a bit of festive good luck right now, it's you.'

Jen responded with a nod. Perhaps this unplanned earring hunt would stop Bonnie from wanting her to open up about her feelings over the David situation.

16

BAR PÁME, PLAKA

'*Ya, Astro!*'

Astro almost jumped out of his skin as he was punched hard in the side by something. Turning around, he was greeted by a grinning six-year-old boy brandishing a lightsabre that was flashing red, green and gold, and intermittently a mix of the three at strobe-esque speed.

'Achilles, be careful of the heaters,' he replied, grabbing the hood of the boy's coat before it touched the flames.

'Do you like my lightsabre?' the boy asked, whisking the glowing stick around and making all the appropriate 'whooshing' noises as it came close to swiping cutlery baskets.

'I love it,' Astro answered, putting his hands on Achilles's shoulders and steering him into what little space there was outside on the steps. 'Where is your mama?'

'Running,' Achilles answered. 'To catch me up. She said she was late to get here so I thought if I got here quickly, she would not get in trouble.'

Astro sighed. Marjorie being a single mum to Achilles was another reason why he was going to endure the Christmas festivities so they could all keep their jobs. Marjorie was a hard worker but Astro also knew that Philippos had taken her on because she reminded him of Eleni...

'You know you should not run away from your mother,' Astro said, manoeuvring him towards the door to the bar. 'She will worry.'

'But I have my lightsabre,' Achilles said, poking it forward and almost catching the ear of a cat sitting under a table.

'I know, but—'

'Achilles! What have I told you about running off? Come here and let me find my grandmother's slipper in my bag!'

It was Marjorie, storming up the steps, red-faced, a large bag hanging from each arm. Astro suddenly felt the boy's presence behind him as if he was a tree Achilles could disappear behind. He remembered that feeling. He also remembered the threat of *yiayia's* slipper.

'He is OK,' Astro said as Marjorie arrived, a little out of breath.

'I can see that,' she replied, her tone frustrated. 'That *Star Wars* sword is giving away his location. Achilles, hear me, you are old enough now to realise that even if you close your eyes and cannot see me, I can still see you!'

Astro was already attempting to peel the bags from Marjorie's arms in a bid to lighten her load. 'Go and get yourself a coffee.'

'I am already late for my shift, and I had to bring Achilles. I do not deserve coffee,' she said, sighing.

'Everyone deserves coffee,' Astro said. 'And I am not going to tell Philippos you were not here at exactly ten.' He shook the bags. 'What is in here?'

'Scraps. Beads. Fabric. Glitter. Things to make this place shine like a Christmas tree. On a budget,' Marjorie explained.

Astro looked in the first of the bags and a plethora of randomness confronted him. It looked like Mrs Calimeris, one of

Marjorie's neighbours, had opened up her sewing box and emptied the contents into them.

'We are going to hang material from the bottom of the late Mr Calimeris's trousers from the ceiling of the bar?' Astro asked.

'Yes,' Marjorie answered. 'But use your imagination. Have you not seen the strings of things across the streets in the Psyrri neighbourhood?'

Of course he had. He spent as much time as he could in that very place. Once a place for undesirables where the very worst members of the gang, *Koutsavakides,* hung out, it was now a rejuvenated area. By day it appeared nothing but residential, but by night the streets were transformed, and the district became a melting pot of music, food and people having fun. However, what interested Astro the most was the street art. Yes, there were still the unimaginative slogans and tags, but they sat alongside real works of genius worthy of a gallery. There were also a couple of his own.

'I hope your imagination is better than mine,' Astro replied, pushing at the door of the bar.

'Astro, can we make smoothies?' Achilles asked, ducking into step behind him and avoiding the path of his mother. 'With honey and chocolate and sprinkles?'

'Achilles,' Marjorie said. 'You should not even be here. You should definitely not be drinking Philippos's profits.'

'We can make a smoothie,' Astro told the boy, leading the way. He looked back to Marjorie. 'We will call it payment for Mrs Calemeris's materials.'

17

TOWER OF THE WINDS

'Geoffrey ask for more budget,' Natalia said down the phone. 'He say that one of his actors has clash with taking mother to bingo club and if he does not give him more money he will not perform in Herod show.'

Jen sank down to the low stone wall and watched Bonnie snapping photos of the historic site they had arrived at. Despite combing over their route from the hotel that morning – and Bonnie had at one point actually got out a comb and pulled apart a ball made up of dust, fluff and a paper wrapper from a straw – there was no sign of the angel earring. Now she was regretting this phone call home. Focusing back on the business was supposed to be taking her mind off the loss of her precious jewellery and what had happened with David but everything Natalia was telling her was only making things worse.

She closed her eyes and took a deep breath, imagining her office space back in the UK. All those decorations waiting to go to events, the calming scent of her latest candle – Milk and Cookies for Santa – her favourite festive playlist... Natalia building a rubber band ball she would never be able to deconstruct. It was time for some honesty. A little, at least.

'Natalia, there *is* no more budget,' she said firmly. 'I already gave in to costume embellishments I wouldn't normally sign off on because I know the historical society will appreciate the attention to detail.'

'What do I say to him? He very rude the last time we speak. He say word like "monumental". This feel like insult.'

'You call him back and you tell him there is no more money and he needs to find another actor who doesn't have a schedule clash.'

'He will say that this actor already know lines. That it will take a different one long time to learn.'

'Natalia,' Jen said, sitting up a little straighter and drawing the interest of a ginger cat creeping along the wall. 'I have complete confidence in you handling this situation. And you have my full support in whatever you decide to do to fix it.'

'Really?' Natalia exclaimed, her words accompanied by a noise that sounded like she had just cracked her knuckles.

'And if you can't find a quick solution then…' She paused as the ginger cat bashed its forehead against her elbow.

'Then?' Natalia asked.

She had no answer. If she had more time she could look into another acting group, but she had worked with Geoffrey for a number of years and even with this current hiccup, he was probably the only thespian ensemble in her budget.

'I don't know,' she admitted with a hopeless sigh.

'Not problem,' Natalia answered. 'If Geoffrey still rude I get brothers and friends to learn lines and dress up in costumes. It will be success for you, Jen. I make it so.'

This was the kind of hope and positivity she needed. The knowledge that her clients would be provided with what they perhaps didn't even know they wanted, no matter what lengths Christmas Every Day had to go to.

'Thanks, Natalia,' Jen said, breathing a little easier.

'So, tell me, how is beautiful Greece and handsome David?'

'Oh, Greece is very beautiful and we are actually at this really cool monument right now so—'

'Monumental? Like Geoffrey says?'

'No, not like however he meant it.' She stood up before the cat could climb onto her lap. 'Listen, Natalia, thank you for catching me up with everything. I know the business is in good hands.'

'I have strong hands,' Natalia agreed. 'Mother always say I could tear potatoes from earth like rotavator.'

They said their goodbyes and then Jen made her way over to the iron fence where Bonnie was attempting a selfie with the world's oldest meteorological station in the background. There were tourists down there beside it, walking around and taking photos, wrapped up in coats and hats.

'This is fascinating,' Bonnie said. 'Did you know that this was built in the first century BC?'

'No,' Jen answered. 'I also didn't know that Geoffrey was going to try and scam me the minute I left the country.'

'What?' Bonnie put her phone down.

'I really need to get back to the UK.' Jen dug her hands in her pockets. 'Since we got here, everything has gone wrong.'

She took a few steps along the cobbles, eyes searching the ground for an earring that couldn't even be here as they hadn't travelled this road before.

'Not everything,' Bonnie said, catching her up. 'Remember the amazing meal we had last night and—'

'Almost getting our belongings nicked after accepting a giant blow-up sweet from a stranger,' Jen interrupted.

'We don't know that. You said so yourself.'

'Yes, well maybe I was naïve. The same as I obviously was about David.' She put a finger to the small sore bump on her chin and then gripped the fence with both hands, fingers curling around the metalwork and looking out over the octagonal stone tower.

'That is nothing to do with you, Jen,' Bonnie said, standing close. 'What happened with David is all on him. *He* is the one who's married. *He* lied to you. About everything and—'

'And *I* didn't realise.'

'Christ, Jen, you can't take responsibility for this. No one would have known. He was *smooth*. He seemed so genuine.'

'Yeah, lesson learned. Good guys don't exist.' And it was strange saying that when she was looking at a structure depicting Greek wind gods, all of whom were male.

'No,' Bonnie said with loud determination. 'I'm not going to let what David's done make you retreat from the pursuit of love.'

'Well, to be honest,' Jen began, 'I have enough on my plate with no home, a failing business and an assistant who thinks the word "monumental" is the new "screw you".' She took a breath. 'And now I've lost one of my favourite earrings and Geoffrey's making things difficult and... I'm craving one of those desperately alcoholic drinks we had last night and it's not even lunchtime.'

For most people, this would be when the tears would come, welling up in her eyes, if not completely starting to stream down her face. But Jen had spent so long stopping that from happening, the process didn't even have a chance to begin. She *never* cried. Ever. All she got was a tightness in her chest, a pressure build-up that had to sit there because release was not going to be allowed. The closest she got to letting emotion go was when she was in bed, covers over her head like her own personal tepee, nuzzling her face into Bravely Bear, where no one could see.

'Well, it *is* the festive period,' Bonnie reminded her, slipping her arm through hers. 'If it's not being full from Quality Street it's making every second drink into an Irish coffee. And we're kind of on holiday.'

Jen shook her head. 'We're not on holiday. The only way I'm getting through being here now is telling myself that this is for work and I'm going to put on a Greek Christmas extravaganza for someone one day.'

'And you will. And that is why, once we've had another one of those alcoholic drinks, we will find somewhere that gives us Greek traditions and the dancing and everything you need to replicate it when we get back,' Bonnie said. 'And I might pick up a few bottles of whatever alcohol is strong enough to get me through a Christmas with Andrea.'

'And you promise you'll sort out flights for getting back as soon as we can?'

'I said so at breakfast,' Bonnie reminded her. 'And no one breaks a promise over eggs and feta cheese.' She hugged Jen's arm. 'Come on, let's go and get a drink.'

18

LYSIOU STREET, ATHENS

'Do you think I can get a pet pigeon?' Achilles asked as they
wandered back towards Bar Páme, Peri at their heels. After
smoothie-making, Achilles had managed to knock all the
containers of fruit onto the kitchen floor and before the chef could
go crazy, Astro had suggested he take Achilles out to play a little
football. He knew Philippos had left him in charge but Marjorie
had this and Astro remembered what it felt like to be a small boy
with plenty of energy. His mother used to take him to the National
Gardens to run around, play chase and look at the animals there –
goats, geese, green parrots in the trees.

'Peri isn't really my pet,' Astro told him, the ball tucked under
his arm. 'Pigeons, they are wild animals.'

Achilles laughed. 'But he is not like a lion or a tiger.'

'No,' Astro agreed. 'But he is still something that should not be
kept inside. He is free.' Although he suspected that this particular
pigeon would not take exception to being confined to his
apartment.

'I want a dog, but Mama says they eat too much, and we don't
have the money.'

'They also take a lot of looking after. Walking them every day, cleaning up after them.'

'So, a pigeon would be better,' Achilles said, making wide eyes.

This kid was super-smart. Astro laughed. 'How about I let you feed Peri when we get back to the bar? Maybe if your mama sees how well you look after him, she might let you feed the pigeons at your apartment.'

'OK,' Achilles said, a spring now in his step. 'And then you can help me make Christmas bracelets.'

'What Christmas bracelets?'

'We have a festival at school and we have to make things to sell to raise money to buy new things. Me and Plato have to make Christmas bracelets but Mama says she doesn't have time to help me, and I have to ask Mrs Calimeris, but Mrs Calimeris smells of donkeys.'

'Does Mrs Calimeris *have* a donkey?'

'No!' Achilles exclaimed. 'It is crazy!'

'Well, I have to work, but you can take Peri up to my apartment and start on the bracelets, and I will come and help you when I can.'

'Really?' Achilles asked.

'Sure.' Astro lowered his voice then. 'Just don't let my uncle see you with Peri. He does not know he sometimes likes to stay inside.'

Before they had even reached the door to the bar, Achilles had picked the pigeon up and hidden it beneath his jacket.

* * *

'It's minus seven here!' Kathleen shouted over FaceTime. 'Minus seven and that bloody man in room thirty is still running around in shorts and a vest shouting about the Dunkirk beaches.' Kathleen's face came closer to the screen. 'Wait, is that sunshine I can see?'

Jen turned the phone screen around, giving Kathleen more of the view as she and Bonnie nursed coffees at a bar at the bottom of the steps. They were a few metres down from Bar Páme, and the area was still busy in the daytime, looking ever more festive.

'It *is* sunshine,' Jen told her. 'But it's a bit colder today.'

'It's not minus seven though, is it?'

'Don't they have the heating on, Kathleen?' Bonnie asked as Jen put the screen back to their faces. 'It was always a good plus twenty-five when I worked there. In fact, I'm not sure it wasn't the humidity that got some of them in the end.'

'Bonnie,' Jen hissed.

'Sorry,' Bonnie said, sitting back in her seat. 'I wasn't trying to—'

'Never you mind, Bonnie,' Kathleen interrupted. 'We all know we're in God's waiting room here. Well, not the bloody man from room thirty I'm hoping. I want him to be first in the queue for whatever Satan has going on below ground. At least in that singlet he'll be appropriately dressed.'

'You're not in any waiting room,' Jen said quickly. 'You've got years ahead of you.'

'Years of eating turkey arse and listening to the ravings of an alleged war hero. Euthanise me now. Can't you get whatever they give to the dogs, Bonnie?'

'Kathleen!' Jen exclaimed. 'Don't say that!'

She swallowed, not liking the idea of a world without Kathleen nor the blasé way her dear friend was talking about it.

'Anyway, enough about my limited life, tell me what you've been up to. David taken you anywhere really fancy yet? Because he's not one to shy away from an opportunity to show off, is he?'

Jen took a second to gather herself. She didn't want to worry Kathleen but keeping the fact she was living at the business premises was already a secret she knew she shouldn't be hiding. Perhaps airing the truth about David would be cathartic all around.

'David isn't actually here,' she said bluntly.

'What?'

'No, he's in Paris. With his wife.'

She kept her expression straight, emotionless, neutral and then she felt Bonnie move a touch closer, a small show of solidarity. On screen, Kathleen was completely motionless too. So still that Jen wondered if their connection had been severed. Until: 'Good luck to her then. You won't have been the first. Nor will you be the last. She's made a rod for her own back with that one.' She tutted in that particular Kathleen way. 'He was never good enough for you, Jen. And the very worst thing was he gave off the impression he was *too* good for everyone. Good riddance.' She sniffed. 'Does Natalia know yet?'

'Er, no,' Jen said.

'Because if you want David's nuts crushed or his fingernails removed, I have faith that that girl will know someone to do it. Probably her brothers.'

'She's not wrong,' Bonnie commented.

Jen nodded, as Bonnie moved the conversation on, telling Kathleen about their day – the changing of the guard and the racing across the pedestrian crossings at warp speed. In some ways, Jen was glad Kathleen wasn't wanting a full debrief of the whole debacle, that she had acknowledged what Jen had told her and then they'd moved on. But in other ways, she wondered what would happen if she *did* say more than the blunt facts, if she *did* admit to someone that David's betrayal actually hurt.

'We'll be coming back soon,' she said, interrupting Bonnie's chattering. 'So, I'll be able to come to the carol concert at the church with you.'

'What?' Kathleen said, frowning. 'I thought you had a few *weeks* off.'

'Well, yes, I did,' Jen started. 'But that was supposed to be for David and me to go to Paris and now—'

'And now what? You find out the little bastard is married and he's been stringing you along so you're going to reward yourself by going back to work?'

'I like work.'

Was that really the answer she was giving?

'Jen!' Kathleen exclaimed. 'I liked work as well but I really needed those two weeks in Ladram Bay every year. And believe me, Gerald knew I needed them too.'

'And she hasn't had a holiday at all for as long as I've known her,' Bonnie chipped in.

'I've had weekends away,' Jen countered.

'Party conferences don't count. That's work.'

'Is this ganging up? Because it feels like ganging up,' Jen said, adjusting her posture in the seat. And Bonnie had promised she was going to look at flights back to London asap. This conversation didn't feel like she was invested in a quick return at all.

'Obviously, it's up to you,' Kathleen said in that tone she used that said the complete opposite.

'Of course, it's up to you,' Bonnie added.

'I just... need to think,' Jen said, swallowing away a knot of tension that had bubbled up in her throat. She felt a bit like she was being railroaded into a situation and was losing control.

'Oh, got to go,' Kathleen said, eyes flitting to the right. 'Bingo's on today. I don't usually play because *some* people here need the numbers read out so slowly it can send you into a sleep. But the prize is Baileys and you know I like a Baileys.'

'Don't we all,' Bonnie remarked. 'Bye, Kathleen.' She waved a hand.

'Bye, Bonnie. Bye, Jen, love.'

The call ended and Jen really didn't know what came next. The FaceTime was supposed to be a check-in on Kathleen but somehow Jen felt it had turned into an intervention to get her to stay in Athens. Was this something Bonnie had instigated on the quiet? Was she *really* looking into flights to get them home?

'I'm just going to pop to the loo and then shall we look at getting that tourist bus around the city?'

Bonnie didn't wait for a response, just shimmied out from behind the table and headed inside. Leaving Jen to catastrophise.

She thought that living at her work premises was going to be as bad as it got but now she was in a country she'd never planned for, having unwittingly been someone's mistress, with Geoffrey trying to sabotage one of her biggest earning opportunities, while her best friend and her substitute mum were nearly forcing her to take a break. It was suddenly a lot.

'*Kalá Christoúgenna!*'

The shout was loud and very close, and suddenly a bracelet was slapped onto Jen's arm. Both terrified and horrified, she leapt from her chair, tearing at the band around her wrist.

'I do not want this! I am not easy prey for a bag snatch! And look! Look in my bag! There is less than a hundred euro, my phone is at least three models behind what's new and the rest is a combination of wipes, sequins, hair grips and a loyalty card for Greg's!'

It was only when the crying started that Jen realised she'd been shouting at a little boy.

19

'Why are you shouting at him?'

It was another voice. Jen looked up and there was Astro standing in front of her. His tone had said he was angry and now his body language was giving off exactly the same vibe. And it was all directed towards her.

'I... he...' she began.

The words weren't coming and when she glanced back to the boy, who could only be about seven years old, tears were streaming down his face, his little chest rising and falling rapidly as he full-on sobbed.

'It's OK, Achilles,' Astro said, putting an arm around the child and gathering him close. 'You have done nothing wrong.' He looked back at Jen again. 'He is making Christmas bracelets for school. He wanted to give some to people here. It was meant to be a nice gift.'

Jen looked to her hand. She was still holding the bracelet. It was like one of those fluorescent glowing ones that people bought for parties, except it was clear and glittery, and hanging from it were rudimentary reindeer and stars made from a mixture of fabric and cardboard.

'I am so sorry,' Jen said, bending down a bit and trying to get the boy's attention. He hid his face in the denim of Astro's jeans as if he was scared of her. Perhaps her actions had been fuelled by the life evaluation she had been doing seconds before the jump-scare, but that wasn't the only reason she had reacted so severely. She stood up straight and addressed Astro. 'Obviously, I didn't mean to frighten him, but it was *you* who told me that pickpockets mark you out with bracelets.' She swallowed. It was no excuse really.

'To know, for the future, those bracelets are not usually ones with cardboard reindeer given out by six-year-olds,' Astro replied.

She nodded. He was right. She had overreacted. She had caused this situation and it was up to her to make it better.

'Can I... get you something?' she asked the boy. 'Something covered in chocolate maybe?'

The boy revealed one weepy eye and sniffed.

'He's already had two smoothies. His mother would be mad at me if he has any more,' Astro answered.

'Oh... well...' She didn't know what else to suggest.

'Can you help me make more Christmas bracelets?'

The boy's whole face appeared now, sniffing, the tear tracks drying up.

Astro said something to the boy in Greek, shaking his head.

'What did you say to him?' Jen asked.

'I ask him why *my* help is not good enough,' Astro replied.

The boy said something, frowning.

'What did he say?' Jen asked again.

'I say,' the boy started. 'That Astro may be good at drawing, but he is not good with glue.'

He splayed his hands out then. All of his fingers were connected by spider-web style glue remnants.

Jen smiled. 'Well, I love making things. Especially Christmas things. I can help.' She put the bracelet back on her arm and held out her hand to the boy. 'My name is Jen.'

'*Ime* Achilles.' He shook her hand.

'Achilles, you should go back to the bar and wash your paint-brushes to get ready.'

'*Endaksi!*' Achilles said, letting go of Astro and sprinting up the steps as fast as his legs could carry him.

'He moves everywhere too fast,' Astro remarked as they both watched the boy skidding across the stone and nearly colliding with a cat before bursting through the door of Bar Páme.

'He's young and fearless,' Jen answered. 'And can speak two languages. You must be very proud.'

'Oh... you think he is... no,' Astro said, shaking his head. 'Achilles, he is not my son. He is the son of Marjorie. The waitress who...'

'Stuck Bonnie's trousers together last night. I remember.' She smiled, somehow getting drawn into full eye contact.

'Last night, I think that you lost something here, at the bar. I was hoping that you would come back so I could return it.' He slipped a hand into the pocket of his jeans and drew something out.

Jen gasped as he held out her gold angel earring.

'Oh my God, I can't believe it! Bonnie and I have been searching everywhere for this. I thought it was gone forever and... well, I can't thank you enough.'

'It is special to you?'

'It was a gift from someone who is special to me.' She fingered the angel's wings. 'Honestly, thank you for not sweeping it into the bin.'

'Listen,' Astro began, his hands going back in his pockets. 'I apologise if I was a little rude to you just now. Achilles, he has always good intentions but sometimes he acts before he thinks.'

'Oh, well, I think we can all be guilty of that,' Jen replied.

'Please, I do not want you to feel that you must spend your holiday here making bracelets.'

'I really don't mind. If it will make Achilles forget the English ogre I turned into and make him smile, then I'm happy to do it.'

'Happy to do what?' said Bonnie, back from the toilets. 'Oh, hi, Astro. Do you work at this bar too?'

Astro shook his head. 'No, I was just passing by.'

'And look,' Jen said. 'You won't believe it, but Astro found my earring.'

'Wow! You're right! I don't believe it! That's great though,' Bonnie said. 'So, what is that we're happy to do?'

'We're going to make Christmas bracelets,' Jen told her.

'What? But I thought—'

'Come on,' Jen said. 'It's for a good cause.' She looked at Astro. 'My reputation actually.'

Bonnie looked none the wiser and she shook her head as if everything had changed in the time it took her to visit the ladies.

'*Páme,*' Astro said, leading the way.

20

'She is like Santa Claus,' Marjorie remarked as she cleared plates with Astro, looking outside to the table they had brought out for Achilles and Jen to do crafts. 'It is magic the way she turns bits of crap into actual jewellery I would wear.'

Astro had been watching Jen more than he had been paying attention to anything else. He knew that because he'd messed up a couple of orders when he'd been trying to listen in to her conversation with Achilles.

'You are not listening to me now. You look at Jen!' Marjorie made that expression she usually made when she'd discovered a titbit of gossip – celebrity or local. And Astro needed to shut that energy down.

Piling another plate on top of the stack that was heavy on his forearm, he leaned in a little towards Marjorie. 'I am looking and thinking of ways I can destroy her red coat.'

'Astro!' Marjorie exclaimed, appalled. But then she dialled it down. 'But I do not really believe you. That is why I gave Philippos the earring to pass to you. To give you an opportunity.'

'And now I have passed the earring back and you have the

opportunity of someone else entertaining your son and making horrible festive things so neither of us have to.'

In a flash, Marjorie had taken his pile of plates and swung around, placing a tray with two coffees in his hands. 'It is time for your break. And Jen deserves a coffee. So, I will take Achilles inside and you can get to know her a bit better while Bonnie is shopping.'

As Astro stood there wondering how this situation had arisen, Achilles was brought into Bar Páme, leaving Jen on her own. She was head down in obvious concentration with what she was working on.

Astro moved forward.

'*Kafes*,' he greeted, putting a coffee down in front of her.

'Oh, thank you but I didn't order—'

'It is from us. To thank you for helping with Achilles's project.' He indicated the chair the boy had vacated. 'Do you mind if I sit?'

'No, of course not,' she said.

He put the tray on a vacant table behind them and set his coffee down. He watched what Jen was doing, a tiny piece of material between her fingers. 'This does not look like a bracelet.'

'No,' Jen admitted. 'After a little discussion we decided to diversify. These are earrings. Inspired by the fact that I almost lost my angel one.'

Astro then saw there were a fair number of these already made. Marjorie was right, they looked professional.

'You made all these?'

'Achilles did some of them once I showed him how,' Jen said, still focused on her work.

'He had the patience to do this?'

'It helps to put some of the mind somewhere else when you're doing work like this.' She looked up from the earring she was making. 'I told him a story. So, part of him was listening to me and then the other part had to work a little harder to focus on the crafts.'

Astro picked up one of the earrings. It sparkled and glittered with sequins, a pinch of bright reinforced fabric holding everything together. 'Everything you needed to make this, Achilles had?'

'Yes,' Jen answered. 'Material, stuffing, cardboard... and we made the hooks from paperclips.' She looked up at him. 'Could you pass me the glue, please? I'll just stick this and then I'll have a drink of the coffee.'

Astro quickly found the glue amongst the array of things on the table and handed it over.

'There,' Jen said, sounding satisfied. She put the earring down and picked up her coffee cup, taking a sip. 'Wow, that's nice.'

'You really like it?'

'You sound surprised. Was I not meant to?'

'Marjorie thinks everyone loves Greek coffee the way she loves Greek coffee. She makes it stronger than anyone else I know.'

'Well, I like it,' she told him. 'A lot more than you like Christmas.'

Astro smiled. 'You are still holding this against me, I can tell.'

'I cannot believe you helped Achilles make the first bracelets. It must have been like persecution.'

'I was relieved you offered to help.'

He swallowed. It *was* hard. She had no idea.

'Bonnie thought I was crazy. She doesn't do crafts. She thinks if you can't buy something from Amazon then it either isn't worth having or doesn't even exist.'

'Where has she gone to shop?'

'She read about Eleonas Flea Market in the guide and decided to start Christmas gift shopping.' Jen sighed. 'It was a bit of a relief really.'

'A relief?'

'Sorry, I shouldn't have said that. It's just things here have been a bit up and down. We weren't meant to even be coming to Athens and I really should get back to the UK for my business.'

'You have a business?'

Jen nodded. 'For a few years now.'

She smiled at him then and he felt it warm his insides.

'But you won't like what I do,' she said.

'Why not?'

'Because I make money from Christmas. It's at the heart of everything I do. My business, it's called Christmas Every Day and that's what I do for people, make every day like Christmas. I organise dinner parties, larger events, proposals, baby showers, all with a festive theme.'

Astro shook his head. 'I do not know if I should laugh or cry.'

'Please laugh,' Jen told him. 'I've had enough tears today with Achilles.'

He swallowed. She wasn't going to be in Athens long. They had had a couple of conversations and he had picked her up off the floor; it wasn't a situation he should feel this disappointed about. But somehow, he was. And he had never known a tourist spend so little time in the Greek capital...

'The Acropolis disappoints you?' Astro asked.

'What?'

'You only arrive yesterday and now you leave?'

He watched her seem to contemplate his question. This was not simple for her. As time elongated, he wondered if she was going to answer at all. Until: 'The reason I came over here ended up being no good reason at all. It was a really bad, ugly, back-stabby, treacherous reason and nothing to do with your lovely city.' She swallowed. 'Although the pedestrian crossings do need a longer countdown.'

Astro wasn't quite sure what to make of her reply so instead he just kept looking at her, trying to work things out from her soft eyes and the curve of her lips.

'Bonnie and one of my friends back home think I should have some time off work but I don't usually do that.'

'Why?' Astro asked.

'Why what?'

'Why don't you usually do that?'

'Because...' She paused again. 'I don't really know what to do if I'm not working.'

Astro watched her inhale and then she took a large gulp of her coffee. In some ways, he could relate.

'God, that sounded awful, didn't it? Who doesn't know what to do if they're not working?'

'When I am not working it seems I am making Christmas bracelets. I think that is worse,' Astro told her.

'Well, tell me what you do when you're not working or making Christmas bracelets,' she said.

It was his turn to pause and think about what to say. Nobody in his life knew just how much art meant to him. That that was where he dreamed his future would lie if everything was different. He opened his mouth to say something, then he had another idea.

'Do you leave Athens before tonight?' he asked.

'Oh, I doubt it. And seeing as Bonnie is shopping, I expect looking at flights has completely slipped her mind amid the bargains.'

'OK,' Astro said with a nod. 'If you have the time, I will show you what I do when I am not working.'

'O-K,' Jen said tentatively.

'Astro!' It was Marjorie calling from the door, beckoning him furiously.

Astro got to his feet. 'Meet me in Monastiraki Square. At midnight.'

'Midnight?' Jen exclaimed in shock.

He smiled. 'They say New York is the city that never sleeps. But really, it is Athens.'

21

MONASTIRAKI SQUARE

Astro hadn't been wrong about Athens still being alive at midnight. As Jen walked into the vibrant square with its multi-coloured cobbles and lines of stone like silver snakes, there were almost as many people here as there had been in the daytime. This square with its bustling metro station was only a few streets away from Hotel Plaka and like many other places here, it sat below the Acropolis, the monument keeping an authoritative eye on proceedings. There were people queueing to buy fruit and piles of different nuts from a blue-painted stall, yellow stands were selling what looked like giant pretzels and interspersed with all the food vendors were sellers holding sticks with moving parts that whizzed and lit up in all the colours. Surrounding the square were bars and restaurants, lights welcoming, the beginnings of Christmas décor around the edges of awnings. Jen took a breath and positioned herself next to a concrete structure in the centre of the square that everyone seemed to be sitting on.

Bonnie had stayed at the hotel and had been almost half asleep when Jen had left her. She had tried to get her to come too, wanting the company, perhaps needing three to make a crowd.

Because otherwise, meeting a man she had only just met, literally seconds after the man she'd thought she knew had been revealed as an untrustworthy, married liar, felt like a risk. One that in any circumstance other than being in a city she wasn't meant to be in, she would not have taken. Why had she taken it? Because what did it matter when things were spiralling in her life anyway? Or because she felt she needed to prove she still had the ability to judge character? Astro seemed genuine and nice, not to mention *very* attractive...

She shivered. It wasn't super-cold tonight; she knew it was nerves. She was worried she was alone at midnight in a festively decorated nightlife metropolis and there was every chance that either she would be stood up or she would never find Astro. At least she could tell herself that was the case if he did stand her up.

Five minutes. That was all she was giving him. If he wasn't here by then then she'd be heading back to the hotel to curl up under the duvet tent-style and hug the pillow as a substitute bear...

'*Yassas.*'

Jen jumped, her over-thinking catching up to the moment. There was Astro, dressed for the first time without his Bar Páme apron over his clothes. Black jeans with boots, and a black T-shirt with a khaki-coloured shirt over the top. Jen took it all in, plus his dark hair, shaved a little at the sides, slightly longer on top, but it was his green eyes that were the standout.

'Hi,' Jen said, unable to stop herself from giving a visible shudder.

'You are cold?' he asked, seeming ready to immediately take his shirt off.

'I'm OK,' she said, pulling her coat closer and fastening the top button. 'Actually, I was expecting it to be colder. It's in minus figures in the UK today and here Bonnie and I have been eating outside.'

'That is the magic of Greece. Warm under those patio heaters belching out power into the sky.'

'Don't say that!' Jen gasped. 'Are they really bad?'

'Relax,' Astro said. 'It is knowledge the whole world over that Greeks, we do whatever we want. Even now it is a fine balance between doing the right thing and doing what we have always done. Recycling, good. Still using donkeys for work, not so good.'

'Next time I'll pick up one of the blankets instead.'

Astro laughed. 'At this time of year, you would get warm from the brightness of the Christmas decorations, remember?'

'It's actually quite subtle here compared to Syntagma Square,' Jen remarked. She looked towards the restaurants with tinsel wrapped around struts of parasols, a few white icicle lights on strings, but nothing seasonally outlandish.

'Subtle,' Astro said, shaking his head. 'Nothing about this season is subtle.'

'Exactly the way I like it,' Jen laughed.

'Come on,' Astro said, nudging her shoulder with his. 'I am going to show you somewhere that will have all the decoration you could ever need.' He took a few steps forward, then turned back to face her again. 'Did you wear shoes you can run in?'

'What?' Jen asked, looking down at her boots. They had a slight heel but were comfortable, however she couldn't remember a time when she'd ever had to run in them. Apart from that one Bar Mitzvah...

'Do not overthink it. Come on,' Astro said, smiling.

* * *

Astro was used to the narrow alleys around this area of Athens, but he was enjoying seeing the changing expressions on Jen's face as she experienced it all for the first time, squeezing past mopeds and plant pots, making turns to routes that looked like they had no end.

'It's so different to the daytime,' Jen remarked as they made a left turn. 'The shops with their shutters down instead of all their things spilling out of baskets and onto the pavement.'

'No space, everyone trying to get you to come into their store. Yes, different,' Astro agreed.

'I like it,' Jen said. 'Handbags swinging from ropes, little soaps wrapped in paper, olive wood salad tongs – Bonnie bought some of those. She's been to Tunisia, and she said that here was like a *souk*.'

Astro shrugged. 'I would not know. I have never left Greece. I had not left Athens until last year. Philippos, my uncle, made us visit an old friend he has in Thessaloniki. The man had five children, sixteen grandchildren and three dogs. I spent the whole visit being jumped on and licked. And that was just the grandchildren.'

Jen laughed. He seemed to be able to make her laugh a lot and for some reason that really pleased him.

'How about you?' he asked. 'Have you been many places in the world?'

'No,' Jen answered as they walked past a small church, its stained-glass door in red and green reflecting the light from within. 'I only just got my first passport.'

'To come to Greece?'

'Paris, actually.'

Astro frowned. As the street widened and she was able to walk alongside him again, he asked, 'What happened? Your flight was diverted to somewhere further away? You got on the wrong plane?'

He was pretty sure the last one was impossible these days.

'It was Bonnie's idea. As I said earlier, it didn't work out quite how it was supposed to.'

He looked at her. 'No?'

'No.'

There was more to this situation, but she was not giving it to him. He was getting to understand that apart from her obvious adoration of all that glitters at this time of year, she was guarded when it came to sharing anything else. Was that simply because they had only just met? Or did it stem from something deeper? Whichever one it was, it only made him more curious to find out.

'So, do you live near to where you work?' Jen asked, changing the conversation.

It was his turn to laugh. 'I live above Bar Páme.'

'Oh, wow.'

'It is just me and my uncle. We renovated our separate apartments together, and now mine is so good sometimes I think he wishes he could rent it as an Airbnb.'

She laughed again and this time when it happened there was a tingling in his gut he wasn't entirely in control of. He *liked* her. Of course, he'd known he liked her because he was about to show her somewhere he'd never taken anyone to before, but this, this was his body recognising he *liked* her. Involuntary maybe, but undeniable.

'Do you... live alone?' he asked.

'No,' Jen said, a wry smile on her lips.

'No?'

'I live with Christmas, obviously.'

'In your home as well as your heart,' Astro remarked, shaking his head. And then he reached out a hand, halting her progress and taking hold of her arm. 'Not that way. It is down here.' He indicated the next path.

'Down there?' she asked tentatively.

He laughed. 'What are you afraid of? Is there not enough light, Miss Christmas?'

'It is *very* dark,' Jen said, not moving.

'I am thinking... let me get the English right... atmospheric?'

'If the atmosphere someone is going for is "creepy".'

'You are scared of the dark path?' Astro asked.

'No.'

'Then let us go,' he said, leading the way.

'Wait for me,' Jen said, following. 'And, just so you know, if there are bats then I am out of here.'

'If there is tinsel, I will be running too,' Astro called back.

22

PSYRRI

Jen really wanted to close her eyes. This alley was narrow, and it was almost like a cave in the dark, walls close, doors to who-knew-where set into the stone. She was rushing after Astro, not wanting to lose sight of him. And then suddenly she was out, following her leader around a corner and then finding herself standing in a square.

There were buzzing bars and cafés, patrons sitting outside and in, and in the centre were tables and wooden chairs under canopies amid the trees, music and chatter in the air. Jen took a breath; there was so much to see, she couldn't take it all in. There was a different vibe here compared to the tightly packed bars in the Plaka district. It was more *local*. Vibrant, yet easy, laid-back somehow.

'This is Psyrri Square. Although it is also called *Platia Iroon* – Heroes Square,' Astro said.

He was close to her now. She realised that she had most definitely been slowly turning around and taking this place in from every angle, like a human carousel.

'Back in ancient times, this was a place for artisans. Potters, tailors, artists, makers of leather goods. In not so ancient times, it was the area of Athens where the gangs hung out,' Astro explained.

'Oh!' Jen exclaimed. 'And I was worried about bats.'

He smiled. 'They are no longer here in the same way they once were. The gangs. I do not know of the bats. But Psyrri is known now for being a place that is being rejuvenated. Yes, it is not yet back to how it once was, but it is regaining a reputation for the arts once more.'

He pointed a finger at a large mural on the wall across the square. It was like graffiti, of faces, looming over the space, grinning wide, painted around high windows.

'This is a combination of photography, collage and painting. By an artist called Alexandros Vasmoulakis,' Astro explained. 'There used to be more colour but sadly it has faded with time.'

Jen turned to him then. 'You like art,' she said, making the connection as to why they were here in this district.

'I like art if it has something to say,' he answered.

Jen looked back to the faces on the building. 'What do you think *they* are saying?'

'That is not the point of art in my opinion,' Astro answered. 'It is not important what they say to me when *you* look. It is important what they say to only you.'

Jen stared again. Were the faces happy? Was it three people? Or were the distorted images the same one person in different guises? It was like surrealism.

'I don't know,' she answered, disappointed in herself.

He nudged her arm again. 'Hey, smile. It was not a test. Not every piece of art will speak to you.'

'But does this one say something to you? When you look at it?' Jen asked.

'Yeah,' Astro answered. He took a deep breath and directed his gaze at the faces. 'This picture, to me, it tells a story of transformation. It is a journey. One woman on the left, her much younger self in the centre and the queen she has become on the right. But, you could read it the opposite way. A successful woman who has lost everything.'

Jen swallowed. The idea of going from nothing to success was nice. Turning it on its head wasn't so palatable given her current cashflow issues and no-roof-over-her-head-apart-from-the-one-she-worked-under situation.

'Oh, well, I very much hope it is the first way you said.'

'You are a very serious person. I understand this from the moment I first see you,' Astro said.

'Really?' Jen asked. 'Even though I was helping to carry an inflatable candy cane?'

'You were carrying this very seriously,' Astro told her.

Was she a serious person? One of those people who didn't really know how to have fun? In foster homes, 'fun' wasn't exactly front and centre. It was only ever about survival. The less you shared with people the less they had to throw back at you. You might be labelled 'strange' or 'a freak' but that was better than anyone knowing the real you or anything about you. Like the fact you had a teddy bear with a torn ear that was the only thing you possessed from your birth mother.

Contrary to that, her whole business had been based on creating social, special, festive extravaganzas. She *practically* made fun! For everyone else...

'Hey,' Astro said, dragging her thoughts back out of the black hole of overprocessing. 'I did not mean it in a negative way.'

'It's OK,' Jen said with a nod, as internally she knitted her guard back together again.

'No, I need to make this right.'

Before Jen could do or say any more, he had disappeared and

she was left turning in circles again, eyes moving from the lively bars to the people dining under the square parasols. And then Astro was back, holding two bottles of beer, their tops taken off.

'A not so serious beer,' he stated, passing one to her.

'Is there any other kind?' she asked. She looked at the label. 'Fix.'

'We are fixing my rudeness. *Yamas*,' Astro said, knocking his bottle against hers.

'*Yamas*,' she answered, taking a swig.

'OK, so we need to walk just a little further,' he said, leading the way.

'No more dark alleyways, please,' Jen begged.

'I promise,' he replied.

Within a few moments, the atmosphere had changed yet again, and the music wasn't Greek stringed instruments but something with a lot more bass. It seemed to mainly be coming from a large black beaten-up speaker stack that was specked with bright pink paint. There were people too, sat on doorsteps, backs against walls or shutters, which were also covered in graffiti. Jen didn't know quite what to make of it. She had certainly never come across anything like this scene back in Little Pickering.

'Astro!'

The second the groups saw them approaching, they were all up on their feet and heading their way. Some had bottles of beer like them, others seemed to be holding spray cans.

Astro was soon enveloped in hugs; handshakes or fist-bumps came from others. It seemed like everyone here knew him.

There was that creeping feeling again that she didn't fit in, shouldn't be here. She took a swig of her beer. Perhaps she could silently retreat...

But before her boots could make any backwards steps, or even any steps at all, Astro turned back to her and was talking in Greek.

'Everyone, this is Jen,' he then introduced in English.

She was greeted with English 'heys' and Greek '*yas*' and one girl offered a high-five which Jen quickly reciprocated. And then, as quickly as they had been introduced, most of the groups returned to what they had been doing before – chilling, having conversations... and were they spray painting these buildings?

'Jen, this is Petros. He is an amazing artist,' Astro introduced.

Jen smiled at a really tall guy, dreadlocks escaping from under the baseball cap he was wearing.

'Hello,' she said. 'It's nice to meet you. But are you really graffitiing these walls and doors?'

'Graffiti,' Petros said with a snigger.

'We prefer to call it art,' Astro told Jen. 'Or self-expression.'

'Or a combination,' Petros said. 'Everything has a place if someone has felt strongly enough to put it on a wall or a door.'

She had never thought about it like that before. Granted, the crude lettering or tags of graffiti she had seen being scrubbed from public spaces weren't attractive to look at for the most part, but maybe that wasn't the point. Perhaps it was an important platform for people to air their views. It was certainly less destructive than breaking windows or keying cars.

'Come on,' Astro said. 'You said you wanted to know where I spend my time when I am not at Bar Páme. This is it.'

He headed down the road in step with Petros.

The street opened up to where more people were gathered, dancing to the music, others moving on skateboards or rollerblades, or spraying colour onto stencils pressed against the wall.

'And this,' Petros said, stopping so abruptly Jen almost walked straight into him. 'Is the finest work of art on this street... in fact in this whole area.' He put his arms out with a flourish as if he was a compère introducing entertainment to a stage.

Jen looked at the work that was taking over the entire length and width of the side of an abandoned building. It was a giant moon, all the light and shade creating perfect dimples and craters as if it was truly textured. But the moon had a persona, a face, and long dark hair cascaded from it. Then there were arms and hands, perfectly drawn hands, reaching out to a boy sitting in a hunched-up position on a rooftop as if he was crying.

As Jen admired the artistry, the music from the boom box faded away and it was as if she was alone with this mural. She felt the sadness and desperation the boy in this painting was portraying. She had felt that same way hundreds of times before. She could have been that lonely, sad child wanting the moon to reach down and put its arms around her.

'Jen?' Astro said.

His voice sounded concerned and she quickly tried to temper the emotion, not let it show, putting her mouth to her bottle of beer.

'I think,' Petros said, nodding, 'she likes *this* graffiti.'

23

'Here,' Astro said later, pressing a metal can into Jen's hands.

She had been quiet since she'd looked at the mural of the boy and the moon, her mood low, despite doing her best to appear upbeat amid the music and the skateboarding. She was hiding in plain sight, her real emotions balled up inside her, locked into a compartment she had sealed tight, a smile on her lips but one that didn't come from her soul.

Astro didn't know her well, but he knew her behaviour because he had been exactly the same, still sometimes was. And the only thing that worked, without someone calling him out and forcing him to open up, was distraction.

So now, he was giving her evasion by aerosol...

'What's this?' she asked, regarding the can as if it could be a component of an alien craft.

'You know what this is,' he said. 'You have seen the others using them.'

'I *do* know what it is,' Jen admitted. 'I just don't know why you've given it to me.'

'No?' Astro said, raising one eyebrow. He took her hand then and pulled her up off the bench. 'Come on, there are no spectators here, only artists.'

'But I'm not an artist,' Jen reminded him as she followed.

'The way you make Christmas bracelets and earrings for Achilles? That is art of the greatest kind.'

He stopped opposite a former shop, its brickwork eroded, its shutter pulled over the frontage. What had been speckled with faded tags from previous spray-painters was now a freshly painted steel grey.

'This is your canvas,' Astro told her.

'I... can't spray this,' Jen said immediately. 'I've only ever sprayed gold and silver glitter on yule logs and fir cones before, not something this big and... something everyone in this city is going to look at and judge.'

'Judge?'

'Yes, I mean, people stand and stare and decide if they like something or not and make comments about it, good or bad, just like us looking at the faces before and—'

'And you care about this?' Astro said. 'You worry about what these people will think about your art?'

'Well,' she began. 'Yes. Because, what if they hate it? What if it's the worst thing they have ever seen?'

'So what?' Astro spread his arms wide. 'Art should only be about how the *artist* feels, it is *their* self-expression. Of course, we want people to love it, or even hate it, but a reaction is like... how do you say... a bonus.'

'But it's a door, Astro, of an old shop on the street, in Greece. I'm not good enough for that.'

'Not good enough to paint your feelings?'

She didn't answer so he carried on.

'And, if you must have someone be your judge, let me.'

From a canvas bag in front of the door, he drew out more cans, sandpaper, charcoals and brushes. He laid them out then took a step back.

'I will get us another drink and then I will come back and make my comments.'

* * *

It took Jen a good five minutes before she even moved. What was this all about? What was she even doing here? She thought of Kathleen. The woman would be absolutely incensed that Jen was here with people daubing things in public spaces, let alone considering doing exactly that herself. But looking again at the blank 'canvas' in front of her, she wondered how cleansing it would be to put her feelings out there. Show the people of Athens a glimpse inside her – anonymously, of course, except for a waiter she barely knew. What was even going to come out? She guessed she wasn't going to know unless she made a start.

Looking at the can in her hands, a dark brown, she stepped towards the shutter.

When she finally stopped she was out of breath. She didn't know how much time had passed or exactly what had happened in the minutes she had quite obviously been working on this mural. Had this finished product really come from her?

It was dark and chaotic, strands of black, brown and grey, spiralling like worms – or the rubber bands Natalia made into balls – burrowing into each other, tangling up, before they turned into fiery licks of flames shooting towards a black volcano. Then, from the volcano seeped Christmas-style lava – stars and angels, Santa, reindeer, pinecones and candy canes – that turned from lava into a rainbow waterfall, which gushed down to a lake surrounded by an oasis of greenery, trees, flowers, even her Bravely Bear with his peppermint-scented belly, smiling...

Oh God. Jen hurriedly stepped forward and put her hands to the image of Bravely, trying to erase it with her fingers.

'What are you doing?'

She jumped. Only when Astro spoke did Jen then realise he was standing across the narrow road, watching her.

'I don't know,' she answered. 'Clearly whatever was in that Fix beer has not fixed anything.'

'I like it,' Astro said, standing next to her now. 'There is a whole story.'

'Well, you gave me the brown paint first, so it felt natural to—'

'Begin with a volcano?'

She couldn't help but smile. The whole scenario was ridiculous.

She watched Astro get closer to her picture and really look hard at it, studying each part. She swallowed, feeling suddenly raw about just how much of herself she had shared in this artwork. He had told her it was about self-expression, and she could so easily have dipped out of doing anything or, alternatively, drawn something that had no meaning. Except, given everything Astro had told her about the people who shared their work in this space, it would have felt like she was going against this area's very principles if she had done that.

'What is the name of the bear?' Astro asked.

'Oh, well, I don't know,' Jen said, immediately closing herself off as her default kicked in. 'He's just, you know, generic. Made up.'

'With one ear?'

Who was she trying to fool? And Astro had already seen her trying to erase the bear with her hands.

She sighed. 'His name is Bravely.'

'With that name, he has to be special to you.' He hadn't phrased it as a question.

She nodded but added no more.

Keep what means most close. Hidden.

'You did this section with charcoal,' Astro commented, pointing at the dark volcano. 'Why?'

'The spray can was too light. It wasn't doing what I wanted.'

'It looks like you stabbed at it. There are dents in the metal.'

'Yes, I... think I did it too hard and I broke some of your charcoals as well. Sorry. I will replace them.'

'Don't be sorry,' Astro said, turning away from the mural and looking at her. 'Never be sorry for creating something with passion.'

His eyes met hers and it was like her insides had been touched by fizzing embers. They were stood so close now and the space seemed to be getting smaller...

'*Astinomia! Astinomia!*'

The shout came suddenly and it was loud enough to make Jen jump. Up the street she saw people scattering, grabbing what they could – skateboards, the speakers providing the music, paints...

'Come on,' Astro said, taking hold of her hand.

'What's going on?' Jen asked as they quickened their pace, speeding down the street into the darkness. 'What were they shouting? Is there a protest? Bonnie read there are lots of protests here.'

'*Astinomia*, it means "police",' Astro told her. 'We need to see if you can run in your boots!'

24

This was not funny. Yet Jen was laughing as they ran, Astro holding her hand, her feet slipping and tripping on broken paving slabs as they zigzagged through the narrow streets. Coffee places and restaurants appeared suddenly in the middle of thorough-fares, Astro calling '*signomi*' as they flashed past waiters carrying trays of food and drink, moving onwards, keeping up the pace.

'I can't... run any more,' Jen told him as a stitch suddenly pained her side and didn't let up.

'Really?' Astro asked.

'Well, how far do we have to go? I know for a fact the English police wouldn't chase this far on foot.' She slowed down, allowing her side a bit of respite. She let go of his hand. She wasn't even sure how the handholding had happened. One moment she had been looking at the crazy spewing up of her feelings on the shut-ters and the next fleeing into the night, Astro holding on to her.

'You are right. We should be OK now,' Astro agreed, slowing his pace too.

The streets were still busy here, stores open selling spices and herbs by the kilo, small intimate bars with mood lighting, kiosks offering beers to take away plus magazines, newspapers and cigarettes.

Suddenly reality hit her. She had drawn graffiti and she had run from the police. This wasn't Jen Astley CEO of Christmas Every Day, this was someone else. Perhaps the someone everyone else had always expected her to be. The foster kid who had to be bad news...

'You are OK?' Astro asked, walking close beside her.

'I just didn't think I would be trying to avoid being arrested tonight.'

'Oh, I thought I give this away when I ask if you can run in your shoes.'

'So, it was always a possibility?'

'Expressing yourself always carries a risk, no?'

Jen mused on that sentence. It was as true as it got. She had opened up a little to David and look what happened there...

'Maybe,' she answered.

'But always you feel better for taking the opportunity,' Astro continued.

'I'm not sure how much better I would feel if I'd been arrested,' she admitted.

He waved a hand dismissively. 'You think I would let this happen? I would have told the police it was all me. Even though you are the one with more paint on your hands.'

Jen looked at her fingers. They were smeared with colour, every shade she had used, and the dark charcoal too.

'Oh!' she exclaimed.

Astro laughed. 'We need to remove the evidence.'

She rubbed at the marks on her skin, but nothing was coming off.

'I have something for it at my apartment.'

'Is that what you say to every tourist you take out for the thrill of a police chase?' she asked.

He put his hands up. 'You got me.' But then he nudged her with his arm. 'Seriously, it did not raise your heartrate? The thought of spending the night with me in a police station?'

'It's always been my dream,' Jen answered. 'I'm surprised it didn't make it into my mural.'

He laughed again. 'Come on. I have white spirit and Greek spirits waiting for us.'

She hesitated. Going back to Astro's apartment. She didn't ever do that on a first date. But this hadn't been a date. And she was not in the market for a date. She was fresh out of a disaster dating scenario with someone Bonnie had thought was going to propose. Besides, Astro hadn't made the initial invitation *sound* like a date.

'Unless you have to get back.' Astro looked at his watch. 'It is almost 2 a.m., I did not realise the time.'

Neither had she. Two hours with him had flown by quickly and their conversation had been easy yet also deep – self-exploratory even. Who said this night had to have a label? It could be anything she wanted it to be. Plus, if she wasn't going to be in Athens very long then she needed to make the most of it, didn't she?

'White spirit for my hands,' Jen told him. 'And a quick *ouzo*?'

Astro clapped his hands together. 'Yes! Come on, Christmas Girl, you are very almost Greek!'

25

ASTRO'S APARTMENT, BAR PÁME

What was he doing? He didn't do this. None of it. Ever. From taking Jen to the place he liked to hang out, to now inviting her into his home. No woman had ever been in his home. From the limited experience he had with women, encounters took place anywhere *but* this apartment. He had climbed out of a few windows and down fire escapes when mothers or grandmothers had unexpectedly woken up, preferring to risk admonishment rather than bring someone to his own bed.

Except this was only about putting turps on Jen's hands and sharing more conversation. Because he *liked* her. How crazy was it to think that? He liked her so he *wasn't* going to try to seduce her...

'It is up here,' he said, grabbing the metal handrail and swinging himself up the spiral staircase. 'Then behind. But those flashing festive lights were not there when I leave. Or that angel. Mr and Mrs Pappas have turned their garden into a grotto.' The small courtyard of the adjoining property was usually only full of plant pots and washing strung out across a line, but now it was shimmering like most of the rest of the city.

'I think it looks very nice,' Jen said. 'But, in my opinion, it could do with *more* decoration. A bit like your bar.'

Astro bit his lip. Jen loved Christmas. He wanted to obliterate it. If there was any proof needed that this was insane then that was it – they were polar opposites.

'Well, my uncle is insisting that changes very soon,' Astro said, turning to check she was managing the steps in the dim light. 'He wants the bar to look more festive than anywhere else so tourists will come to us above other places. But, you know, decorations, they are expensive.'

At the small platform at the top, which led to the door, he reached into the pocket of his jeans for the key. Had he left the apartment in a mess? Was there washing up? His clothes strewn across the bed? Wet towels on the floor? Well, it was too late to worry about that now.

He opened the door and flicked on the light. And then he saw something he hadn't been expecting and the moment their eyes connected, one of them took flight...

'Oh my God! Is that a bat?' Jen screamed.

'No,' Astro said. 'It is a pigeon and he should not be in here. Come on, Peri.'

'It has a name?' Jen said as the pigeon flapped about a bit and then settled on Astro's hand.

'Well... yes, I give him a name because he is a regular visitor.'

It was then Peri began to perform his heart out, ruffling his feathers so they became furrier, cooing like he was a dove, rubbing his face against Astro's hand and tapping his legs up and down as if they were the steps to a dance routine.

'Aww, he's cute,' Jen said, moving closer to him.

OK, so now Peri had Jen's attention, Astro could do a quick reconnaissance of the apartment. There was a T-shirt on the bed, the covers were pulled over but not particularly neatly, the easels were a bit chaotically placed and there were chalks, pencils, glue and glitter all over the small dining table from his work earlier with Achilles.

'I should put him outside. Before he shits in places he has not shit already.' He moved to the window – Peri's favourite perch just outside – and opened it.

A little reluctantly, but resigned to the fact, Peri stepped off Astro's hand and onto the ledge.

When Astro turned back, Jen was already moving over to the easels...

'Do not judge,' he said quickly, stepping after her. 'These are not my best work.'

Really, he wanted to cover them over so she couldn't see at all. He didn't show anyone his work, even hiding it from Philippos.

'Well,' Jen said, moving around the easel to look at the canvas propped on it. 'You judged my artwork earlier so it's only fair I get to look at these.'

His stomach was contracting. He cared what she thought, didn't want to disappoint her. That was crazy.

'Astro, did you really do this?' Jen asked.

She hated it. Why wouldn't she? She had probably asked him if he had done it because she thought it was the work of Achilles. All that talk about judging and declaring that self-expression was the only important thing and he was acting like someone hungry for the Turner Prize.

'It is mine. But it is not finished.'

'It's exceptional,' Jen said. 'Not that I am an expert, or have seen much art but... well, I think it's really *really* good.'

He moved next to her and looked at the charcoal work of an elderly couple that he had first drawn in his tiny book, then refined and made larger here. It had been raining that day. The couple had sought shelter under a canopy, but it had pelted down hard. The old man had held a newspaper over his wife's head. Perhaps a futile attempt, but it had been written all over her face: to her he was a hero. Maybe it wasn't so bad.

'*Efharisto*,' he said. 'Thank you.'

'This one is different,' Jen said, looking at the next canvas, something he had done in acrylics. A mess.

'Do not say this one is "good". I do not understand acrylic or how anyone can have joy when they are using it.' He put his hand to the rough peaks and troughs of what he'd created. He had been angry when he'd done this one. Furious that Christmas was on its way. And now Miss Christmas herself was right here in his apartment...

While he was doing all that thinking and putting his fingers on the hard knobbly pieces of not very much, Jen had moved on to the final piece. Before he even had time to think, she had gasped and put both hands to her mouth as if she were in shock.

'Astro!' she exclaimed.

'What?' he asked, worried he had done something wrong. Had something he'd painted offended her?

'This painting...'

'Again, unfinished, and not my best. I—'

'It's you! You're the artist of the mural Petros showed me earlier.' She looked from the painting to him. 'Of the boy... with the moon.'

He swallowed. She had recognised his style. This painting wasn't exactly the same, but he had been equally emotional when he had started it.

'You never told me it was you,' she continued. 'When I looked at it and it made me... how it made me. You didn't say.'

He hadn't. He had wanted to show her, but he hadn't claimed the art despite his big talk about freedom of expression and how important it was.

'*Ochi*,' he answered. 'No.'

He hadn't realised he was trembling until he heard it in his own voice. What the hell was wrong with him? He went to turn away, but she stopped him, taking hold of one of his hands. It was almost too much.

'We should get the turpentine, for your hands,' he said, that emotion still very much there. It wasn't going away. In fact, it was growing stronger, everything he always felt – loss, burning grief, loneliness, but it was mixing with something he definitely didn't always feel, perhaps had never felt...

'Astro, your mural,' Jen began, her voice as soft as her touch on his skin. 'It wasn't just good. It wasn't like any of these beautiful works right here. It was... another level.'

'Jen, you do not have to—'

He stopped himself from continuing. Because he didn't even know what he had been going to say.

'I felt it,' she whispered. 'It didn't just speak to me, it touched me inside, like it had torn through my skin and ripped open somewhere I thought was inaccessible.'

'You do not have to...' he began again as her fingers held his, feeling as unnatural as it also felt perfectly right.

'I know I don't have to,' she said.

He met her eyes then and what he saw there seemed to be an interpretation of everything he was feeling inside himself. Excitement. Anticipation. Heat. Hurt?

And then, a millisecond later her lips were on his and he was reacting like he'd never reacted before, his mouth a more than willing participant in this moment. His hands moved to cradle her head, fingers in those blonde waves as he deepened the kiss...

Then, suddenly, as quickly as it had begun, it all stopped and Jen was backing away across the wooden floor.

'I... should go... it's late and—'

'Let me walk you back to your hotel,' Astro said, his lips still buzzing, alive but growing colder with every backwards step she took. 'You said it was the Plaka Hotel, right? It is not far and—'

'No, no, it's OK. You don't have to.'

He knew he didn't have to. He now knew she didn't want him to.

She had her hand on the door already and he couldn't have felt sadder. She wasn't waiting for him to stop her leaving. For the second time tonight, she needed to run.

Without either of them saying anything more, he watched Jen slip through the door and speed back down the spiral staircase until her red coat was completely out of sight.

26

PLAKA HOTEL

'Andrea has bought my mum a new washing machine. And it's not just *any* washing machine. No, this is the kind of washing machine that could probably deliver Sky Movies and Domino's pizza at the touch of a button. My mum sent me five photos of it *and* a video. She's never sent me five photos of anything. Not even the time she met Michael McIntyre. And you know how she loves Michael McIntyre.'

Jen pushed her breakfast plate away. They had brought their food and drinks from the dining room up to the hotel's roof terrace. It was warmer again today, as though yesterday's cold snap hadn't even happened, and the sun was strong enough that a coat wasn't necessary here in this bright nook looking out towards the Acropolis. But Jen's mind wasn't here with Bonnie discussing kitchen appliances, it was in a loft apartment with a pigeon, artwork and a sexy and intriguing guy...

'She's bought it as a status symbol, you know. It's not a gift for our mum, it's something to prove to me and anyone else Mum shows the *five* photos and a video to that she is doing incredibly well in her big, important job in London,' Bonnie continued, devouring olives like there might, at any moment, be a national shortage.

'Andrea doesn't have any of your sass, Bonnie. And she struggles to make conversation unless she's telling the room about an important legal victory,' Jen said, cradling her coffee cup with both hands. 'You are a listener, someone who's kind and compassionate, always putting others first.'

'But sass and banter don't buy top-of-the-range-could-take-over-the-world-when-you-sleep washing machines, do they?'

'But maybe Andrea is doing that to compensate, because she feels inadequate compared to you,' Jen suggested. 'You and your mum have a great relationship. Andrea rarely sees her.'

'You think?' Bonnie asked, perhaps a little too excited by the prospect. 'That Andrea could be jealous... of me?'

'Maybe,' Jen said with a sigh. 'I don't really know.' She took a sip of her coffee. She needed to do something. Something more than sitting here not eating breakfast and hoping the winter sunshine was going to cleanse her from whatever had happened last night.

'You're not yourself this morning,' Bonnie said, her full attention and those deep brown eyes fixed on Jen.

Oh no. Perhaps she had said too little; the spotlight was now on her and that was the last thing she wanted. Time to take control...

'Just wondering how Natalia has got on with Geoffrey,' Jen said. 'You know, wondering whether I'll actually be able to honour the booking for the historical society or lose a huge chunk of money I can't do without right now.'

'Natalia is more than capable,' Bonnie said. 'And I'm sure if there was any update on that situation, she would have called this morning.'

'I know she's capable,' Jen said. 'But... she's not me and it's *my* business and it's also my home right now so—'

Bonnie interrupted with a gasp, her knee nudging the coffee table and almost sending her glass of orange juice into a spin.

'Something happened last night! I knew there had to be more to it than a bit of street art.'

A bit of street art. Jen felt suddenly protective towards everyone she had met the night before, having seen them project their passion, their politics, their *raison d'être* on the walls, doors and whatever available space there was.

'Well, it was a bit more than that, it was kind of like if Salvador Dali had a graffiti gang,' Jen admitted. 'And, at one point, we all had to run from the police.'

'What?' Bonnie exclaimed, eyes almost bursting.

This was good. Keep talking about that high drama and they were never going to get into what happened after. Except Jen herself couldn't get it out of her mind. *She* had initiated the kiss. When she *never ever* made the first move. When she had *sworn* she was done with guys. And, as if that wasn't shocking enough, it had been the best kiss she'd ever had. Because something had happened between them which she couldn't even begin to explain. It had felt almost... ethereal.

'I have to admit,' Jen carried on, as she tried to make her brain stop. 'That I haven't run from the police before. Social workers maybe, but not the hardcore stuff.'

'Well, what happened? I mean, I take it they didn't catch you.' Bonnie seemed to muse on the idea for a second. 'What's the punishment for being *with* a graffiti gang anyway? It wasn't like you and Astro were actually defacing property, were you?'

'Well...'

'Jen! Did you spray something?'

Jen put down her cup and waggled her still paint-marked fingers at her friend. 'Not all of it has come off. I didn't even know what I was doing. Astro offered white spirit when we got back to his apartment but...'

And now the story was at this stage, like a train at a signal waiting for the points to change. She either admitted the truth or made up a lie before Bonnie jumped on board the carriage and set the course herself.

'You went back to his apartment!' Bonnie was sitting on the very edge of her chair now.

'I met a pigeon,' Jen said, nodding.

'O-K.'

'And I...' She stopped.

'This empathetic, great listener is dampening down her banter and opening her ears.'

'I need to leave Athens,' Jen blurted out. 'Now. Sooner than now.'

'Because you were chased by the police and there's a warrant out for you?' Bonnie asked. 'Or because you met a pigeon?'

'Because... I kissed Astro.'

Bonnie fell off the chair. The plates and cups juddered in a porcelain cymbal clash as she nudged the edge of the table and her bottom met tiles.

'Bonnie, are you OK?' Jen asked, leaping up.

'Yes! Yes, I'm fine,' she said, getting to her feet. 'And we are not using my arse-plant as an excuse to brush over this.' She sat down on the chair again. 'You *kissed* Astro. Like *kissed* him.'

'Yes,' Jen said. 'Exactly like that. And I feel such an idiot for a whole multitude of reasons. I mean, it wasn't even a date. He was just showing me the art and thanking me for helping Achilles and I went and did that.'

'Well,' Bonnie said. 'What did *he* do?'

What had Astro done? Reliving the kiss, Jen remembered everything Astro had done. From his mouth reacting instantly to hers, to the way he had gently, yet passionately, held her head in his hands, his fingers in her hair...

'Oh, God!' Bonnie exclaimed before Jen could even say anything. 'He did *everything*, didn't he?'

'It was just a kiss,' Jen assured her, knowing her cheeks were already going red. She looked to the Parthenon for some sort of centring. It had stood for thousands of years, it must have seen and heard everything...

'But it wasn't just a kiss, was it?' Bonnie continued. 'Because *you* initiated it. And you don't do that.'

Bonnie who listened and remembered everything...

'And I can tell, the way you're talking about it, that this was a kiss like no other. God! I'm almost jealous.'

It *had* been a kiss like no other. No other that Jen had ever had, that was certain. Nothing like the kind of kisses she'd accepted after a few dates with a guy – expected, pleasant but nothing to recount before you went to sleep. Nothing like any kind of kiss she'd had with David...

'So what happened after you kissed that was so awful you need me to phone the airline again and speed up our return?'

Jen swallowed, looking away from the view and back to Bonnie. 'I ran away.'

'Oh God! You didn't make plans to see each other again?'

Jen shook her head. And by kissing Astro she had only made things awkward. That easy way they had initially had with each other had been blown up.

'Right, well, we need to remedy that straight away,' Bonnie said, getting to her feet.

'No, Bonnie, it's done. I mean, it was stupid of me, I wasn't thinking straight. I don't know if it was some kind of need to kiss someone else because David has been kissing someone else or it was... I don't know, a momentary lapse of judgement but there doesn't need to be a follow-up. It would be better if there wasn't. I can eventually forget the absolute embarrassment of it and Astro can... forget about me.'

But would she forget? About the kiss? About the boy and the moon mural? About the boy who had painted it and had hit the weakest hidden spot inside her she didn't usually let anything touch...

'I mean, he's probably forgotten about me already,' Jen added. 'He'll be thinking "wow, that was weird" and then he'll be back to serving coffees and avoiding Christmas and—'

'I'm not buying it,' Bonnie said, folding her arms across her chest. 'You don't *have* a lapse of judgement. Ever. And now you can't stop talking about him.'

Jen went to make a comment, then, realising she was about to prove her friend's point, she clamped her lips shut.

'Jen, this is a good thing! You *like* him!'

'I don't like him! How can I like him? I'm seconds out of a relationship I thought might be going somewhere and, you know, none of that was even real and I barely know Astro! He's a waiter who hated my inflatable candy cane and—'

'And lifted you up off the ground to see to your injured chin and after all the crazy stuff you got up to with him last night, it's the most excited I've seen you about anything except work and Christmas.'

Oh God.

'Maybe *this* is exactly why the universe sent us to Athens. Maybe David happened to lie to you at this very point so we could end up here in Greece and you could meet Astro!'

'You know I don't believe in that kind of thing.'

'Kathleen does.'

'Kathleen thinks if she doesn't throw salt over her shoulder when she's using it then Joe Biden might press the nuclear button.'

'Well,' Bonnie said, picking up her orange juice glass. 'For the very health of the world, you need to see him again.'

The thought both terrified and excited her. And both of those feelings made her uncomfortable. It seemed she was braver in the dark when there was a pigeon for company...

27

ATHENS' CENTRAL MARKET

Astro was already biting on his bottom lip. Usually, he loved coming here with Philippos, but today the market had turned into another of the city's attempts to inject Santa's soul into everything. Amid the lines of fresh fish – octopus, squid, ginormous prawns, rows of silver fish still moving on the crushed ice – were red ribbons and silver stars and bright balls. There was only one festive Greek custom that Astro did not mind so much and that was the decorated boats – *karavakia,* 'little ship'. Wooden ship ornaments were balanced on counters, wires of fairy lights tied around the miniature rigging and masts. He had once made a boat just like them with his mother out of junk. Twigs, cardboard, string and flags he had fashioned from scraps of fabric. A little like Achilles with his bracelets. And Jen with the earrings...

'I am thinking,' Philippos began. '*Politiki* salad goes on the menu. With fish. Together with the Christmas cookies and... pork in the oven.'

Gourounopoula. It was what his mother used to make every Christmas Day. Philippos had tried to make it so many times since but it was never quite the same. And now he wanted to put it on his festive menu? How did he feel about that? Did he hate the idea because it was another painful reminder of what he had lost? Or could this be something to honour his mother's great cooking? Something to feel pride in?

'I know what you are thinking,' Philippos began. 'That there will never be another *gourounopoula* like your mother's. That every Christmas I have failed to produce anything like the same. That somehow our mother gave my sister all the genes to perfect the family recipe—'

'I do not know if you would like me to laugh or cry,' Astro admitted, putting his hands in the pockets of his jeans as they continued to walk through the hordes of shoppers.

Philippos looked serious then. 'I only ever want you to laugh, Astro. That is all I have ever wanted for you.'

'Yeah, I know. And, we have Chef now, right? So you can't screw it up for the customers.'

'Right. So, tell me, who this girl is you like?' Philippos nudged him with his arm.

'I do not know what you mean.'

Denial. Never got you anywhere but perhaps it would temporarily delay the vivid memories. Ah, no, here they came... the heat of her mouth, the way her hair felt under his fingers.

'Marjorie tells me she is English,' Philippos carried on, stopping at a stall to examine some mullet.

'Marjorie needs to spend more time worrying about Achilles than worrying about tourists I have spoken to.'

'And was this English girl with you when you were chased by the police last night?'

Astro shot his uncle a look, wanting to see if this was guesswork based on his actions in the past, or whether this was based on facts somehow. Philippos's gaze was unmoving. *Skata. Shit.*

'Dimitri was one of the policemen, right?' Astro said with a sigh.

Dimitri was one of his uncle's friends and it always seemed that, of the hundreds of police in the city, Dimitri ended up in his space.

'Dimitri suggests that you do not always hang out at the same place.'

'Dimitri, like the rest of Athens, does not want people like me and my friends to hang out *anywhere*. We paint there because people care less. Would he rather I sprayed Hadrian's Arch?'

'Astro,' Philippos said, shaking his head.

'What? I do not know what you want me to say.'

'I want you to be honest. That is all I have ever asked.'

'About graffiti? About Jen?'

Philippos grinned, rubbing his beard with his hand. 'She has a name.'

'Everyone has a name... and you really do need to have a trim of your beard.'

'And you like this girl,' Philippos continued, pointing to a large fish that the vendor then picked up and offered for inspection.

Astro didn't know what to say. He did like this girl. He had never met anyone who intrigued him enough to actually begin to... care. But it was hopeless. They were from two entirely different worlds and at the heart of hers was a season that had taken everything from him.

'Astro,' Philippos said, taking his eyes away from the fish despite the vendor's best efforts at shaking it. 'Honesty.'

He sighed. 'I like this girl.'

'Oh my God!' Philippos exclaimed, his hand knocking the fish as he reached to grab Astro's shoulder. 'This is happening.'

'What is happening?'

'Love,' Philippos declared, gesticulating like he was a performer on stage.

'You are crazy,' Astro said, shaking his head. 'It is no such thing.'

'You have your mother's heart. Always Eleni would fall in love. With people. With food. With flowers. With life. She would want that feeling for you.'

Astro shrugged, trying to be nonchalant despite Philippos's words peppering him like the hardest hailstorm. 'I love street art. Please ask Dimitri not to set tear gas on me.'

'Be serious, Astro.'

'I thought I only had to be honest.'

Philippos sighed. 'I am saying to you, just, be yourself, follow your heart exactly like your mother did. Her circumstances were not easy, she could not chase dreams, but she did make small dreams out of the path she had been given. And I know the one thing she wanted for you was to have choices, more opportunities than she did. Embrace them, Astro, no matter what form they take.'

He didn't know how to respond. And it felt disconcerting being emotionally vulnerable here in this noisy, hectic marketplace. He suddenly felt like one of those flapping fish, uncertain of what he should do, not knowing what happened next. Was this his opportunity to tell Philippos more? To reveal that his art wasn't just rudimentary signs made with aerosol cans, that he loved to draw, to paint, to depict life and his feelings as they came to him? That perhaps that could play a bigger part in his future?

'As long as you do not spray the front of Bar Páme,' Philippos said, chuckling.

The moment had gone. Astro put his hands back into the pockets of his jeans.

'Jen, she isn't here for long,' Astro told his uncle. 'She has no reason to stay.'

Philippos smiled then, as he signalled to order ten of the fish. 'Then you must give her a reason, no?'

28

THE ACROPOLIS, ATHENS

'Where do you call from? It sound like you are trapped underground. Do you want me to call rescue team?'

Jen had no idea why Natalia would think it sounded like she was speaking from underground, seeing as she was taking this call outside, high up above the city, marvelling at the marble pillars and time-eroded beauty of this iconic monument that stood before her. It was so very different being here amongst the ruins than it was looking at them from their hotel roof terrace. From a distance it seemed like a backdrop made for a movie scene, so spectacular that it couldn't possibly be real. But when you saw it up close, got right next to the abundance of history in these crumbling columns and imagined how much painstaking work had gone into creating it – and in the present day, restoring it – you really began to appreciate why it was one of the most must-visit places in the world.

'I'm actually on the Acropolis, you know, the very famous historical site,' Jen explained. She looked to Bonnie who was lost in the guidebook.

'You break up,' Natalia said. 'I hear one word you say. Is that name of cocktail?'

Oh no, this wasn't good. Maybe she should cut to the chase, see what the reason behind Natalia calling was. Silently she said a prayer to Athena – the goddess of wisdom and warriors who, it was written, protected this city – that this was going to be positive news.

'Natalia, is everything OK?'

'No.'

Don't panic. 'Tell me, what's happened?'

'Geoffrey is pig.'

'Oh, well, I know he can be difficult sometimes and definitely wants to try and get things his way but—'

'No, Geoffrey is pig. He play pig in new Christmas production in Southampton. He take all other people with him to play piglets and gnomes and he say he will not perform for historical society.'

This was the worst news ever! This wasn't just one actor having issues, this was the whole troupe. There was no way she was going to be able to employ a whole team of actors – at goodness knows what price – even if there were still people with availability now. She needed to think. She needed to be the leader she was. Except nothing was coming to mind...

'I do not even know what kind of Christmas production has pigs and gnomes. Even in Ukraine this would not happen.'

Think, Jen, think.

Then it came to her. *Kathleen.* Kathleen might have contacts from her days at Fancy Occasions.

Kathleen had bailed her out before when she'd had to plan a Christmas-Easter fusion for a birthday-cum-wedding anniversary at the Women's Institute. She'd connected her with an expert Easter Bunny for the occasion. If Kathleen didn't know someone, she should definitely know someone who knew someone.

'What you want me to do? I could get brothers to visit Geoffrey.

Brothers would only have to crack knuckles for him to change mind.'

Jen didn't know whose knuckles were cracking in this scenario. 'Leave it with me for a few hours. I'll get back to you.'

Bonnie was waving from higher up the rock, then pointing to some ornate columns over to the left and away from the main structure.

'There is one more thing,' Natalia continued.

Not something else. Jen really didn't want anything else when Bonnie had told her that three days' time was the earliest she could get them back to the UK. She took a deep breath and tried to relish the breeze blowing her hair.

'Just tell me,' she said.

'David. He call here. He say he want to talk.'

Jen closed her eyes. Why couldn't this still-married man just leave her alone?

'He say he want to know where you stay in Athens. I say if I tell him, I have to kill him,' Natalia carried on. 'Am happy to tell him and follow through before he has time to get to the airport.' Natalia had been itching to go down the 'take out a hit' route since Jen had told her about David being married.

'No, Natalia,' Jen said quickly, sending a reassuring wave to Bonnie. 'No, just don't engage and block his number.'

'You are certain?'

'That I don't want to talk to him?'

'That you do not want me to make his penis parts into *varenyky*.'

'I don't know—'

'Ukrainian dumplings, very good.'

'Just ignore him and blacklist his number,' Jen said, sighing. 'And I will get back to you as soon as I can about the historical society.'

She ended the call and took a deep breath. Then she gazed at the structures around her, pieces worn away, bits being put back together. That was close to exactly how she felt right at this moment. But, like the Greek temples, she had two choices, to accept decay and deprivation or to stand strong and fight against it. Like spray painting your feelings on rundown shops in the Psyrri neighbourhood. Maybe this city was going to be the key to her own need for restorative intervention. She would call Kathleen later; right now, she was going to wonder at the relics and enjoy feeling like everyone else here – completely insignificant amid them.

29

ACROPOLIS MUSEUM CAFÉ

'Never trust a man whose eyes are too close together,' Kathleen announced.

'I agree,' Bonnie said, her lips around a piece of *baklava* she had already licked honey from.

They were sitting at a table on the terrace beneath the famous ruins with other rocks of archaeological significance now literally at their feet. The museum had been anything but boring – a magnificent mix of perfect modern design built to constantly highlight the ancient landmark outside through every turn. Everything here you could tell had been thought about so carefully, the placing and direction of all the exhibits maintaining a flow that had made Jen feel like she was actually walking through time. Now they had coffee and these delicious Greek pastries, Jen was trying to address the Geoffrey issue with a FaceTime to the care home.

'I can see why he got cast as a pig,' Kathleen continued. She was wearing an orange paper party hat that kept falling down over one eyebrow.

'Me too,' Bonnie agreed, biting into the *baklava* and giving an orgasmic eyeroll.

'OK, well, what's done is done,' Jen said, steadying the phone as she picked up her coffee cup. 'What we need to focus on now is the future. The very *near* future. Because I don't have anyone to take this job on and it's going to mean creating a dramatic piece from scratch. That's if there are any groups that even have a gap in their festive diaries.' Saying this all out loud also made absolutely everything seem even worse, like talking about it was actually dragging the deadline date closer.

'Or you could change it up a bit,' Bonnie suggested. 'Do something that isn't quite at the same level as trying to create Broadway on a budget.'

'I can't do that,' Jen breathed. 'Because it isn't what the society expects. I've always delivered a showstopping performance that's historically accurate – mainly – and anything less will make them question what's different this year and probably ask for a refund.'

'Well, what's different this year is that Geoffrey's been a shady dickhead and you've—'

'Had my eye off the ball and made the biggest mistake of my life with David,' Jen blurted out.

It was still sore. But now, rather than David's actual lies, her fury was more to do with the fact she'd allowed herself to be duped. And that was at the heart of why she'd run away from Astro last night. Because he could be *exactly* the same. He could be a catfishing connoisseur for all she knew. She could be one in a long string of tourists he befriended. Soften them up with a few coffees, beers and graffiti and then move in for the cash. Except she didn't have any cash. And street art wasn't really a well-known modus operandi for men to flatter women with, was it? She took a breath. Her gut feeling about Astro was that he was genuine, but could she trust her gut any more?

'David is married. That was not your mistake,' Bonnie said immediately, licking sugary goodness from her thumb and forefinger. 'Not at all.'

'And now he's phoning Natalia and telling her he wants to talk and asking where I am—'

'He's what?'

The same short sentence had come from both Bonnie and Kathleen, and half the terrace café had heard it too.

Jen lowered her voice. 'Obviously I told her to ignore his calls and block him... not turn his penis into dumplings... but, you know, this whole thing, this being here in Athens, is down to him and now everything I'd planned to go so smoothly while I'd be in Paris is all falling apart and—'

'Jen, stop.'

It was Kathleen. She hadn't shouted, but she had used her voice of authority, which could probably cut through a high-decibel concert performance if it was put to the test. Even Bonnie stopped attacking the pastry and sat still.

'You're speaking like this is some kind of disaster,' Kathleen said. 'Like it's on the same level as... that awful chap we had at Eurovision before Sam Ryder or... me having to put up with tales from the trenches while they try to force-feed me meat that wouldn't even be good enough for Purina.'

Bonnie gave a snort.

Kathleen's analogies were enough to give Jen a little perspective as Kathleen continued.

'This is one *small* hiccup in your perfectly perfected festive season for your clients. It's not a stack of dominos all falling down at once during a Guinness World Record and... landing on your head and... knocking you unconscious... or falling on the man from room thirty and knocking *him* unconscious or—'

'I get it,' Jen said, interrupting. 'You think I'm making too much of this.'

'I think you're opening the oven door before the cake has risen,' Kathleen said, adjusting her paper hat again. 'And we all know what happens if you do that.'

'It sinks,' Bonnie said. 'Goes flatter than one of my mum's rotis.'

'Quite right, Bonnie,' Kathleen agreed with a nod. 'This is one tiny hurdle, not a—'

'Limbo marathon,' Bonnie said.

Jen looked at Bonnie.

'Sorry, got thinking about my mum's rotis and remembered last summer and Uncle Caspian.' She sighed. 'Never mind.'

'Kathleen, do you know anyone from your days at Fancy Occasions who might be able to step in at short notice and provide actors *and* a story?' Jen asked, crossing her fingers.

'Like Kirk, the Christmas-Easter bunny?' Kathleen asked.

'People exactly like Kirk,' Jen agreed.

'Eggs-actly,' Bonnie added. 'Sorry, couldn't resist.'

Kathleen ceremoniously pulled the paper hat from her head and put a finger in the air. 'I know someone who will know someone.'

Jen could have kissed the screen. This was exactly what she had hoped for. What would she do without Kathleen?

'Give me until tomorrow and I will put my thinking cap on instead of this ridiculous paper crown!'

'Thanks, Kathleen,' Jen said, feeling some sort of sense of relief about the situation already.

'Yes, thank you!' Bonnie exclaimed, as if a weight had been lifted from her shoulders too. 'Now perhaps Jen can pay proper attention to all the amazing things in Athens. And I've already said she has to go back and see Astro no matter what happened last night.'

Jen's heart felt like it had suddenly dropped from her chest. Why had Bonnie brought up Astro? She swallowed, knowing Kathleen was going to latch onto it.

'Is Astro a new planet?' Kathleen asked with a chuckle. 'Next to Uranus?'

'Astro's just a waiter at a nice little bar,' Jen informed her. 'That area of Athens is beautiful, Kathleen, you'd love it. Tiny tables all close together under canopies with patio heaters so no one gets cold; there's Greek music and cats and lots of Christmas decorations and lights and—'

'And this Astro is *just* a waiter? Bringing you drinks,' Kathleen said, already forming that all-knowing expression.

'And food sometimes,' Jen added. 'Not expensive meals because I'm on a budget but—'

'Bonnie,' Kathleen called.

'Yes,' Bonnie said, dipping her head back into shot.

'I agree with you. She has to go back and see this Astro, no matter what happened last night.'

Bonnie squealed and clapped her hands together as if a master plan had been formulated.

'Kathleen—' Jen began.

'Now you listen to me,' Kathleen interrupted, blustering on. 'You only get one life. One. And you've always done a bit too much thinking and not enough doing in my opinion. I know this David was rotten fruit, but I can already tell you like this "just a waiter". Because you told me everything about the surroundings of the bar he works in and nothing about him. "Classic Jen," as Gerald used to say.'

'Classic Jen' had been one of Gerald's favourite phrases. Every time she tried to shy away from telling news – even good news – she would ramble about unimportant things until it very slowly – sometimes even over days – finally came out. Another 'classic' case was the fact that she could never accept praise for anything. A fantastic testimonial for Christmas Every Day and Jen knew she would feel nothing but tight embarrassment and declare it really was a team effort and profess that actually the stars of the event had been the guests who had joined in so enthusiastically. Was it 'Classic Jen' that she hadn't told Kathleen she was bedding down with Elsa and Anna's *Frozen* costumes and a cardboard cut-out of Buddy from *Elf*?

'I didn't give you that little bit of cash to have any of it left when you come back. Go out with this Astro! Take a gamble! If you won't do it for yourself, do it for me, an old woman wearing a paper hat who had to listen to at least twenty cracker jokes earlier, half of them exactly the same.'

Jen took a deep breath, trying to internally manage the absolute reticence that was already grabbing hold. She nodded as fiercely as she could. 'OK.'

'Right, well, as I said, I will take charge of your actors' problem and I will ring you with an update as soon as I have one. I just need to find the right little red book.' She pointed a finger at the screen again. 'And when I do ring back, I want to know more about this waiter than what his bar snacks are like.'

It seemed Jen's afternoon had been planned for her.

'I cannot reach everything! I need steps!'

Achilles had been grumpy ever since he'd got back from school. And he would not stop talking about Jen. *When is Jen coming back? Everyone loved the earrings and we need to make more. Why do you not know when Jen is coming back? Can we go to her hotel and ask her to help again?*

'Achilles,' Marjorie said, spinning around with the steaming platters of grilled meats she was taking outside. 'You need to be quiet. People come here to relax, not to hear your loud shouting.'

'I am helping Astro with the Christmas decorations but I cannot reach and some fall apart in my hands! They are so old!'

Astro picked Achilles up and popped him onto a chair so he could reach the hook on the stone fireplace.

'This angel was one my mother made with my grandmother,' Astro explained. 'It is a peg, and she drew on the eyes and the smile and the clothes are made from Christmas napkins.'

'How old is it?' Achilles asked, carefully lowering the string onto the hook so it sat just right.

'Nearly twice as old as me.'

'Hello, Astro.'

At the unexpected sound of the voice, Astro jolted the chair and had to hurriedly steady Achilles as he turned to look at her. Jen was standing in the bar looking just as beautiful as she always did. Even with that festive red coat on.

'I... did not hear the door open,' he said in reply.

He was an idiot. What kind of greeting was that?

'Jen!' Achilles said delightedly, leaping from the chair, using Astro to lean on, and onto the ground.

'Hello, Achilles,' she greeted as he offered her a hand to high-five. 'Finally, Bar Páme is getting Christmas decorations! I did not think it was going to happen.'

'It is happening. Just a little slowly,' Astro answered.

She was here. She had come back. She wasn't yet on her way back to the UK.

'Oh, these are—'

'They fall apart,' Achilles said, picking out some disintegrating tinsel from the even more disintegrated carrier bag. 'See,' he said as it drooped onto the tabletop.

'They are a little out of date,' Astro admitted.

What was going on? He was now ashamed of these decorations he didn't even want in his life?

'I think we should buy all new ones,' Achilles stated.

'Achilles,' Astro admonished.

'Well,' Jen began, taking the bag from him and looking inside. 'Not everything has to be bought new. Like when we made the bracelets and earrings.'

'You can make *these* old things like new?' Achilles asked, eyes wide like saucers.

'With a bit of help from nature,' Jen said.

Achilles frowned.

She looked at Astro then. 'Are you too busy to leave the bar for a while?'

'I did not have a lunch break,' Astro told her. He was already untying his apron.

'If your mum says it's OK, do you want to look for things to make decorations for the bar?' Jen asked Achilles.

'*Ne!*' Achilles shouted with excitement, running off.

Astro knew that the boy's thrill was replicated in his own expression. He couldn't seem to stop being glad that Jen was here.

'You have time for this?' he said, trying to give off cool and calm.

'I am making time for this,' she confirmed.

The statement had been delivered positively, yet not quite confidently. Perhaps, like him, her mind was reliving last night and that kiss. *She* had kissed *him*. But he had responded quickly, with a degree of passion he didn't know he possessed. Now, as they looked at each other, the atmosphere was already charged as if his thoughts and feelings were visible to her in the air...

'*Signomi.*'

One of his customers was beckoning him, breaking the intensity of the moment. He smiled at Jen. 'Give me one minute.'

31

ANAFIOTIKA

'I can't believe you have oranges just growing on trees here in the winter,' Jen said as Achilles plucked some and put them in a bag a lot sturdier that the one holding the festive decorations at Bar Páme.

Night was beginning to fall now and streetlamps were starting to come on in this little village, just above the street where Bar Páme was located. It was made up of winding narrow alleyways barely wide enough for one person to walk through, let alone for anyone to pass side by side. At first, Jen thought it was like the paths in Psyrri, dimly lit and leading to potentially bat-filled door-ways, but with every step upwards there was a new treasure to be discovered. Rogue fruit was one of the things Jen was going to make use of, twigs they had already collected from trees that were blighted, and she was hopeful of finding pinecones, nuts and fir sprigs on the ground.

'We have lemons that come in the winter too,' Astro told her.

'We do!' Achilles chirped. 'Mrs Calimeris sits in the garden and she has this long stick with a big knife at one end and she pokes it up into the tree and slices the lemons down.'

'It is true,' Astro said, nodding. 'I have seen her do it.'

'What are we going to do with the oranges?' Achilles asked, swinging the bag from his hands as they turned another sharp corner, passing a little cottage with lights in the shape of a sailboat in the window.

'We are going to make decorations. Like a Christingle, but it doesn't have to be religious. The three spokes that the orange will sit on can represent anything you like.'

'Me, Mama and Mrs Calimeris,' Achilles suggested.

'We can make one for your mum too if you like,' Jen said. 'The more things we can collect, the more we can make.'

'I am going to find the big trees!' Achilles shouted, running on ahead.

'Achilles,' Astro called after him. 'Not too far.'

'Will he be OK?' Jen asked as Achilles disappeared out of sight around the next corner and who knew where beyond.

'He knows this area well. And people here know Marjorie and Achilles. If only for their sad situation.'

'Sad situation?' Jen asked, her interest piqued.

'Marjorie was told when she was very young that she would never have children. So, when she unexpectedly became pregnant it was more than a shock. She was not ready to have a child; it was supposed to be an impossibility. And then she was told it was twins. She got married to the father, but he did not stay and... she lost one of her babies.'

'Oh,' Jen said. 'That's terrible. I don't know what to say.'

'Marjorie is strong and fearless with most things because she has already battled so much already. She adores Achilles but it is hard being alone and working and having someone with so much energy to take care of. That is why we all try to help a little bit.'

Jen swallowed. Marjorie's story made her own sadness seem a bit smaller. Yes, she may have grown up being 'cared' for by people who seemed only interested in the local authority handouts. But then Kathleen and Gerald had come into her life. And now she had Bonnie and Natalia and her business. They were all good, strong things. Letting these people in had been the making of everything that had come next for her. Perhaps that was the very reason she was here with Astro, making time, seeing if maybe he could be someone she let in too. Except her return flight, the one she needed to get on for the sake of her business – the most stead-fast thing of all – was only a few days away. Was there a point to starting something that was going to finish so soon?

'You are OK?' Astro asked, pausing by a potted palm decorated with white lights on the step in front of a small blue door.

'Yes,' Jen said, nodding. 'I was just... thinking about a friend I have at home in England. She helped *me* when I needed someone. She... gave me somewhere to live and a job and... even now I defi-nitely need her help more than she needs mine.'

'That is a good friend,' Astro said as they rounded the next corner, almost disturbing a tabby cat which was washing itself. 'What is her name?'

'Kathleen,' Jen answered. 'She's eighty-two. She's not that mobile any more but if someone puts on a sixties' song, she'll try her hardest to get up and dance. And she tells me what I should do, a lot, and I always listen.'

'She is like a mother to you?' Astro asked, the path widening a bit and allowing them to walk next to each other.

'I guess she is,' Jen said. She shrugged, maybe to brush off the mother mantle. For her it had always held negative connotations. And Kathleen's influence had been anything but negative.

'You do not have a mother?' Astro asked her, leading the way off left to narrower paths again.

This was touching on the parts of her life she never discussed with anyone, the parts she used all her conversational avoidance skills to get out of. One joke, one lie, whatever worked better than the truth. She took a breath.

'No,' Jen said. 'I don't.'

That short simple sentence was as honest as she had ever been and her heart contracted at the enormity of it. He had shown her his art last night, he had introduced her to a pigeon and his mouth had taught her that there was so much more to a kiss than she had actually ever realised.

Their shoulders close together as they walked on, she felt Astro take a deep breath.

'I too have no mother,' he told her. 'And also... no father.'

Jen looked across at him, her heart now thumping for the voids in his life that were so very similar to hers.

'Neither do I,' she whispered into the dark.

Before either of them could react to anything they had said, there was a shout from ahead. It was Achilles, yelling in Greek and waving his hands as if he was drowning at sea.

'What is he saying?' Jen asked.

Astro smiled, shaking his head. 'He say that we have been offered to stay for dinner at a house where he is. It is cabbage rolls and *tsigereli*.'

'What? Invited in for dinner? By a stranger?' Jen exclaimed. Surely this wasn't normal behaviour, to ask a child and two people you hadn't even seen yet, to come and have food with you!

'There are no strangers in Greece, Jen,' Astro told her. 'Come on, I love cabbage rolls.'

32

ANAFIOTIKA

It was the tiniest little home where the sitting area, dining area and kitchen were all in the same space, with a doll-sized bedroom and bathroom set off to one side. But the second Astro and Jen squeezed into the main room, the smell wafting from the oven and hob was enough to make Jen realise exactly how hungry she was. Achilles already had a hunk of bread hanging from his lips when they came in and looking at the two chairs at the small table, Jen was left wondering if this offered meal was a real invitation, a hopeful invention from Achilles, or perhaps they were going to be given a paper plate to take away.

However, what space the home lacked inside was close to doubled when it came to the outside. A *plaka* stone patio came off the backdoor, a low wall on all sides offering views over what looked like the whole of Athens. White square buildings like sugar cubes stretched as far as the eye could see, interspersed by mounds of hard rock speckled with green. There was a bigger table here, with a cloth over it that didn't quite make the ends, and a halved metal drum was providing the heat, a roaring fire inside. There were three cats – one sleeping on a chair with one eye open, the other two looking at their guests with a large degree of suspicion – and a dog excitedly chasing a ball he had started to nudge with his nose back and forth to Achilles. In plant pots Jen recognised herbs – oregano, basil and rosemary – and then others with flowers, still vivid reds and oranges, despite it being winter.

'This is crazy,' Jen remarked as one of their hosts, Mr Sinrades, pulled a chair out for her.

'Why crazy?'

'I don't know these people and they've just invited me into their home, invited the *three* of us into their home and they're going to feed us. She whispered so only Astro could hear.

Astro smiled as he sat down next to her. 'Is that not what your Kathleen did for you?'

He had a point. Except it had taken her time to build up a rapport with Kathleen and Gerald. These lovely people did not know her at all. *There are no strangers in Greece.*

Jen's phoned chimed in her bag. It was Bonnie.

So tired. Ordered food from room service. Text me if you need to be rescued but I don't think you will. Xx

Jen hadn't planned to be out all evening and she knew Astro had to get back to the bar, but now there was no reason to go back to the hotel just yet...

'Everything is OK?' Astro asked.

The Sinrades had started lighting candles down the centre of the table as if this was their own personal taverna. Fairy lights in all the colours suddenly lit up the pergola overhead and Achilles gasped as though it was a firework display. Did they do this every night for people who happened to be passing by?

'Yes,' Jen said. 'Everything is OK. Bonnie went shopping and now she's gone back to the hotel and—'

'You have to go?' Astro asked. 'It is OK. We can—'

He was already rising from his chair. She put a hand on his arm to stop him.

'No, I don't have to go. I can definitely stay,' she told him. 'If I'm not keeping you from your work, that is.'

'You *are* keeping me from my work,' Astro said honestly.

'Oh. I—'

He smiled then. 'But we are also keeping Achilles out from under the feet of Marjorie and my uncle, and Chef, who my uncle is always terrified will quit if Achilles spills anything else he has spent hours making perfect.' He paused then, his to-drown-in eyes meeting hers. 'And also I am enjoying your company. If that was not obvious.'

There was that flash of heat again, sitting somewhere south of the pit of her stomach...

'Mrs Sinrades says we can take berries for the decorations,' Achilles said, bounding over, a large frond with tiny red fruits dangling from it in his hands.

'That's great,' Jen said. 'Shall we put them safely down somewhere before the dog eats them?' She reached out a hand and took the branch.

'I am not sure Philippos will be happy about berries,' Astro said. 'If they drop on customers or if they could stain the furnishings...'

'Do you not have faith in the Christmas expert?' Jen asked, putting the berries to one side away from anything that could damage them. 'We will coat them in glycerine. Or, if I can't find that here, then clear nail varnish will do.' She smiled. 'This is not my first time using nature to make decorations. In fact, last summer I was in charge of a Christmas-themed wedding in a barn in the woods. The grooms both loved Christmas and wanted a winter wedding but they wanted the warmth of July, their guests to be in sunshine not rain and their photos to be beautiful outside shots. I made it happen, including snow that didn't make anyone cold and wet.'

Astro shook his head. 'I did not realise how many strange people there are in England.'

'Are you calling me strange?' Jen asked. '*And* my customers?'

'No,' Astro said, as plates of food were put in front of them. 'Just that, if you want a Christmas wedding, why not have this at Christmas?'

Jen shook her head, smiling. 'You really have zero idea of what the weather in the UK is like right now. We would not be sitting outside to eat – ever. And inside, those that can afford to would have their heating up to maximum and those that can't would be swaddled in normal clothes, followed by a Christmas jumper and then possibly a dressing gown and a hat.' She sighed, remembering how beautiful that wedding in the woods had been. 'Christian and Jakob got the perfect weather and their perfect winter-themed party all in one.'

When she had finished talking, Astro simply stared at her, the steam from the full plates rising up into the evening air. Even with those beautiful eyes it was a little bit disconcerting. Had she said too much? She knew he didn't like Christmas…

'You very much love your work,' he said softly.

Jen nodded. 'I really do.'

'It is good. To love what you do every day so much.'

He looked a little wistful then. It was obvious to Jen that working at Bar Páme was not where his passion lay.

'You would like to spend all your time on your art,' she said.

'*Fisika*. Of course. But it is impossible.'

Jen opened her mouth to ask him why, but their hosts interrupted, speaking in Greek.

'Mrs Sinrades says we must eat before the food gets cold,' Astro said, picking up his knife and fork.

'It does look delicious. What was it called again?' Jen asked, staring at four fat sausage shapes covered in a yellowy/cream-coloured sauce and a large steaming mound of green vegetables.

'Cabbage rolls. In Greek they are called *lahanodolmades*. And the vegetables are *tsigereli*, a mixture of things that grow here, spinach, and this one I think you call dandelion?' he said, putting some on his fork.

'Really?' Jen exclaimed.

'We will cook anything that is not poisonous,' Astro told her. 'Like what does not kill you makes you stronger, no?'

Next, Mr Sinrades pulled out a violin and began to play.

33

The meal was delicious, and after the main course and a dessert of chocolate *halva* – a super-sweet, super-crumbly nutty concoction – which Achilles had eaten the majority of, Astro and Jen had offered to take care of the clearing and washing up, but their hosts did not let them do a thing. The moment that Achilles had fallen asleep on a wooden bench, the dog at his feet, Astro knew it was time they left. But, before they made any move, he couldn't resist sketching the tired boy in his pad.

'Do you carry that everywhere?' Jen asked, arriving at his shoulder.

For a second, he considered shoving it back into his pocket, the way he would usually if anyone asked him what he was doing. But then he realised, this was Jen, the person he had already shared his mural with. Someone he had told a little of how art was important to him. The woman who had seen three of his awful canvases in his apartment. She had seen his best and his worst.

He nodded. 'Most of the time I am at the bar. But, yes, it is with me. With some pencils that put holes in the pockets of my jeans.'

She sat down next to him, watching him work. He could see

her in his peripheral vision, her eyes going from Achilles to Astro's drawing and back again.

'You really do have a gift,' she said. 'You look at something and you draw or paint it in such a way that... it comes alive.'

'I do not know if that is true,' Astro answered, his pencil brushing the paper. 'And I have a feeling that Achilles will not be coming alive to make the walk back to the bar and I will have to carry him.'

'You know what I mean,' Jen said. 'Don't brush off the compliment.'

'I have a pencil. Not a brush.'

'Ha, ha,' Jen said. 'Very funny.'

He looked at her then, knowing she was going to be smiling, wanting to see her face light up the way it did when she made that expression.

'It is exactly like your mural in Psyrri,' she told him.

His mural in Psyrri. That was, without doubt, the work he was most proud of. That high-rise personal expression only his peers, and now Jen, knew was his. Other street artists signed their pieces with their name or their tag; the great ones were photographed for travel magazines and *his* had been photographed too. But he had never wanted the acknowledgement, the fame for something he had only depicted because he had needed to get it outside himself...

'You really could make money from your art. You know that, don't you?' Jen said as his pencil continued to bleed onto the paper.

'I do not think so,' he answered quickly.

Could he? Because, in his opinion, everything he had made since the mural had been nowhere near the same level. Besides, it was a dream. People like him did not achieve notoriety in the art world.

'Why not? I mean, to begin with, you could do some artwork for the walls of Bar Páme, put prices on them. It's something a lot of artists are doing in the UK instead of putting paintings in galleries. People come in, they have something to eat, a little wine, they sit next to this amazing picture and they think "I would love to have that in my living room" and if it's for sale, they buy it.'

Astro looked up from his pad. 'You make it sound so easy.'

'Not easy... but definitely possible. What is it they say? I forget the completely right words but something like, the difference between a dream and a goal is action. Dreams you think about, goals you get working on. You should make your art a goal.'

She looked so enthused by the idea, but how could it ever happen? He worked at Bar Páme, the business his uncle was striving to keep going and Philippos had put a roof over his head for the past seventeen years. He also knew how much his uncle loved the bar; it was Philippos's entire life! You couldn't make other plans when someone who had supported you without question needed your help with different goals. Plus, he didn't think he was any more skilled than his friends. They all had talent worthy of recognition.

'I do not have anything of the right standard to put on the walls of Bar Páme,' he finally said.

'I'm sure your uncle would disagree.'

'You do not know my uncle.'

'I know he wants Christmas decorations around the place. Why not artwork?'

'Because... it would not be his style.'

'Why not? I mean—'

Astro snapped the sketchbook shut, dropping the pencil to the table. 'Because he does not know I draw or paint. Only that I graffiti and get chased by the police.'

He hadn't meant to snap at Jen and in the candlelight he saw that happy expression he loved so much drop.

'I... didn't mean to say it hard,' he said.

'It's OK,' Jen replied, sitting back in her chair and scrunching her napkin in her hands.

'No, it is not OK. I just... don't tell my uncle about it because it is easier. And... I do not want him to think that I will one day do something else and leave him on his own at the bar.'

He swallowed as those thoughts hit the air and stabbed at his heart. Yes, he might threaten to quit sometimes, blow up about things he did not like, but there was no chance in the world he would abandon his uncle.

'I understand,' Jen said simply, pulling her chair closer to his.

'You do? Because it sounded stupid to my own ears.'

'No, I know exactly what you mean. Neither of us have parents. I am guessing that you want to look after the person who has always been there for you, guiding you, supporting you. But...'

She let her sentence trail and he knew she was waiting for him to fill the silence. But it was his choice whether to say anything at all.

He picked up the pencil, let it carry on fleshing out the curve of Achilles's legs, the dog's head at his feet, the bright red trailing flowers over the whitewashed wall, until he felt ready.

'But you think it is wrong to not tell him about my art,' Astro said, looking at Jen.

'Not *wrong* necessarily. Just that someone who loves you and I assume has supported you through whatever happened with your parents, I'm sure he would want to be your biggest supporter in your talents.' She paused before continuing. 'Maybe I don't know your uncle, but I know that Kathleen always encouraged me in the things that made me happiest, *still* encourages me.'

He didn't answer. Perhaps this was all because he had never

opened up to Philippos about anything. From the moment he'd lost his mother their relationship had been based on schoolwork, making meals together, playing football in the park until he was old enough to drink ouzo, serve ouzo and help his uncle up the stairs after too much ouzo. Neither of them talked about their feelings. It wasn't the Greek male way. They chatted a lot about AEK's latest results, a little about alleged corruption within the government and the rest was snatched conversation when they were working.

He nodded. 'Maybe you should come to dinner. Meet my uncle when he is not the man shaking up cocktails or yelling about late orders.'

'Oh, well, I would like to, but I feel really guilty about leaving Bonnie so much already and—'

'Bonnie too, of course,' Astro replied. Before she had a chance to make a decision, he spoke again. 'And our dinner, it will be late, after the bar has closed.'

She didn't get to answer because with a crashing sound that shook them both, Achilles suddenly rolled and fell off the bench and onto the ground, his head hitting the patio with a thud.

34

BAR PÁME, PLAKA

'*Yassas, Mama!*'

Astro lifted Achilles high up into the air, then over his head, placing him down on the ground after the boy's ride back from the small village atop Astro's shoulders.

Marjorie gasped, hurriedly ditching the tray of empty bottles she was carrying, and rattled out some rapid words in Greek. Jen didn't need to know the language to understand that Marjorie was upset/crazy mad. Jen also knew the reason was the egg-shaped lump on the side of the boy's forehead.

When he'd fallen, everyone had jumped into action. Astro lifted him up, sat him on his knee and examined the injury whilst Mrs Sinrades rushed for ice in a tea towel and Mr Sinrades offered everyone but Achilles some Metaxa for the shock. Achilles was fine despite crying his eyes out, bruised but fine, but it having happened on Astro's watch, Astro had taken Achilles to a medical centre to get him checked out.

'Did you see what happened?'

Marjorie was addressing Jen now and all the customers were

paying far more attention to this commotion than they were to their conversations.

'Yes,' Jen said. 'But it happened quite fast.'

'How did he fall?' Marjorie demanded, eyes a furious mix of concern and rage. 'Like this?' She smacked the very flat of her hand to a table and it made a horrid thwack.

Jen wasn't sure how to answer.

'Marjorie,' Astro said. 'Achilles is fine. I—'

Marjorie continued to stare at Jen. 'Or was it more like this?' She thumped the side of her hand on the tabletop. It was still hard but perhaps slightly less dramatic.

Was there a correct answer here?

'The second one,' Jen offered.

'Are you sure?' Marjorie asked, almost accusing.

'Marjorie, this is no one's fault and Achilles is fine. I took him to the medical centre. A doctor checked him over.'

'He gave me sweets with reindeer on them,' Achilles said. 'Astro, can I go upstairs and see if Peri is there?'

'No!' Marjorie roared. 'You will stay where I can see you.' She looked hard at Astro then. 'You took him to a doctor?'

Astro nodded. 'Yes.'

'I do not believe you. Why do you lie to me?'

'Marjorie,' Astro began. 'I—'

'He isn't lying to you,' Jen jumped in, struggling to keep hold of their bag of Christmas nature and Achilles's branch of berries. 'We went to a medical centre. We had to wait quite a while which is why we're much later than we planned to be and—'

Marjorie was shaking her head. 'No, I know how much it costs to see a private doctor.'

'I paid for it,' Astro blurted out. 'Not with money. I said there would be a free meal here for the doctor and his wife.'

'So you mean Philippos paid for it!' Marjorie exclaimed. 'And I am now in more debt to your uncle.'

'It is not that way,' Astro insisted. 'We are family. The most important thing is that Achilles is OK. That would have been what Philippos wanted. Why do we not go and ask him?'

Jen watched as Astro headed towards the door of the bar, scooting around a white fluffy dog on a lead that was tied to a table leg.

'Philippos is not here. I am working all these tables inside and out alone until Makis gets here and he is late and now I am stressed and freaking out about Achilles,' Marjorie rapped out at pace.

'Well, where is he?' Astro asked.

'He said he had to go out. He said he was phoning you.'

Jen watched Astro dip a hand into the pocket of his jeans and pull out his phone. She knew what she had to do.

Touching Marjorie gently on the arm, she stopped her from going back into Bar Páme. 'Marjorie, give me your apron. I'll help Astro. You take Achilles home.'

'No, Jen, you are not here to—'

'I'm here to help,' Jen interrupted. 'Let me help.'

She swallowed, hoping to inject enthusiasm into her expression.

'I've done this before... back in the UK I actually worked at Greg's. You know, it is a—'

'I have heard of the pastry with vegan sausages,' Marjorie replied.

It was a technicality. Jen had once minded the counter for all of five minutes when Greg had to run down Little Pickering High Street to chase the postman. And Marjorie had assumed Jen meant Greggs with two gs. But that wasn't what was important.

'You are certain you want to help?' she asked, her gaze

suddenly as severe as Natalia's had been when she had suspected one of the elves had lied on his CV.

'*Ne*,' Jen answered in the affirmative. It was about all the Greek she knew.

'I am leaving before you change your mind. Come on, Achilles,' Marjorie said, simultaneously untying her apron, dumping it in Jen's hands and shepherding her son towards her.

Achilles didn't look particularly happy about this, screwing up his face, the bump thankfully looking less inflamed now. 'But what about the Christmas decorations? You said—'

'I'll come here again tomorrow,' Jen said quickly. 'I won't start doing anything until you're here after school and you can help me.' She looked at Marjorie, suddenly realising she was making decisions for someone's child. 'If that's OK with your mum.'

'It is OK,' Marjorie said. 'As long as there are no steps to fall from or poisonous berries he can eat.' She made to leave. '*Ta léme.*'

'*Yassas*, Jen,' Achilles said, waving a hand, a smile on his face.

Jen waved back and then, once they had disappeared into the group of people making their way up and down the steps amid the bars and *tavernas*, she realised exactly how many customers there were and some of them were already beckoning her.

35

EN ROUTE TO PLAKA HOTEL

It was almost 2 a.m. and these late nights/early mornings in Athens were starting to become a habit. Jen thought the city was just as beautiful at this time as it was during the day. As she and Astro moved through the streets, there was less traffic, the Christmas lights standing out as they lit up trees, the sides of businesses, window frames of bars, some still open, some closed until tomorrow. She stifled a yawn and Astro noticed. Wrapping an arm around her shoulders, he drew her close until she could feel his body heat transferring to hers. It all felt incredibly natural despite the fact it usually took a lot of time before she let anyone do that. With David it had taken her a month to let him even hold her hand...

'It is cold again,' Astro said.

'I'm finding it does that here. One moment it's like spring, the next it's dipping into UK autumn temperatures.'

'Wait for the Greek winter. We *do* have one,' Astro told her.

And it was likely she *wasn't* going to experience it as she was booked on a flight back to London in three days – actually, given the time now, it was only two days.

'Listen, I am sorry for you having to help at the bar tonight,' Astro said as they continued to walk in step past the shops that all had their shutters closed for the evening, cats loitering on their stoops.

'There's nothing to apologise for,' Jen replied. 'I *offered* to help. I could see Marjorie was worrying about Achilles and she had obviously been running around trying to do everything and it was my suggestion that we went out looking for festive things so you weren't at the bar. She needed to take him home and I didn't mind pitching in.'

'You were great,' Astro said.

Jen laughed. 'Oh, Astro, I was awful! I broke a plate, a bowl and almost the toes of that poor woman when I trod on her foot.'

'It is a hazard of a job when so many tables are packed into a small space, that is all.'

'You are way too kind. I don't think your uncle would have shared the same opinion.'

'Well, he was not there.'

The way Astro had said it was a bit severe and Jen felt it through him – he had straightened up, core stiff.

'Is everything OK?' she asked as they crossed the road and entered another street that was usually burgeoning with leather goods hanging from rotating stands.

'I do not know,' Astro admitted. 'I think there is something going on with him.' He sighed. 'In all the time we have lived and worked together I have never known him to disappear like this. This is the second time this week. Yes, the first time he told me he was going but, I do not know, it is not normal for him to do this.'

'Do you have any thoughts about what it might be about?'

'Many thoughts,' Astro answered. 'All of them not very good.'

'Are you going to talk to him about it?'

'No,' he said, shaking his head. 'If it is something important, he will eventually tell me. If it is not, then this behaviour will stop and everything will return to how it was.'

'You don't want to know,' Jen surmised.

'I do not want to know something bad,' Astro said. 'And, if we are honest, if it was *not* something bad he would have told me already.'

All too soon they had reached the hotel and, as they came to a stop, Jen realised she really didn't want the evening to end. Despite the drama with Achilles and the disaster-filled service she'd performed at Bar Páme, she had had the best night. Finding items to make Christmas decorations with, eating sublime traditional Greek food they hadn't had to pay for, enjoying Mr Sinrades's violin, but most of all loving Astro's company.

'We are here,' Astro said, standing opposite her now.

'Yes.'

And then neither of them said anything more. Athens seemed to hold its breath too, not a sound coming from anywhere in the very early morning air. Jen's heart was beating hard but whereas last night, before she'd fled from Astro's apartment, it had been a rhythm that had felt as scary as it had felt sexy, now it felt more assured, still full of anticipation but almost confident of what it wanted...

'Jen,' he said, the low tone sending shivers through her.

'Yes.'

'Did I... do something wrong last night? To... make you leave?'

Was that what he thought? She was already shaking her head, desperate to take that feeling away from him. Whatever she had felt then, that indecision, that usual sentiment she got that this closeness wasn't right for her, it wasn't quite in reach now and she had no desire to stretch and see if she could touch it.

'No,' she whispered. 'You did nothing wrong.'

'I thought,' he said, shifting a little on his feet in a sign of nervousness. 'That I had got the situation wrong. That I had made a mistake and—'

'You didn't make a mistake,' she assured him. 'And... I would really like it if we didn't make a mistake again.'

She didn't dwell on how that sentence might have been confusing and instead she reached for his hand – those beautiful long-fingered hands she had watched painting, drawing, carrying plates and trays, picking fruit from trees, the hands that had caressed her hair last night.

Entwining his fingers with hers, he gently rested his forehead against hers and it was the strangest sensation to be that close to someone in that way.

'I want you to know that... whatever this is... it has never happened to me before,' Astro said, his words warm on her skin.

'Me neither.'

'Really?'

'Really.' She swallowed. 'But, Astro, I'm going back to the UK in two days and—'

'Sshh,' he said, pressing a finger to her lips. 'Let us not waste any time thinking about something bad when we are here with something good.'

As he moved his forehead from hers and tilted his head ever so slightly, Jen was already remembering how his mouth had felt the night before and sparks were tickling her insides in anticipation. She didn't have to wait too long. A second later, Astro's lips were on hers and as their mouths moved as one, she was catapulted into a head rush even stronger than before. And this time she wasn't running anywhere.

36

MOUNT LYCABETTUS

'Bonnie, I thought you said there was a cable car train thing to get us to the top!'

Jen was already absolutely out of breath from following Bonnie's lead as she guided them to the summit of this 277 metre crop of limestone. Bonnie had woken up early, full of enthusiasm for the day, and Jen hadn't had the heart to tell her she'd rather strike climbing this landmark from the agenda because of her late night with Astro.

'That's what the guide says but, you know how these things are with accuracy. They practically expect you to have a compass in your handbag.'

'Are you sure we're going the right way to get to the top, at least?' Jen asked, hands on her hips as she drew in much-needed air. The air was so cold today she could see her own breath in front of her. They had powered up streets lined with tall residential buildings, each apartment with a balcony shaded by large awnings, some orange, others a deep turquoise green, a sheen of frosty condensation on top. Now they were walking up a rough track that only seemed to be track at all because a path had been worn by people obviously as crazy as they were or those who also couldn't find the train to get them to the top.

'Well,' Bonnie said. 'I'm following Google Maps – a bit, because it keeps moving off centre – and hoping that these well-walked trails keep on going and don't peter out because people got so far and then had to turn around.' She sniffed. 'And if Andrea can do a sponsored walk up Snowdon with nothing but some designer coat that couldn't keep a mouse warm then I'm sure I can get to the top of this hill without needing to call the coastguard.'

As Jen caught her breath, contemplating why Bonnie would need the coastguard in this scenario, she realised this wasn't only a morning stroll or a visit to another Athens landmark.

'Bonnie, wait for me,' Jen said, starting to walk again and determined to catch her friend up.

'I think it's this way,' Bonnie said, peeling off left to a track that was looking all the more craggy.

'Stop a second,' Jen said, breathing heavily already but trying to reach Bonnie's arm and get some purchase.

'I can't stop because my inner thighs are killing, and if I stop I'll notice and then I won't be able to make it to the top, and if I don't make it to the top I can't share it on my socials and Andrea won't see it!'

There was so much in that sentence and Bonnie quickly realised it, stopping next to a tree, despite what she'd said about her thighs. She gave Jen the expression she adopted whenever she needed a release.

'Did something happen when you were shopping?' Jen asked. 'When I was with Astro?'

'Yes,' Bonnie said, sighing. 'While I was looking for *the* perfect Christmas gift for Mum and Dad, Dad shares to his Insta story a reel of him and Andrea at the gym! Dad never shares anything to his story unless I'm there to help him! And he's never invited *me* to the gym!'

'Oh, Bonnie...'

'I know I wanted to come here to get away from Andrea, but when I opened the door to leave I didn't think she was going to barge her way through it and *replace* me!'

'I'm sure that isn't what's happening. And *no one* could replace you, Bonnie.'

'I thought, come here with you, prove to Andrea that I can be independent and not the stay-at-home sibling with no ambition. I don't know, be all boss bitch at the same time as she's just come back from London with this break-up sob story. But one tear from Andrea's eye and my parents are both suddenly behaving like Kris Jenner – Momager.' Bonnie heaved another sigh. 'Any second now they're going to be putting up the Christmas tree without me and Andrea's going to be allowed to put Fairy Fatima on top!'

Jen stayed quiet as she watched Bonnie rush through all the stages of anger, disappointment, envy and upset in only a few expressions. Finally, she spoke.

'Bonnie, what actually happened between you and Andrea to make you feel this way? Ever since I've known you you've had this kind of rivalry but you've never told me when it started or what caused it?'

'*She* caused it,' Bonnie said bitterly. 'And I hate her.'

Everything about the tone of Bonnie's voice was saying that behind the words was actually a very different emotion.

'She went to university and she got her fancy new friends and she got her degree and the high-powered job and the top-notch apartment and... she left me behind without even a glance back.'

Jen put an arm around her friend's shoulders, never having seen her quite like this before. What had always seemed like light sparring between siblings had now turned into a deep bitter trench in their relationship – a trench that Bonnie had been standing in for a lot longer than Jen realised.

'I think you miss her,' Jen said. 'I'm guessing you had a good relationship, a *great* relationship before she left home and then she had other things in her life and—'

'You can say it,' Bonnie said. 'I do *resent* her. I know it. She probably knows it. She's someone who suddenly went from dunking battered chicken balls in a polystyrene cup of sweet and sour sauce on the sofa with me at the weekends, to eating parfait at The Savoy with her clever work colleagues.' She sniffed. 'I didn't even know what "parfait" was. I had to google it! And it looked disgusting! But I was still jealous. That the parfait and the other people all got to spend more time with her than I did.'

'Bonnie,' Jen said, drawing her into an embrace now. 'Have you told Andrea any of this?'

'No!' Bonnie said, seeming appalled at the idea. 'How can I tell her that? She'll know then, that I've been jealous of her life there. But it's not really jealousy of what she has or what she's doing.' She sighed. 'I feel like this because I want her to still want the life we all had when we were a family of four. She moved out and moved on and she forgot about us, forgot about me. And I know how pathetic that sounds but there we are.'

She let Jen go.

Jen could relate in some way with regard to wanting stability and familiarity. Any brief few weeks when stability had been hers at a particular foster home, she would allow herself to give it a fresh chance, whisper to Bravely Bear that maybe this time he could have a visible space on the bunk bed, but it had never ever lasted. Circumstances would change and she would have to move somewhere else, or another child would arrive and make her life a misery and she would retreat into her shell.

'It's OK to feel how you do,' Jen told her.

'Is it though? Because saying it out loud to you has made me sound like a whingeing unstable twenty-something who's acting like they're still in primary school.'

'I think there's one thing standing in the way of you getting your relationship with Andrea back on track,' Jen said.

'Andrea?'

'No,' Jen said, shaking her head. 'Pride.' She took a breath. 'From my limited observations, both of you have that in common. You're both too proud to admit that you miss each other, because you're too busy trying to out-do one another and pretend that you're loving life when, in reality, neither of you are happy with how things are between you.'

She suddenly realised she might have been a little too blunt and honest.

'Sorry, Bonnie, maybe I know nothing. Maybe—'

'No,' Bonnie said, visibly deflating. 'I mean, I don't know from Andrea's side obviously, but I know that I really wish she wanted to spend time with us again, yet the second she came home I was straight to thinking it was to inject her superiority over us.' She gasped then, hands on her cheeks. 'Do you think she actually has split up with someone called Jules? Because I *really* thought it was a ruse for Mum's attention.'

'I think you need to talk to her. Have an honest conversation.'

Bonnie sighed. 'Yeah, and I shouldn't be trying to power up this virtual mountain to prove something with no idea where it's going to lead us. Especially when my fitness regime consists of watching *SAS: Who Dares Wins* with loaded cookie dough ice cream.'

'You don't know where this is going to lead us?'

'Well...'

'Bonnie!'

'OK, so, I am going to… think about speaking to Andrea. If she has time for me between selfies with our dad and dumbbells.'

'Bonnie!'

'So are we carrying on upwards or are we going back down for much-needed frappé and cake?'

Jen looked ahead of them at the continuing trail, the summit of Mount Lycabettus still appearing some way away. The Jen who had arrived in Athens on a whim but still very much needing someone to tell her she was doing the right thing would have chosen the path down to civilisation. But the Jen who had done art on a shutter door, worked a shift at a Greek bar and was being told by Kathleen to take a break, wasn't someone who gave up.

'You said there was a restaurant at the top, right?'

'I did say that. Currently regretting saying that because I think I know what's coming next.'

'Come on, the guide says a spectacular view is waiting, doesn't it?'

'It does,' Bonnie agreed. 'But remember it also said there was a funicular railway to the summit.'

Jen put her arm around Bonnie's shoulders. 'Well, let's see how we get on and I can tell you about dinner tonight.'

'You've picked a place?' Bonnie asked.

'Something like that,' Jen said as they got going again.

37

BAR PÁME, PLAKA

Astro had maybe an hour until Chef got there and he needed to have everything cleaned down and be out of his kitchen space well before then. He carefully used two cloths to get the earthenware pot out of the oven and as the heat started to burn his hands, he instantly regretted not making a better, thicker material choice. He couldn't drop it. He could *not* drop it.

'Astro! What the hell!'

It was Philippos entering the kitchen. In milliseconds, his uncle had picked up two rubber mats and had grabbed the pot from him, putting it down on a wooden board on the worktop.

'Are you crazy?' Philippos asked, looking at Astro as if he might have invited lions to dine rather than just got a hot pot from the oven with inappropriate equipment. 'You could have hurt yourself!'

'I was OK,' Astro replied. 'I could have done it.'

'What is it?' Philippos asked, looking at the pot with suspicion.

Astro picked up one of the rubber mats that Philippos had used and lifted off the lid. All at once Philippos was inhaling and then closing his eyes as the aroma filled the air. Astro had to admit, it did smell good.

'*Gourounopoula*,' Philippos said.

'Do not worry, I am not going to be the one cooking for our customers. I am very happy to leave that for Chef but...'

He stopped talking, swallowing as he realised how important tonight was to him. Inviting someone to meet his family. He hadn't ever done that before. And yet it was so temporary, Jen's trip almost already at an end...

'But?' Philippos asked as Astro hadn't finished his sentence, nor added to it.

'I have invited Jen to dinner.'

'Great,' Philippos said. 'This place needs to be full until Christmas. Takings high and profit higher, yes?'

Despite all this bravado about 'love' at the market the other day, his uncle didn't seem to have understood.

Astro tried again.

'I didn't mean as a customer. I meant I have invited her and Bonnie to dinner with us. To eat with us.'

'When?'

That hadn't been the exact first response he had been expecting. 'Tonight.'

'Ah, Astro, I cannot do tonight. There is somewhere else I need to be,' Philippos said, already making moves towards the door to the bar area.

Again! Something was definitely going on. And perhaps it was time to voice that concern. 'Where else do you need to be after we close?'

'I will be leaving around ten and I will be back late,' Philippos said, pushing the door. 'Makis will be here to cover the bar.'

Astro felt anger bubbling up. His uncle was avoiding the question and was walking away.

He quickly followed. 'Where are you going?'

'I'm sorry I can't be here to have dinner with Jen,' Philippos said, moving behind the bar and beginning to prep. 'Can we make it another night?'

'No,' Astro said. 'Because she is leaving soon. Back to the UK.'

'Really? She is not here for Christmas Day?'

Astro gritted his teeth. It still pricked that everyone's thoughts at this time of year revolved around one solitary day. One day out of so many better ones! And it seemed that since Philippos had insisted the bar was coated in festive finery and Astro had had to relent, his uncle had virtually forgotten how difficult Astro found the season!

'No,' he said again. 'She is not here for Christmas Day and it was important to me that she had a meal with us, as a family.'

'Have you even had a meal on your own together yet?' Philippos asked, picking up a tea cloth and wiping down the beer taps. 'I mean, you don't want a middle-aged man getting in the way of your time. You should take her out. A nice restaurant with a roof terrace and a view over the city.'

Astro bit his tongue. They had had a beautiful meal last night, with a view over Athens, Achilles running around with the Sinrades's dog, lights wrapped around the herb garden. It wasn't the venue that was important in this situation, he wanted to mark Jen as important in his life, someone he liked enough to show all the sides of him, introduce to the one member of his family he had left.

'I made *gourounpoula*,' Astro reminded him.

'I know,' Philippos said. 'And it smells so much more authentic than mine. And if it was any other night then I would eat with you, but I cannot tonight.'

'Why?'

'I told you, Astro. I have to be somewhere else.'

'And you have not said where.'

Astro stood his ground, staring at his uncle, wanting to hear something other than a skirting around the issue.

'I think I can hear the delivery guys,' Philippos said, rushing from behind the bar. 'I must go and check.'

And before Astro could say another word, his uncle had left.

38

ASTRO'S APARTMENT, BAR PÁME

'Achilles, remember to only put the nail polish on the berries,' Jen instructed. All the materials and Christmas nature goodies they'd foraged for yesterday were laid out on Astro's dining table as Jen and Achilles got them ready. The boy was back from school and had been highly excited when Jen and Bonnie had arrived. The bar was busy so Astro had suggested they assemble everything up here and then, when it was quieter, they could start decorating.

'It's a sizeable apartment, isn't it?' Bonnie remarked, strutting around and seeming to take it all in. 'With a Juliet balcony too. What's the bathroom like?'

'It is small,' Achilles said. 'And the pipes make a lot of noise. There is no bath.'

'That's a shame,' Bonnie said.

'It's not for rent,' Jen reminded her. 'It's Astro's home.'

And she felt suddenly protective over it. It was nice here, comfortable. She loved the aged wood floor and the amount of light the windows let in. She also loved seeing some of Astro's things about the place – one of his sweatshirts was neatly hanging over a chair, mismatched coffee mugs draining in the kitchen area, a stool he used as a nightstand holding books. His art, she noticed, was gone.

Bonnie shrieked. 'Argh! What's that? There's something banging at the window! It's big! With wings!'

'It's Peri!' Achilles announced with much excitement, getting down from the table and running towards the window.

'What's a Peri?' Bonnie asked. 'And what are you going to do now?'

'I am going to open the window and let him in. He is Astro's pet,' Achilles announced, his little fingers already around the latch.

'Still don't know what he is,' Bonnie said. 'And don't pets tend to live in the house full time? And, if they have wings, usually in a cage?'

'Achilles, wait a minute,' Jen said, getting up too. 'We don't want Peri to fly in and start eating our decorations. Especially when we've now coated them with something not for birds. Let's put some of this seed in a bowl for him and he can stay out there until we're finished.'

She grabbed a packet from the side of the kitchen area – it was all written in Greek but there were pictures of birds on it so it had to be seed – then took a clean bowl from the drying stack and poured some in.

'Let me do it,' Achilles said, taking the bowl from her and rushing to the window again.

'Eww! It's a pigeon,' Bonnie said, mouth downturned.

'Bonnie, you work at a vet's,' Jen reminded her. 'You must have seen lots of birds.'

'Domesticated ones. In cages, as I said. Ones that don't survive from eating scraps found on the floor.'

'Peri is a nice bird,' Achilles insisted as he carefully opened the window, popped the bowl on the wide sill and gave Peri a stroke on the head as he started to tuck in.

'And Astro lets it come in here,' Bonnie said, appearing to look at the apartment with a whole new perspective.

'Sometimes,' Achilles answered, shutting the window and coming back to the table.

'Well, I know I said you should give Astro the green light, but if he's the kind of guy to live with birds then I might have to reconsider that opinion.'

Jen's face was flushing before she felt the intensity of Achilles's eyes. She knew what was coming next and there was no way to stop it.

'What is the green light?' Achilles asked. 'And why are you giving it to Astro?'

'It's... er... something that—' Jen started.

'The green light,' Bonnie said, pulling up a chair next to Achilles and picking up the twine they were wrapping around the nature pieces, 'is something we put up as a decoration at Christmas time in England. Isn't it, Jen?'

She nodded. 'Yes, it's an old tradition, um, connected with the fact that British people like sprouts so much.'

This was ridiculous! Why was she lying to Achilles? Why hadn't she just said that it meant being friends with someone?

'What is sprouts?' Achilles asked.

'You don't eat sprouts in Greece?' Bonnie exclaimed.

'They are food?'

'Little green balls like tiny vicious cabbages. Always make you—'

Before Bonnie could elaborate any further, they were interrupted by Jen's phone starting to ring. A side-eye to the screen told her it was the nursing home. Usually, her heart would drop a little at this, but Kathleen had been in bolshy spirits when they'd spoken yesterday. This would be an admin-related query, something like Kathleen needing more tights – she did tend to go through them.

'Hello,' Jen greeted.

'Hello, Miss Astley, it's Matilda from the nursing home. It's about Mrs Ockenden.'

It wasn't about tights. It was about Kathleen herself.

She held her breath.

'I'm afraid to say... well... she's gone missing.'

39

BAR PÁME

'Why don't you go and sit with her? Because you are little use to me when you are chewing your nails and looking at her waiting for news and not delivering drinks and meals.'

Astro took his finger from his lips, quickly sanitised his hands from the nearest pump and tried to remember where his tray of drinks was going. No, he had forgotten.

'Table six,' Marjorie said, heading off to take her own order to customers.

'Right,' Astro said, turning in the correct direction.

Once the food and beverages had been distributed, they met back in the middle of the steps through the bars on either side of the path to the base of the Acropolis which was getting more and more Christmassy by the minute. Soon the atmosphere would be replicated inside Bar Páme once Achilles and Jen's decorations had been added to the mix.

Except the berries and ferns were not the primary thing on Jen's mind now. Her thoughts were only on the whereabouts of Kathleen.

'This is not her mother who is missing,' Marjorie said, wiping down an empty table and straightening chairs and cushions for seating on the floor.

'No,' Astro answered. 'But I think this is the only person like a mother Jen has had.' He sighed. 'The only person she has ever cared so hard about.'

'Oh my God,' Marjorie said. 'I hope and pray only positive things.'

'Yeah, me too,' Astro said, taking another look over at Jen who had been sitting at an outside table for over an hour now. She and Bonnie both with phones to their ears or fingers to their keyboards, trying to find any information about Kathleen's whereabouts.

'It is a lot for Jen to think about,' Marjorie remarked, handing Astro a tray of used crockery.

It was a lot and very selfishly he knew how limited Jen's time in Athens was. Was this going to cut things even shorter? Would she have to leave now? Today? He needed to not think about it. But he was. And when he wasn't thinking about that, there was only one other thing on his mind.

'Marjorie,' Astro began as he helped her clear another table.

'Oh no, that is your serious voice. The one you use when you are about to ask me something I definitely do not want to answer.'

'There is something else that is a lot.' He sighed. 'There is something going on with my uncle and I want to know your opinion on what it is.'

Marjorie picked up her cleaning materials and a tray and began to head back to the bar. Astro matched her stride.

'Marjorie, please, if you know something, you have to tell me. Like what you said about unpaid bills.'

'Sshh! I don't know anything.' Marjorie avoided his gaze, suddenly seeming to have the urge to preen a newly made wreath that was hanging on the door.

'But you think something? Have heard something? Because Philippos is avoiding conversation with me when I ask him directly. Three times this morning he has heard the delivery truck and needed to investigate.'

Marjorie shook her head. 'I need this job, Astro, and getting involved in gossip is not the way to keep employment. I learned that from watching the waitresses at my last place. *Everything* has ears.'

'Marjorie, this is me. We are always honest with each other, right?'

She pushed open the door to the bar and bustled through; Astro followed, hot on her heels.

'Marjorie—'

'Sshh!' she ordered, taking Astro by the arm. 'Do you want him to hear?'

She indicated Philippos, who was busy behind the bar, serving customers sat on stools there. She pulled Astro into the stone nook where the wine was stored.

'Now,' she began. 'This is not coming from me. It is just something someone who I will not name has said to me.'

'O-K.' Astro said, waiting with bated breath.

'Well, the rumour is... that...'

'Marjorie, just tell me!'

She sighed. 'My source thinks that Philippos... he is seeing someone.'

'Seeing someone?' Astro knew he had said it as if the words did not make sense to him.

'My God, Astro, like dating!'

'A woman?'

'Yes, a woman!'

Astro hadn't been 100 per cent sure of his uncle's romantic preference because, in all these years, he had never ever known him to date *anyone*. He flirted with the customers, both men and women, wildly sometimes, but as far as Astro knew, there had never been anyone special in his life. Where was the time? The bar took up most of the moments they had... But then Astro remembered the conversation he had had with Philippos at the market. He had talked about love. Was that because *he* was pursuing it?

'You know that new dance club everyone was talking about a few months ago?' Marjorie continued.

Astro shook his head as he tried to take on board this potential news. 'Like Studio 24?'

'No! Nothing like Studio 24. This is not where you arrive drunk, get more drunk and dance like you're the drunkest you have ever been. This is where they teach you to dance. It is called Sequence.'

Now Astro felt this really couldn't be true. His elbow nudged a bottle of Merlot and he turned, gripping it with his hand to steady it. Sure, his uncle would sway about at festivals, attempt the traditional dances, but he had zero rhythm and always forgot the order of the steps.

'You are saying Philippos goes to this place? I do not see it.'

'I said the same at first but...'

'But what?'

'But we all do crazy things when we like someone, right?' She stared straight at him. 'Like accepting Christmas into the bar.'

He bristled at Marjorie's words because whenever he dwelt on that fact he felt a deep feeling of disloyalty to his mother. As though he was disrespecting her memory.

'Astro,' Marjorie said. 'I should not have said that. I was only—'

'It's OK,' he replied. 'I get it. It's just... if this is true, if he has met someone, why is he keeping it a secret from me?'

'There is only one way for you to find that out,' Marjorie said, taking a step back into sight.

'I know. To ask him, outright.'

'Oh no!' Marjorie exclaimed. 'I was not going to say that!'

'Then what?'

'Tonight, when he is leaving again, maybe you should follow him.'

40

ATHENS NATIONAL GARDEN

Sitting still didn't ever work for long when Jen was problem-solving. Her mind might have been racing but her body had started to knit itself together, her back hunched, her shoulders tight with tension. All she could think about was moving, walking, doing something while they waited. Waited for an update about Kathleen. So they were here, in the city's national gardens, an oasis of green amid the greys and whites of multi-storey buildings around Syntagma, right behind the parliament building. The temperature was rapidly decreasing and the light of the day was beginning to fade, while Bonnie did her best to keep spirits up...

'These are the tallest palm trees I think I've ever seen,' she announced as they strode through the gates, heading towards the dozen or so specimens at the end of an area with beautifully coloured bedding plants all set in rows.

'Mmm,' Jen answered.

'And apparently there's a lake here with ducks and geese and terrapins.'

Jen couldn't be bothered to give that statement any answer at all. She knew Bonnie was trying to keep things light, give them both a distraction from what was going on at home, hope for the best, perhaps prepare for the worst. No, she couldn't think about the worst at all.

'Jen, you need to breathe,' Bonnie said suddenly, shaking her arm quite roughly as she drew her to a stop.

Jen looked at her friend and it was then she realised her chest was tight, sore even, and pressure was building. But she couldn't release it. She was suddenly struck with a reel of memories. Being cornered by bullies at one of her schools. *She's a care kid. More like no one cares kid.* Hiding in her wardrobe when one of the other foster children threatened to set fire to the house. *We're spare parts no one wanted. Spare parts that don't fit anywhere.*

'Jen! Your lips are going blue! Breathe! Please, breathe!'

She could hear the fear in her friend's voice but the whack on the back came right out of nowhere and such was the shock, Jen didn't have a choice. An exhale flew from her, followed quickly by an inhale and soon after, light-headedness. She swayed.

'Whoa! OK, let's just come over here and sit down,' Bonnie said, gripping onto Jen's shoulder and directing her to the left where there were metal benches with wooden seats.

'No,' Jen said, trying to regulate her breathing now. 'I don't want to sit down. I just want to keep moving. Otherwise I don't feel like I'm doing anything except waiting for bad news.'

There, she'd said it. Her fear that bad news was coming. Why wouldn't it be? Because that's how it had always been for her. She always felt she was only one step away from things going wrong again. But this was December now and Christmas was all about good! It made everything brighter! If she couldn't rely on that, what could she rely on?

'Kathleen is as strong as an old goat,' Bonnie said, still holding onto Jen. 'She's probably got really annoyed by that man raving about Dunkirk and just went out for a walk.'

'Bonnie, it's been hours,' Jen reminded her. 'And it's so cold in the UK at the moment.' She was shaking now, from a mix of worried adrenaline and her body's desperation to keep its essential functions going. 'Where would she be? What would she be doing?'

'I don't know,' Bonnie admitted. 'But, you know, wherever she's gone is likely to be familiar to her. You heard what the police officer said.'

The police officer. Yes, the home had called the police and Jen had gone through every place she could think of that Kathleen might have wanted to get to – the cemetery where Gerald was buried, the old premises of Fancy Occasions, the bingo hall in the neighbouring town, the library. Natalia had left Christmas Every Day and had rounded up as many people as she could to scour the village, including the fields and, even worse, the river banks...

'I can't help thinking that no one is trying as hard as I would be if I was there,' Jen admitted. 'And also I'm thinking it might be... my fault.'

'Jen, you know she wants you to be here and—'

'And I got her all worked up about finding an alternative to Geoffrey's acting group. I should have been able to solve my own problems. I shouldn't have gone to her about it. And if something's happened I will never be able to forgive myself.'

'Breathe, Jen, please, just keep breathing,' Bonnie said as they walked, passing under a pergola covered in strings of vines without any of their leaves or bounty. 'I feel certain she's going to be fine and I reckon Greg is going to find her. The scent of his Christmas gingerbread tea cakes she likes will have her coming out of wherever she is before too long.'

No sooner were the words out of Bonnie's mouth than Jen's mobile phone began to ring. For a second she stalled as she felt every emotion zip through her – joy, desperation, hope, dread.

Then she was moving to get it out of her bag. When she was holding the phone in her hands she saw that the number didn't belong to anyone she knew.

'Answer it,' Bonnie ordered.

Jen stabbed at the screen with her finger. 'Hello.'

There was a pause until finally words.

'Jen, don't hang up.'

Jen gasped, eyes wide with shock.

'What is it? What's happened?' Bonnie demanded.

'It's David,' Jen whispered.

'What?' Bonnie roared. 'Give me the phone! Give it to me!'

Jen battled to stop Bonnie from wrenching the device away, turning her back and moving down one of the other paths through the park, green parrots flying over her head.

'I'm going to hang up now,' Jen told him, her teeth gritted. 'I need to keep this line open. I'm waiting for an important call and you need to stop calling Natalia too. We have a lot going on and—'

'What's happened?' David asked. 'You sound upset.'

'I *am* upset! I'm *very* upset! And it has nothing to do with you any more so I'm going to go now and I'm going to block this number, whoever's number it is you're calling from and—'

'I've split up with Claudia.'

For a second Jen thought of the only Claudia she knew – Winkleman. But very quickly she realised David had to be referring to his wife. And as Bonnie arrived by her side, she put the call on speakerphone. She was going to get rid of him quickly and she wanted her best friend to hear everything.

'My... wife,' David continued. 'Claudia is my wife. *Was* my wife,' he clarified, as if realising Jen wouldn't know who that was.

'David, I really don't know why you're telling me this,' Jen said. 'I have no interest in what you do or don't do. I thought I'd made that clear. I'm hanging up now and blocking this number, as I said.

And please don't call me again on another number as I'll just have to block that one too.'

'Jen, please, give me—'

'No!' Jen roared. 'Kathleen is missing and—'

'Kathleen is missing!' David exclaimed. 'Are you serious?'

Jen swallowed, her mind going from full to blank and back again. *Kathleen was a missing person. The police were looking for her.*

'David, it's Bonnie,' Bonnie interrupted. 'As Jen just said, you need to stop calling. She doesn't want to talk to you. It's over and done, no matter what your current relationship sitch is. And, as she's also just said, her priorities are elsewhere right now so—'

'I can help,' David butted in again. 'I can help find Kathleen. I know people.'

'What? In a mafioso kind of a way?' Bonnie asked.

'Rather the opposite actually. I play golf with the chief constable. I can give him a call. I can make sure they're prioritising finding Kathleen over, I don't know, chasing kids who've graffitied the town hall.'

Jen swallowed, the graffiti comment hitting home. She wanted to end the call, her phone shaking in her trembling hand. But a direct route to the head of the local police. The focus on the search for Kathleen escalated and more urgent. She couldn't turn that down. However, she wasn't naïve enough to think that David's help wouldn't come at a cost.

'Let me give Tony a call. He'll shake things up and make sure there's a positive outcome, I'm sure.'

A positive outcome. What did that even mean? How about 'make sure Kathleen's found safe and well and back to moaning about turkey arse before the day's over'?

'Jen,' Bonnie whispered, 'what do you want to do?'

She had no choice. This was Kathleen, the person she cared most about in the whole world.

She sighed. 'Make the call.'

'OK,' David answered. 'I'll get straight on it. Right this second. And I'll call you right back after I've spoken to him.'

As the connection ended, Jen looked at Bonnie. Her expression was giving absolutely everything away.

'You don't have to say anything,' Bonnie said, putting an arm around her shoulders. 'I know.'

41

BAR PÁME, PLAKA

Astro had been trying to call Jen any chance he got between service and helping Marjorie and Philippos fix more Christmas decorations to the interior of the bar. But now she was standing in the doorway looking cold, pale and a shadow of the person who had lit up like a festive display herself the first moment they had met. Under his breath he whispered a short prayer that there had been *no* news rather than bad news.

'Jen,' he said, rushing forward.

'Hi.'

'Is there—'

'There's no news,' she said, exhaling. 'And I'm really trying not to panic knowing that it's definitely dark in the UK right now.'

'Hey,' he said, putting an arm around her shoulders. 'From what you have told me about Kathleen I do not think she is the kind of person to let the dark get in the way of whatever she has gone out to do.'

'Ordinarily I would agree,' Jen said. 'But she's a lot older now and there's medication she has to have and where has she gone?

Because she has no family and most of her friends are in Little Pickering and Little Pickering is not that big.'

'Come, come and sit,' Astro urged her.

'I can't sit. Because I've also done a deal with the devil and I know that Kathleen will hate that I did that and doubly hate that I did that for her and... oh my goodness!'

She was looking up now, at the ceiling. The berries, fir sprigs and other things they had collected the night before were cascading down as if the bar was now a winter forest.

'Astro, this looks fantastic,' she said. 'It's like a festive woodland. Oh, and you've put the Christingles around too. Did Achilles make them on his own?'

Astro plucked one of the oranges from the windowsill and turned it upside down. 'I do not think they will last the season. He put many holes in the wrong places so they would not stand up, but we got there finally.'

'You helped him?' Jen asked.

'With Peri. Although he wanted to eat more than help.'

'I'm so sorry I had to go I—'

'Shhh, it is OK. You have many things happening.'

'I know and I don't think I'm going to be in the right head space to have dinner with you and Philippos tonight,' Jen admitted. 'I'd be thinking about Kathleen and waiting for the phone to ring and, well, that isn't fair on anyone.'

'It is OK,' Astro said, putting the Christingle back. 'I understand. Someone you love is missing and anyway, my uncle, he says he will not be around tonight so...'

He had left the sentence hanging for two reasons. The first was he didn't really know what to say in explanation. The second was the thought of Philippos keeping things from him made him annoyed and he didn't know if he even had the right to be annoyed.

'Has something happened?' Jen asked.

He shook his head. 'I do not know.'

'You can talk to me,' Jen said as the door opened and a customer came in, bringing a shot of cold wind with them.

'I still do not know what is going on with him. Marjorie thinks that maybe he is... seeing someone and they are... dancing together.'

What was wrong with him? He made it sound as if his uncle was doing something sinister, like suddenly he was a major player in an illegal arms organisation. He was possibly going to a dance academy and dating! It wasn't a crime!

'I am sorry,' Astro said. 'This is stupid. To talk about something like this when you have more serious things happening.'

'I want to know, Astro.' She reached for his hand and slid their fingers together.

She wanted to know. What was important to him. What he thought about things and why he thought that way. He had never had anyone in his life who had done that. And that knowledge was weaving its way through him like a warm sensation, getting hotter and driving straight to his heart. He gently teased her fingers with his.

Then a ring tone broke the air and Jen let him go, hand racing for the zip on her bag.

'*Signomi!*'

It was a customer calling to him but Astro was going nowhere until he knew if this call was news of any kind.

'Hello,' Jen greeted, her face holding so much tension.

Astro prayed again as he kept his eyes on her. Then suddenly he knew as her expression altered.

'Oh, thank God! Oh... thank you so much. I don't know what to say. Is she definitely OK? Yes... OK, yes, I understand. Yes, I will. OK, thank you. Thank you, bye.'

The call ended and Astro could see exactly how much emotion Jen was internally fighting to hold back. He didn't wait. He put his arms around her and hugged her tight as she shook.

'It is good news, yes?' he asked, mouth close to her ear.

'Yes,' she answered, her voice jagged. 'It was the police. They've found her. In Portsmouth. I don't know what she was doing there or even how she got there. They are taking her to the hospital to be checked over but they said she was really moaning about all the fuss which means she has to be OK because moaning is literally her favourite pastime.'

'This is good,' Astro said. 'This is so good.'

'It is good. It's the best news and I feel like...' She eased herself away from him then. 'So relieved. Just so incredibly happy.'

As much as her desperation had been written all over her when she'd come into the bar, now it was her joy that was close to palpable. And he felt that relief resonating inside himself.

'I mean, I won't feel completely 100 per cent OK until I've spoken to Kathleen myself but...'

'But she is OK,' Astro said. 'She is safe.'

'Yes,' Jen breathed. 'Yes!'

'*Signomi! Parakalo!*'

It was the customer again and Astro couldn't pretend he wasn't in the middle of service for much longer.

'Jen, I have to work now but later, maybe now Kathleen is OK, you can come to dinner? I know it was supposed to be with my uncle but—'

'Yes,' Jen answered. 'Yes, I would really like that.'

'OK,' Astro said, nodding. 'Good. *Ta léme argótera.* I will see you later.'

42

HOTEL PLAKA

With a large glass of white wine on the table in front of her, Jen waited for the FaceTime to connect. This evening she and Bonnie were bundled up in coats, the complete opposite to their first night here on the roof terrace of the hotel when they'd worn short sleeves. It seemed that Greece really did have wintry weather sometimes. Yet the pull to be close to the Parthenon was still too strong to ignore or give up because of the temperature. There was a calming vibe about this space with its plants and soft lighting, and calm was exactly what Jen needed.

'She's not answering,' Jen said as the ring tone continued.

'Give her a minute,' Bonnie said. 'She's had a big day.'

That was true. And so had Jen. She felt it physically, like someone had pushed her into traffic and a zillion of those speeding Athens yellow taxis had all driven over her. Bruises were on the inside if not showing on her skin.

'Hello!'

The voice was one Jen hadn't been expecting and then the visual came up. It was Natalia, wearing a white Santa beard.

'Natalia?'

'Yes, I am here. Sorry, I have come straight from bazaar. After searching fields for Kathleen, Michael call in sick so I have been Santa Claus and Merry Poppins today.'

Michael, one of their principal workers, was sick again? He had been sick for three days the week before Jen had flown out to Athens. And he was down to lead the reindeer performance for the Knowles' engagement party...

'You want me to fire Michael? Both brothers can do excellent reindeer impersonation, or we can find real deer and make red nose.'

'Can we talk about this later, Natalia? I just really want to see Kathleen.' Jen was back to worrying again.

'She is here,' Natalia said, the camera swaying about a bit. 'She is very angry. I think she want to stay longer in Portsmouth with sailor.'

'She was with a sailor?' Bonnie asked.

Then Kathleen was on screen, her hair immaculate, dressed in one of her smart jumpers, a row of pearls at her neck and a blanket over her knees, but the expression on her face wasn't giving pleased-to-see-you vibes. Jen didn't care. Her friend being safe was all that mattered.

'Hello, Kathleen. You really don't know how pleased I am to see you. I was so worried and—'

'*You* were worried,' came the chippy response. 'I could say exactly the same thing.'

Jen felt Bonnie looking at her but she kept her eyes on the screen. What did Kathleen mean? What had *she* been worried about? Was there something no one had told her about the hospital check-up? Something underlying or slow growing that had crept up on them?

'I don't know what you mean,' Jen said. 'Why don't you tell me about Portsmouth and what you were doing there.'

'Oh yes,' Kathleen said, mouth still very much set to harsh. 'Let me tell you what led me to Portsmouth, shall I?'

Was it her imagination or did Kathleen sound annoyed at *her*? She reached for her glass of wine and took a large gulp.

'I was looking for one of my little red books for the name and phone number of one of my old contacts,' Kathleen began, leaning forward in her seat and putting her face very close to the camera.

'O-K,' Jen said.

'And then I remembered that you had some of my things that I didn't have room for here.'

A chill ran down Jen's spine.

'So, I went to your flat,' Kathleen confirmed. 'And I met a nice young man called Thomas and he told me that *he* lives there now.'

Jen didn't know what to say but she watched Bonnie pour some more wine from the carafe into Jen's glass.

'You have boyfriend called Thomas?' Natalia asked, only the edge of her beard visible. 'Is quick work.'

Jen shook her head, thoughts tumbling like someone had emptied a container of Christmas baubles from the top of a staircase. What did she say? How did she explain what had happened with her flat? How did she justify keeping it a secret from Kathleen?

'Thomas said he's been living there since September. So, my question to you is, where have *you* been living since then?'

Jen didn't know what to do. She stood up. Then she sat down again. How could she have this discussion when Natalia was right there and Bonnie was next to her and Kathleen seemed so *so* angry and disappointed.

'Natalia,' Bonnie said, breaking the enforced silence. 'I'm going to call you. There's something I need your help for.'

'OK,' Natalia said. 'Kathleen, I leave you to talk to Jen. I come back with second puddings.'

As Bonnie made the call to distract Natalia, Jen took her phone and walked to the other side of the terrace. The truth now was that it was her fault that Kathleen had gone AWOL. *She* had done this.

'Are you going to answer me now then? I take it Natalia didn't know either but Bonnie quite obviously does.'

'I only told Bonnie since we arrived here.'

That was a tiny white lie but it hadn't been long before Athens. But perhaps that shouldn't have been her opening gambit. She sensed trying to justify anything right now wasn't going to work.

'And when were you going to tell me? Easter? Spring Equinox?'

And there it was.

'No,' Jen began. 'I just... wanted to get my busiest period out of the way and then I was going to... reassess.'

'Reassess what?' Kathleen yelled. 'Whether you told me about your living predicament or actually doing something about it?'

Jen had no answer. She knew Kathleen was only raising her voice out of concern, but it felt so similar to how she had been shouted at and belittled scores of times before. *Wear your best clothes before the social worker comes. Smile or there won't be anything to smile about from now on. Why are you so stupid?*

'Jen,' Kathleen said, tone softer. 'Why didn't you tell me? Don't you trust me any more?'

And now Kathleen sounded hurt, as if Jen keeping this secret from her had physically wounded her.

'No. I mean, yes.' Jen leaned against the barrier of the terrace, looking out over the city. 'Of course I do. I just didn't want to worry you.'

'Because I'm old and in this place? Because you think my marbles are more lost than Elgin's?'

'No... because I wanted to fix things myself and I knew you would offer to help.'

'Of course I would have offered to help. Because that's what families do, Jen.'

Family. That alien word that had never had a place in her life. The dictionary definition never relating to any of the experiences she had had in the care system. The only memory she had of her mother was a blurry outline of a face and blonde wavy hair like hers, accompanied by crying, shouting, more crying, a whispered voice calling 'Jen-Jen', softer words and then Bravely Bear and that scent of peppermint. Then those things stopped and other people appeared and the only thing Jen learned was that it was better if you were invisible. And if you couldn't manage invisible then mute and compliant were the next best things. Thoughts and feelings, they were better off hidden, if you dared to even let them grow and expand inside...

'We *are* family, Jen,' Kathleen continued. 'You're the daughter Gerald and I never had. I know we never formalised anything but I thought you understood that. When you came into our lives if felt like the greatest gift, a young girl who just wanted to hide in tinsel; it was a dream come true.'

Jen swallowed. She wasn't just hiding in tinsel now, she was actually sleeping in it. And she still didn't know how to respond so she took a second, her eyes going from Kathleen's face on screen to the rooftops glittering with fairy lights as far as the eye could see.

'Tell me, how bad is it?' Kathleen asked. 'And don't fib, because I will know if you do.'

'It's not a disaster... yet,' Jen admitted, her attention back on Kathleen. 'But I needed to make the decision about the flat because the lease was coming to an end and finances were tight and it was a sure way to save almost a thousand pounds a month. Besides, you know, sleeping in the office isn't sleeping on the streets, is it?'

'You're sleeping in the office! I presumed you were staying with Bonnie!'

'I really didn't tell Bonnie until recently,' Jen said.

'Well, I don't like it,' Kathleen said, folding her arms across her chest. 'Sleeping where you work isn't healthy.'

'But you and Gerald had the apartment above Fancy Occasions,' Jen countered. And then she thought of Astro and his lofty room above Bar Páme as well.

'That's different,' Kathleen said. 'We didn't bed down with the Disney dress-ups. And there's no point denying it. You and Bravely Bear will have been using all those sleigh-ride blankets to get cosy under.'

'No,' Jen replied. 'Well, maybe one.'

'Listen to me now. When you get back from your Greek holiday, we will have a proper talk about the business and your living arrangements because I've already been through losing a home and a business and I'm not about to let the same thing happen to you.'

'Kathleen—'

'No, shh, go and finish your glass of wine and get ready for the next one. There's nothing more to say now and Natalia will be back with our second puddings shortly. I'm going to go now.'

'No, Kathleen, wait, just tell me... what were you doing in Portsmouth?'

'I'll tell you what I *wasn't* doing. I wasn't being a vulnerable missing person like the police labelled me.' She sniffed. 'I couldn't find the contact details for the person I wanted to ask about your performance needs, but I remembered they lived just off Albert Road. So I got on the train, thought I would know the street when I saw it and I could ask someone.'

'Kathleen! You know how crazy that is? To do that and not tell anyone.'

'If I told anyone they would have tied me to my bed or given me one of those injections they give people when they're too vocal. Anyhow, I found the street and a few knocked doors later I found young Willy.'

'What?'

'Willy Junior,' Kathleen said. 'His dad, Willy Senior, died in 2018.' She sighed. 'So, I wasn't able to find a solution for you and I didn't even get to have fish and chips before two policemen said the chief constable was personally looking for me.'

David's favour she was going to regret accepting. He had already messaged her on whatever phone he was now using saying he was so pleased Kathleen had been found safe and sound. She knew that wouldn't be the only contact he'd make but how could she block him again now after the strings he had pulled on her behalf?

'It doesn't matter,' Jen said. 'About the performance. It's not going to happen. I just need to be upfront with the historical society and see what alternatives I can offer them.'

'Well, I still wouldn't be too hasty. Why not let Natalia and me have a brainstorm while you're over there.'

'My brain is very ready to storm,' Natalia announced, appearing on the screen as Bonnie arrived at Jen's side, putting their wine glasses on the edge of the terrace.

'OK,' Jen said. 'But, promise me, Kathleen, no more leaving the home.'

'What? Ever?'

'Until I get back. At least can you promise me that?'

'I suppose,' Kathleen said. 'If you promise me that you'll tell me next time you're in trouble and we can work things out together. And that you'll let me help you sort your living situation.'

She nodded, despite it feeling a little bit awkward to agree to support, even after all this time, even after what Kathleen had just said about how she felt about her and family.

'You have trouble with living situation?' Natalia butted in. 'I have spare bed in flat. Brothers are storing cheeses right now, but these will be gone before Christmas.'

Jen started to say her goodbyes. There was no way she was going to be cosying up to a camembert any time soon, no matter how desperate things got.

43

ASTRO'S APARTMENT, BAR PÁME

'This is so lovely,' Bonnie remarked, sipping from a small tumbler Astro had filled with white wine. 'And you promise that the pigeon won't be joining us for dinner.'

'Peri has been fed but, you know, pigeons they are very hungry creatures,' Astro replied as he put a steaming pot in the middle of the table.

'I also know my sister ate one for a starter once.'

'Bonnie!' Jen exclaimed.

'It is OK,' Astro replied. 'To make Peri into a meal, it would involve Bonnie getting very very close to him, looking into his eyes, perhaps stroking his feathers to make him feel safe—'

'All right! You can stop now! I didn't know I had a pigeon phobia, but I do know that it's a real thing and not something to be laughed at.'

When they had arrived at Bar Páme and Astro had shown them up to his apartment, Jen was astonished to see it had been transformed from how it had looked earlier that day. Gone were all the branches and berries, the fruits and bent-up coat hangers; instead, the table was right by the Juliet balcony, granting them a view of the bars opposite and those now very-familiar steps, always filled with a steady stream of people. Throughout the apartment there were candles in every corner providing a beautiful glow as well as a warm gourmand fragrance that was verging on being a little bit festive. What was also Christmassy was the strings of fairy lights around window frames and doors, the painting above Astro's bed. Yes, they may be subtle touches, but Jen knew what a big thing that was for someone who didn't seem to want to let Christmas in...

'Are you ready?' Astro asked, tea-towel-covered hand poised on the lid of the pot.

'Is this a pre-dinner magic trick?' Bonnie said. Then she gasped. 'The pigeon isn't going to jump out of there, is he?'

'I'm ready,' Jen said, her stomach reminding her that it couldn't be more prepared.

He lifted off the lid and as he stepped back to put it somewhere else, Jen could react to nothing else but the insanely rich and fragrant aroma coming from the large hunk of meat squeezed into the ceramic pot. Garlic. Rosemary. Somehow simply the essence of every great Greek meal they'd had since they'd been here. She closed her eyes and savoured the scent.

'Oh my God,' Bonnie said, inhaling loudly. 'This smells so good. Your chef is a master.'

Jen looked to Astro who was busying himself bringing over another pot that she could see contained the crispiest roast potatoes. And then it hit her, as she watched him setting things into place, topping up Bonnie's wine glass then hers, then his, untying the Bar Páme apron he'd had on over his jeans and the black button-down shirt he was wearing... Everything felt better, *was* better, when she was with him. She swallowed, acknowledging the depth of that feeling and drinking him in. That short crop of dark hair, his eyebrows that sometimes spoke a language all of their own, those green eyes and those lips that could be soft and gentle but also firm and passionate. He was fierce and opinionated – hating Christmas, wanting to spray his emotions over the walls of the city – yet also so calm and grounded – looking after Achilles, always working hard, often to his own personal detriment. They were so aligned...

'Jen? Are you OK?'

She jolted in her seat. 'Yes, I was just...' She felt her face heating up.

'Thinking that those roast potatoes look better than my mum's Christmas ones? Because that's what I was thinking,' Bonnie said.

'We should cheers,' Astro said, holding his glass of wine towards the centre of the table. 'To the happy news that Kathleen is OK. *Yamas*.'

'Definitely cheers to that,' Bonnie said, clinking her glass with Astro's.

'*Yamas*,' Jen said, raising her glass in the air and trying to collect herself.

It had been an emotional time. So much had transpired in the short period she had been here and soon she would be leaving again. She was really going to miss this place.

'Please,' Astro said. 'Help yourselves to everything and I will carve the meat.'

And Jen now knew that Astro was the thing she was going to miss the most.

* * *

'Well, that food was fantastic,' Bonnie said after they'd all eaten as much as they could.

It had been. The pork had had the softest texture, like layers of deliciousness that had fallen apart on Jen's plate and then melted beautifully on her tongue, releasing those delicate herb accompaniments. And the roast potatoes! Golden brown with crisp edges and the fluffiest consistency on the inside. But there was something extra about it, a definite care in the flavours and a flourish in the presentation that was leading Jen to think that these pots of tastiness were not exactly the same as those the Bar Páme chef put on the menu...

'It was really delicious,' Jen told Astro. 'Would you like us to clear up? Wash the dishes?' She was already getting to her feet.

'*Ochi*,' Astro said immediately. 'No, please, I will move everything from the table and I will wash it later.'

'No, we'll help,' Bonnie said, standing up and picking up plates and cutlery and heading over to the kitchen area.

'You can't say no to Bonnie,' Jen said. 'She's like a force of nature.'

'Like the Christmas decorations in the bar,' Astro said, collecting other crockery. 'Fir branches and berries made into stars.'

'Do you *really* like them?' Jen asked. 'I mean, I know if you had the choice you wouldn't want them there but—'

'I like them,' Astro admitted. 'I had reservations at the beginning but... it is not glittering so much it can be seen from space.'

Jen smiled. 'Not everything involving Christmas has to be about bright lights or Santa Claus or religion. For me it has always been about... a feeling... a kind of warmth spreading through everything.'

She swallowed. She hadn't ever really put into words exactly how Christmas made her feel. It felt important, defining even, that she was sharing it with Astro.

'So!' Bonnie announced, coming back to the table and unintentionally shattering the mood. 'Who is working at the bar while you're here with us?'

'Well,' Astro said. 'My uncle has gone out dancing. But Marjorie is here and Makis and I called a friend to cover for me. It will cost me doing the shopping with his *yiayia* one weekend but—'

'Your uncle's gone dancing? Where?' Bonnie asked, swigging back what was left of her wine. 'Because I love dancing! Is it Greek dancing though? Because there's no way I can swing my legs like those soldiers outside the parliament building.'

'I think it is maybe salsa. Something Latin,' Astro said.

'Really? I love salsa! Can we go?'

'Bonnie!' Jen exclaimed. 'Astro invited us to dinner and—'

'And now we've finished dinner and it was fantastic and we can burn it all off by getting our hips moving on the dancefloor. It's perfect!'

Jen looked to Astro. She knew how he felt about his uncle keeping this dancing/possible dating from him.

'We could go,' he said. 'If you would like to.' He looked at her then. 'Jen?'

Now she knew he wanted to because it was written in his expression. Whether it was because he wanted to dance or because he wanted to investigate what his uncle was doing, she wasn't quite certain. But she nodded.

'Yes,' she answered. 'Let's go dancing.'

44

SEQUENCE DANCE CLUB

'This place is crazy!' Bonnie squealed as they entered a large warehouse-style building that was covered with Christmas decorations, from industrial metal beams above them housing spiralling gold shapes that span around in the air, to large white frosted trees poking out from every corner.

The air was thick, and the atmosphere was alive as what looked like hundreds of people danced together, some performing as one giant group, others in different circles taking turns to spin into the middle as Latin beats bled from the sound system. Astro didn't quite know what to make of it. This was really where his uncle had been coming? To dance with all these people who seemed to know exactly how to move? As he watched them – step perfect, twisting in and out with each other, hips as slick as professionals – he wondered if perhaps Marjorie was playing a prank on him. Would she be laughing at the fact he had believed her and come down here? Would his uncle laugh too when they discussed it later at Bar Páme?

'Astro, shall we get drinks?' Jen asked.

'*Ne*,' he answered. '*Páme*.'

Bonnie was leading the way in a dance-cum-walk and Astro followed her, one eye scanning the happy revellers for Philippos.

'It's so busy,' Jen remarked.

'What?' Astro replied.

'I said, it's so busy!'

'Yes,' he answered, nodding.

He could hardly hear her above the music, though that was not unexpected; before, when he had been to clubs, it hadn't been for conversation.

'Are you OK?' Jen asked him, a little louder.

He nodded. 'Yes.' But he knew he sounded far from convincing. Perhaps this was a mistake. What he really wanted was to spend more time with Jen, time where they could talk and be heard by each other, time that was rapidly running out...

'Ouzo,' Bonnie said, passing shot glasses back. 'The barman said we have these while he makes our cocktails.'

'Cocktails?' Jen queried.

'On me. We need to go big before we go home, right?'

Astro downed the ouzo in one then he grabbed Jen by the hand. 'Let's dance.'

'What? Astro, no, I don't know how to.'

He smiled at her. 'Neither do I.'

'Give me your coat,' Bonnie said, whisking it off Jen's shoulders.

He was going to be selfish for once, think about what he wanted, not what he felt he should be doing. He wanted to spend more time with Jen, wanted to get to know her on a deeper level. Maybe there wasn't time or perhaps time didn't matter. Maybe it only mattered that their connection was strong enough for them to feel safe with each other. He had already told her he had no parents... Was Miss Christmas going to be the person he opened up to about why he repelled everything about the season?

'Astro,' Jen said, laughing. 'I can't do this.'

He smiled at her obvious happiness as she tried to replicate the movements of the pulsating bodies around them, and he squeezed her hand. He loved seeing her smile. He loved the purity of her, the way she embraced everything with a positive outlook.

'You're not dancing!' Jen squealed, tugging his hand until he fell into her, their bodies colliding.

As he put his arms around her, moving his hips against hers, he was suddenly struck with another thought. She had made everything better for him in such a short space of time, but what had he done for her? Was her Athens experience enhanced from meeting him or was he making things more difficult? She had so much on her agenda – her business, Kathleen, her past – that volcano she had depicted in graffiti he didn't know enough about. Was he giving to her or taking away?

As he turned Jen around in a spin that was far less accomplished than the one he'd seen another couple perform he saw him. Philippos. His uncle was across the room, sitting at a table in the corner and he wasn't alone. With him was a woman with auburn hair...

So, it was true. Philippos did come here, *was* here and he was with someone, exactly like Marjorie said. What happened next? Did Astro take this knowledge back to Bar Páme and ask his uncle about it then? Or did he go over there right now? Confront him where there was no denying it? But confrontation... His uncle wasn't doing anything wrong. However, the keeping it a secret from him didn't sit right, particularly when he had told Philippos a little of what he was beginning to feel for Jen. Why would his uncle not want to tell him about someone in his life?

'I am... just going to go over there for a second,' Astro told Jen, letting her go. 'I will be back. I will find you.'

Without waiting for her to reply, he made his way across the floor, drifting around the space heaving with gyrating bodies, part trying to steer clear of them, yet part using them as cover. He didn't want Philippos to see him and bolt.

He shook his head, trying to straighten his thoughts. His uncle wasn't a dishonest person by nature, perhaps this was nothing, so new that Philippos didn't yet know what it was...

But then, despite his best efforts, Philippos saw him and there was no halting the locking of their eyes.

Astro held his uncle's gaze as he drew closer to the seating area and watched as the first expression of acknowledgement turned into something akin to fear. And then his uncle moved on his seat like he might be about to flee and Astro found himself speeding up, weaving around the dancers and the Christmas décor.

But Philippos didn't retreat. He walked towards Astro with purpose, until they met and his uncle put a firm hand on his shoulder.

'Astro.'

'Yes,' Astro answered, nodding. 'I am here.'

Now Philippos nodded. 'I did not think you liked to dance.'

'I thought the same about you.'

'I now wonder who is looking after my bar.'

'I now wonder who the woman you are with is.'

Astro was tempering emotion that he couldn't quite distinguish. It wasn't quite anger, it wasn't quite upset, but it was messing with him and he did not like it.

Philippos drew in a long breath that elongated his frame and then he let out a sigh. 'You know, don't you?'

Know? That his uncle was with a woman? Wasn't that obvious to everyone here? Now his uncle had his fingers in his beard, pulling at it like he always did when something was on his mind.

'I would like to hear it from you,' Astro challenged. 'Not from the gossip of the city.'

Philippos shook his head. 'Always the gossip of the city.'

Astro didn't want his uncle to stop talking now. He had to play this right.

'But is the gossip correct?'

'That depends what you have heard.'

Now Philippos was looking at him with suspicion, as if he had realised that Astro did not know the full extent of whatever the situation really was.

'I have heard enough,' Astro said. 'To know that you have not been honest.'

The music changed to something slower, the sultry drumbeat pulsing through Astro's body.

'Honesty,' Philippos said. 'How can I be honest with you at this time of year?' He put his hands out as if to highlight the festiveness. 'So many memories. So much we are missing.'

Astro swallowed, his mother's face right there in his mind, the last time she had hugged him, the final goodnight...

'You do not want honesty, Astro,' Philippos said. 'You only want to hear that things are how you need them to be. In your comfort zone. Unchanging. The same life that you are used to.'

'That is not true!' Astro exclaimed. 'You think I want to feel dread every winter? That I want to remember the time of year that took my mother from me?'

'Wake up, Astro!' Philippos boomed above the music. 'It was not Christmastime that took your mother from you! It was something she did not know she had, mixed with not taking care of herself. Too much hard work and late nights, looking after a young son. Why do you think I try to help Marjorie? Why do you think that this decision has been the hardest one I have ever had to make?'

Astro had no come back for this. Was his uncle saying his mother's death was somehow *his* fault? And what did he mean by having to make a hard decision? Dating? He felt both under attack and more confused than ever.

'Who is that woman?' Astro asked, indicating the auburn-haired individual Philippos had been sitting with.

'That is Angela.'

'And Angela, she is coming to live with us?' Astro blurted out, even to his own ears sounding like a spoilt child.

'What?'

'Well, creeping out of the bar and not saying where you are going, learning to dance... this is love for you, yes?'

Philippos was shaking his head again as dancers began to fill the space around them. This wasn't the place to have this conversation but it was happening all the same.

'I have no idea what you have heard now, Astro. But no, I am not in love with Angela, or with anyone, but, maybe one day, I would like to be. That is why I am doing this.'

'Doing what?' he asked.

'You know how things are with money. I tell you I need all the customers I can get, not just to boost my profits but to make Bar Páme an attractive proposition.'

Now Astro's thought process was pounding. This was not about dating or dancing.

'There is no easy way to say this and that is why I have put off saying anything.' Philippos sighed. 'Astro... I am looking to sell the bar.'

The news hit Astro like a speeding train.

45

PSYRRI

'Where are we going?' Bonnie asked, trotting in the high shoes she was wearing as Jen tried to keep up with Astro. He was angry and upset, Jen could see it written right the way through him. What he had said to her when he got back across the dancefloor had been close to unintelligible. At first, Jen had thought it was the volume of the samba music pumping through the speakers that was making Astro hard to understand. But she very quickly realised he wasn't able to communicate effectively, had emotions thicker and deeper firing off inside him that he was trying to manage and light words weren't able to be strung together properly. And then he'd fled, bursting past the dancers, heading for the exit. Grabbing hold of Bonnie, with no explanation, Jen had rushed them the same way, not wanting to lose sight of him.

'We're going to where he feels safe,' Jen answered, almost like she was talking to herself and not Bonnie.

'Back to Bar Páme?' Bonnie asked. 'Are you sure it's this way?

'No,' Jen said. 'Not back to Bar Páme.'

'What happened in the club to make Astro feel he wants to be somewhere safe? Because I don't think I have a complete grasp of the story and it's becoming more complex than an episode of *Westworld*.'

Jen sighed as Astro turned a corner ahead of them, jostling a string of bright fairy lights around a door frame. 'I don't entirely know but it's something to do with his uncle.'

'Not being funny, Jen, but I really can't jog any further in these shoes.'

'If he is going where I think he is going then it's not far.'

* * *

Astro couldn't think, was barely noticing the pavement ahead of him, his feet moving fast and leading him on muscle memory alone.

Philippos wanted to sell the bar. His uncle's words were echoing around his brain, seeming like they were bouncing off one part and cannoning into another, the implications unknown. How was this happening? He had put everything into being there for Philippos as his uncle had been there for him since Eleni had died. The bar was their home. It held them together as a family. It wasn't Astro's dream, but it was *duty*. And now his uncle was throwing that away? Just like that?

He stopped in front of a rusty iron door that was bent out of shape at the bottom. Prising the metal apart with his hands, he stuck his arm in up to the elbow, feeling around in the dark. *Where was it?* Then his fingers found what they were searching for, and he dragged the canvas holdall towards the gap in the door. As he tried to manoeuvre the bag, he finally got some proper leverage and heaved it out of its hiding place. This was something he could always rely on. Something he had taken charge of. Perhaps that was all there really was. Yourself.

Fuelled by anger and disappointment, he marched through

the walkway, seeking a release. He knew exactly where he was going with this bag of paints and spray cans. He was going to add the finishing touches to his mural.

It was only when he was face to face with the boy, the woman and the moon on the side of the building that the enormity of what he was about to do hit hard. He shook a black aerosol, purposefully, the rattle of the can like some kind of eerie death knell. And then he pressed his finger onto the button, tightly, a pulse under his skin. All he had to do was add a little more pressure...

'Astro! Stop!'

He held still, eyes focused on the painting. He wanted to do this. Because what did any of it matter? No one stayed forever. No one kept their promises. He held the can closer to the wall.

Bar Páme was the one thing that had always been there. Philippos and the bar, solid, good things to cling to...

'Astro, put the spray can down!'

It was a voice of reason. It was Jen, the girl he had only just met but couldn't now imagine a few hours here without. But what good was he to her, really? She was everything, full of spirit, living proof that some people, *good* people, could pick themselves up from losing their parents and make something better, stronger. Right now, all he wanted to do was deface his work, erase it, black out this public outpouring. Soon he would be without a home, without a job, and his uncle would be where? Thessaloniki perhaps? Maybe Philippos would not stay in Greece at all.

Waiting no longer, he pressed the top of the can with force and out blasted a mist of black spray, landing on the pyjama top of the boy.

'Astro, no!'

Suddenly it felt like he was under attack. Arms were around him, strong, gripping hard and not letting go. He wanted to fight, to break free but he knew he was already losing the battle. What was the point? What did it change? What he had heard would still be true and his mother would still be gone.

'Please stop,' Jen begged. 'Because a minute's worth of anger might feel good for sixty seconds but when it's over you're going to regret it in much less time than that.'

'Can I let go of this spray can now?' Bonnie asked. 'Because I don't want to stain my fingers.'

It was only then that Astro realised Bonnie's hand was wrapped over his, while the whole of Jen's body was clinging to him. Suddenly he was awash with embarrassment and shame. He detached himself quickly.

'I... do not know what I was thinking,' he mumbled, as thoughts set off in all kinds of directions. 'I should not have... brought you here.'

Back in the dance club, he had thought about being selfish, going after what he wanted, being with Jen and ignoring his responsibilities at the bar. But now he realised he had been selfish from the beginning. He had leaned into their connection for his own benefit, as if the universe owed him this. Well, he knew one thing for certain, the universe owed Jen something much more than him.

* * *

There was something in his expression that Jen recognised. *Retreat*. He had shown his raw emotions here and now he was uncomfortable with that. It was something she related to so much but usually it was when she was exposed to someone she didn't trust. She knew she hadn't known him very long, but she knew, on her part at least, that he was someone she trusted. She had thought the feeling was reciprocated.

But what exactly did he mean when he said he shouldn't have brought her to the Psyrri neighbourhood? Did he mean tonight? Or did he mean ever?

'I should go,' Astro said, beginning to make tracks backwards.

'Go where?' she asked.

'Anywhere but here. Anywhere where I cannot destroy things.'

Did he mean his beautiful mural? Or did he mean something more? She was trying to think quickly. She didn't want him to go. She didn't think he should be on his own and she had no idea if anyone would still be at the bar now, or if Philippos was on his way back.

'We could go to our hotel,' Jen rattled out. 'It has a lovely roof terrace, doesn't it, Bonnie? We could get a drink there where it's quieter and talk and—'

'Goodbye, Jen.'

Not goodnight. *Goodbye.*

The millisecond it took for her to take that one word on board was time enough for Astro to turn on his heel and sprint up the street.

46

PLAKA HOTEL

'Did the wings arrive?' Jen asked, phone close to her ear as she strode out around the roof terrace. It was cold but bright, the early sun bringing the temperature up a few degrees but definitely still coat-buttoned-up weather now. It was their last day in Athens and Jen had woken up early with a real sense of unease weighing on her chest. Nothing felt quite right and it was a different sensation to the one she'd had when Kathleen was missing. This one was manifesting itself as a real sense of emptiness, like someone had taken something out of her that had burned bright. Right now though, the only thing she could do was prepare to go home and that had begun with a call to Natalia to see if everything was going OK with the events she'd booked in.

'You know about new menu at Greg's all the way from there?' Natalia asked, sounding shocked.

'What?'

'The festive wings. With chargrilled sprouts and cranberry glaze. And the ones he make like Santa. Horseradish cream for beard and hot sauce to make bone look like hat.'

'No, Natalia, I meant the angel wings for the Christmas christening. Remember Mrs Butler was very precise about how big the wings should be.'

'I remember,' Natalia answered. 'She want them to look like swan not angel. I had to measure width of church door.'

'Yes, that's right,' Jen confirmed. 'So, did they arrive?'

'Where?'

'At the office? You ordered them, right? After we did the measuring and we discussed it.' Now the emptiness was being overridden by panic. The christening of Mrs Butler's third grandchild was in three days. Mrs Butler was one of her best clients. Jen had organised countless events with festive flair for her over the past two years from gender reveals to the funeral of the late Mr Butler who had wanted to be brought into church to the tune of 'Walking in the Air' from *The Snowman*.

'I order braids of fake angel hair and ribbons. The Mrs Butt take care of wings with span of Boeing 737.'

Jen felt like her heart had just been thrown out of that aircraft with no parachute. Natalia was usually so organised. *Jen* was normally so organised. How had this been missed? She knew the answer. Because she had been caught up in the philandering whirlwind that was David. And Paris. How far away did Paris feel right now?

'Natalia, *we* were supposed to order the wings and we need them fast or Mrs Butler will be livid.'

'What is "lee-vid"? It sound like new feature on TikTok.'

'It means angry,' Jen continued. 'Violently angry.'

'Like Putin. I understand.'

'We need those wings and if they don't have the right size now then we are going to have to improvise by... ordering extra and sticking them together or... using things from my stock to fix it.' She sighed. 'I'm going to be back tomorrow so—'

'Please,' Natalia interrupted. 'I feel this is my fault. I will fix.

Even if I have to get brothers to find real swan.'

'Please, Natalia, don't do that. I—'

'I go now. Fix problem. Do not worry.'

And with that last sentence imparted, the call was ended. Jen let out a sigh. What was it with people not letting her say what she needed to say? The same had happened last night with Astro. She knew he was upset, angry with everything, but she had wanted him to tell her how he felt, not run away or say goodbye...

'I got the biggest hunk of feta cheese I could take without looking greedy, the heavenly tomatoes, the cheese pastry puffs and tzatziki obvs. Oh, and someone is bringing us two strong coffees.'

Bonnie had said all this whilst putting a tray with plates of food on one of the low tables. Eating was the last thing Jen felt like doing.

'I know what you're thinking, but a Greek breakfast is not something you turn down, particularly on our last full day. So come and sit otherwise I will have to eat it all. And I really could.'

Jen sighed again and pulled up a chair. 'Natalia's forgotten something crucial for Mrs Butler's baptism in three days.'

'The baby?' Bonnie asked, taking the plates off the tray and setting out knives and forks.

'Not the baby, the angel wings.'

'Surely the baby is the only crucial thing at that kind of event.'

'Not when you're Mrs Butler and you have a reputation to keep up. Like I have too. Because if I lose the business, I won't even have a corner to sleep in. I'll be... I'll be... looking for a room at an inn. Maybe not even a Premier one.'

'Loving the festive analogy but that would never happen. *I* would never let that happen and neither would Kathleen,' Bonnie said, digging a fork into a tomato.

'I know and I appreciate that, I really do, but I don't think you realise how important being self-sufficient is to me.' She swallowed, that tightness in her chest building as she thought about all the times she'd only had herself to rely on. It was the backbone of who she was. 'It's my business, and David, well, he was a distraction a bit like... being here was a distraction.'

'So we're calling Astro "being here" are we?' Bonnie asked. Her stare was direct as she put the tomato piece into her mouth and began to munch.

'I just think that after last night and... everything... like Paris and... David and... Kathleen going walkabout and... Natalia and the wings and the fact that as soon as we get home I'm going to have to go and see the historical society and tell them I can't deliver on what I promised and hope they still let me provide them with a great evening but knowing that even if that happens I'm going to have to give them a partial refund and—'

'So you can say "David" but you can't say "Astro".'

'Stop, Bonnie, please,' Jen begged. 'I can't think about Astro at the moment.'

'Why not? Because, OK, I get the whole attitude and aggressive graffiti-can wielding was a bit full-on last night but I can see how much you care about him, how him being upset was upsetting you.'

'And we're going back to the UK tomorrow,' Jen reminded her. A waiter arrived with their coffees.

'So, you need to see him today. Find out what's going on with him and remind him how much you care.'

'No,' Jen said. 'I don't have time. I have to check through every event I have booked from now until the end of January and double down on every tiny detail because now Natalia's forgotten this, I can't trust that she hasn't forgotten other things and you also said you wanted to get the metro to Piraeus today and—'

'Excuses,' Bonnie stated, waving a dismissive hand in the cold air.

'Not excuses,' Jen countered. 'Valid reasons.'

'I say again, excuses. And I should know because I've been making excuses of my own when it comes to Andrea.' Bonnie heaved a sigh. 'I spoke to her before I got this breakfast.'

'Did you?' Jen sat forward in her seat.

Bonnie nodded. 'I decided that my usually unspoken jealousy was getting in the way of remembering that Andrea is my sister. A sister that I love very much despite all her deeply annoying traits and her current clinging on to our mother like she's Rose from *Titanic* on that icy doorframe.'

'And how did it go?'

'She really has split up with her girlfriend.'

'Oh! Jules is female. I mean, not that it matters.'

'She cried,' Bonnie continued. 'A lot.'

'Oh, Bonnie.'

'Yes, I know, I do feel like a villain from a pantomime. Worse than that actually.'

'But did you sort things out?'

'Not quite yet,' Bonnie said, picking up her coffee cup. 'But not because I'm backing away from it, or ignoring the way I think her successes always make me feel inadequate, but because she literally couldn't stop crying and, you know, I'm not about to kick someone when they're down.'

'I'm glad,' Jen said. 'That you've at least spoken to her.'

'Mmm,' Bonnie said. 'So that leads us back to you, doesn't it? Speaking to Astro today. Before it's too late.'

Jen looked out over Athens, her eye immediately drawn to the Parthenon. Was she looking at *it*? Or was it looking at *her*? Questioning? Curious? Understanding? She didn't really know, except she suspected it had been witness to millions of people thinking about their next move.

'Maybe, given everything, it's already too late,' Jen replied.

47

ASTRO'S APARTMENT, BAR PÁME

A sharp pain on his cheek brought Astro to consciousness. What was that? Opening his eyes, he felt that gritty, sore, scratchiness that came from dehydration and not enough sleep. The sleep he *had* got had been courtesy of half a bottle of ouzo and he was feeling the after effects of that too.

'Peri,' he croaked, turning his head. That was the pain; the pigeon was jabbing him with his beak. How had he got in? Or had he been here all night?

Shifting in his bed, his head spinning, he sat up and surveyed the apartment. What had happened here? It was like a tornado had ripped through it. There was the table he had set for dinner, still in place by the balcony doors, but the rest of the space was chaos. Paper, paints and easels were scattered across the boards and the small offering of festive décor he had put here for Jen was broken into bits.

Jen. Now his head pounded. He had left her in the street. She had seen him exposed. His rawest feelings right there to be dissected. He had hated that.

'You are alive!'

Astro juddered as a stick was jabbed forward, almost catching him in the eye.

'Achilles. What are you doing here?'

'Making certain you are alive! Mama has gone for the doctor.'

'Oh, shit!' Astro said, standing up now, Peri taking flight and beginning to flap around the room. 'I do not need a doctor.'

'That is what Mama said you would say,' Achilles said, continuing to swipe the stick around the room. 'Ah! What has happened here?' The stick dug into a Christmas decoration on the ground and Astro watched as Achilles lifted the snapped and broken decoration in the air. 'Was this Peri? Did he make *all* this mess? It is very much for such a small bird.'

Astro could lie. It would be easy to blame a pigeon. But what was that going to teach Achilles? He shook his head and pulled the sleeves of his sweatshirt down, some kind of defence mechanism.

'I did it.'

Achilles screwed up his face in disgust. 'You broke Christmas and you threw paper everywhere? And you did not wash your dishes? Mama says that people who do not wash their dishes will not be blessed by the Greek gods any longer and Poseidon might decide to drown them.'

That was dark but no less than Astro thought he deserved, if truth were told. And the fact Achilles had also said he had broken Christmas was hitting hard as well. Jen was Christmas. Had he broken her too?

Suddenly, Philippos burst into the apartment, out of breath, his apron drooping, half tied around his waist, an anxious expression on his face.

Peri rose up at that very moment, a wing catching the edge of his uncle's beard.

'What is going on here?' Philippos asked. 'Marjorie says you need a doctor.'

Astro sighed. 'I don't need a doctor. I just need some tablets for my headache and for everyone to leave me alone.'

'He has broken Christmas,' Achilles announced, still waving the remnants of decorations on the end of his stick. 'And will be killed by Poseidon soon.'

'Achilles,' Astro said. 'Please could you take Peri outside and tell your mother not to call a doctor?'

'Can I make crepes? And milkshakes?' Achilles asked, dropping the stick.

'Only with supervision,' Philippos answered. 'Make sure your mother is with you.'

Achilles deftly caught Peri in between cupped hands then went running to the door, quickly followed by the sound of trainers thudding down the stairs.

'I will clear up the mess,' Astro said, already beginning to pick up a pair of jeans and a hoodie.

'Astro,' Philippos said, sighing. 'I am not concerned with the mess. I am worried about you.'

'You are?' Astro snapped. 'Because I am sure last night you were at a salsa club telling me you are selling Bar Páme. And I am not sure that fits with being worried about me.'

Philippos shook his head. 'Are you serious, Astro? Because you are sounding a lot like an angry child and not the sweet little boy I took into my home without question many many years ago.'

'You are resentful now? You think that if I had not been here you would have been Latin dancing your whole life?'

'Astro, that is not fair,' Philippos said.

'Well? What *is* fair? Is it fair that my mother died? Is it fair that I have spent my life working in this bar to make you happy? That I thought it was a family business, one you loved and one that I respected? That for me Bar Páme is the only home I really remember because all my memories of the apartment in Exarcheia, all the memories of my mother, are becoming fainter and further away as every year passes?'

'Astro—'

'I do not know what you want from me,' he declared. 'I have never really known what you want from me. Am I just like another employee but one you cannot fire because I am the nephew you were forced to bring up? We don't talk! We never speak about how we feel or what is going on in our lives! And I have to find out about your plans to sell our home in the middle of a throbbing nightclub! At Christmas time!'

'Are you done? Or are you going to throw those jeans back on the floor?'

Astro looked at the jeans in his hands and tossed them onto the bed. His heart was racing but he had run out of steam, didn't know what else to say. Nothing was making him feel better and none of their words so far seemed to be putting them on the path to solving anything.

'I am no good at this,' Philippos admitted. 'I have *never* been very good at this. Having a family, *any* family, it was never in my plans. I could not even look after the pet fish your mother and I had as children. But, when I would forget to feed the fish, your mother would be there giving them too much.' He sighed, pulling out one of the chairs from the table. 'I think perhaps that is where the answer lies when it comes to life. Life is not about the extremes, it is about the finding that place in the middle where everything is balanced.'

'You are a great Greek philosopher now?' Astro mocked.

'No,' Philippos said, sitting down. 'I am saying there is very little that I *am* good at. Astro, I was not made to be a father. I do not think I am even cut out to be a good uncle. I am selfish. I am happiest doing my own thing alone. The bar, it did mean everything to me but, as I said before, times are hard, and I am not getting any younger. I am at the stage in my life where I wonder what else there might be for me, or rather, what little there might be left for me if I do not make changes.'

Astro slumped down onto the bed. 'It was just a shock. I went there thinking that Marjorie could not be right that you had a girlfriend and then, well, it was so much worse.'

'Why did you not just ask me?' Philippos asked.

'Because, every time I tried, you pretended to hear the delivery van.'

Philippos nodded his head slowly. 'Because I am not good at doing the right things.'

Astro looked at his uncle now. There were lines around his eyes that he didn't remember being so deeply etched before, a definite spattering of grey in his beard. He had not seen these physical changes because he had not been looking. It had all been about *his* discomfort, *his* grief, *his* challenges.

'You *are* good,' Astro told him. 'And you do do the right things. Most of the time.'

Philippos smiled. 'Now you sound like your mother. Always she would give a compliment and then very quickly take it back again.'

Astro sighed. 'I do not know her like you knew her.'

'And that is my fault,' Philippos said. 'Because I have stupidly thought it is better to move forward than to look back.'

'But I have so very few years that I remember to look back on.'

'I know,' Philippos said, a hitch in his voice. 'And I need to remember that reminiscing doesn't have to mean grieving all over again.'

Astro let that sentence sink in. Losing his mother had been the saddest thing, but he did feel that his life was always focused on the empty space there was now rather than the smiling, upbeat and positive influence that used to occupy it.

'What are these?'

He realised then that Philippos had leaned over and picked up something from the floorboards and was now holding a canvas in his hand.

The artwork he usually hid.

Astro was off the bed and over to his uncle with a speed that made his already dizzy head spin faster.

'It is a mess. Like everything else in here. But I will clean it up and...'

He knew it was fruitless to keep talking. He made a grab for the canvas but Philippos moved it out of his reach.

'Did you do this?' Philippos asked, the words seeming to catch a little in his throat.

Astro looked at the black and white painting in his uncle's hands and inhaled sharply. It wasn't one of the pictures he had previously been working on. It almost felt as if he had never seen this before, yet it was no doubt his work. Not only was it his style, he also, somehow, instinctively felt it belonged to him.

'I... do not remember,' he answered truthfully, a finger finding a curve of the line of the face.

'You do not remember?' Philippos asked. 'This one? Or these others?'

It was only then that Astro looked at the other drawings littered across the floorboards. Some of them were presumably face down, nothing more than blank sheets, others were seemingly complete, a few unfinished. All of them were of the same thing, or rather, the same person. *Jen.*

Astro didn't know what to say. It was like the crazed scribblings of a mad person, deep charcoal lines, others stabbed in oil...

'Astro, you have this talent,' Philippos began, his eyes a little glazed. 'And I did not know.'

Astro shrugged then. 'I guess we all have our secrets.'

'Well,' Philippos started. 'There is no hiding two things here. Your great artwork and the way you feel about Jen.'

And, for that, Astro had no answer.

48

BAR PÁME, PLAKA

'Remember when we first got here,' Bonnie said as they started up the steps lined with bars and tavernas on either side, bustling with lunchtime trade. 'How warm it was?'

'I do remember,' Jen answered. 'We sat outside in short sleeves and thought Greece had summer all year round.'

'And now it's freezing.' Bonnie shuddered, taking a moment to dip into the range of one of the working-overtime patio heaters to her right. 'Like you can tell Christmas is just around the corner from the fact I now wish I'd packed more substantial underwear.'

Christmas was just around the corner. Ordinarily, just that fact would make Jen feel so happy that, as they flew through Advent in a whirl of events and occasions, every day became a little bit brighter than the day before. She injected the festive season into her daily life all year round but when the actual time came it was usually better than anything else. However, things felt different this year. She'd lost her structure. She'd lost her way. She'd lost her mind at times...

'David's been phoning me,' she said with a sigh, thinking back to how she'd accepted his help in finding Kathleen. 'On three separate numbers to the one he called me on before.'

'I mean, a man with access to one burner phone is a bit suss, but multiple... get in the bin.'

'You think I should block them all?' Jen asked.

She knew what Bonnie was going to say but, for some reason she needed to hear it out loud.

'Yes! Hell, yes! I mean, surely he's going to run out of options soon. Or you might have to think about changing *your* number. But,' Bonnie continued, pulling Jen to a halt beside another flaming heater, 'before anything else, I think you need to stop letting David live in your head rent free and concentrate on the here and now. Athens. Bar Páme. Astro.'

'David's not living rent free in my head,' she insisted, breathing in the delicious aromas of Greek food coming from literally every door around them. 'I just feel that he helped find Kathleen and maybe I owe him something for that.'

'Something,' Bonnie said, the expression on her face making it clear she thought that Jen was almost certifiable.

'I don't know, a favour, or—'

'Stop right there,' Bonnie ordered, putting a firm hand on Jen's arm. 'You owe that man nothing. Yes, he may have called in a favour to find Kathleen but honestly, Jen, I feel he only did that so you would feel like this. Indebted to him somehow, giving him the time of day, letting him invade your thoughts, making you second guess yourself.'

'I'm not second guessing myself because of David.'

'But why are you second guessing yourself at all? Jen, you're the most organised person I know. And you're worrying about literally everyone except yourself.'

'I don't like to let people down. Loyal clients. People that are expecting the high-quality Christmas Every Day usually provides. Kathleen. I don't like disappointing Kathleen.' She sighed. 'And I feel that, no matter what she says, she *is* disappointed that I couldn't keep my flat.'

'Kathleen loves you, Jen. Like a mother.'

A mother's love. Something she had never understood. Had her mother loved her once, before she was taken into care? She must have cared a little to have chosen Bravely Bear for her, for there to be the vaguest memory of laughter amid the shouting and the tears.

'Maybe we should just have a drink here,' Jen said, her eyes going to a vacant table for two a little to their left.

'No,' Bonnie said firmly. 'We're going to Bar Páme. You're going to have a conversation with Astro and you two can get back on the holiday romance track before we have to leave.'

But what was the point really? She cared about Astro, she really did. And meeting him had opened up the doors to her heart wider than they had ever been before. She had quickly recognised how different those feelings he'd evoked in her were to anything she'd had before – from their first conversations, to spray painting her emotions in the middle of Athens, to their evening of fabulous traditional food in the garden of strangers, to those kisses...

'I can hear what you're thinking, you know,' Bonnie said, guiding her away from the heater and back to the next run of steps. 'You're thinking that you're too busy or that because you're going back to England tomorrow there's no point.'

'Well—'

'Jen, I can see how much you like him.' She led the way upwards, passing by those coming down. 'You're different with him.'

'What do you mean?'

'I mean, I've never seen you without your guard up, not with anyone. And I'm not gonna lie, when we first met Astro I thought you were going to punch him with the candy cane, but over the days you've spent together, or when we've talked about him, there's a sparkle in your eyes, a smile quick on your lips and just this fizz about you... a bit like how you get when you're pulling Christmas crackers, you know, the good ones with the manicure sets in.'

Before Jen had a chance to check herself, there was an upturn of her lips. Simply *thinking* about Astro brought about an uplifting response.

'OK,' she said, taking a deep breath.

'OK?'

'You're right. I really like him. And I feel that whatever connection we have is worth a conversation to find out what's going on with him. And to see if there can be something, despite the distance.' She sighed as nervousness took hold. 'And, if not, then... at least I will have tried.'

'That's the spirit,' Bonnie said. 'Christmas or otherwise.'

'OK,' Jen said again, stepping onwards and upwards. She could see Marjorie, silver tinsel woven into her hair, a full tray in her hands with bottles and plates on it. This setting was starting to feel so familiar.

She strode on until she had reached the outside seating area of Bar Páme.

'Hello, Marjorie,' she greeted as Bonnie sat down at a vacant table.

'Oh!' Marjorie exclaimed. 'Thank God you are here! He has been whining all day. "When is Jen coming?". "I need Jen". "I can't do life without Jen".'

Really? She hadn't pegged Astro as the whining type.

'He walk around with face like devil even after more milkshakes than he should. He cannot focus on work. He cannot even focus on that stupid pigeon!'

'He wants to see me?' Jen asked, her heart raising a little.

'He does not want to see you, Jen. He *need* to see you! Ah! Here is the sad boy now. See! A smile already back on his face!'

Jen's heart quickly fell back down to where it was supposed to be when she saw it was Achilles coming out of the bar, plastic bags swinging from his hands.

'Jen!'

'Hi, Achilles,' she replied, injecting as much enthusiasm into her voice as possible. 'Goodness, what do you have there?'

'Almost everything from Mrs Calimeris's sewing box. She says we can use it all to make more Christmas jewellery for the school event. You *are* coming to the event, right? It is on Saturday and the whole of Athens is coming and—'

'Achilles! Not so loud! And what have I told you about making your stories too big? The whole of Athens will not be there. It is a school market not Anna Vissi at the Olympic stadium.'

Saturday. She would be gone tomorrow. But she couldn't think about that now.

'Marjorie,' Jen said tentatively.

'It is OK if you do not have time to make earrings on your holiday. I tell this to Achilles already, but he does not listen.'

'It's not that,' she replied. 'It's... well... is Astro around?'

'He is not here,' Achilles announced. 'But he is not dead. But he did need medicine this morning.'

Jen wasn't quite sure what to say to that but, before she could try, Marjorie jumped in. 'There was a situation this morning. He's gone out with Philippos. I'm supposed to have Makis coming to help but...' She indicated the busyness and the lack of other staff.

'Do you know when he'll be back?' Jen asked, her stomach knotting like a bad attempt at knitting.

'From the expressions on their faces, I hope it is not until they have sorted things out. *Ne, perimene!*'

And with that said, Marjorie rushed off to serve her customers, leaving Jen with Achilles who was shaking the bags from his neighbour again.

49

HOLY CHURCH OF THE DORMITION OF THE VIRGIN MARY CHRYSOSPILEOTISSA

Astro had not been near this church since his mother's funeral, but here he was, standing outside in the ever-colder weather, looking up at the tiled domes against the thick cloudy sky. It had been Philippos's suggestion and although Astro had thought of a zillion reasons why this outing wasn't something he wanted, he hadn't voiced any of them. Instead, he had pulled on an extra hoodie, put on his trainers and left Bar Páme with his uncle.

Inside there was no one but them and the Greek icons looking down from the walls in a rich palate of reds, blues and golds, aged with time. It didn't matter whether you believed in God or not, whether you went to church regularly or not, being inside a building like this did something to a person. The air felt thick with reverence, as if it was full to bursting with eons of confessions, slim candles flickering in the half-light. Despite the church's emptiness, Astro felt judged, as if eyes were on him. *Astro Salvas, you, the boy who woke up on 25 December to find his mother cold in her bed, what are you doing here?*

Astro shivered. Maybe this was a mistake. They both should be at the bar right now. Then he remembered, what did it matter? Philippos was selling the bar.

'We should light a candle,' Philippos said, reaching for the small stack.

'We used to light one for *yiayia* and one for *pappoús* even though I never met them. Do you still do that when you go to church?'

'Sometimes,' Philippos replied. 'But not here. I have not been to this church since...'

The sentence needed no explanation. Or perhaps it did.

'Why is it so hard to be here?' Astro asked. 'We go to Mama's grave. Why should it be difficult to come into the church where her service was?'

'I do not know,' Philippos said. 'Perhaps it is because here was where her friends gathered to cry for her, to cry for you, where she was delivered into the arms of God. The memories of that day are not easy.'

Astro could see the emotion running through his uncle, from the way his large hands were shaking as he held the candles to the way he had tripped a little over his words just then.

'Your mother always talked honestly, didn't she? Said whatever was on her mind regardless of how anyone was going to feel about it.'

Astro looked at his uncle. 'She did that with you too? I thought it was only me.'

'She did that with everyone,' Philippos whispered, a faint smile on his lips. 'Good-naturedly always, but fiercely too. And it did not matter if you were the priest or the person she was serving drinks to. Everyone got the same treatment.'

'Why did she not work at Bar Páme when you started it?' Astro asked.

Philippos sighed. 'I asked her to. I said we could be joint partners. She was the hardest worker I knew.'

'And she said no?'

'She said that she wanted to earn her place in life, her way. She never wanted to be indebted to anyone, even her own brother. She was always so independent. Independent until the end.'

This was the most his uncle had ever talked about Eleni, and it seemed poignant that it was here in the church where they had said goodbye to her.

'Astro, I want you to know that I have not made any firm decisions about selling the bar.'

'No?'

'I do not know.' Philippos shook his head, still holding the candles between trembling fingers. 'The offer came a little out of the blue and at the beginning I almost said no... I know I should have talked to you about it. But, at the time, I just thought it was a decision I needed to make alone –for both of us.'

Astro shrugged, as if he was pretending it didn't matter. 'It is *your* business, not mine.'

'But it could be yours. One day. And, perhaps, until then, if you wanted, *we* could be partners. I know I said that things were not going as well as I hoped but, perhaps there is another way. I could ask Angela if she might consider being a shareholder rather than the new owner and with her injection of funds we could—'

Astro was already shaking his head. It was a quick reaction, but it was an instinctive one. No matter how he had felt last night about the shock of Philippos's desire to sell, the morning had brought about different sentiments. 'I don't think that is the right thing.'

'No?'

'No,' Astro said. 'I do not think it is what you want or need and I do not think it is what I want or need either.' He put a finger above the flame of a burning candle in front of him. He left it there until it started to become hotter, holding it until he could no longer stand the intensity. But he didn't snatch it back, he simply lifted it slightly higher, until the sensation was still painful but bearable. 'Perhaps it is time we both let go of what is essentially holding us back.'

Astro looked at his uncle, to see if he could gauge his reaction, but Philippos had his head bowed, staring at the candles in his hands.

And then he spoke.

'The bar, it is all I have known. You know *yiayia* and *pappoús* had nothing but an account in the bank with barely anything in it when they died? Your mother, she bought the most expensive dress she could afford with her share and she said she would make it last forever.'

'The bright blue one?' Astro asked as a vision came to mind of his mother dancing in the living room, peacock-blue chiffon billowing out as she spun around and around.

'The bright blue one,' Philippos confirmed. 'I used my money to pay the first month's rent on Bar Páme, not even knowing if I would be able to pay the second month or make it work.'

'But you did.'

'Yes,' Philippos said. 'I did.'

He mused for a second before lighting the two candles in his hand then putting them into the sand on the lower level.

'But, I think, when we lost your mother, I held on to the bar because it was something I needed to get through life, to help get *you* through life. It was a constant. I had you to make sure I got up in the morning to take you to school but I had the bar waiting for me to make sure that when I came back I didn't have time to cry, to fall back into bed and hide away.'

'And I held on too,' Astro said. 'To that routine, to that familiarity. Because it stopped me having to make any hard decisions about my life. You were there. Bar Páme was there. There wasn't time to think about anything else.'

'And now?' Philippos asked. 'You think the time has come? To think about something else?'

'I know that existing somewhere, doing the things you have always done simply because you have always done them shouldn't be the way life is.'

'No,' Philippos agreed.

'Perhaps, sometimes, a situation presents itself because it's meant to be,' Astro suggested. 'Maybe because the person who has to make the decision would not have actively sought a different path unless the opportunity fell into his lap at a salsa bar.'

Philippos shook his head. 'I still do not know why Angela likes it there. It is very hot and everyone dances like they are on a stage.'

Astro picked up a candle and lit it from the flame of the ones Philippos had lit. But instead of placing his next to the two representing his *yiayia* and *pappoús,* he placed it on the higher level.

'Who is that candle for?' Philippos asked. 'You pray for someone?'

'It is for Mama,' Astro answered.

'But, Astro, you remember the candles on the top shelf are for prayers for the living?'

'I know,' he replied, holding onto the wax stick and watching the flame dance a little like his mother had. 'But, you know, she lives within us. Does that not count?'

He didn't wait for a reply, making sure the candle was completely straight and its flame burning well before finally, he let go.

'What happens now?' Philippos asked.

'Well,' Astro said, taking a breath. 'I think there is something I should show you.'

50

THE OLD TAVERN OF PSARRAS, PLAKA

'I don't care how cold it is,' Bonnie remarked. 'I refuse to sit inside when there's this beautiful setting out here.'

The setting *was* beautiful and there was no doubt in Jen's mind that of all the walking and touring they had been doing since they got here, these few streets beneath the Parthenon, almost forming the base of the Acropolis, were her very favourite part of Athens. Here, under a now dark sky, at what claimed to be the oldest taverna in Plaka, there were wooden tables under soft lights from lanterns on the walls and the bare branches of the trees, painted white at their base. Checked cloths were draped over the tables, cutlery set out and tealights glowing in glass pots. On the door to the restaurant was a festive wreath and in each window was a spray of white, as though snow had fallen in the corners.

'Are you sure, Bonnie?' Jen asked. 'Because the roaring fire they have inside did look cosy.'

Inside was just as beautiful as out, with its stone walls and traditional fireplace, dark wood furniture and black and white photos adorning the walls. The waiter had told them the actor,

Laurence Olivier, had once dined here, amongst other famous
names.

'Minus four in Wiltshire today,' Bonnie reminded her. 'Absolutely no chance of sitting outside there until mid-May so I'm
going to button up and enjoy a seat on the Plaka cobbles and
watch the Greek world go by.'

Jen couldn't deny that sounded good. Even if the Astro-shaped
part of the Greek world was still absent. Earlier, she had helped
Achilles make some more jewellery for his school event whilst
Bonnie visited an Athens flea market for more potential Christmas
gifts to take home. Then Jen had broken it to the little boy that she
wouldn't be in Greece on Saturday. His fierce little face had got
very red very quickly and there had been a lot of bashing the glue
pot on the table and screwing up material tighter than it should
have been before he somewhat reluctantly realised that no matter
how angry he got, Jen was still going to be getting on a plane
tomorrow.

Tomorrow. She had never even planned to come to Greece this
winter, yet thinking about leaving was making her sadder than she
could ever have imagined. She had so much work to get on top of
when she got home but, in the meantime, all she could think
about was how things currently were with Astro. She had texted
him. No response. She had left a message with Marjorie to ask him
to call her. So far it had been complete radio silence. Maybe this
issue with his uncle and the bar was so serious he couldn't focus
on anything else. Maybe he just needed time. But time was the one
thing Jen didn't have. Perhaps it wasn't meant to be.

'Stop it,' Bonnie said as they pulled up chairs and sat down.

'Stop what?'

'All that thinking you're doing. I can literally see the thoughts
going round and round like a carousel. *Has Natalia solved the angel*

wings problem? Is the historical society going to fire me? Will Kathleen
nick off out the fire escape the minute a carer's back is turned?'

'Actually,' Jen said. 'I wasn't thinking about any of those things.
But thanks for reminding me.' She sighed and picked up a menu.

'Sorry, I didn't mean to—'

'It's OK,' Jen said. 'I know you're trying to keep me together in
your unique Bonnie way but... all I'm really thinking about is
Astro. And I'm struggling with that because I *should* be thinking
about all those other things.' She let a breath go. 'What's
happened to me?'

'You don't really need me to spell it out for you, do you?'

'What?'

But, in reality, she knew exactly what Bonnie was about to say.

'You're falling in love with him.'

* * *

The food was fantastic. As was customary in Greece, they had
started with lovely rustic bread and then ordered *tzatziki* and *tara-
masalata* to accompany it. Bonnie had opted for veal cooked slowly
in the oven and Jen had decided on cabbage rolls like she'd had at
the Sinrades's home. White cabbage leaves had turned into tightly
packed fat parcels of ground beef, rice and mixed herbs, covered
in that creamy lemony sauce. And now they were sharing a thick
walnut cake named *karidopita* which was full of rich spices and a
warming syrup.

'This is delicious,' Jen said, closing her eyes as she chewed the
mouthful of dense, cinnamon-drenched cake.

'It really is,' Bonnie agreed. 'I'm going to miss the vibe here.
I've not been anywhere in the world yet that's such a mix of
cosmopolitan and traditional. Like, at one bar it's high-end cock-

tails and the next it's retsina or there's ridiculously elaborate salads with avocados made into flowers and then there's thick chicken breast pieces on a stick.'

Jen smiled. Yes, that was what she had felt about this trip to Athens too. It was a city of beautiful contradictions. That was also a bit like Astro. At the beginning, he had just been a waiter at an eclectic bar, on the surface at least, but as each fine layer melted away like light phyllo pastry coating a slice of Greek *baklava*, Jen had seen there was so much more to him. But now she was starting to think she might never get to know him even more deeply. And she *really* wanted to.

But was it what Bonnie said? Was it the beginnings of love?

Before she could dwell on it further, her phone began to ring. Maybe it was Astro at last. That thought had her unzipping her bag and pulling her phone out.

'Is it Astro?' Bonnie asked, obviously sharing the same thought.

Jen looked at the unknown number. At best, it was new business or Kathleen with an update. At worse, it was a cold call. But the part of her that was less optimistic was saying she knew exactly who it was.

'Jen?' Bonnie said, fork stuck in what was left of the pudding.

'I think it's David.'

Bonnie let go of her fork and it clanked on to the plate. 'Don't you answer.'

'But if I don't answer he'll just keep calling.'

Before Bonnie could say anything else, she answered.

'Hello.'

'Jen... for a second I didn't think you were going to pick up.'

'David,' Jen began, getting to her feet. 'Before you say whatever it is you've needed to get another phone number to say, I want to talk first.'

Bonnie triumphantly rolled a fist in the air and then Jen put a little power into her walk, moving away from the table and across the cobbled street.

'Jen, I really need to tell you this though—'

'David! I'm not kidding,' Jen said, exasperated. 'What I want to say is... there is no way back for us and I need you to understand that. What you did, calling in a favour to help find Kathleen, was ever so nice and I am so grateful, but, given everything, my gratitude isn't going to be shown in the form of a second chance.'

'Jen, listen to me, I know we didn't start off with the truth, on my part at least, and I know how wrong that was, but this whole situation has only made me more determined to make the right choices going forward and—'

As she listened, she wasn't seeing snippets of their relationship playing out in front of her, she was seeing glimpses of all the time she'd spent with Astro. The months with David didn't mean anything compared with the days in Athens with Astro. And that said everything.

'It's good to want to make the right choices, David,' Jen said, stepping towards a tree bedecked with fairy lights. 'But you need to understand that I'm not a choice you can make.'

'Don't say that, Jen. Please, we had some fantastic times together and we could have so many more, without the weight of deceit on my back and—'

'No,' Jen interrupted. '*I* don't want that. Because...'

She stopped talking as she realised she was standing just above the start of the steps that led down to all the bars that lined both sides, their tables full, the cushions on the steps all occupied, the Christmas decorations more abundant than they'd ever been. She could just about see Bar Páme and yet even that faint edge of one of its parasols was enough to quicken her heart.

'Because what we shared together was so... superficial. It was nice. But it wasn't ever substantial, was it?'

It didn't matter if David replied or not. She knew how *she* felt. Whether Astro wanted to see her again or not, *that* brief encounter had meant the world.

'Jen, I've got a flight booked to Athens. I leave first thing in the morning. I'll be there by lunchtime.'

Jen shook her head. Typical David trying to take control.

'I have a flight booked too. Back to London.'

'Then I can pick you up from the airport. We can go to Paris like we planned. I'll arrange everything.'

'No,' Jen said, this time not holding back. 'I'm only going to say this once more, David. We are over. Done. And I don't want to keep in contact. To thank you for your help with Kathleen I'm going to send a hamper to your secretary. I'm sure she doesn't get paid nearly enough for navigating the potential clashes in your diary.'

'Jen, I—'

'Goodbye, David.'

She ended the call before he could say anything else and, right at that moment, looking down on her favourite place in this extraordinary city, she had never felt more empowered. Until...

'Ugh!' Jen winced as something wet hit her forehead. A finger to the skin showed her a white paste which did not take a Greek scholar to identify. And then the culprit was at her shoes.

'Peri?'

The pigeon doffed its head and flapped its wings, but one of its legs didn't look particularly stable.

'I paid the bill,' Bonnie said, arriving at Jen's side. 'Has David been dispatched? Ugh! Is that Astro's smelly bird? Why does it seem to be the only pigeon in this area? Get away from me, I have nothing but loathing for you!'

'I think it's hurt,' Jen said.

'Then we'd better find its master, hadn't we?'

It seemed Fate was definitely laying out its cards.

51

ASTRO'S APARTMENT, BAR PÁME

As he tidied up his apartment, Astro felt caught between exhausted and strangely alert. He never would have imagined talking to his uncle the way they had talked to each other earlier. It was almost as if they had needed the explosive coming together in the salsa club before they could both react to the fallout and then regroup. Nothing had been decided about the future, Bar Páme or otherwise, but Astro felt an unfamiliar, but not unwelcome, shift in the dynamic between them. It was less elder versus younger and more like they were now family members with respect for one another's opinions. But now he had finished washing dishes and putting away clothes, his attention was on the dining area, still set up like it had been the previous night when he'd made his mother's pork roast.

Jen. Beautiful, insightful Jen. What right had he to start something he could never finish? Something that was destined not to grow by the nature of so many things – their geography, their short time in the same country, their opposing views on Christmas... He shook his head, picking up one of the small garlands Jen had made with Achilles. What was wrong with him? *Their opposing views on Christmas?* It wasn't like one of them was pro-war and the other was not. He had got her messages – a text, then one left with Marjorie – but he didn't know what to do next. He was rapidly concluding that what he wanted to do was perhaps not what he *should* do.

Suddenly the door burst open and as if he had conjured her into the scene, Jen was rushing into the room, something cupped in her hands.

'Sorry... for not knocking... but he's making a funny noise now and I think he's in pain.'

It took him a few seconds to realise that it was Peri in her hands and that the pigeon was making a sound not unlike a blender on slow speed.

'What happened?' Astro asked.

'I don't know,' Jen said. 'We were, Bonnie and I that is, having dinner and we were just finishing and Peri was just there and—'

'Hey, Peri. It is OK. *Ela*, come.'

Astro cupped his hands around Jen's and as their skin met in a glancing touch, instantaneously his mind wasn't on the pigeon but on the fizzing connection. He hurried the exchange, trying to ignore the rush inside himself, and transported Peri to the edge of the table.

'It's his leg, I think,' Jen said, following, looking concerned.

'I think it's broken,' Astro said, watching Peri struggle to put weight on it, one half of him closer to the ground than the other.

'What do we do? Do we call a vet?'

Astro was shaking his head as his eyes roved over what was left on the table. Paper serviettes... the metal casing from around a wine cork... that Christmas decoration. 'We need to make a splint. Something to give support while it heals.'

'You can do that?' Jen asked as Peri seemed to sit down.

'I do not know,' Astro answered. 'I have never done this before.'

What could he use? Everything seemed unsuitable. And would Peri even stay still enough for him to do anything?

'What about this?'

He turned to see Jen holding out a cotton swab.

'It's a bamboo one,' she said. 'We could cut it to size and hold it in place with something... I don't seem to have my tape in my bag for some reason.'

'You always have tape in your bag?' he asked, taking the cotton bud.

'Yes,' she replied. 'Usually. But I haven't seen it since I got here. Otherwise, I would have been the one to tape up Bonnie's split trousers that first night and—'

'I have some,' Astro said. 'I use it on my canvases.'

'Oh, OK. That's good.'

'Will you watch Peri while I get it?'

'Of course.'

* * *

This felt so awkward to Jen. Why did it feel so awkward? For some reason, they had gone from feeling as comfortable as anyone could feel around someone to not knowing how to communicate. Although tending to a pigeon with a broken leg didn't lend itself to being a perfect situation for heartfelt interaction. They were sitting at the table now, about to perform the procedure on the bird.

'Are you sure it's OK to give a bird paracetamol?' Jen asked as Peri nibbled at the mix of seed and crushed-up white tablet.

'As sure as I can be that a portion of it is going to help with his pain. Can you hold this in place? While I put on tape?'

'OK,' Jen said. 'I just don't want to hurt him.'

'It is OK,' Astro said, scooping Peri up. 'You hold him and I will do it. Put him on your arm like this.'

'It's OK. Peri,' Jen spoke softly as the bird struggled to get comfortable. If she was honest, she was struggling to get comfortable too because they were together in close proximity, but the vibe was off. It was almost like they were strangers.

'I... got your messages,' Astro said, his concentration on the bird and the short stump of bamboo he was trying to attach.

'You didn't reply.'

'I did not know what to say.'

Jen swallowed. That didn't sound positive.

'But perhaps I should have begun with an apology for how I behaved last night. I was juvenile. Worse than juvenile. Not even Achilles would have gone running from the club looking to graffiti.'

'Maybe in a few years,' she said, trying to keep things light-hearted.

'Yes,' Astro replied. 'Maybe.'

Now Jen wondered if he was still talking about Achilles or whether there was another meaning to his words.

'But I am sorry for rushing off, for acting like an idiot, for not being mature, for—'

'You were angry and upset. Life can get you like that sometimes. It's OK.'

'But it is not OK,' Astro said with a sigh. '*I* do not think that is OK.'

'OK,' Jen replied, then instantly regretted it. It didn't feel like the right response. But perhaps there *wasn't* a right thing to say.

'Right, Peri, let us make this feel better.'

Astro said nothing else as Jen focused on keeping the bird still and as comfortable as possible as she watched Astro gently apply the stick and add strips of tape to keep it in place.

'Is this going to work?' she asked, breaking the quiet of the room.

'I really do not know.'

It felt as though they were talking about more than the situation with Peri's leg.

'There,' Astro said finally. 'I think that is the best that we can do.'

'Should I let him go now?'

'Yes,' Astro said. 'He will do one of two things. He will stupidly try out his leg and walk on it as if he has been cured or he will fly.'

Jen tentatively removed her hold and waited with bated breath. Instead of doing anything, Peri remained still, leaning against Jen's hand.

'He likes you,' Astro said.

'Maybe his leg is hurting too much for him to move.'

'No, he definitely likes you,' Astro said.

The atmosphere seemed to charge again and Jen's stomach felt as though it was circling like the flakes in a snow globe. Finally, Peri made his move, away from Jen's hand and up to where the seed and what was left of the painkiller were waiting.

Jen had never felt more like she was running out of time. She needed to not waste a second more.

'Astro, I'm going back to the UK tomorrow.'

'Tomorrow?'

She nodded. 'Yes.'

'I knew that it was soon but...'

'But?'

He got to his feet and walked towards one of the balcony doors looking out over the rooftops. Jen swallowed. They weren't strangers; she could tell just from his stance that he was battling with how he was feeling. She stood up and moved next to him.

Physically close but she could feel the emotional distance widening as every second ticked by.

'Astro,' she began. 'I have so much to do when I get home. My business needs me, Kathleen needs me, although she would never admit it, but I don't want to leave Athens with any regrets.'

He sighed. 'You have not seen the Parthenon? Most sightseers think that is the only thing we have to offer.'

'You know that's not what I mean.'

'Yes,' he said, putting one hand on the doorframe. 'I know that is not what you mean.'

'Then help me out here because I don't do this. I never feel like this. It terrifies me. And, right now, I'm thinking I am making a fool of myself because you feel... so far away.'

There was a knot in her throat now, a blockage that was growing and starting to cause tension. Maybe this was a mistake, to open up and show herself to Astro, spray painting feelings she didn't usually admit to herself, to start to fall in love...

He moved then, turning his body towards her and looking deep into her eyes. It was so intense she started to hold her breath.

'Come with me,' he said, reaching for her hand.

52

STREFI HILL, EXARCHEIA

Jen hadn't questioned where they were going and Astro hadn't elaborated. He had just held her hand tightly and they'd walked through the streets of the city, which was becoming more festive as the days counted down to Christmas and the weather grew colder. Shops were bright with lit-up gifts on display, hot doughnuts and pastries were being queued for, buskers performed on street corners, yellow taxis still drove too fast, buses snaked their way up to stops and the scent of coffee, sugar and spices emanated from every restaurant door. The huge Christmas tree in Syntagma Square was the backdrop to many a selfie pose and the soldiers still stood guard out the front of the parliament building. But now they were in a different area altogether, one that Jen hadn't visited before. On initial impressions, this was probably not on the immediate hit list for tourists. What most people expected of Athens was the history, the relics, the photo opportunities with monuments as old as time. This area was something less discovered, perhaps a secret locals kept to themselves. Everyone they passed by seemed to have a certain flair about them. There were many that looked like students, strolling into cool cafés playing music with a strong baseline, the overall energy a mix between bohemian and arty with a touch of anarchy. Graffiti was abundant. Some of it was beautiful, like Astro's and his friends, others were made up of dark, spiky, Greek letters Jen didn't understand but could sense the bitterness from. As for the shops here, well, they weren't selling souvenirs. These wares were an abundance of artwork, vintage clothes and vinyl records. Still Astro kept walking until finally they reached some steps and he let go of her hand.

'This is Exarcheia,' Astro told her as if he was a tour guide.

'It's very different to the Plaka district. It's even different to Psyrri.'

'Yes,' Astro agreed. 'This is where I grew up. My mother, she rented an apartment here, took whatever she could afford when she was pregnant with me. So, my first seven years were spent hanging out here.'

'You were definitely influenced by the art,' Jen said, indicating more paintings on the wall next to the steps.

'Maybe.' He shrugged. 'Some people, they do not like this area of Athens. It is most likely not on your map with a star rating to visit.'

'Why not?'

'Because it is too real. The people that live here have actually lived. They struggle. My mother, she loved people. Any people. The more diverse the better. Here there are many migrants, refugees that no one wanted. They came here without anything, not even hope, but this area is where they have settled. My mother would always be exchanging food with people. Something from our culture, traded with a dish from theirs. One of my favourite things to eat was *morghe zaferani*, a saffron chicken. My mother's friend, Damsa, used to make it for us.'

As if suddenly realising they were stood still on the steps, Astro began to move upwards. 'The government doesn't like Exarcheia being this way. They want to move people to camps now, camps with poor conditions. The police come here, evict from the squats.' He sighed. 'That is one of the reasons I don't come here any more. My mother, she would have hated what is going on. She would not understand why people can't live and let live. Neither do I.'

'I think your mother would be proud that you share her values,' Jen said, following him until they came out onto a dusty path surrounded by trees and scrub land. Somehow it had gone from harsh city to nature in the space of a staircase. She was finding that much of Athens was like that. She breathed deep, the cold night air filling her lungs, only the stars above lighting their way.

'I spent the day with my uncle,' Astro continued. 'I know that sounds crazy because I spend every day with my uncle at the bar. But, today, we talked properly for perhaps the very first time since I came to live with him.'

'That's so good,' Jen said.

'It is good,' Astro agreed. 'Neither of us know quite how to go forward. But I am finding that where I thought I was getting by, going through life the way I should, that it is not at all what I have been doing.'

'No?'

She didn't really know what to say but she knew how important it was to listen. This was Astro being raw with her. Every time he had opened up before it had been somewhere away from Bar Páme, as if he needed the space for his thoughts to fly free.

'No,' he echoed, as they continued along a path that seemed to be getting narrower, close to indistinguishable from the brush surrounding it in the dark. 'That is what I want to talk to you about.'

Jen's heart scudded then. Whatever he was going to say was going to have an impact, good or bad. But did she try to pre-empt it? He may have been the one to bring her here but that didn't mean she didn't get to have her say.

'I think I know what you're going to tell me.' She spoke before she could think about it any more.

'You do?'

She nodded as the whole blanket of Athens rolled out in front of them. 'You're going to tell me that you wish things could be different and—'

'No,' Astro interrupted. 'I do not wish things could be different. Not with us.'

Mounds of thick rock appeared before them, hunks of solid balls forming a pinnacle where the city lay at its feet. Athens in all its bright white glory was shining from below, stretching as far as the eye could see. Dotted amongst the crags were other young people, talking, smoking, sipping coffees or beers.

Astro headed away from the groups towards a more solitary place and Jen followed, watching her step.

'Are we allowed to be here?' she asked.

'*Ne.* It is a park. But, at night, it is hard to see the edges so, we will take care.' He plumped down onto the rock, sitting with his feet dangling.

Carefully, Jen moved over the stone until she was able to stoop down and sit next to him. It was colder up here, with nothing to protect you from the chill breeze, and she shivered, drawing her knees up and in towards her body.

'I used to come up here with my mother,' Astro said. 'She would bring a blanket and pack a lunch big enough for twelve people and she would point at the buildings down there and make up stories about the people that lived there. I don't know... Mr Michalidis loves to eat fish but his wife hates the smell so every Friday he goes to his favourite taverna and orders a platter that could feed an army. Or... the little girl who lives in that apartment there loves to dance and one day she is going to perform as the star of a ballet.' He shook his head. 'It sounds stupid now I have said it out loud.'

'No,' Jen said immediately. 'It sounds nice. It sounds like she loved you ever so much.'

'The truth is, I am always so scared to remember her because all it does is make me sad. But, if you stop thinking of someone, if you do not remember all the good they put into the world then it lessens the impact they had in the time that they were here with us.'

Jen didn't know what to say. Her experience of loss was the hazy outline of her mother's face, barely remembered. Then it was Gerald and although she had felt that keenly, she had hurt more for Kathleen's grief than her own. Loss was hard to connect with when you had never really had anything in the first place. Perhaps the way she felt about her beginnings was sadness for the start she might have had if her circumstances had been altered. But absolutely anyone could say that, no matter what their situation.

A minute ticked by and then Jen replied, 'You were lucky to have someone who loved you so much, even if it was for the shortest of times. That should be something you always cherish. And good memories, they are always important.'

He turned his head then, went from looking out over the buildings to looking directly at her.

'You do not have good memories, do you?' he asked.

'No,' she admitted with a sigh. 'Of my parents I have no real memories at all. I've never known who my father was and my mother... well, she was called Nell and I was taken into care and away from her when our social worker found her high and me alone in a bath full of cold water.' She shuddered. 'I don't remember that, and I'm not meant to know, but people get sloppy with their paperwork sometimes.' She shrugged. 'After that, I only have memories of being an inconvenience, in the way, someone that receives the bare minimum and never any real affection. So, that's why I've always clung to Christmas. And I know people think that it's an obsession but for me, growing up, it really was the only time of year that felt slightly better than the rest.' She sighed. 'My foster families got happier, maybe not for the whole of December, but on Christmas Day, we all could pretend that things were OK, that our situation was acceptable, just for a few hours. That's why I longed for Christmas, that's why whenever I'm feeling down or overwhelmed, I default to burying my face in tinsel, listening to uplifting carols and burning candles that smell of pine, chestnuts or yule logs.'

'How long did you live with foster families?' he asked.

'Until I ran away the last time when I was sixteen. The local authority was meant to put a pathway in place but, for me, all pathways led to Kathleen and Gerald.' She sighed. 'No one came knocking on the door. It felt like everyone just metaphorically gave a sigh of relief. Including me.' She took a beat, held eye contact. 'I've never told anyone any of this, Astro. I've always felt that it would make them think differently about me. Bonnie knows I was in care, but I've never told her anything about what I remember of my mother or any of the tough stuff. It's something I find hard to talk about but I want to be completely honest with you. It feels right to be honest with you.'

He nodded. 'And I want to be honest with you too.'

She watched him look to the sky and take a deep breath.

'The reason I despised this season is because... my mother, she died on Christmas Day.'

And then suddenly she understood so much more. He held his head as if this admission was making it hurt. Now she knew why the decorations going up around the city, the festive food on the menu and his feelings about the season were so painful. And here she had been thinking he was simply a Scrooge figure who was overworked or just didn't enjoy celebrating...

'She read me a Christmas story,' Astro began. 'She went out to work, I went to sleep and in the morning, I went to wake her up, to wish her Happy Christmas and... she was cold.'

'Astro—'

'I only remember that she was cold, and I wondered why she was so cold when she was under the blankets, and I thought that if only I could make her warm, she would open her eyes again.'

His voice was raw with emotion and Jen wanted to do something, touch him, put an arm around him, but she also didn't want to crowd him in this moment of vulnerability.

'So, I guess, in the same way that you look to Christmas for salvation, I had been looking at it as a monster. A living thing that surrounded my mother and suffocated her like it was the actual cause of her passing.'

'And now?' Jen asked.

'And now, what?'

'Well,' she began, shifting her bottom on the rock so she was more comfortable. 'You're talking in the past tense. You said "despised" rather than "despise". And you said that you *had* been looking at Christmas like a monster. As if you don't feel the same way any more.'

Astro sighed then, long and slow. 'I showed my uncle my mural today.'

'Really?'

'I did not ever think I would do that. But we went to the church where we had the service for my mother when she died and we talked about Bar Páme and how, maybe, we have both clung to it in our own way and, perhaps, to be able to move forward we need to think about a new direction or, at least, changing things up.' He shrugged. 'I do not know the right path yet, but I thought about what you said about my art, sharing it with Philippos and putting it on the walls of the bar and... I thought he should see what I had made in memory of my mother.'

'And what did he think?'

'He cried,' Astro said. 'He said it was the most beautiful thing he had ever seen. He told me I should be a world-famous artist.'

'You really should,' Jen agreed.

'I do not know that. But what I do know, is that I have some work to do. But first of all, on myself.'

Jen swallowed, feeling – and somehow knowing – that this was when her heart was going to take the real hit.

'I do not want to hate the time of year that my mother always made so special for me. It should be a time for joy and laughter and all the things that Achilles drives me crazy with. It should be about the lights and the trees and the pork baked in the oven and songs on Christmas Eve, exactly all the things my mother loved. Exactly the things *you* love.' He took a deep breath. 'But it does not come easy. I need to learn to love it again. And that will take time.'

Again, the one thing they did not have.

'I understand,' Jen said, swallowing away the emotion that was welling up at speed. She *did* understand but she didn't want to. Because although he had yet to say it, him taking time, pausing, trying to live with his grief in a different way, was going to mean the end of what they were just starting.

'You do?' he asked, turning on the rock and looking at her.

'You're saying goodbye again,' Jen said. 'And I get it. You think that you need to do this on your own and I understand that, I really do, because my whole life I've made doing things on my own the biggest overarching theme so, you know, I really do know a little bit of how you're feeling and... I admire you for wanting to make changes and I'm so glad you and Philippos are talking properly at last and that maybe your art will get to be admired by many more people and—'

'Jen, you are crying,' Astro said, reaching out for her.

She put her fingers to her face, needing proof and there were hot, fat wet droplets streaming from her eyes and trailing down her cheeks. She didn't know what to do. She had spent her whole life succeeding in keeping the tears at bay and now she didn't know how to make them stop.

'Jen, I don't want to make you cry,' Astro told her. 'And I feel that where I am in my life right now, that is all I am going to do.'

'I understand. Completely. I do.' She was nodding now, although everything she was feeling inside was a negative rather than a positive and the physical affirmation couldn't have felt more wrong.

'No, I do not think you do.' He took her hands then, his long, lean fingers swamping hers and holding on tight. 'Meeting you, it has been like nothing else for me. Nothing else. And, I know if we had not met, there would be no way I would be trying to make these changes or thinking about things differently. I owe that to you, Jen. I owe a lot to you.'

She didn't trust herself to speak. Right now she didn't trust herself not to shed *all* the years of tears she had been storing in a crying reservoir. She needed to hold on, just simply hold on…

'And I know now that I am not worthy of you, Jen. Not as I am.' He smiled but it was coated in sorrow. 'You are this bright burning torch of light, perhaps like the star on top of the Christmas tree in Syntagma Square. And we have this connection that I do not know if I will ever find again.'

She couldn't hold on. She needed to let go. She needed to stand up on this rock and walk away because *this* was losing someone. It might be dressed up in the most beautiful of words but it was, without any doubt, the end.

Astro squeezed her hands. 'You showed me love and you gave me hope and—'

'I can't do this,' Jen said, letting go of his hands and getting to her feet – doing it so quickly she wobbled and had to put her arms out like a tightrope walker to keep her balance.

'Jen, take care.' Astro got up too as if he was going to steady her.

'I need to get back to the hotel. I need to pack for my flight.'

'Jen, please, don't leave like this. Let me walk you back.'

'No,' she answered, heart aching, soul stinging. 'It's fine. I can find the way. I seem to know Athens quite well now. So... well... thank you... for your company while I've been here and... I hope Peri gets better soon and... say goodbye to Achilles for me and... good luck with everything.'

And then, as if Astro was a client who had booked her services for a festive-themed function, she held out her hand in formality.

Astro shook his head, an expression on his face of combined devastation and bewilderment. 'I am not going to shake your hand.'

'OK,' Jen said, somehow managing to maintain equilibrium. 'Well, goodbye.'

She didn't wait for a response.

Turning away, not caring about her footing on the rocks, she rushed off, knowing that at any second her heart was going to break in two.

53

HOTEL PLAKA

The siren sound was so loud it was as if someone had blasted a high-pitched, out of tune trumpet right by her ear. What was that?

'Is that the fire alarm?' Bonnie asked, bolt upright, the silk headwrap she wore over her hair for sleep falling down over her nose.

'I don't know. I don't think so.' In her still-sleepy state, Jen was just trying to work out where it was coming from. Then suddenly another one sounded, exactly the same. Turning her head towards the nightstand, she realised it was emanating from her phone and the screen was lit up with the largest looking text message she'd ever seen. Detaching it from the charging lead, she brought it closer.

'What is it?' Bonnie asked, putting her legs out of the bed and taking the one stride over to Jen's.

'It's an alert. It's all in Greek. Hang on, there's an English translation below.' Jen read on in her head. 'Oh, God!'

'What is it?' Bonnie asked. 'You can't say "oh, God" with no context.' She leaned over Jen until she was basically in the bed too.

Then the room was filled with noise again, this time from Bonnie's phone. 'Argh! It's got me too! Tell me!'

'It says there's a red warning for snow!'

'What? In London? My mum hasn't said anything and you know what she's like about snow, she'd fill a bath with it if she could.'

'Not London. Here! This area of Greece! Oh, God, a potential threat to life,' Jen continued. 'This is bad!'

'Well, you did say last night it was getting even colder. Sounds like we're getting out at the right time!'

Jen swallowed, remembering last night. That astounding view over Athens no tourist was ever going to find, Astro opening up to her about his mother, her opening up to him, but then the knowledge that if she had stayed any longer, she would have had to listen to him end things. She hadn't needed to hear any more, she had known inside.

'How are you feeling this morning?' Bonnie asked, pulling at the covers arched up like a tent and getting into bed next to Jen and resting her head on her shoulder.

'Like getting back to Little Pickering is what I need to do,' she said. 'To make sure Christmas Every Day is fulfilling all its obligations. To take Kathleen to the carol concert. To have one of Greg's new chicken wings with chargrilled sprouts. To delete my dating app.' She sighed. 'I know you're not going to agree but I don't think looking for someone right now is what I need.'

'No,' Bonnie said, lifting her head from Jen's shoulder. 'I'm not going to disagree. Because you actually found someone much better when you weren't looking.'

Jen couldn't meet Bonnie's eyes. Astro hadn't been like anyone she had ever swiped on. He hadn't even been like anyone she had ever met. And it was going to take time to get over that.

'Is it really over, do you think?' Bonnie asked softly.

'Yes,' Jen said. 'I mean, it was fraught with difficulty to begin with. He lives here and I don't and...'

'So, it was only the distance. A cheap flight away.'

'It was more than that, Bonnie. It was where he is in his life right now, the fact that he hasn't grieved for his mother properly and that's held him back from being the person he wants to be. He doesn't know himself yet, so he doesn't have the space to get to know anyone else at the moment.'

'That's what he said, was it? That he didn't have the space to get to know you?'

'Well, not in those exact words but I could feel that from him and—'

'Because you know him,' Bonnie interrupted. 'Really well. Like you have a strong, solid connection.'

'Yes,' Jen admitted. 'But some things aren't meant to be, are they?'

Bonnie got out of the bed and gave a sigh. 'I suppose I just don't want you to regret coming to Athens with me.'

'Oh, Bonnie, how could I regret it?' She put her phone back down. 'It wasn't Paris but in so many ways it was better. Phenomenal food, the Parthenon, the parks, not getting mown down on a pedestrian crossing.' She swallowed as all the other places she'd spent time with Astro at came to mind – collecting nature decorations in Anafiotika, spraying painting in Psyrri, Bar Páme.

'Maybe, if we're not too terrified of them, we could get one of the buses to the airport,' Bonnie suggested. 'Unless it's cold. I don't fancy waiting at a bus stop if it's cold.'

Jen watched her friend throw back the curtains then and the change of light in the room was immediate. Suddenly it was a lot, lot brighter, *whiter* even.

'Oh my God!' Bonnie exclaimed. 'Oh my God, Jen!'

Jen scrambled to get out of bed now, covers flying, bare feet padding across the floor. The scene that met her was like nothing she had seen before.

Everything was covered in snow. And not the light dusting that icing sugar might make; this was thick, inches and inches, across their balcony, on the chairs and table, and it was still falling from the sky.

'I think that alert was a bit bloody late,' Bonnie said. 'I've not ever seen snow this thick.'

'Me neither,' Jen agreed, getting right up close to the glass and looking down towards the road below. There was no traffic, not even a moped, the tarmac covered with snow, crisp and fresh, without tracks or marks. It was like Athens had been turned into a winter wonderland. But as much as she wanted to revel in the whole Christmas aesthetic, she was equally also worried.

'So, do you think this might cause an issue with our flight?'

Bonnie had taken the words right out of her mouth.

54

BAR PÁME, PLAKA

'Have you looked out of the window? Don't *open* the window because it might actually come into the bar! There's snow! So much snow! It looks like we are in the middle of the Arctic Circle.'

Astro continued to wipe down the tables, checking each and every basket for the correct amount of cutlery, making sure the menus were clean, readjusting the festive centrepieces they now all had. It was ironic that he cared about the bar more than ever now, wanted things to be perfect, when his uncle was close to thinking about selling the business.

'What are you doing?' Philippos asked, buttoning up his shirt and adjusting the waistband of his jeans.

'I am preparing the bar. You look like you are getting dressed. Something that should be done in your bedroom, no?'

'Why are you preparing the bar? Have you not seen the snow? No one is going to come out in this! Schools will be closed! Roads will be closed!'

'Greeks will still want coffee,' Astro replied. 'I have already cleared the worst of it from the tables outside and off the top of the parasols so they do not break under the weight and—'

'OK, what has happened?'

'Peri has broken his leg,' Astro offered. 'I am keeping him in my room for a while.'

'And that is the thing you tell me to distract me from the thing that has really happened,' Philippos said, pouring himself a mug of coffee.

'I do not know what you mean,' Astro said, rubbing his cloth across a shelf that he knew he had already cleaned twice.

'Astro, I know you think that we do not communicate properly—'

'And you agreed.'

'Yes, but that does not mean I do not pick up on some of your familiar traits of avoidance.'

'Do you think Marjorie will be able to come in today? Or do you think she will have to stay at home with Achilles?' Astro asked, changing the subject.

'I think that as the bar will be closed or, at the very least, less busy today, that it might be a good opportunity for me to meet Jen,' Philippos said. He put his coffee to his lips and took a sip before carrying on. 'You do not have to cook. Perhaps I will make one of my famous baked fish dishes.'

Of course Philippos would bring up Jen now.

He was working his way around the bar, erasing dust that wasn't there just because he needed to keep moving to stop himself from hurting.

'Astro?' Philippos queried. 'You are going to get blisters on your fingers if you keep scrubbing at things with them.'

'Jen is leaving today,' he said quickly.

'What? Is it the end of her holiday? Or did something happen?'

Did something happen? Yes, something happened. *Everything* had happened. From the second she had stumbled up the steps outside with that stupid giant candy cane, his whole life had changed.

'She has a life in the UK and a business and it's a busy time of year for her so...'

'So...' Philippos mimicked.

'I do not know what you want me to say.' He folded his arms across his chest.

'I want you to talk to me the way we promised we would talk to each other from now on. Honestly,' Philippos reminded him. 'Like two adults who are related to each other and who should take time to care about how the other one is doing.'

'It would not have worked. I... don't know how to be with someone in that way. I have no experience of it. I would be no good at it. I am not good for her.'

'You know what I hear?'

Astro shook his head.

'All I hear is that you love her,' Philippos said bluntly. 'I hear that she is the most important person you have ever had in your life since your mother.'

Astro met his uncle's gaze then, his eyes burning with emotion. 'It does not matter if I feel that. To acknowledge that means I am thinking only of me. I have to think about her. What is good for her.'

'Astro—' Philippos began.

The door to the bar opened with a bang, one of the wreaths Jen had made falling with a thump to a table.

'Have you seen the snow?! Have you seen it?'

Achilles bounced into the room dressed from head to toe in a padded snowsuit, which was already damp, looking as if he had been rolling in the snow on the way from his home to here. Marjorie followed, the expression on her face making it look like she wished she could attach reins to the energetic boy.

'Have we seen it?' Philippos said. 'We cannot open windows for fear of it coming into the bar.'

'Are we opening?' Marjorie asked. 'Please say yes. Because otherwise I will have to watch Achilles almost burying himself every five minutes. I am considering buying a shovel to carry around.'

'We are opening,' Astro confirmed, picking up the wreath.

'Astro wishes to keep busy,' Philippos said.

'Can Jen come and make snowmen outside the bar? Or we could make a Saint Vasilis!' Achilles said excitedly.

'Jen has gone back to the UK, Achilles,' Astro informed her, toying with the decoration between his fingers.

'What?' Marjorie exclaimed. 'When did she go? Last night? Did you go and see her?'

'She is leaving this morning.'

'I don't think so,' Marjorie stated as she began unbuttoning her coat.

'What do you mean?' he asked, reaching to re-hang the decoration.

'Have you not turned on the TV today? It is not only the schools that are closed, some of the roads are closed too, even the main roads. There are no buses. And the airport is shut. No flights in. No flights out. It is not something they can easily clear and the snow is still falling.'

This information hit Astro like *he* was the snow and the detail was a plough pounding its way through it.

'It is certain that Jen will not be going anywhere today,' Marjorie clarified.

55

KALIMERES BISTRO, PSYRRI

'Well, this place is a find, isn't it?' Bonnie said, sipping at her cocktail.

'What I'm finding is apparently when it snows here all roads close and all public transport is cancelled, yet coffee shops and bars can withstand anything,' Jen remarked.

She had a coffee, a strong one. Bonnie had turned to alcohol the moment they had found out that not only was their flight back to London cancelled, but that getting a new date for their return right now was near-on impossible. As it got closer to Christmas, flights were already full, and they had yet to work out what they were going to do. Bonnie was opting for the let's-have-a-cocktail-to-take-the-edge-off-the-situation path as they thought about where they were going to stay. They had had to check out of their hotel as it was full going forward and their next plan was to look at Airbnbs close by.

'I love that light fitting,' Bonnie said, gesturing above their heads. 'Do you think it would look good in my bedroom?'

The light fitting looked as if someone had strung ice cubes together and put a bulb in the middle. It was as decadent as the rest of the décor with its black and white striped awnings over outside tables today speckled with snow, then inside white stone walls mixed with floral wallpaper. There were Christmas touches all around too – leafy garlands with red bows wrapped around the banister of the stairs, lights and baubles hanging strategically to catch attention.

'I think your bedroom is pretty amazing already,' Jen said truthfully.

'Andrea said that when we spoke on the phone,' Bonnie said. 'She said that I'd coordinated it better than she had ever coordinated her apartment in London. "Perfectly" she said. That's high praise from Andrea.'

Jen didn't have a proper bedroom to coordinate. She had a sofa bed and rainbow-coloured bear. She didn't even have a hotel room to sleep in tonight. And if they *did* manage to find somewhere, she couldn't let Bonnie pay for it again. She also had a million things she had planned to do when she got back to Little Pickering and now that wasn't going to happen today, nor did she know *when* it was going to happen.

But at the very forefront of her mind was Astro. Last night, going home had been inevitable, a sure and certain fact that come today she would be on a plane heading away from Athens and everything that had happened here. Now that *hadn't* transpired, it was giving her options. Or perhaps not. What did it change?

'Hello,' Bonnie said, waving a hand in front of her face. 'I was saying that maybe we're going to have to call on friends if we can't find anywhere to stay.'

'Friends?'

'Jen, I don't want to freak you out any more than you're already freaking out right now, but if we can't find anywhere we can afford to stay in this city and if we don't ask for help, we might be sleeping in the Monastiraki metro station.'

Bonnie meant Astro. Asking Astro if they could stay in his apartment when last night she had crumbled because he rather nobly said he wasn't ready for a relationship. How was she supposed to face him? She wasn't meant to ever face him again. She was supposed to be halfway to passport control by now.

'We could call the British Embassy,' Jen suggested. 'Isn't this the type of thing they're meant to help with?'

'I don't think finding a B&B is at the top of their priority list to be honest.'

'We can't ask Astro,' Jen said, feeling suddenly uncomfortable on her seat.

'These are not ordinary circumstances, Jen. If we bed down on a bench in the snow we could die! And I know those soldiers stand outside the parliament building twenty-four-seven not getting frostbite but, even after a few sessions at Pure Gym, I am not conditioned for alfresco living like that!'

She didn't want to die, but the thought of asking Astro for help made her feel like that nauseous ten-year-old again in front of her schoolteacher trying to explain that she couldn't hand in her homework because one of the other foster children had spat all over it.

'You said things ended amicably. That it was because he wasn't in the right place for a relationship,' Bonnie continued. 'It didn't sound like you couldn't still be friendly enough to beg for a bed for a few nights.'

Jen didn't immediately respond. Bonnie might know the way she felt about Astro was unprecedented, but Jen suspected Bonnie didn't quite realise exactly *how* deep her feelings went. The fact she had *cried*. It wasn't a case of not feeling comfortable asking Astro for this favour, and it was more than simply seeing him – those green eyes, the way his eyebrows creased in when he really listened to you. Being near him – watching him interact with the world, carefully draw what was all around him – would be torturous. But, then again, Bonnie had paid for this trip, supported her through everything with David, during Kathleen's flit from the care home, through gnome interviews and blood-spattered knaves. Her best friend didn't deserve to worry about where they were going to sleep because of her pride and her aching heart.

So she took a deep breath, cupping her hands around her coffee. 'OK. After our drinks, we can go to Bar Páme. We can ask Astro for help.'

But as she sipped at the thick froth and got the first hit of coffee underneath, she wondered if this was a decision she was going to regret.

56

PSYRRI

'I have never seen so much snow! Even on the television!' Achilles announced.

Somehow, and Astro wasn't quite sure how, he had been tasked with the job of entertaining Achilles. Marjorie had convinced him that if he tired the boy out with snow play now, then the novelty of the extreme and exciting weather would soon wear off and everything could get back to normal. Astro wasn't so sure. On their walk here, Achilles had wanted to build a snowman on each street corner and had somehow been gifted pastries from every eatery owner he had smiled at.

'Do you think it will stay until Christmas?' Achilles continued.

'I hope not,' Astro answered, trudging forward, the snow up to the top of his boots in parts of the path.

'Why do you hope not? Do you not love it?'

'When you get older, Achilles, snow will mean different things. For adults it is a difficulty. The roads are dangerous to drive on. Plans have to be changed. Schools are closed.'

'Schools are closed so everyone can enjoy the snow! Even the teachers! And it is good that Jen's plane cannot leave! Now she can come to the Christmas experience at my school tomorrow and you can give her a green light.'

'What?'

'Has she not given you a green light yet?'

'Achilles... I do not know if Jen will be able to come. Things with planes, they are difficult.'

Achilles folded his arms across his chest even though he had a snowball in each gloved hand, looking cross. 'Why do you say that *everything* is difficult?'

'I just mean that perhaps the airport will be better tomorrow and she might have to take another plane quickly in the morning.'

He swallowed. Was that what he wanted? To avoid the fact that she was here today and hope that tomorrow things would be as they should have been? Even if they did not make contact with each other, both of them knew that the other would know a flight out today was impossible...

Achilles hurled the snowballs at the shutters of an abandoned shop where they made a loud slam before splattering onto the pavement.

'Grown-ups are stupid. Why do they not enjoy anything? Mama sees the snow and she starts to swear and says to me all the things that can go wrong. All I want to do is lie in it like a bath!'

And with that said, he launched himself backwards into a pile of snow and lay down, fanning out his arms and legs and making a snow angel of epic proportions. As he laughed and got snow in his eyes and his mouth as he continued to move his arms and legs like pendulums, Astro looked to the shutters on the other side of the street. One mural in particular. Jen's mural.

His feet seemed to be moving before his brain had asked them to and a few seconds later he was standing in front of the picture she had made. He put his fingers to the artwork and remembered how he had watched her create this. Her initial reticence, then the letting go, until finally this finished piece. He traced the outline of her bear, Bravely, all the colour and the hope coming from this one possession and this one time of year. What she must have been through. How it had shaped who she was. It was like an opposing image of his own feelings, her hope and light stemming from the time of year he had always felt so darkly about...

'I like the bear.'

It was Achilles, his entire padded bodysuit soaked in snow, his fringe underneath his hood dripping, now standing next to him.

'I like the bear too,' he agreed. 'He is called Bravely.'

'Did you do this painting?' Achilles asked, wide-eyed.

'No,' Astro said. 'Jen did it.'

'The lines are not very straight,' Achilles concluded.

'Achilles, when you draw a picture for your mama, do you worry about how straight the lines are? Or do you want to make a nice picture that means something to you and will make her smile?'

Achilles looked sheepish then. 'The second one.'

'This bear is a toy Jen has had a long time. That is why she painted it. It means a lot to her.'

'And Jen means a lot to you,' Achilles said.

Astro didn't reply and Achilles huffed an annoyed sigh.

'I do not know what is wrong with everybody,' he stated, flapping his arms out. 'Christmas is coming soon and everyone is mad or sad or saying that things are difficult. Why can't everyone just be happy?'

It was a question that only a child with that upbeat outlook on life would ask. But it did give Astro immediate perspective.

'You want to use spray paints?' he asked.

'What?' Achilles exclaimed. 'You are going to let me spray on buildings?'

'No,' Astro said immediately. 'Your mother would kill me.'

'Awww!'

'How about we make a picture in the snow?' Astro suggested. 'We can build something and then we can spray it different colours.'

'I will make a deal,' Achilles said, water still dripping from his hair.

'I do not know if I like the sound of that.'

'I will make a snow picture with you and you will ask Jen if she can come to my school tomorrow.' He folded his arms across his chest, giving off the vibe of a master negotiator.

'Achilles, you make it sound like I need *you* to help *me* make a snow picture.'

'I think *you* need *me* to help you make things happy with Jen,' Achilles countered.

Astro had no answer for that. 'Look,' he began. 'I will promise that if we make a picture together and take photos to show your mama then, if I see Jen, I will ask her.'

'If you see Jen you will ask her what?'

It wasn't Achilles replying. It was a voice Astro hadn't expected to hear here, or in fact, ever again.

'Jen!' Achilles shouted, jumping through the snow and looking a little like Neil Armstrong bouncing across the surface of the moon. 'Your teddy bear is cute! Why does it have a funny ear?'

'Well, I think he was born like that,' Jen replied, stepping closer, trainers not doing so well with the slippery terrain.

'Toys aren't born! They're made!'

'Except the ones that Father Christmas brings,' Jen told him. 'They're special and they are all tiny little baby toys when they start out in life.'

Achilles snorted. 'So my big racing car was a small one to begin with?'

'Why is that funny?' Jen asked, right alongside them now. 'You grow, don't you? Why not toys? With a bit of Christmas magic?'

Astro watched Achilles, the boy's expression saying he was taking on this information and thinking about it a little. He wanted him to believe the story, wanted him to be gifted a fairy tale.

'We are going to make a snow picture with spray paints!' Achilles declared. 'You can help too!'

'Listen, Achilles, why don't you get started making something we can paint on and I will come and help show you how to spray in a second,' Astro said.

'There is the biggest pile over here,' the boy said, running off.

Then it was only the two of them and the quiet streets. Astro didn't know what to say, but his whole body seemed to be telling him that simply *seeing* Jen again, having her stand here so close, was unpicking every decision he had told himself he must make.

'So, the snow happened,' she said, stomping her feet on the ground.

'It did,' Astro replied. 'Unexpectedly. I mean, we have had snow in Athens before but this time the warning came too late and, well, there it was.'

Why wasn't he saying anything better and more meaningful?

'My flight is cancelled,' Jen continued, dropping her gaze to the ground. 'And our hotel is fully booked so we had to check out and... well... I hate to have to ask but do you know anywhere that might have somewhere Bonnie and I could stay?'

'*Fisika*,' Astro answered straight away. 'Of course.'

'Really?' she asked, looking back up at him.

'Jen, you are staying with me.' He quickly rephrased. 'I mean at Bar Páme. We can find room. Make it work.'

'Thank you, Astro. It should only be for a night or so, if we can get seats on another plane when the airport reopens. I wouldn't have asked but...'

She stopped there as if she didn't know what she had been going to say. Either that or she *had* known what she was going to say but decided not to carry on. Whichever it was, it only served to highlight how far away they were from where they had once been.

'*Páme*. Let us spray snow with Achilles and then we can make room at the bar, yes?'

'OK,' she agreed with a small smile.

'OK,' Astro repeated.

'Did someone say "spray snow"?' Bonnie asked, appearing from around the corner with a shopping bag on each arm.

'Astro says we can stay at Bar Páme,' Jen said to her friend.

Astro smiled, trying to ignore the fizz of anticipation in his stomach. It was just Greek hospitality, giving whatever he had to help someone in need. It was definitely, *absolutely* only that.

57

BAR PÁME, PLAKA

'Natalia, please tell me that Mrs Butler is OK, and that she isn't going to want a refund over the wingspan issue.'

Jen got the sentence out of her mouth and then closed her eyes and held her breath as she waited for the response. It was evening now and she was sitting on the edge of Astro's bed, which was now dressed in clean sheets and blankets he had insisted she take. He had planned to set up a rather uncomfortable-looking sofa bed in his uncle's room until he and Philippos had realised it was never going to fit without being crazily close to the existing bed or in the doorway to the bathroom. So the lumpy, blue barely-cushioned-at-all construction was currently near the kitchen area of the apartment and that's where Astro was going to be sleeping. Bonnie had jumped at the chance of staying with Marjorie and Achilles as soon as the offer had been made. Jen knew this was a ruse by her friend to give her and Astro some alone time and Marjorie was equally and enthusiastically on board – Achilles not quite so much. Right now, Bonnie was dropping off her cabin bag at their apartment and coming back here later to help at the bar.

At the moment Astro was working. Jen was going to go downstairs to lend a hand as soon as she had checked in on Kathleen and Natalia. Kathleen hadn't picked up, so Natalia was first.

'There is no wingspan issue to ask refund for,' Natalia said. 'The problem is no longer problem. My brothers help.'

Why Jen's first thought was that ill deeds had befallen Mrs Butler she didn't know but before she could voice another thought, Kathleen interrupted.

'And I helped!'

'Kathleen! What are you doing at the office?'

'Helping,' Kathleen said, coming into shot. 'And don't worry, the home knows I'm here.'

'Well, we told grey lie,' Natalia said, picking up her rubber band ball and passing it from hand to hand. 'We say is funeral of sister. We have to be back before dinner is served. They say I can have plate tonight. It is not arse of turkey.'

'Praise be!' Kathleen said, raising her hands in gratitude.

Jen didn't immediately have words.

'So, you text flight is cancelled, and I see Athens on news. Famous ruins like they are part of ice castle.'

'Yes, it's quite thick snow here,' Jen remarked, her eyes going to the window and the white tiled roofs like icing over a Christmas cake. 'It's still snowing now but a bit lighter. Tomorrow there may be more but after that, it is meant to get warmer so hopefully then we'll be on our way home.'

'Well, there is nothing for you to worry for here. Wings are all organised and delivered for fitting. Mrs Butler phone to say they are perfect and much more authentic than she could dream of.' Natalia laughed then. 'She say she almost think they are real feathers.'

Kathleen began to laugh too. Jen decided not to ask any more questions about that.

'OK, so I just need to call the historical society and tell them they will have to make alternative arrangements.' She sighed. 'Or accept that there won't be a big dramatic piece this year to accompany the dinner.'

It was a huge deal. A large sum of money she wouldn't get in her business account, as well as a high probability that the group would not book Christmas Every Day again for next season...

'I have thought about that,' Natalia stated, bouncing the rubber band ball on the desk as if it was a miniature basketball. 'As soon as it snow there and you become trapped I have idea. I think to myself, 4D experience.'

'I went on one of them when they were brand spanking new,' Kathleen said, wheeling in closer to the screen on one of Jen's office chairs. 'It was a trip to a theme park and, as an alternative to the actual rides that made you go doolally, they had one with a screen of a rollercoaster. You watched it like you were on it and then the chairs all tipped up and down and there was air blowing in our faces. Gerald near-on lost his glasses when water sprayed at us.'

Jen had no idea what they were both talking about, and she really hoped Natalia hadn't given Kathleen any of the festively flavoured liqueur that was only meant for clients.

'You do not need rollercoaster,' Natalia continued. 'You need snow and... customs of Greece... the big ruins that look like ice castle... smiling children in clothes from old centuries... the sights and sounds of Athens... and, of course, dancing flash mob.'

Now Jen's brain was firing. What exactly was Natalia suggesting?

'Natalia has had some of that funny drink you keep in your client cupboard,' Kathleen said, by way of explanation. 'What's she's trying to say is... do you think you can get something together *there* for the historical society? In Greece? Even a few of the things Natalia said? Some traditional dancers? The historical costumes? The historical sites? Are you getting it now?' Kathleen asked. 'You're in the midst of one of the most historical places in the entire world. This could turn out not to be a compromise for the society but an *improvement*.'

Now Jen's mind was racing. More speed, less instability. Possibility. Could she find those things at short notice in a city that was struggling to keep moving with the extreme nature-dump? How would it really work? Filming what was going on here and it appearing on a screen in the UK... It would have to be a better quality than this FaceTime call...

'I can see things now,' Natalia began, hand around what looked like a wine glass. 'We turn down lights, we drop temperature of heating, put on air conditioning, we drop confetti, so it feels like snow. You tell story of historic things – battles – I can scrape knives together like swords. Dance – we can get people up and joining in with short tutorial. Is there something they can make? People on screen make craft and we have things to make the same here...'

Jen's brain was working overtime now as she realised this wasn't just one of Natalia's usual slightly out-there ideas, this was *inspired*. If she could gather together all the components before the event night...

'Where are you? This look like log cabin not hotel? And is that bird behind you?'

Jen looked to the nightstand and saw that Peri was there, nibbling at the edge of a leather-bound book. His broken leg didn't seem to be hampering his ability to get around too much.

'This is Astro's apartment and—'

'Ooooo!' Kathleen interrupted with all the finesse of the finest builder catcall.

'It is snow magic,' Natalia said with a firm nod. 'You think it stop everything, but really it make everything happen.'

58

BAR PÁME, PLAKA

'I think we have record takings!' Philippos announced as he finished counting the day's money ready to be put into the safe. 'It is crazy when the city is half-closed.'

'And the snow is still falling,' Astro added as he began to close up the shutters.

Jen was giving the inside tables another wipe down. She had cleared the outside ones too, but it seemed pretty futile when they were only being re-covered in fresh snow.

'Thank you for your help tonight, Jen,' Philippos said, slamming the till shut with a flourish. 'And Bonnie too.'

'Well, I think Bonnie encouraged the extra shots of brandy in everyone's coffees but I'm not sure how many she actually had herself too that she didn't pay for.'

'She try to pay before she leave with Marjorie to get gyros,' Philippos replied. 'I say no. You both work for free, to help, and I very much appreciate that.' He put a hand to his chest. 'Really.'

'We should be the ones thanking you. For letting us stay at short notice,' Jen answered, straightening one of the decorations on the wall.

'If Bonnie really has had so much Metaxa she will not be thankful for Marjorie's sofa when Achilles wakes at 6 a.m.,' Philippos said with a laugh. 'Hey, listen, you two, Chef has left some chicken fricassee in the oven, take it, eat it.'

'What about you?' Astro asked.

'I am going to have another look over the accounts. Maybe have a Metaxa myself. See if I can make a list of pros and cons.' He rubbed his beard. 'Do not worry. Any enlightenment that comes my way I will share with you in the morning.'

'Are you hungry?' Astro asked, turning to Jen.

She nodded. 'I'm always hungry. Especially when it's cold.'

'Let's go then,' he said, leading the way.

'*Páme*,' Jen replied.

Philippos chuckled. 'She learns Greek. Very good!'

* * *

The chicken dish was delicious. In a clay pot, it had been covered in bright green spinach and finely chopped spring onions, and was resting in a sauce not unlike the one her cabbage rolls had been served with the previous evening. But although the conversation flowed, like when they had spray-painted snow earlier, it all felt more like small talk. It felt that as well as having a pigeon in the room, there was also an elephant.

Now they had moved from sitting at the table to sitting on the small sofa bed Astro would be sleeping on tonight. He had poured red wine but, even with the beginnings of an alcohol buzz, the atmosphere was a little off.

'So, are you able to come to Achilles's event tomorrow?'

'He asked me about ten times when we made the rainbow reindeer in the snow,' Jen said.

'And you did not say yes...'

'Well, I don't make promises I can't keep. I didn't really know if we would have any luck getting a flight tomorrow but, as it stands, the airport hasn't reopened yet.'

'Does that mean you will come?'

Jen nodded. 'Of course I'll come. He's very excited about it. I do hope it goes well.'

A heavy silence cloaked the room again, the only sound the flickering of a candle on the dining table. There was that feeling of awkwardness again...

'I'm quite tired,' Jen said, making a move to get up.

'Jen, just, wait a second,' Astro said, putting a hand on her arm.

The touch sent a shockwave through her and whether he felt it too or not, he withdrew his hand as quickly as he had put it out there. She stayed still.

'I just wanted to say that... things between us feel... I do not know... different.'

'Yes,' she agreed with a nod.

'I do not like it.'

'Neither do I, but perhaps that's just the way it's meant to be.'

Her heart was hammering against her rib cage as she tried to avoid looking into his eyes. He had made his decision for all the best reasons and perhaps, if she was honest, falling so hard for someone so quickly after her experience with David might not have been right. What she needed to do was support the decision he'd made, not think of herself and her own disappointment at the relationship not developing, no matter how hard that felt.

She took a breath. 'I think it's time I told you the real reason I'm here in Athens.' She swallowed. 'I was actually meant to be in Paris.'

'What?' He turned his body towards her.

'When I arrived here I thought... I had a boyfriend. We were supposed to be going to Paris but then he had to work... or said he had to... and he told me he was here in Athens and Bonnie persuaded me that this could be the new Paris and, well, cutting a long story short... he was married.' God, it sounded so disgusting. Quickly, she followed it up. 'Obviously I had no idea. I mean, I'm not the type of person to do that. I would never and he... he was actually never someone I was ever completely honest with. He didn't know where I had come from or my circumstances and—'

'Jen—'

'No, I just wanted you to know because, well... now *I* know that he was not important to me. I can see that so clearly. And, what you said about wanting to take time and to work on yourself... I get that, I really do, because that's what I should be doing as well.' She nodded. 'It makes sense to... have some breathing space and really take time to figure out next steps.' She sighed. 'And I should have told you... before now... about David.'

Astro shrugged. 'You say you realise he was not important to you. And you did not paint him on the walls of Athens, you paint your Bravely Bear. That tells me everything I need to know.'

Now the air was charged again as she did meet his eyes. There was no doubt that being here with him was far from ideal, but there hadn't been any choice. And now she was left looking into his beautiful eyes trying desperately to hold on to her resolve so he could maintain his.

She got up then, quickly and, as she did, she spilt her glass of wine *and* Astro's.

'Oh my God! Oh! I am so sorry! Quick! Quick, take off your hoodie before it stains!'

She already had her hands at the hem of the hooded sweat-shirt and was heaving it upwards until he had no choice but to wriggle out of it, the T-shirt he had on underneath coming with it, leaving him bare-chested...

Jen took a breath, the hoodie in her hands now, her eyes not doing a very good job of concentrating on the task at hand, lingering on the lean, contoured-in-all-the-right-places torso right there with her...

'Vinegar!' Jen said hurriedly, eyes still not on the sweatshirt. 'We need to soak the stain with vinegar. Do you have some?'

'I think so,' Astro said, heading towards the kitchen area.

It was then that Jen looked to the sofa bed and realised that it too was covered in red wine. There was no way Astro was going to be sleeping on that tonight.

59

Jen closed her eyes for what felt like the millionth time, but sleep was as far away as the UK. Astro was lying next to her, no longer bare-chested but wearing a grey marl T-shirt that fitted so well it didn't take much imagination for Jen to be recalling the topless scene of earlier. They'd got as much red wine out of the hoodie as possible before putting it in the sink with detergent to soak. Then they had turned their attention to the sofa bed. But both of them had known it was going to be too stained and damp for anyone to rest on it that night. So... they had agreed to share the bed. Except this wasn't a king-size, this was some kind of narrow-European-double-that-wasn't-really-a-double, and Jen felt like she was clinging to the edge, as if the Astro side was really a volcanic crater that meant certain death if she slipped into it. She turned over, still very much on her edge, but facing the shape of his back which she could just make out in the dark.

'Are you awake?' she whispered. It had taken her a good few minutes to pluck up the courage to speak at all. Maybe it was the combination of the dark and Astro's close proximity that was giving her the courage now.

'No,' he replied.

She smiled as he rolled over, shifting his body until he was facing her.

'You cannot sleep,' he stated.

'Neither can you.'

'Usually, when I cannot sleep, I go to Psyrri and I paint.'

'I make hot chocolate and listen to the top hundred best Christmas songs.'

He laughed and the sound warmed her. It was gentle, light, but somehow incredibly sexy...

'Do you think your uncle will sell the bar?'

'I do not know.' He sighed. 'I do not think that he knows yet.'

'What will you do if he does?'

'The first thing I will do is make sure that the new owners know that Marjorie is the very best worker and tell them they should not only keep her on, they should pay her more.'

And there it was. His kind soul. The way he cared about people. One of the many qualities she loved about him.

Love.

'But, what about what *you'll* do? Will you find another bar?'

'I do not know that either.' He sighed again. 'Maybe. Because I will need to find somewhere to live, and I will need to pay the rent.'

The very thing that Jen hadn't been able to do on her own apartment. She put a finger to her earlobe and pressed the angel earring for some kind of celestial solidarity.

'I had to give up my apartment.'

'What?'

'I had to decide between my business premises and my home. I chose Christmas Every Day. To be honest, apart from feeling disappointed that I hadn't managed to keep both of them, it was an easy decision to make. I was never going to turn my back on something that's had *my* back for as long as I can remember.'

'So, you live where you work? Like me?'

She smiled into the dark. 'You would hate it. I have tinsel everywhere, even in the toilet.'

'I would not hate it,' Astro whispered. 'Because you love it.'

Was it Jen's imagination or were they now closer together in the bed? It suddenly felt like if she stretched out a finger it would reach him.

She closed her eyes and took a long, slow breath inward, trying to channel inner peace and restful thoughts. The fluttering of wings had her snapping her eyes open again.

'Is Peri all right?' she asked.

'*Ne*,' he answered. 'He likes to sleep on my book of paintings by Wassily Kandinsky. He will settle soon.'

Again, Jen shut her eyes and tried to tell her body it needed to rest. As soon as Astro was asleep, she could make a dome out of the covers. *Think happy, gentle thoughts.* Except all she could think about was the fact she was lying next to a person she cared so very much about, someone she found stupidly attractive, a man with so many intriguing facets of which she knew she had only just scratched the surface. It was torment. She wanted nothing more than to slide across the sheet and press herself closer.

'Astro,' she whispered. 'Will you hold my hand?'

She held her breath, waiting for a response. But all she could hear was the kind of sound that told her Astro had fallen asleep.

60

ACHILLES'S SCHOOL, PLAKA

It had snowed all night, lightly, but the wind that had come with it had brought its own issues. It had turned the banks of snow into spiralling whirlwinds, flicking up the fresh powder and spraying it anew. As Astro stood outside the school, the area having been swept as much as possible, Christmas trees at the entrance and eager children with red cheeks, handing out what looked like maps of the inside with all the different areas of interest, he remembered exactly why he knew it had snowed all night.

He'd watched it. Because he couldn't sleep in the bed next to Jen, not without it crucifying him. He looked at her now. She was with Bonnie, Achilles, and Marjorie, rushing back and forth with the over-excited boy who also seemed nervous for some reason, hands full of things – Christingles, pieces of wood made into candleholders, calendars.

When Jen had asked him to hold her hand last night his heart had soared. And that's when he had known. Despite everything he'd told her while they'd been sitting on the rocks overlooking the city, knowing he really *did* need to work on himself, there was something inside screaming at him. He didn't want to call time on this. He wanted to hold on to whatever this was, nurture it, embrace it hard. Perhaps he wasn't in the perfect place, but was anyone ever really in that position? But, despite feeling that way, he didn't want to go fast too soon. He had hurt her already. He didn't want to do that again. And, more importantly, he wanted *her* to be sure. He could have held her hand, reached out almost selfishly, quickly put them back together again, but in the dark, half-asleep, something had told him to wait just a little longer.

Jen was helping Marjorie attach a beard to Achilles's face whilst Bonnie dabbed at the boy's cheeks with glittery paint.

Jen was someone who made other people's lives better. A fixer. A nurturer. She was someone who never judged him, only accepted him for who he was, even when he knew he wanted to be so much more. Her thoughts, her feelings, her values – he had learned so much from her since she had been in Athens. They had shared such a similar past, such hard and difficult childhoods, yet she had risen out of it still carrying hope, managing so bravely.

Bravely.

He thought of the mural then. He knew in that picture he had seen inside Jen's mind and he knew that was a place she didn't let anyone in easily. Was there a chance they could turn this around? A chance to tell her that although he was committed to becoming better, to trying to properly work through his grief now and look for new beginnings, that maybe it didn't have to be the sole choice?

'Astro! Do I look like a king or Saint Vasilis?' Achilles yelled across to him.

He waved a hand. 'You look like them both!'

'You are more handsome than both,' Marjorie shouted back.

'Ugh! *Mama!*'

Astro looked to the old school building, bedecked in sparkling garlands, a sign strung across the front advertising the event, people swaddled up in thick coats against the winter weather. In reality, the event should have been cancelled. The airport was still closed, bus services were non-existent and only those brave enough were getting into their cars. However, Astro knew how hard Achilles and his friends had worked on their creations and he suspected the go-ahead had been given because the tears and tantrums of the children would have been worse than any loss in footfall. Besides, feet were one of the only ways to travel right now and if the citizens of Athens could make it out for coffee, then maybe they could make it here too.

'It's bloody freezing!' Bonnie announced, stamping her feet on the ground, and tucking the scarf around her neck into her coat.

'That is true,' Astro agreed. He hadn't seen her approach as he was still watching Jen and Marjorie toy with Achilles's costume.

'So, Jen would hate that I'm going to talk to you about this, but I wouldn't be her true best friend if I didn't. Because I want what's best for her. Always.'

'O-K,' Astro replied, his heart rate rapidly increasing.

'Are you seriously done?' Bonnie asked, gloved hands on her hips. 'I mean, I'm all for being the best you can be, but are you really going to kiss goodbye to the chance of something with the most wonderful person I know?'

'You are right,' Astro responded. 'Jen would hate that you are talking to me about this.'

'Well, what am I supposed to do?' Bonnie said, arms flailing about. 'Because you're both as bad as each other. Both too damaged by all accounts to put any faith in unique possibilities gifted by the universe.'

'Has she said something to you?'

Did Jen know that he hadn't been asleep last night? Had she seen him from his position by the window, looking at her, longing to curl her hair around his fingers, to not only hold her hand but to wrap her up in his arms and never let go?

'Nothing since she arrived back at our hotel in floods of tears when she never ever cries and told me that her heart was breaking. Since then, she's moved back to being Work Jen. *That* Jen focuses on everything and everyone that *isn't* her. And it's not helped by the fact that she's now trying to organise an event here in Athens to be beamed to the UK probably via an Elon Musk satellite. It's all needing traditional dancers and a history trail of the city and something culminating in an extravaganza at the Parthenon which might not even be possible but, as my sister, Andrea, once sat next to the Greek Prime Minister at a dinner I'm going to ask her to pull whatever strings she has available to make this happen for Jen. But...' Bonnie stopped talking and pointed a gloved finger at Astro. 'While I'm doing all that, I want you to think about Not Work Jen. That Jen deserves the moon and an entire freaking galaxy. And she likes you... *more* than likes you... more than I've ever seen her like anyone before. And, yeah, it's crazy that we're here by chance and it's even madder that we're having this conversation in actual Greek snow but, Astro, if you feel for Jen like I think you do then don't let this chance be missed. Jen has had so many missed chances in her life – through no fault of her own – and she is the absolute worst at taking a second for herself. She's probably not going to tell you how much she cares, because she wants to put you and your needs first. Do not let her.'

She really liked him. She was putting his feelings first. He had broken her heart.

It was a lot to take in. But it was nothing that he didn't already know on some level. He really liked her. He wanted her feelings to be nothing but happy going forward. His heart had been so heavy when she'd left him at Strefi Hill.

'Right, well,' Bonnie said, putting her fingers to her hat and pulling it down. 'I've said my piece and, in fact, all the pieces, so I'm going to head inside before my hair freezes.'

She made to leave.

'Bonnie,' Astro said.

She turned back.

'*Efharisto*,' he said. 'Thank you. For the pieces.'

'OK.' Bonnie nodded. 'No idea how you're going to put them all together but... I'll leave it with you.'

Astro took a deep breath and watched everyone moving inside. He knew what he was going to do. He just hoped it wasn't too late.

61

The large hall at the school had been decorated beautifully. When it came to festive décor, Jen was forever internally critical. Obviously, she wouldn't ever voice her thoughts, but she acknowledged the difference between a room that had been put together with little thought for co-ordination and the end result and something that had been thoroughly planned. This was definitely the latter. Paper spirals of silver and gold cascaded down from the ceiling, angels revolved on wheels made from wire, and there was a real fir tree in one corner filled with decorations she assumed the children had made. Many of them were of a similar style to hers, perhaps crafted by her little protégé, Achilles.

'I hate all this,' Marjorie muttered.

'What? Christmas?' Jen asked, a little taken aback.

'No, not Christmas. School events.' She sighed. 'There are two types of Greek mother. The ones who have paid for expensive items from the store instead of helping their children make them. And the others who have made them *instead* of their children, using the kind of skills only an architect should have.'

'Oh,' Jen said, looking at the group of women Marjorie was talking about.

'I know what you are thinking. You are thinking what group I am in,' Marjorie continued, chewing on the corner of her thumbnail. 'Because *you* are the one who has helped Achilles make decorations and jewellery, not me.'

'I wasn't—'

'I am not in any group. I have little money and I have no skills in this... crafting.' She sighed again. 'I think that I always let Achilles down.'

'Oh, no you don't!' Jen said immediately, turning to face Marjorie. 'You are the best mother to him... from what I've seen.'

The conversation was touching a nerve and even though it probably wasn't her place, Jen felt compelled to continue.

'You have provided him with a roof over his head, food, school, care and, most important of all... love.' She gazed over at Achilles now. He was presenting his jewellery wares with a flourish, absolutely intent on doing a great job. 'From the first time I met him... after I made him cry because I thought he was going to pinch my bag that is... he's never been without a smile on his face. He laughs and he grins and he looks after Peri the pigeon with care and nothing in life seems to faze him. And I'm sure that's down to you, Marjorie.'

The woman shook her head. 'I do not know about that. Always I think I could be doing more.'

Jen put a hand on her arm. 'I didn't have anyone growing up. The people that were supposed to take care of me didn't really want to. Trust me, everything you're doing for Achilles is more than enough. And everything you've said about those groups of mums tells me that what they *think* they're doing for their children, they're really only doing because of their own insecurities.'

Marjorie seemed to muse on her statement for a moment, her gaze going to and from the other parents.

'I very much want to see the ornaments made by Konstantina sell for only a euro. She tell everyone they were made with real gold thread from her grandfather's best priest robes.'

'Goodness! That is extra,' Jen said.

'Oh, what is Achilles doing now? Is he trying to get that man to buy a whole bag of things? I know it is all for the school to buy new books and art supplies but this is like extortion, no?' Marjorie headed across the hall. 'Achilles!'

Jen smiled, watching Marjorie interact with her son. She turned around in a bid to find out where Bonnie had got to but there was Astro. She swallowed. Last night, sharing a bed with him, had been as tough as it gets when all the feelings she had inside were so intense. You could tell yourself it wasn't wise, wasn't right or sensible, but that didn't magically turn those feelings off. And this morning, before coming here, they had both focused on the needs of Peri – topping up bird seed, checking his leg, playing him his favourite Ariana Grande song – and danced around everything left unspoken. Then it had been time to meet everyone here.

'I bought you a coffee,' Astro said, holding out a small paper cup.

'Oh, thank you.' She accepted it, feeling a little awkward.

'I do not know if it will be good. A group of kids Achilles's age are making it. There is someone supervising but...'

Jen took a sip of the dark liquid. 'Ooh, it's strong but I like it like that.'

Somehow a silence descended between them, only the sounds of the general chatter and notes of music from a small band in the corner to be heard. Until Astro spoke again...

'So, Bonnie told me you are doing an event here in Athens.'

'That's the very new, very fresh, not-really-thought-through idea right now. I don't even know if it will be possible but everyone who isn't me seems to think it can work.'

'She said you need traditional dancers, perhaps someone with historical knowledge to make a trail through the best sites of Athens.'

'Something like that. In the snow. When nothing is really making a trail anywhere at the moment.' She sighed. 'The more I think about it, the crazier it sounds. I don't know how long the snow is going to stop me from going back to the UK. But, if the snow goes too soon, I lose the opportunity to make it part of an event I have run out of options for so, well, it's a dilemma.'

'Which is the reason you should let me help,' Astro told her.

'I can't ask you to do that.'

'I know,' he said, a smile already forming at the corners of his mouth. 'You don't ever really want to ask anyone for help.'

She knew she was going to blush before it kicked in. He really did know how her mind worked.

'Well, I'm still a little bit sore about the fact my assistant, Natalia, came up with the idea and not me. I'm supposed to be the brains behind the company and I was floundering for quite some time.'

'Is that not why you have an assistant? To help you?'

'Yes, but—'

'So she is helping. Like she is meant to.'

'But I'm usually the ideas person and—'

'And you do not have to do everything on your own. That is kind of what you have been telling me ever since you arrived here.'

She knew Astro had a point. Obviously, he was right. But when it was ingrained in her to always take everything on her own shoulders, that relying on others was a mistake. It was hard to shift that mentality, even now.

'Let me arrange the dancers,' Astro said. 'There is a group

coming here, to the school. The man in charge I know. He went to school with Philippos.'

'Astro... my budget for this is quite tight. I do not know how much they usually charge but—'

'Relax, Jen,' Astro said, putting a hand on her shoulder. 'We can work everything out.'

We can work everything out. She looked into his eyes and felt a sharp pang of regret. Was that really even possible at this stage?

'Let me help you,' he said. 'And Marjorie and Achilles will help too. And my uncle and Mr and Mrs Sinrades and anyone else I can find.'

'Astro, I can't ask that—'

'I know, Jen. But, as I said, you're not asking. I am offering and so will everyone else when they find out that this famous Christmas girl from England needs to put on a show in their city.'

Famous Christmas girl.

She knew how Astro felt about Christmas but somehow the way he had said it now made it sound like it was her biggest attribute and she was some kind of celebrity. Like she was worth something. She swallowed. She knew her worth but she also knew that sometimes her need to be a lone solider made her overlook the best intentions from those around her. Those who really cared.

'OK,' she said with a firm nod. 'Then, after this, we need to do some brainstorming.'

'OK,' Astro answered. He took a sip of his drink. 'And I will make certain there is more strong coffee.'

62

PLAKA DISTRICT

Three days later

The air was freezing, so cold it was too cold to snow any more. But, because of the drop in temperature, the snow thankfully remained. The airport had opened back up the previous day but the flights were still fully booked as airlines attempted to catch up. That was a bit of a relief as now that Jen was fully invested in providing the historical society with a Greek Christmas walk-through, she needed to stick around. It was also good to see that Athens was back to being a hive of activity. Those Athenians who had been snowbound were heading back to work, buses were up to full speed again and the city was once again a mecca for festive sightseeing and Christmas shopping.

'Natalia, can you see this whole area fully?' Jen asked. She was testing the technology ahead of tonight's performance. Having never done something in real time that was going to be broadcast on a big screen to an audience in another country, she had needed to undertake a lot of research, with the help of Bonnie, whose no-nonsense translating of the film-making terminology had made it possible. If she'd had more time and if she wasn't using up everyone in the vicinity's goodwill, plus her small monetary budget, she would have pre-recorded the whole thing in case the live stream went down. But everyone had jobs, other things to do; they were all assembling this evening and they had one shot at it.

'Natalia!' Jen called, looking into the camera. 'Please answer! The signal hasn't gone, has it?'

'I have toffee stuck!' came the response as Natalia's face moved in different shapes and forms. 'What do I do? I need teeth!'

'Oh no,' Jen said. 'Have a drink? Soften it up a bit?' She didn't have time for a sweet crisis. She had very limited time to put lots of things in place and Natalia's noises as she tried to dislodge the toffee was drawing strange looks from passers-by in Syntagma Square.

This was where they were going to show the traditions of Greece, including Achilles and some of his friends telling the story of Saint Vasilis and one of the street vendors showing how you make *koulouria* – the sesame bread rings that were sold on every street corner here. Then, on the hour, they would showcase the changing of the guard outside the parliament building. It was still a performance that Jen loved as much now as the first time she and Bonnie had watched it – so regimented in all the best ways, sad and serene, yet also powerful. Then it would be a wander through the best street art areas in Psyrri – highlighting that Greece and its capital weren't only about ancient relics and arte-facts. Then it was on to Anafiotika, the troupe of traditional dancers leading a dance up the tiny, winding streets with scarves, to Mr and Mrs Sinrades's garden. There, traditional musicians would play, before everyone who had taken part thus far – excluding the soldiers at the parliament building who would have had no idea they *had* been taking part – would head up to the Acropolis and into the Parthenon.

Jen still couldn't believe all this had come together in three days and how many people Astro had managed to get on board here. Both he and Bonnie had been a whirlwind of activity in different ways, ways that Jen was certain would cause a bigger cyclone to swirl in an opposing direction, but it seemed she only had to mention the need for something and one of them would offer an immediate solution as if nothing was too much trouble. Exactly like what had happened with them being allowed access to the Parthenon after it was officially closed. That was down to Andrea. It seemed sitting next to influential people at five-star hotels in London carried enough sway to get you a golden key from the Greek officials...

'Toffee is gone from teeth!' Natalia informed her. 'I think it is stuck on lung now... but I can speak.'

Jen had almost forgotten what she had asked her assistant. 'So... can you see everything? Or are there areas the camera isn't getting?'

'I see... giant tree. I see fountain! There is fountain when it snow?'

'It wasn't working for a few days but it's back working now. Good. Can you see the steps?'

'Yes, I see many steps. There is less snow there.'

There was a lot less snow and where there was more footfall it was beginning to get sludgy and grey. She had gone from wishing the snow away to hoping there might be a little more before tonight's performance. Not too much that it would hamper things but a light dusting to make everything brighter, whiter and that little bit more magical.

'Yes, there is less snow, but I think it's going to be fine.'

'You do not think,' Natalia said. 'You *know*. Like I know I am never playing the Christmas bingo with Kathleen again.'

'Oh, you didn't play bingo with Kathleen, did you?'

'This is what I say. She talk between the man calling the festive things and I do not know if I am marking my stuffing or my baubles.'

'Is she OK with me not being back for the carol concert? I mean, she said she was and there isn't really anything I can do but—'

'She is mad,' Natalia answered. 'Only because she hates my singing. I try to follow words but "bleaks" and "midwinters" and "Wenceslas", they are not real words, are they?'

'So, you're going with her? Oh, Natalia, thank you. I mean, everything you've been doing with Kathleen while I've been away is just so much more than I could have hoped for.'

'I like strange angry old lady. She remind me of grandmother in Ukraine. They have the very same being rude and hairs on chin.'

'OK, right, well, when I get to the next location I'll video message you again and we can work out the best place to set up the camera there.'

'OK. So, shall I wait for next location before I tell you about issue with menu?'

Jen's heart dropped. 'There's a problem with the menu? For tonight?'

'I did not say "problem", I say "issue". It will be fine. I have Ukraine deli on speed dial.'

A sharp icy wind hit Jen's face, forcing her to take a deep breath and steady her stance. 'OK, well, yes please, wait until the next location.'

Her phone vibrated as Natalia disappeared. It was a message from Astro and before she could check herself, her heart was rising like a nearly-mended pigeon who had been given all the seed. She needed to quell that feeling, particularly when she had this all-important event to focus on.

Everything good in Anafiotika. No need for you to check the route through Psyrri either. Achilles thinks Peri should have a costume like he does. Marjorie thinks her nails should be manicured before she appears on camera. Bonnie is being Bonnie. My uncle is talking of shaving. He has had a beard for as long as I have been alive. What are you doing to us, Miss Christmas?

What followed were a set of emojis. A pigeon, painted nails, a man with a beard and a Christmas tree. Astro sending anything Christmas related to her was barely believable when you thought back to the beginning of their story.

Jen sighed as she looked out over a snow-dashed Syntagma Square. *Their* story. It wasn't so much a full novel, more a short story perhaps heading for a friendship conclusion. But perhaps that was all either of them needed it to be. It had been something strong, something good, something true. It was certainly something neither of them had expected and it had been something that had made them both re-evaluate their lives. For Jen, this time with Astro had taught her that no matter how compatible a man appeared on paper – or rather digitally on an app – nothing compared to getting to know someone in person and basing your judgement solely on that. Having superficial things in common – like both enjoying the same type of shows on Prime Video or having once learned French – was not a full-proof yardstick at all. And she felt that she knew Astro more than she had ever known David or any other of her previous dates. Perhaps it was simply because she had never planned for this time, this place, or this person. Maybe it was because the universe had intervened.

She shook herself then, putting a hand to the top button on her coat and making sure it was fastened tight. This event and the speed in which it had all come together was starting to make her think that Christmas magic *was* real and not just something she usually made happen for others.

Ducking her head against the chill wind, she headed out of the square.

63

PSYRRI

Astro looked at his phone screen. There had been a brief burst of the three bubbles that said a reply was imminent and then nothing. Maybe he shouldn't have called Jen 'Miss Christmas'. Why had he mentioned that Philippos was thinking of getting rid of his beard? It was hardly great material to lay the groundwork for asking Jen on a date later tonight. That was his plan. Not his only plan. But if she didn't agree to the first part then the rest of it was going to have been for nothing. He sighed. No, it wouldn't have been for nothing because emotionally, with his whole heart, he would have taken a chance. And if that was all it turned out to be then he was still grateful for that.

Putting the phone back in the pocket of his jeans, he began to climb up the ladder that was propped against the wall of an old, crumbling hotel.

'I like the ropes!' a shout came from above.

Astro smiled. It was Petros, hanging up high, a wide canvas belt around his middle from which paints, spray cans, brushes, sponges, and any implement you could imagine were dangling or poked loosely into pockets.

'You know you are only meant to use the ropes to move along the platform, not swing from them like you are in a circus act,' Astro said. He stepped off the ladder and onto the platform that was somewhat precariously balanced on scaffolding he and his friends had constructed two nights ago. Thanks to a small tower they had acquired some time ago and other pieces of junk added to it, they could reach the bricks easily. This was as high as they had ever been.

'How long do we have left?' Petros asked, spraying a section in a copper colour.

'Before we need to be out of here? Or before someone calls the police?'

He put his hand to the brickwork right in front of him, smudged to create texture. This piece needed to be finished faster than anything he had done before, but it also had to be perfect. If it wasn't how he had envisaged it, then he'd feel nothing but the deepest, darkest disappointment. He had to give this everything and more.

'I thought you had created an arrangement with your uncle's friend?' Petros asked, referring to something he was holding in his hand and then marking out a line in chalk.

'There is a loose arrangement,' Astro replied. 'But I did not exactly tell him we would be painting the side of this hotel.'

Petros laughed, his dreadlocks shaking. 'What *did* you tell him we were painting?'

Astro thought back to the conversation with the policeman as he had caught Dimitri at his usual coffee spot early the other day. He had been specifically non-specific, carefully making sure not to drop the words 'street art' or 'graffiti' into the chat. It hadn't taken more than a few sentences before his uncle's friend had made it clear that he understood and for Astro to stop talking, as the less the man knew, the less he had to deny should it come to it.

'This hotel has long been in need of a face-lift,' Astro answered.

'Now he agrees!' Petros said, the hand holding a brush gesticulating to the sky, the other wrapped around the rope he was less than securely tied to. 'We have been telling you this for the past twelve months. Possibly more. And you always said no.'

Astro whipped a small knife from Petros's pocket and used it to chip away at the brickwork. What Petros had just said made it sound like Astro had decreed that this large perfect blank canvas was unavailable to his friends. As though he had been keeping it for something. It was crazy to think that was true...

'Hey! You will make that blunt!' Petros said, wriggling on his line and trying to grab the knife back. 'If you are wanting to break the bricks, use this chisel.'

Astro swapped the tools and shook his head, a smile on his lips. 'You are always so prepared.' He dug the tool into the brick then smoothed the crumbs of dust as they disintegrated.

'Except for this,' Petros admitted. 'Three days, Astro. For something of this scale, with this much detail.'

'I know,' Astro said, pulling pieces of plaster away with his fingers. 'I have asked a lot of everyone. Too much. Everyone's time and materials and all the risk – not just from the heights but, well, you know.'

'What I do know,' Petros began, his dark eyes entirely on Astro now. 'Is that this is the first time since you created the boy with the moon that I feel all your emotions, your heart and your soul have truly been in your art.'

Astro made to respond, opened his mouth, not knowing whether his immediate reaction was going to be to confirm or deny it. But then he thought twice. He knew Petros was right. He felt it too. Designing this mural, then setting the project in motion, getting his friends to understand his vision and the speed needed to deliver it, heading down here every night after work at the bar until dawn began... it had been as exhausting as it had been necessary. With Jen in his bed, her swirls of hair fanned out on the pillow beside him, one hand to her cheek, lips slightly parted, he'd also welcomed the excuse not to be there and be tormented by everything that could have been. Everything that he had decided he wanted to try to restore...

'You don't need to say anything, Astro,' Petros said, eyes back on his work. 'This picture, it speaks for itself.'

Astro knew it did. He'd stood back on his approach here and looked at the very-near-to-completion artwork and tried to see it as a neutral, a street-art enthusiast or an ordinary passer-by. But it had been impossible. It was just so powerful to him. Each part of it hit him hard, every component reaching inside and punching its way through his body. But there were still parts he wanted to enhance as Petros boldened sections they'd discussed at around 3 a.m. this morning. However, they were running out of time now.

'You have until maybe ten tonight,' Astro told him. 'But remember, it has to be completely covered up between seven thirty and eight o'clock.'

'I remember,' Petros replied. 'We are to behave like real artists as the procession passes through. No loud music, all looking tidy, no spraying political statements that could be caught on camera. I do not know why we are being featured at all.'

His friend had said it wryly, but Astro knew there was a hint of truth behind it.

'Petros, it is important to Jen to show her clients more of Athens than is in the traditional guidebooks. They are a historical society, yes, but she also wants to introduce them to something new. Anyway, one day we *will* be old enough to stand alongside Zeus and Dionysus as part of the history of the city.'

'Is she not ending the tour with the Parthenon like everyone else?' Petros asked, one pierced eyebrow raising up on his forehead.

'Yes, but, come on, everyone *needs* the Parthenon and it has snow! Even you have to admit it looks great with snow.'

'I admit that maybe it's kind of cool to be breaking the law and having that sent over the internet to the UK.'

'See!' Astro said, slapping his shoulder and making him sway on the ropes. 'Being a felon *and* helping out a friend. It's a win/win.'

'Not if you carry on breaking up bricks like that,' Petros answered. 'We don't have that long.'

It was true. Astro rubbed his fingers over the granules he had dislodged, refining some corners, roughing up other segments. This would definitely have to be sprayed now, but it was better this way than before. Over time, the bricks would deteriorate further and it would give this section life, an ever-changing fluidity, which was exactly what he had been aiming for with the entire project. It was being painted to last. Something to be admired and photographed for many years to come, exactly like the other crumbling ruins.

'I will get the other cans,' Astro said as he reached for the ladder again.

'Of paint?' Petros called. 'Or Fix?'

'Maybe I will get both,' Astro replied.

64

SYNTAGMA SQUARE

'Repeat after me,' Bonnie said, holding Jen's shoulders as light snow fell like divinely provided confetti from the sky. 'This is not the Royal Variety Performance.'

'This is not the—' Jen stopped talking. 'Why am I meant to be saying that this isn't the Royal Variety Performance?'

'Take a deep breath,' Bonnie encouraged again. 'And say "whatever happens at least there are no fake blood cannons".'

'I'm glad for that,' Jen said. 'But I'm not going to say it.'

'Have a slug of ouzo,' Bonnie said. 'I bought a couple of those travel-sized miniatures that are never good value, but I can fit one in each coat pocket.' She held one up and Jen swore she could smell the liquorice scent hit the air.

'Why do I need a slug of ouzo?'

Her eyes were on everyone on standby here in the square – the dancers, the man making pretzels, even the soldiers across the street who she was worried would suddenly decide to abandon tradition and head home before she had filmed them. They were minutes away from beginning this ridiculously-complicated-speedily-put-together event which was either going to elevate her to goddess-like status in the festive-planning arena or it was going to be the beginning of the end of Christmas Every Day and she was going to face a future where she might have to beg the nursing home to let her apartment-share with Kathleen.

'Because you're shaking,' Bonnie stated bluntly. 'And it's not from the cold because seeing as it's snowing again, the temperature has actually risen not dropped. So, it must be nervous anticipation and we don't want the camera shaking, do we?'

It was only when Bonnie had vocalised it that Jen realised she *was* quivering. She didn't get like this before events! But, then again, that was probably because she had always arranged them far in advance, with every detail thought through at least three times. She hadn't had that luxury here but what she had had was more support than she could ever have envisaged. This hadn't been Classic Jen, the lone entrepreneur not wanting anyone to lend a hand because who could you trust as much as yourself? This has been a Jen who had accepted assistance almost willingly, someone who had nearly delegated tasks without gnashing her teeth...

'OK,' she said. 'Give me the ouzo. I'll have just the tiniest bit.'

But before she could even put the bottle to her mouth her phone was ringing.

Natalia.

'Oh my God! Why is Natalia ringing me? She should be making sure the canapes are going out.'

Since the Athens event had been pulled together, Jen had made some tweaks to the menu being served to the historical society in the refectory of the local cathedral. As well as the canapes featuring aged cheddar, she had managed to procure others featuring goats' cheese and oranges – so similar to the bright fruits still ripe and lush on many of the trees they were going to see on the tour. The starter was still salmon but now with a confit of figs, the main course a hog that had been roasted for hours with lemon and oregano roast potatoes and seasonal vegetables, and for pudding they had the society members' favourite, traditional trifle, but there was also now Greek *baklava* instead of mince pies to go with after-dinner coffees. Jen had Greg to thank for the *baklava*. He said he had never made it before, but he was up for the challenge and Jen knew he hadn't let her down. He had sent photos of the crispy and gooey trays of pastry-wrapped deliciousness earlier and it all looked divine.

'Breathe,' Bonnie said. 'And answer it.'

Bonnie was right. Jen needed to keep her head, the way she usually did. She answered the call.

'Jen… is that you?'

'Natalia, why are you whispering?'

'I am in crypt.'

'What?! Why aren't you in the refectory making sure everyone is having a good time? Are they having canapes, because we are going live in no time at all and—'

'We have situation,' Natalia rasped.

'A situation? What situation?'

Jen didn't need a situation. She needed happy, smiling, history-obsessed customers chowing down on fine festive fayre with a little Greek influence.

'Geoffrey is here.'

'What?'

'He arrive. With others. He say he will perform for cut price. I make phone call to theatre where he meant to be. They have problem with plumbing and have cancelled shows. We are second option for him.'

Now Jen's head was revolving with anger more than anything else. Geoffrey had ditched her at the first opportunity, knowing he would be leaving her in turmoil. Now he wanted to swan back in?

'I tie him up,' Natalie informed.

'Sorry, what?'

'I tie him up. My brothers make others leave. Most are unharmed. I put Geoffrey in crypt but he is crying like baby and the noise is distracting. I have turned up Christmas music mix with bouzouki greatest hits but he cry loud... even with gag in mouth.'

Jen had no words and Bonnie was looking at her curiously. Her assistant had someone *imprisoned* in the cathedral. She needed to think quickly. Make a decision that was best for everyone. She swallowed as all the thoughts started to gang up on each other. A decision that was best for everyone? Or, perhaps this time, a decision that was best for her...

'Are the society aware of Geoffrey or anything that's going on?' Jen asked.

Bonnie mouthed the word 'Geoffrey' and put her hands to her face in a show of despair.

'No,' came Natalia's reply. 'And Kathleen is watching him right now. She has knitting needle and crochet hook.'

Kathleen was there. Why was Kathleen there?

You don't have time for this.

'Keep him there,' Jen found herself blurting out. 'Until after the event.'

'Good,' Natalia said. 'I only call you before you call me and wonder why I sound like I am in dark cave. When brothers come back I will leave Artem here and Kathleen can help me with fake snow.'

Jen had heard more than enough. However, she knew her assistant's heart was in the right place and she only had the good of the company at the centre of all her decisions, no matter how crazy those decisions might sometimes be.

'Natalia, you're doing a great job and I so appreciate everything you're organising while I'm away and—'

'Is pleasure. Really,' Natalia interrupted. 'I like the being in charge.'

Being charge? She *wasn't* in charge!

'Jen! Plato says he will not sing unless he has food!'

It was Achilles tugging at her sleeve now. She needed to end this phone call and concentrate on making this tour of a city she had really fallen for the best event it could be.

'Natalia, let me know when the society are all sat down and we'll get this underway. Speak soon.'

She put her phone back in her pocket and turned to Bonnie.

'Please don't make me explain about Geoffrey now,' she said before her best friend could make any comment. 'We have work to do.'

65

PSYRRI

'Astro! I cannot make the sheet fix!'

Astro's friend, Cora, was struggling high above them. His heart was racing now, and he knew it was all his fault. Everyone had spent too long putting unnecessary finishing touches to the artwork because he had demanded it. Now they were in danger of not being ready when Jen, the camera and the entourage of performers arrived for the next section of the tour. Plus, if the covering wasn't put over then the impact he had hoped for would be lost.

'I am coming,' Astro called upwards, rushing to the ladder.

'Astro, take care,' Petros warned. 'One of those rungs is getting really shaky.'

He didn't have time to think about anything other than covering up the partial exposure of the mural in double quick time. After powering up the rungs, he was up and onto the platform fast, despite the flurries of powdery snow in the air. Cora was on the ropes, holding the edge of the dust sheet-cum-tarpaulin, trying to fix it onto a peg Astro had hit into the brickwork himself.

'I thought I could reach,' she explained, breathless. 'But the cover is heavy and—'

'It is OK,' he replied. 'You go back down. I will fix it.'

'Are you certain?'

'Yes, honestly, go.' There wasn't room for two people to be up here stretching for the same space.

He waited for Cora to move to the platform then squeeze past him to get to the ladder then, once he was sure she was safely on her way down, he made a grab for the rope. Everything was dry up here now and hopefully the bottom section was too. At least the light snow wasn't likely to penetrate the wrappings.

He picked up the end of the tarp and, wrapping his legs around the rope, he shimmied up it, his core straining as he tried to hook the cover into position. Finally, with one last effort, he managed to get the material over the hook and the picture was wholly concealed.

He took a breath, smoothing a palm over the tarpaulin and sending out a whispered message to the universe. He closed his eyes.

'Let this work.'

The next thing he knew, he was slipping from the rope.

* * *

'What's the time, Bonnie?' Jen asked. 'How long has it been?'

Her friend looked at the screen of her phone as they rushed up the narrow streets into the Psyrri district, a trail of people behind. Everything in Syntagma Square had gone really well as far as the Greek side of things was concerned, but Jen was still on edge about everything back in the UK. Had there been any technical glitches? Was the spirit of everything translating through video link? Were the society happy? And then there was Geoffrey in the crypt…

'Oh! I forgot to start the stopwatch!' Bonnie exclaimed. 'Shall I start it now?'

'Bonnie!'

They were meant to be timing the intervals between the sections of entertainment. The group had to walk to and from locations, get set up for the next section and Jen wanted every-thing perfectly managed.

'It has been only seven minutes and thirty-five seconds,' Achilles answered, showing Jen the numbers on his watch.

'Oh, Achilles, thank you! You didn't need to do that, but I am ever so glad you did.'

'I can do it too,' Plato chirped up.

'We do not need you to do it too, Plato,' Achilles admonished, adopting a grumpy expression.

Jen took a breath. She was waiting for a call from Natalia to cue the start of the next event – the artists here – but it really all had to fit in with estimated timings for when the society were being served the next courses of food. It was a lot to juggle and the last thing she needed was two scrapping children and a friend who couldn't seem to set a stopwatch. She halted her thoughts. That was a little bit mean. Bonnie had pulled out all the other stops for her, including the highlight of the event, the private tour of the Parthenon…

She put a hand on her friend's arm. 'Don't worry about the stopwatch. We just really need to wait for Natalia.'

'Want another slug of ouzo?' Bonnie offered, producing one of the mini bottles from her pocket.

'Astro!'

Now Achilles was running forward, getting his toga-style costume covered in sludge. And there was Astro, and behind him all his friends who were going to put on a demonstration of how they turned these decaying walls into art.

Jen's insides were already reacting to seeing him, despite her better judgement.

'Hey, Achilles,' Astro replied. 'How did everything go at Syntagma?'

The question had definitely been addressed to Jen. She smiled, ready to reply.

'It was so good!' Achilles jumped in. 'I now know how to make pastry!'

'And I stepped like the soldiers!' Plato announced, bringing his leg up and then slapping it down to the ground, spraying slush everywhere.

'It's been quite hectic,' Jen said.

'I am just going to take some photos of everyone for your website,' Bonnie said, phone already poised. 'Ones that will hopefully be sitting next to a glowing testimonial from the historical society.'

'Or next to my police mug shot when everyone finds out I condoned an imprisonment.'

'What?' Astro asked.

'Come on, lads,' Bonnie said to Achilles and Plato. 'Let's get some photos of you doing spraying too. Traditional costumes meets... I don't know... Banksy?'

Achilles and Plato hurried after Bonnie, both desperate to be first to be photographed.

'The rivalry,' Astro joked. 'I remember what it was like to be their age.'

'Me too,' Jen said. 'I think I was around that age when I perfected my skill of giving good Chinese burns should they be called on.' She smiled. 'Sorry, that wasn't very peace and goodwill, was it? How are things going here? Is everyone ready?'

'We are ready,' Astro agreed, nodding.

'And no one's going to swear on camera, are they?'

'What do you take us for?' He raised an eyebrow. 'You make us sound like law breakers.'

'Well, you did make me run from the police once.'

'My reputation precedes me, I get it. But we are going to be on our best street artist behaviour for your event and—'

'And I am going to pay you in spray cans or paints or brushes or whatever you need so everyone can keep doing what they're doing,' Jen said.

'Jen, you do not need to do that. Everyone is happy to show their work to people in the UK.'

'I know,' Jen said. 'But, please, let me do something for you.'

She wet her lips. She shouldn't say she was doing it for him. It implied that there was still a romantic connection between them and, as much as she might want that, it obviously wasn't meant to be. She rephrased. 'For everyone.'

Her phone began to ring. *Natalia*. She looked at the screen and waited. Five rings. That was her cue. She had five minutes to get everyone ready for the next scene.

'We need to get everyone in position,' Jen told him. 'Make sure everyone is in shot and then we'll be going live.' She looked up at the old building opposite. There was some kind of covering she hadn't noticed before over one whole side of it. 'What's happened there?'

'Where?' Astro asked.

'That building that looks like a hotel. There wasn't all that stuff draped over it the last time I came down here. Is someone going to renovate it?'

'Oh, wow, I did not notice that. I have no idea what is going on there at all. *Páme*. Let's get everyone together.'

'Astro!'

It was Petros calling him.

'Give me one second,' Astro said. 'I will be right behind you.'

As Jen headed off towards Bonnie, the children and everyone else who had followed them up from Syntagma Square, Astro looked at Petros who had hastened towards him.

'What are you doing, brother?' Petros asked, putting a hand on Astro's shoulder.

'I'm doing what I said I would do. Helping Jen make this event... a success.'

'You just fell the height of that hotel,' Petros reminded him. 'No more than fifteen minutes ago.'

'And I landed on a canopy.'

'Briefly. Before you fell through it and onto the ground. You should be at the doctor's office.'

'I'm fine,' Astro assured him. 'Please, Petros, I need to do this.'

'You are a crazy person.'

'I know that,' he agreed, trying to tune out the pain in his side.

'Promise me, if you start to feel anything bad then—'

'Petros, I'm not going to promise that. I told you, this event, the mural we all put together, they are the most important things.'

Petros grunted, seemingly dissatisfied with Astro's responses. 'Is there anything you're going to let me do?'

'Yeah,' Astro replied. 'Do you have any painkillers?'

66

THE PARTHENON

Jen had thought she couldn't be more awed by the Parthenon than the first time she and Bonnie had visited. But tonight, with no one present but their party, with the spotlights illuminating the ancient marble and making it glow like it was ethereal, the dancers performing, the children singing and the snow lightly falling, it was as if they were all pieces of a beautiful Greek-style festive snow globe.

When the tour came to the end, there was applause from everyone who had taken part: Mr and Mrs Sinrades, who had made food for them after they had all wound through the tight lanes of Anafiotika with the camera; the street artists who had not only created a fantastic collaborative picture using every different art repertoire anyone could imagine; Achilles and his school friends singing carols; the dancers; the man and his delicious *koulouri*... It really had been the most magnificent coming together of everything Jen had found since she'd been in Athens. She really didn't know who to thank first.

But, before she could thank anyone, her phone was ringing.

Her heart might still be hammering with adrenaline, but the rest of her was running on sheer joy.

'Natalia,' she greeted.

But she didn't get a 'hello' or a sinister whisper from the crypt, the only sound she could hear were whoops and cheers and extensive clapping. It was still ringing pleasantly in Jen's ears when finally Natalia said something.

'Do you hear stamping of feet also?'

'I hear happy customers,' Jen replied.

'Ah! You cannot see them. One second. I fix.'

With a touch of the screen, Natalia was there to see and then she swung the camera around to show the refectory looking like a glorious winter Narnia with fake snow-covered firs and a glowing lamppost, their snow carpet looking more realistic than Jen had ever seen it, the table settings perfect. But the best thing of all were the glowing, smiling faces still applauding so heartily.

'We wait for *baklava* and coffees to be served, but they say it is best event!' Natalia shouted. 'Can you hear me?'

'Yes!' Jen exclaimed. 'Yes, I can hear you! And I am so so pleased. Thank you, Natalia for doing such a wonderful job and I will—'

'I have to go, Kathleen wave at me that coffees are coming.'

And that was all Jen was going to get. The call disconnected and she was left on her own opposite the Erechtheion – looking directly at The Porch of the Maidens, famous for its columns that were statues of women supporting the roof with their heads. Strong women had made this event the success it was – Natalia, Bonnie, Kathleen, Jen herself. She watched everyone joining together and chatting, people she didn't know that well who had come here tonight to help her with the production and to make Athens the shining star, the children making snowballs which she was certain was against the rules they had signed up to to be allowed to be here privately... It was a moment to enjoy, to savour, to be proud of.

'It was a success.'

It was Astro's voice, close behind her. Jen turned to greet him.

'Yes, it was a great success! Natalia said everyone loved it and apparently, they said it was the best event they'd had. Perhaps I should organise all my events at short notice. It seems I get better feedback that way.'

'It is really great,' Astro said. 'That the traditions of Athens made your customers so happy.'

'Thanks to you,' Jen said. 'You were the biggest part of getting all these different components to come together. And I know how busy you are at the bar and how much you have going on and you've already let me stay in your apartment, so I mean it when I say if there is anything I can do for you in return then let me do it.'

He smiled, those beautiful lips she'd had the pleasure of tasting, curving upwards, snowflakes from above landing in his hair. 'I was hoping you would say that.'

'There is something?'

'There is something,' he replied, perhaps a little nervously.

'Well, ask me.'

'Jen,' he began. 'I know this is going to sound a little bit crazy when I know what I said but... would you... go on a date with me?'

The shivers running up and down her spine now were nothing to do with the wintry weather, it was a white-hot rush that Astro had been gifting to her since almost the very beginning. There was only one answer she was going to give and she wasn't going to waste any time debating with her inner self about it.

'Yes,' she said breathlessly. 'But when were you thinking? Because I don't know when my flight—'

'How about now?' Astro suggested.

67

LITTLE KOOK, PSYRRI

'Where are we going? There aren't going to be bats, are there?'

Astro smiled at Jen's comment. 'No bats are planned but, you know, you can never guarantee anything with wildlife.'

'Or Ukrainian assistants, apparently. Is it down here?' Jen asked, indicating the next street.

'Yes, but wait,' Astro said, touching her arm, suggesting she stop.

'What's wrong?'

'Nothing is wrong,' he said, dipping his hands into the pockets of his jeans. 'I am just... building the anticipation.'

'Now I'm a little bit terrified that there *are* bats and they're going to flap out at me and I'm going to become like Bonnie when she sets eyes on Peri.'

Astro smiled. 'Trust me when I say you're going to like this.'

Trust him. Perhaps that was too much for this moment. Why should she trust him? What had he done to earn it? He knew he had blown hot one minute and cold the next. He had been indecisive and arrogant about his own feelings. Maybe he didn't deserve another opportunity...

'Should I be excited?'

He could already tell that she was. Her energy was up, her eyes were bright and she was riding a wave of success from the event, which was definitely showing in her body language.

'I think you are going to be surprised,' he said. 'Come on.'

He led the way, only having gone a few steps when the festiveness descended as if the owners of this themed café had arrived on a sleigh direct from Christmas heaven.

'Astro,' Jen gasped. 'What is this place?'

He was more interested in the look on her face as she took in their surroundings than the decorations. This was exactly what he had hoped for and, having braved looking at the photos on the internet, he knew the street outside was only the tip of the iceberg.

'Read the sign,' Astro said.

'Little Kook. Oh my God, I love it! What is it? Because it's beginning to look like somewhere I want to live!'

He laughed then but stopped as a pain ripped through his torso. Those painkillers Petros had given him had worn off some time ago now. He was hoping the sugar high he suspected was coming from the café was going to sustain him until he could get some more.

'Are you OK?' Jen asked.

She wasn't looking at the glittering stagecoach ahead of them now but was focused on him. He smiled quickly. There was no way he wasn't going to give her this night, a full-on Christmas night.

'Just, you know, worrying that, when we go in, an alarm might sound and detect a Grinch,' he answered. 'That I will melt into nothing but a pile of glitter.'

'I think it's sweet that's the worst ending you can think of.'

'I am hyperventilating right now.'

That was a bit close to the truth, but he managed to deliver the words with a smile.

'Come on, I believe there is a lot more to see inside.'

* * *

As they continued down the street, the decorations became more and more festive with every step. Jen wanted to stop and look into each little window, admire every ballerina, every trumpeter, sit in one of the golden chairs outside that was lightly speckled with snow, but the magnificent stagecoach and tall nutcrackers were waiting at an elaborate entrance guarded by two real people in costume – one a fairy princess, the other in uniform like one of the large toy mice hanging from the wall.

Jen smiled a greeting and Astro began speaking in Greek. A few seconds later and they were being guided inside the café. Those few small steps and Jen was overwhelmed again, trying to take it all in at once. It was like she had walked straight into a festive fairy tale. From the imposing grandfather clock and the giant beanstalk that was in the centre of the room, spiralling up towards a chandelier in an open ceiling, to the golden reindeer, rotating snow globes and glowing stars. It wasn't so much a café but an old curiosity shop, the kind of place that Jen had always sought out, the kind of place that Kathleen and Gerald's Fancy Occasions had been. The kind of place she tried to emulate with Christmas Every Day.

'Jen? Are you OK?'

Astro's voice jolted her for a second, drawing her back from feeling like she was enjoying Alice's Wonderland or waiting for a seat on Humpty Dumpty's brick wall.

'Sorry... it's just... beautiful here... magical.' She took a breath. 'Someone has put a lot of time and energy and love into this. They must feel—'

'The same way you do about Christmas,' Astro said.

'Exactly,' she agreed. 'See! I'm not the only person who wants to embrace little mice in gingerbread houses and post-boxes for the letters to Santa.'

'Come on,' Astro said. 'We are sitting upstairs.'

68

The decoration not only continued upstairs, but it got even *more* Christmassy. A long table with golden swirls and patterns under its lacquer, worn with age, was in the middle of the room and above it, hanging from the ceiling, were vibrant giant baubles of red, gold, and green, shining silver and gold glittering icicles, fairy lights, musical notes and mischievous-looking elves. Away from the big table were other smaller tables with golden edged chairs that sat like thrones, with red velvet cushions, beside angels, Father Christmases and swans with golden bows tied around their necks. Other seats were made from tartan fabric with red cushions. Playing cards, lanterns and snowflakes were dotted around the ceiling and gnomes and goblins pulling cheeky expressions dangled in every corner.

Music played, emanating from all around the room. It wasn't Shakin' Stevens or Mariah Carey though, this was regal, orchestral, a mix of something like a Hans Christian Andersen story and *Bridgerton*. And, right now, Jen couldn't get enough of it. There were so many *details*. She only had to blink and her eye caught something else she hadn't noticed before. But then she realised she hadn't paid much attention to Astro since they'd sat down, nor had she even glanced at the nutcracker menus.

'Sorry,' she apologised. 'I just can't believe this. I had no idea that there would be something like this here in Athens.'

'Ah,' Astro said. 'Maybe it was not here before you arrived. Maybe it has sprung up very quickly like Jack's beanstalk.'

'Ha. Ha. Very good,' Jen said, smiling. She actually couldn't stop smiling. She opened the menu and laughed as she read the choices. 'Princess with rosy cheeks? Dragon's lava?'

'I was going to have "wolf, wolf, here I am". Vanilla cake with peanut butter and tahini and passionfruit marmalade.'

'That does sound delicious but... I think it's going to be princess with rosy cheeks for me.'

They placed their orders, including two decadent-sounding hot chocolates, with one of Santa Claus's foot soldiers and then they were left all alone – if you didn't count the elves and the angels!

'Thank you, Astro,' Jen began. 'For—'

'Please, Jen, do not thank me. I do not feel there is very much for you to thank me for.'

She watched his face cloud over and that expression he wore when he was deep in thought etched itself in the space between his eyebrows. She much preferred it when he laughed, when his eyes lit up and widened, when delight drove the formation of lines.

'All your friends painting that fantastic modern depiction of the historic sites for the walk-through in such a short space of time for a start. For helping me arrange for the children to be here and for getting the dancers and speaking all the Greek to the *koulouri* man and Mr and Mrs Sinrades and giving me somewhere to stay while it snowed and—'

'And for what I said to you at Strefi Hill. For making you cry.'

'Well,' Jen said quickly, her gaze dropping to the table. 'That was days ago now.' She swallowed. 'And you can't be upset about something just because it's the truth of how someone else feels.'

'But it was not the truth,' Astro said fast. 'Not the *whole* truth. Because I should have said it better. I should have said more and —' He stopped himself, putting a hand to his hair, frustration the only sentiment showing across his face now. 'I do not know. Perhaps I do not deserve for you to listen to the rest of it now.'

'Well, what if I *want* to hear it?' Jen asked.

He seemed to be overwhelmed by whatever he was keeping bottled up – not to mention the fact he was sitting inside a virtual grotto, tinsel glittering and shining, baubles spiralling and spinning.

'Do you?' Astro asked, as if needing clarification. 'Want to hear it?'

'Yes,' she said decisively. 'Yes, of course.'

And her heart was telling her exactly the same. Whatever he was about to say, it mattered to him and that meant it mattered to her. You didn't share this kind of crazy instant connection with someone and just stop caring because things got complicated.

He reached across the table for her hand and took it in his. She had always thought he had really nice hands, lean fingers, big flat palms, skin smooth. And their size dwarfed hers, his hand covering hers entirely, wrapping over it like Christmas present paper.

'Before I said all the things I did say, Jen, I should have said this,' Astro began. He took a breath. 'You are the most incredible person I have ever met. To have had a bad beginning in life, to not know your family, to go through everything you have and to still be the wonderful person you are with your successful business and—'

'Oh, well, I don't know about that.'

'I *do* know,' Astro insisted. 'Believe me, I know. Because I see you. I've been seeing you from the start. And the more I got to know you, the more I wanted to keep seeing you.'

'Astro,' she said, squeezing his hand. 'I want to tell you something, before you tell me anything else.'

'What is it? Is something wrong?'

She heaved a big breath. 'I am not 100 per cent together either. I also need to work on myself. Because... living inside a Christmas bubble, it's not healthy, is it? And I've made that my everything because I've had to. For survival. Because without that season of hope, that rush of planning, the glitter and the lights and the snow and the great food, I dwell on all the bad memories. They all come rushing back and I feel worthless and insignificant and stupid and all the other names everyone called me when I was younger.' She sighed. 'But I need to learn not be fearful of those memories and to stop hiding away from those thoughts. Because *I* need to be my saviour, not a man in a red suit riding in a sleigh.'

The pressure that had built up in her chest was finally released and she realised she had been gripping Astro's hand like it was a stress toy. She went to let go but he held on tight, kept holding on.

'You're supposed to let go now,' she said. 'Now you realise what a shambles I am. I'm sorry I accepted the date because that was really selfish of me and—'

'Come on,' Astro said, standing up, still clasping her hand. 'I want to show you something.'

'What?' she asked, rising too.

'Just let me tell them to hold the cakes and then we'll go outside.'

69

PSYRRI

The snow was falling again but not a harsh, hard storm-like flurry; this was lighter, softer snowfall, the kind with snowflakes that lay for a second on your coat and then instantly melted away. Like Astro's heart had melted across the table from Jen at Little Kook. She had finally *really* opened up to him and it was at that moment he knew without any doubt how he felt about her. He *loved* her. His mind could admit now what his heart had already known a lot longer. She was *real*. She was as mixed-up and had been as tossed about on the sea of life as he had but where he had turned his grief into misery and focused anger at everyone and everything, Jen had wrapped her past up in a Christmas gift box and tied it with a golden bow. They were the same. But also different. They could make each other stronger.

He held her shoulders now, having guided her from the café to the decaying hotel with her eyes closed. And now he waited.

Taking a second to look at the finished mural, he inhaled a deep breath. He had seen this picture take shape over the past few nights but now, completed, it was something he was completely proud of. His vision, his work, and the work of his friends, here on the walls of the city forever, or, at least, until someone tore the hotel down...

'Open your eyes.'

He watched her look to the building and it was as if he could see her take in every individual section all at once and then start from the top again and work down slowly, evaluating every piece.

It was her. It was all her. From the giant sprayed portrait at its centre, to the many different images surrounding it – copied from the drawings and paintings he had made in his apartment – Jen was its heart. There was the giant inflatable candy cane and the bracelet Jen had thought was marking her for bag snatching, the berries and ferns they had picked with Achilles, the oranges they had made into Christingles and her angel earrings. Then there was Kathleen – he had sketched her from a photo Bonnie had sent him – and Bravely Bear; there was Fix beer and Peri and there was even a bat.

'Astro,' Jen finally breathed. 'I don't have the words. How did you—'

'With a lot of help,' Astro answered. 'And a lot of love.'

He swallowed at his admission, but he wasn't going to backtrack on it.

'No one has ever done anything close to this for me before,' she said as tears snaked down her face.

'What you told me just now,' Astro said, as the snow fell down around them, 'I already knew it inside. Because when you see someone, when you draw them, you see the joy and the pain no matter what they think their face is saying. And, for you to tell me how you feel, it only makes me love you more.'

She turned away from the mural then and faced him, eyes wet with tears, cheeks a little red from the cold. She had never looked more beautiful.

'You keep saying "love",' she whispered.

'I do, don't I?'

'I notice there is no Christmas in the mural apart from the candy cane.'

'I take small steps. And I did not boil in Little Kook,' Astro reminded her. He took a breath. 'It is not there in the picture because Christmas, it is not *all* you are, Jen. And I believe there is the whole world out there waiting to see which part of it you decide to pick next.'

He wholly believed that. Yes, he had wanted to tell her exactly how he felt and *show* her how he felt with the visit to the themed café and this artwork, but what came next in her future was for her and her alone to decide.

'Right now,' Jen said, looking into his eyes. 'The only part of it I want to explore is you.'

'Really?'

'I've wanted to tell you that. Since the first night I stayed in your apartment. But... I was scared to. Because as much as I wanted you to know how much I cared, I also didn't want you to know because that meant I was vulnerable.'

He held her hands. 'And you have been thinking you are less vulnerable keeping those feelings inside, shut away.' He shook his head. 'I am just the same.'

She squeezed his hands. 'I've been clinging on to the edge of your bed trying not to touch you.'

'I have been getting up as soon as you fell asleep because I could not stand not to touch you.'

'Oh, Astro, can this work? You and me?'

'It is already working,' he replied, letting go of her hands so he could brush his fingers through her hair. 'Like Christmas magic.'

'Like Athens was where I was always meant to be this Christmas,' Jen said as he trailed a finger down her cheek.

'And you coming here, it was my greatest gift ever,' Astro replied.

He kissed her then and she wrapped her arms around him, holding tight. Whatever the future held for them, it started now with love and hope and possibly a cracked rib – but he wasn't going to mention that now. And he knew that somewhere up above, amid the stars, there was a woman in the moon looking down at her little boy and smiling.

70

CHRISTMAS EVERY DAY OFFICES, LITTLE PICKERING, WILTSHIRE, UK

Christmas Day

'I think Dean Martin sang it better. And he was dishier. They don't make them like they used to.'

'I agree, Kathleen,' Bonnie answered. 'I've been waiting for a golden-age Hollywood film star to walk into the vets ever since I saw one of the customers was called Frank Sinatra. It was six months before I realised that was the name of the poodle not the owner.'

'Poodle is not dog,' Natalia scoffed. 'Poodle is like rabbit. Too soft. No bite.'

Jen sat back in her wheeled office chair and took a second to really commit this day to memory. The dining space in the centre of the main room she had created out of every table the office owned, the extra chairs she had borrowed from the gym, the plates of food each guest had had a hand in making, as she had no cooking facilities except a gas burner and a toaster and of course the avalanche of decorations that poured down from the ceiling, coating the walls and rising up from every inch of space. She had taken inspiration from everything she had seen in Athens – the present-wrapped doors, the garlands made from nature, the overload for the senses like Little Kook.

She had arrived back in the UK only two days ago and almost everyone she cared about was here to share Christmas Day with her.

Almost everyone...

'Gerald always wanted a poodle,' Kathleen remarked, paper hat askew. 'I said it would be less mess and effort if I just went back to having a perm.'

'Gerald sound like nice man,' Natalia said, stabbing a sprout with her fork.

'He was very nice,' Kathleen agreed, nodding and making the hat collapse a little more. 'And good-looking. But looks don't last, you know, Natty, you need to think of the bigger picture.'

'I dream of arms like Oleksiy Novikov. That is all.'

'Natty?' Bonnie remarked. 'Why don't I have a nickname?'

'Oh, you do, Bonnie. I've just never let you hear it,' Kathleen said, chuckling.

'Well, moving on,' Bonnie said, unperturbed. 'If we're talking about big pictures, what did you two think of all the faces of Jen on the side of a hotel in Athens?'

'I'm not a fan of graffiti myself,' Kathleen said first. 'Back in the day, there were all these shaky black images of a bald man with a long nose looking over a wall. I mean, who wants to look at that? But, I have to say, those pictures of you...' Her voice trailed off and Jen could see that Kathleen was getting emotional.

'Kathleen, you can't cry on Christmas Day,' she said, picking up the bottle of sparkling wine they were sharing.

'I can do what I like,' Kathleen said, patting her eyes with a serviette. 'Always have. Always will.'

'We are the soul sisters,' Natalia said, nodding.

'You looked so beautiful in those paintings, Jen,' Kathleen continued. 'There was Classic Jen but there was also so much more. All the expressions I see you wear; it was like Astro had known them all and captured them exactly right.'

Jen's heart swelled because her friend was absolutely correct. That's how she felt every time she looked at the mural. After that first viewing, they had rushed through the snow-dashed streets to get back to Astro's apartment, their to-go desserts in hand. But it hadn't been that kind of dessert on either of their minds.

As Kathleen, Bonnie and Natalia started to rate each of Greg's festive dishes – some of which Jen knew Bonnie had yet to taste – she put herself back at Bar Páme, in that room with the man she loved and a pigeon who, for once on that occasion, had kept quiet.

Astro had used the sofa bed's cushions to prop up the duvet and that's when Jen realised he must have seen her make that bedding igloo when he hadn't been sleeping next to her. Knowing her, seeing her, without her even being aware.

She smiled to herself as she put her lips to her glass of wine. He had undressed her and then she had started to undress him, only for him to slow her down. There she had been, thinking she was a seduction queen and that her nakedness was driving him crazy, only to realise that one side of him was covered in angry black bruises. She'd stopped, shocked, and made him tell her what had happened.

He had fallen from a hotel for her.

That alone, without everything else he'd done for her since she'd landed in Greece topped anything Paris might have had to offer. And she was giving no apologies to the Eiffel Tower!

He'd kissed her, beautifully persistently, told her the damage she was going to do to his heart if they stopped now was going to be worse than anything else he had received from the fall. It had been too easy to agree. And she was so glad she had. Everything had felt so natural with Astro. She hadn't overthought anything, or worried about being a certain way, like she always had in the past. Touching him, holding him, dropping her guard with him, it wasn't like anything else. It was unique, special, exactly like him.

'I think Christmas Father fat muffins were the best,' Natalia concluded. 'Brothers bite off heads first then suck out all the insides.'

'Wasn't that what they threatened to do to Geoffrey in the crypt?' Kathleen asked.

'He get off lightly. I release him mainly unharmed. And, when he tell me he press charges, brothers say they press other pieces of him until they drop off if he speak of this again.'

Jen's phone began to ring and she shot back on the wheely chair, diving for the windowsill where she'd left it on charge next to her festive carousel lamp, the reindeer rotating gleefully.

'That will be Astro,' Bonnie announced, helping herself to more stuffing balls.

'I have not seen Jen like this,' Natalia stated. 'What is it you say here? That she is love-vomit.'

'Lovesick, Natty,' Kathleen stated. 'Sounds a little bit less vulgar when we're eating.'

Jen frowned. 'It's not Astro. It's a number I don't recognise, wanting to FaceTime.'

'Oh God!' Bonnie exclaimed. 'You don't think it's David again, do you?'

Kathleen cleared her throat. 'If it is then *I* want a few words with him.'

'It won't be David,' Jen said. 'His secretary called to thank me for the gift basket I sent her and said he's cleared time in his diary for someone called Laura. So that leopard hasn't changed his spots but also, thankfully, he won't be clawing at my door any more.'

She pressed to accept the call and watched the screen.

'*Yassas, Jen! Kronia polla!* Merry Christmas!'

Jen beamed as Achilles's face filled the screen, his expression looking like a highly mischievous elf.

'He doesn't have the pigeon with him, does he?' Bonnie asked as Jen came back to the table.

'Is that Bonnie?' Achilles asked. 'She leave her hair scrunchies here! My mum is wearing them!'

Marjorie appeared then, quickly whipping something out of her hair as Bonnie joined Jen in leaning over the screen.

'I will get them back to you, Bonnie,' Marjorie said.

'Don't worry,' Bonnie said immediately. 'Keep them! That one looked really nice on you.'

'I am trying different styles,' Marjorie admitted. 'Trying to look like a bar manager not just a waitress.'

'Oh my God! Are you doing it?' Jen asked her.

Before Jen left Greece, Astro had said that his uncle was thinking about a different approach with regard to Bar Páme. That maybe it wasn't a case of just keeping it or selling it. The third option was for Philippos to retain ownership but spend less time actually working in it and employing a manager – or rather promoting someone. The longevity of this idea was of course dependent on how well the bar continued to do, whether it was viable long-term. But, it seemed, things were starting to be put in motion.

'It is only a trial. A few months. We will see,' Marjorie said, trying to play it down.

'Mama says that she is going to get more tourists coming to Bar Páme than they have visiting the Acropolis,' Achilles said excitedly.

'Achilles! Must you repeat everything I say?' Marjorie snapped.

Ignoring his mother, Achilles walked around with the phone and showed Jen Peri, who was looking much chirpier. 'Look at Peri! His leg is better and he likes to sit on my car and I push him about!'

'Ah! I'm leaving this conversation now,' Bonnie said, backing away.

'How come you have Peri at your apartment?' Jen asked.

Achilles rolled his eyes as if she should know the answer. 'Because Philippos does not like him in the bar.'

That *was* something she knew but...

Her thoughts trailed away as her intercom buzzed.

'I'll see who it is,' Bonnie said, heading to the landing.

'You need to go now,' Achilles told her, bringing the phone back around so Jen could see Marjorie too. 'Maybe there is a green light coming.'

'Yes, Jen, you need to go. Merry Christmas! And maybe you can come back to see us for the event we love to celebrate more than this day – Epiphany. Men dive into water for golden crosses. Bonnie would love it!'

'Bye! *Ya! Ya!*' Achilles said, waving a hand and then disconnecting faster than the speed of light.

Jen felt bamboozled from all the Greek energy filling the room and then, just as quickly, disappearing again. And there was someone at her door.

'Is there any cranberry sauce?' Kathleen piped up. 'I can't eat turkey without cranberry sauce at Christmas.'

'Jar with contents that look like blood? I saw it under pile of mess from pulling crackers,' Natalia replied.

'Jen!' Bonnie called as she rushed back into the room. 'It's a special delivery that needs signing for.'

Jen frowned. That was ridiculous. There were no deliveries on

Christmas Day and the only parcel she'd been waiting for had arrived on the twenty-third.

'Come on! Before he drives away again!' Bonnie called, hassling her. She was waving her arms as though she was a foreign policeman directing traffic.

'Jen!' Bonnie screamed.

'This had better be good because our turkey is getting cold,' she said as she flashed past Bonnie and headed for the stairs.

Speeding down the steps, hand grazing the tinsel wrapped around the banisters, she got to the front door and threw it open, ready to suggest that the delivery man really took a day off and went home to his family or friends. But when the cold air came rushing in and the scene hit her, it took her breath away.

'*Yassas*, Jen. Happy Christmas.'

It was Astro. Standing in the doorway of Christmas Every Day. Here in Little Pickering.

She couldn't believe it.

'I... spoke to you last night. You can't be here now. You said you were going to make *gourounopoula*.' She couldn't tear her eyes away from him – like if she did, he might disappear.

'I did make *gourounopoula*,' Astro told her. 'Bonnie said everyone was bringing food today. So, we are bringing food.'

'We?'

'*Yassas*, Jen.'

Her eyes finally left Astro as her eyes sought out the owner of the second voice. It was Philippos, standing behind his nephew, bags at his feet, waving a hand. Now she really *couldn't* believe what was happening.

'Not so long ago, Astro had asked me to make time for a meal with someone important to him,' Philippos said, picking up the bags and stepping forward. 'Someone who he was already hoping would be part of our family. I did not make the time and, for that, I

deeply apologise. But I am here now, to make that right. So, I am
going to take our things and go inside and find the person who
helped make this happen while you two behave like people in love
should behave.'

Saying nothing further, Philippos smiled at Jen, then headed
past her inside.

Jen was completely overwhelmed, all her senses overloaded. It
was hard to decide which reaction to have next.

'I thought there weren't any flights and I know how expensive
it can be—'

'You have Bonnie to thank for that,' Astro said. 'Well, her sister,
really. She knows many people, including someone with the use of
a private plane. We land at somewhere called Boscombe Down
and a car was there to meet us.'

Jen put her hands to her face then. 'That's literally up the
road!'

'I know,' Astro said. 'Christmas Day in the UK is crazy!'

Jen laughed, so much joy bubbling up inside her.

'But I did not care what transport got us here. I only knew that
I *had* to be here. Because if there is only one thing I have understood about Christmas, it is that it is about family. And how can
you celebrate that when a big part of it is somewhere else?' He
smiled. 'I would have travelled by donkey to get here if I had to. I
would actually have travelled by bat.'

Jen couldn't wait any longer. She needed to hold him, squeeze
him, feel the warmth of him next to her. She rushed into his arms
and he caught her, holding her close.

'I've missed you,' Jen breathed.

'It has only been days,' Astro reminded her.

'I know,' she replied. 'But... I've never missed anyone before.'

That sentiment hit her fiercely as she held on to him, revelling in all the feelings she had always thought other people took for granted, feelings that had been absent from her life for so long.

'I feel the same,' he said. 'There are five more drawings of you in my sketchbook that I need to add to the side of a building.'

She laughed, breaking their embrace. 'Five! Astro, you need another muse.'

'Maybe,' he admitted. 'And maybe, when I find one, you can help me look at art colleges. I have started some research. Some are in Athens. Others are... in the UK.'

'Really?' Jen exclaimed. 'Is that what you've decided, to pursue your art? Because you know I think you should, but I know it's also—'

She was halted by his mouth, which was smothering hers in the very best way. He kissed her, super slowly, and delightful goosebumps broke out on her skin.

'Let us talk about it,' Astro said, holding her hands in his, 'together.' He smiled. 'But right now there are people I want to meet. Kathleen, because I have only seen a photograph, and a certain teddy bear I have only seen as street art.'

'Natalia is here too,' Jen reminded him.

'Ah, yes, the woman who gags people in holy places.'

Jen squeezed his hand. 'I still can't believe you're here. This is... my favourite Christmas of all.'

'And it started with a candy cane,' Astro said with a smile.

Jen put her arms around him again, breathing in the December air and giving him one last hug while they were alone.

'And, best of all,' she whispered, 'it ends with you and me. With us.'

ACKNOWLEDGMENTS

A big THANK YOU to the following:

Tanera Simons and Laura Heathfield from Darley Anderson.

Editors, Emily Yau and Candida Bradford and everyone at Team Boldwood Books – there are far too many amazing members to mention individually!

My friend, Sue Fortin, for being a daily motivator.

My friends in Athens, Greece, I saw during my winter research trip.

Akis Petretzikis and Diana Alexaki – for feeding me and welcoming me at Kitchen Lab.

Dimitris Papageorgiou – for meeting up and giving me a little tour and many stories!

The hotels – Hermes and Plaka.

Everyone at these bars/tavernas – The Clumsies, Lyra, The Old Taverna of Psarras, Klepsidra Café and many others.

My readers! I'm always so grateful for your support, the comments you make on social media and your wonderful reviews.

ABOUT THE AUTHOR

Mandy Baggot is a bestselling romance writer who loves giving readers that happy-ever-after. Mandy splits her time between Salisbury, Wiltshire and Corfu, Greece and has a passion for books, food, racehorses and all things Greek!

Sign up to Mandy Baggot's mailing list for news, competitions and updates on future books.

Visit Mandy's website: www.mandybaggot.com

Follow Mandy on social media here:

 facebook.com/mandybaggotauthor

twitter.com/mandybaggot

instagram.com/mandybaggot

bookbub.com/profile/mandy-baggot

ALSO BY MANDY BAGGOT

Under a Greek Sun

Truly, Madly, Greekly

Those Summer Nights

In the Greek Midwinter

Boldwood